THE STONE OF ONE IRON & OMEN

BOOK THREE
OF
THE RUNEWAR SAGA

J.D.L. ROSELL

Illustration © 2022 by René Aigner
Book design by J.D.L. Rosell
Map by J.D.L. Rosell
Map elements by StarRaven (on DeviantArt)

ISBN # 978-1-952868-32-0 (hardcover w/ dust cover)
ISBN # 978-1-952868-31-3 (IngramSpark trade paperback)
ISBN # 979-8-377300-68-7 (KDP Print trade paperback)
ASIN # B09QXXHPN6 (ebook)

Published by Rune & Requiem Press
runeandrequiempress.com

CONTENTS

WITTERLAND

TREACHEROUS SEA

XEN'TIA

JIN'TO

JADE SEA

SHURA MOUNTAINS

BAEG'ARD

ZAKOWA

ARAI OCEAN

ENEA
THE MIDDLE LAND

THE ELDWALD

HILL HUMMOCKS

WAAST THELAC TU

TAGARTEN

ISOLSI

NORTH VINAXI

SOUTH VINAXI

SUN OCEAN

SUMERLAND

To my wife, Kaitlyn.
I've run out of clever words to convey my gratitude
for your constant support and insightful critiques,
so I'm hoping it's the thought that counts.

PART I
OMEN

"Fate goes ever as fate must."

— Seamus Heaney, *Beowulf: A New Verse Translation*

PROLOGUE

Ganiah Phaza swept into the tent and bowed deeply before sauntering forth. The Shadowed cringed before his passage, though they tried to hide it. Rarely had he raised a hand against them, yet his mere presence was enough to instill fear.

He smiled. Such was the potency of power.

But he served a greater mistress. To her, he had given all, down to his very name. The Ibis, Great Oyaoan called him, and so Ganiah Phaza became.

The giantess paid him no heed as he approached, her head bent to the sand scattered over the fine rugs. Scarab beetles danced atop their orbs of dung, carving shallow lines with their movement. Divinity's rotten scent hung rank in the air and shimmered upon his queen's wagon-sized hands.

So she dines and divines once more.

"Great Oyaoan," he said in her tongue, "your servant begs you to know what visions the Sun bequeaths upon you this dark day."

The giantess neither acknowledged his words nor looked up. Her eyes, black and fathomless as rainforest caves, gleamed with the muted light from the steaming braziers to either side. She let a finger drift toward the sand, falling short of touching it, though her movement caused the beetles to scuttle away.

The Ibis watched and waited. He had sought her council in how to command the karah and the chief general to act for their ongoing campaign, but he had served the giantess for nigh on three decades. A translator did not endure so long without a healthy capacity for patience.

One of the Shadowed edged forth, their head bowed and a cup raised before them. The Ibis took it without a word and drank deeply, his lips curling at the taste. The watered beer of the Syptens was far too sweet for his liking. He wished for a moment he were back in their hidden palace among the overgrown jungle, a goblet of sour black-wine in hand.

Those days are gone, he reminded himself, *never to return. Not until the Great One saves us all.*

His conviction renewed even as he took another sip. Though he couched their mission in religious terms, both he and his queen knew this to be wholly strategic. Fail to strike forth when they did, and the world would be ripped from their grasp.

If only the true enemy would come down to face us.

He started as Great Oyaoan abruptly straightened. She was not the tallest of her kind, nor the cleverest, but her qualities had nevertheless made the others yield. Ruthlessness paired with knowledge made for a potent tincture, one that could cure even a giant's fractious nature.

"Flames," the queen spoke at last. "They all fall to flames." She lacked an eloquent tongue, as was true of all giants, but the power with which each word was spoken gave her speech a certain resonance.

"Who, Great Oyaoan? Who shall fall?"

"Ishilva," the queen continued, deaf to his query. "Near. I must have it."

"Of course, my Resplendent Queen. Where shall I order our soldiers to march?"

Her gaze fell on him. Despite his long service, a part of the Ibis always trembled at her attention. He was useful to her, but every tool could be replaced should they rust beyond usefulness.

"West. To conquer. To claim."

He bowed deeply. "At once, Great Oyaoan."

She continued speaking even before he had risen. "The beetle. She grows tusks. The Sun shines upon her."

The Ibis kept his brow from wrinkling. What light could that cringing woman cast off? Yet he had enough wiles to know Sehdra Karah was not as guileless as she tried to appear. If his queen had foreseen issues with her, he would be a fool to overlook her actions.

"Then I will see she is kept in the shade. Unless you prefer the weed be pulled out at the root?"

The giantess beheld him for a long moment, long enough for him to wonder if a fresh vision had stolen over her mind.

"Watch," she said at last. "Wait. She brings fire and blood."

"To our enemies?"

But his hopeful inquiry went unnoticed. Oyaoan slumped down again to stare at the sand. His audience was over.

He pondered her words as he bowed and departed, giving his cup to one of the Shadowed as he swept out. *Fire and blood.* With such omens, he would be obliged to watch the little goddess closely indeed. Whatever his queen's purpose in preserving her, Sehdra Karah could spell no good for their cause.

But she is not a cause for fear. Not compared to them. Outside, the Ibis tilted back his head to stare up at the stars, thinking of the coming war long foretold. Of those who would bring unspeakable sorrow to these shores.

Fire and blood.

He smiled, shook his head, and strode away. His bent legs creaked with every step, but he did not look to his guards and servants for a chariot, though they trailed close behind. He had much to mull over this night, and massacres were best contemplated with a hearty dose of pain.

1. THE COWLED

*Despite a long tradition of women warriors, often called
shieldmaidens, gracing the legends of the Seven Jarlheims,
most of their names have been struck from the histories.
This is a foolish notion on many accounts, to my mind.
When we revise the facts of the past, how can we ever
truly find the truth of the present?*

- Commentary on Djurian Culture, by Alfjin the Scribe

Two cloaked figures hurried down the rain-slicked streets, hoods pulled low and shoulders bowed. Stains marked their clothes, making plain their late fortunes. It was a common enough sight in Oakharrow these days; few men prospered under the Jotun, and fewer still stood tall where their heads might be parted from their necks. This pair was nothing much of note.

So Egil hoped as he followed his companion.

He cast a wary glance around. His hopes had been realized thus far. Barbars thronged the streets, and spies could be found in those who had once been neighbors, yet their enemies were disorderly and chaotic. They could not account for every movement in the city.

But though he hunched over and avoided the eyes of passersby, a forge-fire roared within Egil. He felt like a thief prowling the streets, sniffing out his next victim, shameful and sinful. This was not how a warrior should hold himself. This was not how his father, Yaethun Brashurson, once in line to sit upon the Oakstone, had raised him to behave.

It was thanks to Bjorn Borson that this was Egil's lot in life now.

That the exiled heir was responsible, he was certain, and had only grown more so during the long months since the return home. *If he'd stayed, if only he'd stayed...* Had Bjorn not sought vengeance among the Teeth, Egil would not have been honor bound to accompany the sprites-damned quest. They would not have been outside the city when the Jotun attacked. He, Egil Yaethunson, would have been here to protect his home.

Perhaps he would have only died defending it. But a glorious death would have been a better fate than this.

He roused from his thoughts as his companion paused and turned back to face him. His icy eyes narrowed against the wind, already tinged with cold again, though he did not seem to feel it through his leathery skin. A thin linen hood, dark and nondescript, clung to the stubble along his shaved head. Egil hardened his thoughts at a single glance from the man. He'd be damned if he let Vedgif Addarson catch him moping.

"It's here," the elder muttered. "The Wolf's Den."

"But is she here?"

"We'll find out inside."

There was nothing for it but to follow. The older man nodded to the door guard, then entered inside the worn decrepit door and into the dark interior. Egil had to stop from wrinkling his nose. He had seen his fair share of filthy taverns, but the Wolf's Den more resembled a latrine, and smelled like one as well. Its wattle-and-daub walls were stained with smoke, and ash streaked across the hearth sputtering in the far corner. The figures huddled at the crooked tables glanced up at their entrance, but looked away as quickly, each careful to mind their own. A barmaid, or perhaps a whore by her state of dress, swaggered between the tables without attracting business of either kind, an empty tray clasped in her thin hands. The barkeep did not rise from his stool, but only watched them from behind dark, greasy curls.

As far as Egil could tell, every last occupant was Vurg.

He forced his fists to relax as he followed Vedgif to an empty table and sat. All the most defensible positions in the place had been taken, so they were forced into the open, no walls to protect their rear. He and the elder sat opposite of each other, a silent understanding passing between them to watch each other's backs.

After a long pause, the sultry barmaid drifted their way. "Anythin' for you, loves?"

"Ale," Vedgif answered. Egil grunted his affirmation.

The woman took a step away, then paused. "Nothin' more?" She gave a significant look down at her bosom, which spilled forth from a lazily fastened shirt.

Egil looked away, his stomach stirring with anything but desire. The elder spoke for them both. "Not today."

The woman only shrugged. "There's the loft, if you change your mind."

Her eyes lingered on Egil before she turned away. Vedgif gave him an inscrutable look, then turned back toward the entrance.

"When is she coming?" The space between Egil's shoulders itched, half-expecting a knife to lodge there at any moment.

Raucous laughter burst out from the bar. The elder frowned in its direction as he grunted, "Soon."

Egil kept his silence, though he smoldered within. *Waiting on the likes of her...* Oakharrow had fallen far in a few brief seasons.

The barmaid soon returned with their ales. Taking a sip, Egil only just stopped himself from spitting back into his pewter. The beer, sour to begin with, had a distinct undercurrent of nightsoil. Scowling, he pushed away the cup and crossed his arms.

The front door burst open.

Egil had halfway risen, his hidden knife drawn, before he saw who entered. A woman stood in the doorway, face shadowy with the light from the hearth. Only her smirk was plain to see. She was tall, though not very broad. Hair flowed like lava down her back. Wolf fur lined her shoulders, and iron lamellar armor spread down her chest.

Egil sheathed his knife and scowled as his face flushed. *Jumping at women...* Still, this was not the woman he had expected.

The warrioress scanned the room, then paused as she saw the elder. She advanced on them with clumping footsteps, the door creaking closed behind. Egil saw then that she was martial in more than just her armor. Her nose had a bend to it from being broken and poorly set, and a raised pink scar edged down her left temple. The woman grinned as she neared, showing she had replaced at least one tooth with a red-gold one. In some ways, she reminded him of the Skyardi scout they had chanced upon in the Teeth, Hoarfrost. But Hoarfrost had been frost-bent; there was little doubt the woman before them was filled with as much fire as her tresses implied.

Stopping next to their table, the warrioress looked between Vedgif and Egil, then settled her gaze on the elder. "You're the two I came for."

Vedgif appeared unmoved, but the woman had the advantageous positioning, and Egil had spent enough time with him to see that he tensed. His response, however, remained measured. "What do you mean?"

The flame-haired woman flashed another smile, then turned to fetch a stool. The scraping on the wood as she dragged it over made Egil's hair stand on end. Sitting, she turned her gaze on him, blue eyes seeming almost to burn as they bored into him.

"You're gentle on the eyes. All you Thurdjurs this pretty?"

Before Egil could think through his outrage, Vedgif intervened. "Who are you?"

Slowly, the shieldmaiden peeled her gaze from Egil and settled it back on the elder. "Bodil the Blaze. I'd have thought you'd know that, Rook."

There it was — confirmation she knew exactly what she was doing. She spoke without tempering her volume; her swagger could fill a room on its own. All signs pointed to an aggressor and not an ally. But Egil did not draw his knife, nor would he, until Vedgif signaled he should.

The old warrior's gaze remained steady on the newcomer. "Yes, I know you. The first woman to join a green hunt, twelve years back, then the first to lead one."

"Not the first, Rook. The first to be acknowledged."

The Blaze's smile pulled taut. Egil wondered why he had never heard of this warrioress before, but only for a moment. Even if shieldmaidens appeared in the ancestral stories, warriors would not wish to discuss a woman fighting men's battles. It was a marvel she had been allowed to join to start. Though, to look at her, it would not have been easy to stop her.

"Ruthless, they call you," Vedgif said. "Heard tell you earned your name by torching a summer settlement of the Woldagi, burning women and children along with the houses."

Bodil laughed, the sound as harsh and abrupt as a rap on wood. "And men, Rook. Don't forget the men."

Everything about this woman made Egil's skin crawl. There was no glory in killing innocents, not even barbars, yet she reveled in her infamy. His hand twitched under the table, but still, he waited.

As the eagle waits to dive.

If Vedgif was horrified by Bodil's bloody past, his expression remained devoid of it. Leaning in, he pitched his voice softer, drawing the warrioress in.

"What I wish to know, Bodil the Blaze, is why a renowned Balturg shieldmaiden follows an unblooded Vurg girl?"

Bodil grinned again, her red-gold tooth flashing. "You have not met her, Rook. You wouldn't ask that if you had."

Egil had been told to stay quiet, but words pushed out of their own accord. "Then take us to her. Take us to Edda Of'Skarl."

Vedgif's brow creased, but Egil ignored him, holding the warrioress's gaze as she turned slowly toward him. Her eyes ran lasciviously over his chest and arms. Though she was no great beauty and held no attraction for him, he still had to refrain from swallowing.

"So the pup can yowl after all," she said softly. Egil scowled, but Bodil continued before he could speak. "It's Skarldaughter, pup, not Of'Skarl. Lord Edda does not belong to any man, least of all her dead father."

So many objections pressed behind Egil's teeth he could

not decide which to say first. He had never heard of a woman rejecting her own name before, much less using the address "lord." He had heard talk that Edda fashioned herself as a jarl; here was plain proof of it.

And pup. Given half a chance, he would have been happy to show her how wrong she was. But they needed her and this strange daughter of Skarl Thundson. Egil clenched his jaw tight and only kept the woman's stare.

"My companion speaks true," Vedgif said, drawing Bodil's gaze away. Though his brow remained creased, his tone gave away none of his disapproval. "We would have an audience with Edda — Lord Edda. We have much to offer one another."

The warrioress seemed amused by their discomfort, her smile lingering. "I've my doubts about that. But you're fortunate — Lord Edda has taken an interest in you and wishes to speak further."

Glancing about them, Bodil leaned forward. For the first time, Egil saw she was not wholly comfortable herself. There was a tenseness to her shoulders that spoke of a readiness for action. "We share an enemy, after all," she continued softer. "And one cannot have too many friends in such times."

Before either Egil or the elder could respond, the Blaze braced her hands on the table and stood, causing the suspect furniture to wobble and the ale to dance in their cups.

"Come," she said, loud enough for the entire room to hear. "We'll go now." Bodil eyed Egil's full ale. "You going to finish that?"

He had barely shaken his head before the woman seized the cup and threw back her head. Moments later, she slammed it down on the table and cuffed her mouth and chin free of foamy dribbles.

"That's better! Nothing like ale in your belly for war talk."

The warrioress turned and strode for the door. Egil looked at Vedgif, but the elder was frowning after Bodil, a thoughtful look in his eyes. Only once she reached the entryway did he slowly stand and return Egil's gaze.

"Keep on your guard. And hope the daughter is not as bloodthirsty as her father."

Silencing his doubts, Egil rose and followed the elder from the tavern.

2. ALLIES & ENEMIES

И

He left in the night.

I did not stir. Torvald often rose at midnight to stand at the balcony. I saw no signs of what he intended. Yet every word he spoke, I copied down. It was as if, even then, I knew he would not remain with me for long.

- The diary of Siva Of Torvald, Wife of King Torvald Geirson, Matron of the Harrowhall, the Last Queen of Baegard

As she walked the halls of the Elkhorn for the last time, Aelthena wondered if she had ever been more eager to leave a place.

She had seen her fair share of suffering. She had been a prisoner in Lawspeaker Yaethun's home, a refugee in Frey's parents' house. She had fled Oakharrow and spent a week with the scantest of comforts.

But here in Lord Petyr's castle, she was a pariah. She was a jarl's heir no longer, but a disgraced recipient of charity, for King Ragnar had granted her amnesty until the warriors left for the next battle. By all appearances, her ambitions had foundered, her prospects beached and sunk. She had no authority on which to stand, nor allies remaining by her side.

But she had always been a woman fighting for a place in men's circles. It had always been an uphill battle. And in this case, she did not begin at the bottom of the valley.

Bastor had sworn an oath to her when he confessed his unrelenting hatred for his father. No matter what the false king said, neither of them would relent to Ragnar Torbenson. They would defy him and free Baegard from his tyranny.

So long as Bastor remained loyal to her and their cause.

Aelthena had not spoken to the prince since his father stole the crown, and what she saw from afar was scarcely reassuring. Alabastor Ragnarson played the part of the devoted prince well; too well, to her mind. He was charming with the couriers from the west: Jin'to had come calling, courting Baegard in the wake of its victory over Ha-Sypt and plainly hoping to gain a strategic position over its longtime rival, Xen'tia. He was strict when enforcing his father's harsh ordinances: the restrictions on food, the drafting of able-bodied men to Baegard's defense, the seizure of loose coins wherever they could be found. He was even sober, and since the Battle of Dragons — as more than one skald called the rout — she had not seen him drink anything more potent than watered ale.

Yet she clung to his earlier words. *I have hated my father since he burned those blocks.* Bastor resented him, and in some ways, had more right to anger than she did. He would not abandon her.

The prince was not her only uncertain ally. Because of her ostracism, Aelthena had not dared to approach those jarls, or even the jarls' widows, most likely to be amenable to her cause, as she feared to evoke the wrath of their new king. Yet her moment would come, and soon, if she judged correctly. Sigrid and Nanna would join her coalition; a women's alliance might finally see fruition. Though, in Nanna's case, that might mean little. The power of Aelford now lay with her son, a young man with all the brashness of his father and none of his hard-won experience. He was hardly the ideal target for her schemes, but with his mother's influence, Aelthena might still succeed.

Though she assumed them all allies, just now, they were as reliable as the skies in spring. *They'll abandon you*, an insidious voice whispered from the recesses of her mind. *As they did before.*

Cloistered in her shadowy corner of the castle, it seemed to Aelthena as if everyone had forgotten what had occurred during the brief siege. How Syptens had entered the Elkhorn, and two jarls fallen in battle — those most closely aligned with Aelthena and who opposed Ragnar's election. If anyone wondered if treachery was to blame, they whispered their suspicions out of her earshot.

Aelthena had not forgotten. She would never forget, not until the day she drove a dagger through the king's stone heart.

No doubt Ragnar suspected her lingering resentment. Much as she hated him, she had to admit he was a clever and perceptive man. It made it even more worrisome that he had not moved against her. The king was plotting something; that she did not know what made her more paranoid still.

Yet she had a ward against her doubts, a balm for her despair. Though all the world was set against her, Aelthena clung to the one who was not, and Frey had not spent a night since recovering from his wounds not in her bed.

For the first time in a long while, Aelthena felt free. She

had dissolved her engagement to Asborn, and though it had come with dire consequences, it had finally released her from obligation. People might whisper now, calling her "fallen" or coarser names, but she did not care. Here at the world's end, she had found a kernel of happiness, a rare bloom in the brightest of times, and she would let none trample it.

As she made her way to her destination, Frey walked a step behind her. She glanced over her shoulder to see his smile. That smile: both infuriating and tantalizing at once. As his eyes crinkled and his brow raised, a warmth stirred in her belly. They promised pleasures awaiting her that night, should she survive that long.

Facing forward, Aelthena blew out a breath and cleared her mind. She had to focus on the oncoming confrontation.

For she had come to beg.

She refused to remain here under the king's watchful eye any longer. One way or another, she would leave this place and make for Oakharrow, and it was far better if she did so with Bastor's army. Then, she might find opportunities among the jarls and the jarls' widows to win over allies.

But to travel with the procession, she needed an invitation. And since the prince had not deigned to extend her one, Asborn was her remaining option without compromising the rebellion before it had begun.

Aelthena reached the final corridor and was taken aback to find a guard waiting outside the intended door. She should have expected it; he was a jarl now, after all. The keeper, wearing a heavy tunic with a scarlet bird emblazoned upon the chest, eyed her and Frey. A hand rested on the hilt of his seax, but he made no move to draw it. He was an older fellow, gray proliferating throughout his braided beard, and part of his nose missing from a long-healed wound.

"Mistress Aelthena," he said gruffly. "The jarl is expecting you."

Mistress. Even her title had fallen. Yet the other part of the statement was more alarming. She had not warned her visitor of her intentions.

"Good," was all she said. "I am pleased to hear it."

The keeper looked at Frey. "Your man will stay out here."

Frey nodded, though he wore a mutinous expression. Satisfied, the guard turned and rapped on the door thrice. A muffled call came through, and the grizzled keeper opened the way.

Bracing herself, Aelthena stepped into the chamber.

There was little to remark upon within. The quarters were much like her own, albeit grander: gray stone walls and floors formed of blocks, a table with four chairs, a cold hearth. Her father had resided here until his removal, so she had visited it dozens of times. But before the trappings had been of the Elkhorn, the green bull elk sewn everywhere in sight. Redecoration had commenced, but been taken down to prepare for the departure on the morrow, so it had become barren once more.

Her focus moved to the room's sole occupant, who had his back to her as he stared out the far window. Though lithe, the heavy cloak about his shoulders, made of the white coat of a greatbear, made him seem larger. Anger shivered through her at the sight of it.

He wears the Winter Mantle even when it is too warm for it.

With an effort, Aelthena held her voice steady as she spoke. "Asborn."

Asborn Eirikson looked over his shoulder. He had never been an imposing figure, but the hard planes on his sallow face made her tense. Once, she had smoothed away those lines on his brow; now they seemed permanently carved in.

"It is Lord Asborn," he said. "As you well know."

The greeting was a poor portent for the conversation to come. Aelthena turned back to close the door. She gave Frey one last reassuring look before she pushed it closed with a resonant clunk.

When she turned back, Asborn finally faced her. His cherry-red hair, once worn long, was now cropped short; to fit under a helm, she assumed. He did not wear armor just then, however, but a fine tunic emblazoned with the red hawk of his kin. His belt, however, hung heavy with sword and seax, and he wore her father's cloak.

Once, she had loved him. But that man had ceased to exist.

"Lord Asborn, then. You were expecting me?"

He stared at her for a long moment. "Our king has spared you once more. Why is beyond me. You conspired against him. Openly defied him. You refused his right to rule. Yet here you stand."

She focused on the only thing that mattered in his words, the thing that hurt least to think about. She would not rise to his goad, nor explain how little Ragnar's treatment of her was a mercy.

"Spared me? How?"

"How, *m'lord.*" His eyes narrowed. "I thought you were so well informed. You have not heard?"

"No. M'lord."

She felt almost as if she did not occupy her body, but hovered somewhere outside of it. A small, cruel smile claimed his lips as he stepped closer. Once, his nearing would have warmed her blood; now, it chilled her through.

"The Eternal Night is falling, Aelthena. It is not just the baseless cries of doomsayers in the streets. Giants of Fire and Frost have returned. If we are to endure, Baegard needs a strong and cunning leader. We need Ragnar as king. Your defiance would kill us all if he let it."

The illusion of impassivity cut away in a moment. Aelthena closed the distance between them and stared up into Asborn's eyes as she spat out the words.

"I'd rather Baegard burn than let him have it."

His facade cracked. A flush crept up his neck to his cheeks. Aelthena held his gaze. She had known him before his ascension; she knew him still. He could never match her.

Asborn took a step back. "You've made that clear."

He seemed about to speak again, then looked aside with fists clenched. Aelthena repressed a smile. She would not lower herself to his base cruelty.

"How did Ragnar spare me, Asborn?" she repeated.

This time, he did not meet her eye. "You're to ride with the expedition tomorrow, and among the highborn. Prince Alabastor has commanded it be so."

It took her a moment to wrap her mind around that. She had known of the campaign, of course; even excluded from planning and politicking, it would have been impossible to avoid hearing of half of Baegard's forces marching on Oakharrow, while the other half stayed in Petyrsholm to ward against further Sypten attacks. But with the dearth of communication, she had not dared hope she would take part in the action. This could easily give Aelthena a chance to claw back into power, a possibility that could not fail to escape Ragnar.

"Did he?" she restrained herself to saying.

Asborn's eyes found hers again. "Don't think I forgot how you two conspired together — or tried to. I can only be thankful the prince proved loyal in the end."

She fought down a smile. Though she had questioned

Bastor's loyalty before, she no longer would. Nothing Asborn did now could deflate her burgeoning hope.

"Thank you for telling me."

Asborn nodded curtly, then moved to the window, a clear sign of dismissal. It stung, but she was in too high a mood to be brought down. Aelthena began to leave, but as her hand rested on the door handle, she hesitated.

She had loved him once. Though she no longer recognized the man he had become, she had to believe he was still in there, buried beneath his anger and hurt.

"It doesn't have to be like this, Asborn," she spoke toward the door. "We don't have to be..." *Enemies,* she almost said, but she hoped they had not devolved that far.

"It does. You made it so."

Aelthena lingered a moment longer, then sighed and opened the door. She had chased enough hopeless causes to know their look.

Back in the hall, she ignored the keeper and nodded at Frey. The guardian fell in step with her as they strode down the hall.

"So it went well," he observed.

Aelthena glanced sidelong at him. "As well as expected."

"That's better than it could have been."

"Were you worried, my guardian?"

"It's my job to worry."

"You were never much good at it before."

"I didn't have something to lose then."

Aelthena remained facing forward. People were passing by, bustling about the preparations to leave the next day, yet she could not entirely hide her feelings.

"Does the lady blush?" Frey teased softly.

She ignored him, hoping it would make the fire in her face fade as well. "We're riding with the expedition. Among the nobility, no less."

"That's... unexpected. Bastor's behind it?"

"Who else?"

"So he's not entirely a bastard — or not just. It's a victory, Aelthena, and one we sorely needed."

"A small one."

"A victory of any size is a fine thing just now."

She repressed a sigh. "I know. It will have to be enough."

Aelthena pulled her thoughts away from the subject. There would be plenty of time to scheme on the road once she was out from under Ragnar's thumb. For now, she had more practical matters to attend to.

Soon enough, she would take back what was hers. And no one — not Ragnar, not Asborn, nor any giant or Sypten — would stand in her way.

3. THE BURDEN OF PRIVILEGE

All understand the burdens of poverty; one has simply to see the poorness of their station. But the burdens of privilege remain unseen, and they weigh on my shoulders, day and night.

- The diary of Siva Of Torvald, Wife of King Torvald Geirson, Matron of the Harrowhall, the Last Queen of Baegard

Charming, do you not think, Highness?"

Bastor roused at the query. Though he strode through the hallway in the company of a dozen others, he had been lost to his thoughts.

And gods know I'm not given to being thoughtful.

"Yes. Very charming." He wondered if his cheer rang falsely in his companion's ear as it did his own. If she even cared.

Tove Of Petyr only smiled. "I am glad you think so. Just because we make war does not mean we must look like barbarians!"

He did not bother asking what she chattered about. The daughter of Lord Petyr had often trailed behind him since his new title had been slapped on his name. When he had been the mere jarl's heir, most had wanted little to do with him. After all, Sypten blood ran through his veins, and his reputation had long ago lost its shine. For a prince, however, it seemed many shortcomings could be forgiven.

He glanced at the jarl's daughter. She was fair by most standards, though her features were more severe than he preferred. But Tove's tittering banished any beauty she might have possessed.

Too late, he looked away, his attention encouraging her to speech.

"We might also fix up something nice for a tent, for socializing in the evenings. Perhaps feasts might not be possible, but certainly dancing could..."

Bastor did not even pretend to listen now. He felt horribly thirsty all of a sudden, and not for the watered beer he had restricted himself to.

One strong drink, where's the harm?

He knew the harm; his past was littered with evidence. He was no misbegotten son lurking in the shadows now. Bastor was the firstborn prince, heir to the new King of Baegard. His present actions carried more weight than ever before, and, for once, he did not wish to burn it all to the ground.

He had an important position, and by it influence to forge a better country — gods, perhaps a better world. Bastor smiled at the thought.

What good could a Sypten bastard do?

Only part of him believed the derisive voice. His power was ill gotten, yet even evil could be turned to good. Ragnar, after all, had saved Petyrsholm through every manner of deceit. The price of princeship was high; being the dutiful son only bolstered his father's tenuous reign. Yet it was one Bastor would willingly pay if he could achieve his aims.

Tove was only part of the cost, for she was not the only barnacle clinging to his every step. Other highborn daughters, and even a few young mothers, hounded him every chance they could get. In one move, he had become the most desirable match among the jarlheims, and no maiden would pass up the opportunity. It was all he could do to repel their advances, particularly the ones that tried to ensnare him in a bedroom. Pleasant as the diversion might prove, the consequences were too dire to ignore. All it would take was one woman claiming pregnancy and his fate would be sealed.

It was enough to drive a man to drown in mead, if he could only allow it.

All things considered, the departure for another front was almost a relief. Tove seemed intent on accompanying the expedition, but most of the other women would not. He could escape them for a time and throw himself into a war he knew how to fight.

Dreaming of blood... Some things never change.

Reaching the end of a long staircase, Bastor noticed his destination ahead and turned back to his followers. "Stay here, if you please — I won't be long. Mido, the bags?"

As his retinue muttered reluctant compliance, a thrall stepped forward. Mido, a short and slight Sypten with a soft manner and a sharp mind, had been gifted to him by Lord Petyr for his good fortunes. That, at least, served as the jarl's official explanation. Privately, Bastor suspected the Jarl of Petyrsholm had been angling for his daughter's betrothal from the start. Though Bastor at first held Mido at a distance, suspicious that he might spy on him for his old master, a few shared drinks and his reputation among the castle's servants had bridged the divide. The awkwardness of power dynamics aside, he liked to think they were fast becoming familiar.

Mido brought out the two requested bags, their contents jangling inside the violet silk, and offered them with a slight smile. Unable to give even a nod lest the nobility behind him take offense, Bastor gave him a meaningful stare instead, then turned forward to stride away from the others.

"Why does he bother with thralls?" someone muttered from behind.

Anger flared through him. Had fortune not favored him, the same would have been said of himself. But perhaps Baegard would have the misfortune of seeing him king. Then, things would be different; he would make sure of it.

For the moment, he set his mind to what little he could do. Passing through the door, the bustle of the kitchens swept over him in a gush of steamy warmth. Scullions chopped; bakers baked; and head cook Pyhia oversaw it all from her stool at the near corner, eyes narrowed and brow furrowed. There was something wholesome to honest work, especially when he himself engaged in plots and schemes from dawn to long after dusk. Even more, after weeks of cloying attention, it was refreshing to be ignored.

But it could not last. Only moments after he entered, a cooking woman carving a hog glanced around. Her eyes widened, and her head lowered, bloody hands and knife ignored.

"You honor us, Highness!"

At her cry, the rest of the kitchen staff came to a slow halt. One by one, they echoed her. With each bow, Bastor's mood fell lower.

What a burden, this privilege.

When the room had fallen silent but for the hissing of cooking dishes and the crackle of oven fires, Bastor raised a

27

hand. "Please, rise. Don't burn the pot bottoms on my account."

The staff needed no further prompting. At once, they leaped back to their tasks, though not without nervous glances over their shoulders.

The head cook had scooted off her stool and approached. She, at least, seemed no more cowed than before his rise in circumstances.

"Highness," she said with a distinct lack of reverence, "what brings you back down here?"

There was more than a bit of accusation in that query. Bastor only just repressed a wince. For a moment, he felt like the boy he had been growing up among the kitchen staff at Lynx Manor. The chef then had been severe as well, though not unkindly.

He held up the silk bags, their contents shifting. "I had promises to keep before I depart, Pyhia Faa."

A touch of warmth returned to the cook. "By your hand?"

The question would have been seen as impetuous by other highborn. For Bastor, it was a compliment. He would never be one of the Syptens, not with the gulf in status between them, but he could hope they would not resent him.

Bastor smiled. "It wouldn't be a proper gift otherwise."

Pyhia gave a curt nod, then turned and shouted over her shoulder. "Ipu! Fetch the trimmings!"

The young serving girl bobbed her head, but stared at Bastor before scurrying away. Bastor averted his eyes, remembered fury flaring. He hoped his father had not forced Ipu into more odious acts. Since the previous occasion, when Bastor had entered the king's chambers to find the girl half-clothed, he had avoided his father whenever he could. After all, there was nothing he could do to prevent it; the king could do as he pleased, on the whole.

For now.

The dark thoughts were banished as three children burst from a pantry and scurried over to him. At the head cook's severe look, they bobbed their heads, then ignored Bastor's esteemed title as thoroughly as they would an irksome chore.

"What did you bring us, Uncle? Prince, I mean," the shorter of the boys, Neith, amended, though his eagerness was unabated.

Bastor grinned. "What do you think?"

"Blocks!" both boys answered.

He had little choice but to hand them over at once. The kitchen boys scrambled to pick their bag first. As they settled the matter, the last of the children, Bennu, stepped forward and crossed her arms.

"What about me, Bastor Faa?"

"You must call him Highness or Prince, Bennu," the girl's mother corrected from nearby, where she stirred a pot and scowled at her daughter.

Bennu ignored her, her fierce gaze never shifting from Bastor.

With a sly smile, he drew out another silk bag that matched the first two. "Can't keep your blocks in just anything, can we?"

Eyes wide, the girl uncrossed her arms to accept the purple bag, running her fingers over the fabric. He would have made a high wager it was the finest material she had ever held, and perhaps the softest as well. More importantly, all the kitchen children were in parity — a necessity to keep their chaos contained.

As the children scurried off to play with their blocks,

the head cook approached again. "You'll be leaving soon, I hear?"

"Tomorrow."

"Well, may you have the gods' fortune surviving."

"The same to you, Pyhia Faa. We all need a bit of luck these days."

Bastor gave the kitchens one last look, then turned back the way he had come. It could well be the last time he saw any of them, even if he survived the coming battles.

Yet he would not forget for whom he fought.

Bastor entered his father's quarters. By their look, he would have been hard pressed to say they belonged to a king. The violet lynx had been stripped from the table, walls, and chairs, leaving tan stone walls behind. The divan remained, however, as did the young man reclining upon it, a plume of smoke curling from his mouth.

Ragnar the Younger grinned slackly up at him. "Brother."

Bastor only nodded, then looked for their father. He could not have said which he preferred: his younger brother's company or the cloyingly sweet sycophants he had left outside the door.

"Where's Father?"

His brother gave an exaggerated shrug. "Am I to be my king's keeper?"

Before Bastor could think of a reply, he heard rustling from the adjoining room. Tensing, he turned as his father emerged. Though he was now the crowned king, Ragnar Torbenson seemed much the man he had been before. He still carried himself in that rigid way, still had the same proud contemptuousness and cold calculation. His bright eyes latched onto Bastor like an eagle's talons on a fish. Even now, it took an effort not to flinch.

"Crown Prince Alabastor. You join your kin at last."

Bastor could not keep his lips from curling. Even in private, his father wanted to maintain formalities.

How sorry I'll be to disappoint.

"Ragnar," he responded simply.

When no honorifics followed, nor even familial affection, the king frowned. Yet he had never had the patience to squabble.

"Your troops are prepared to leave on the morrow?"

Bastor shrugged. "I should hope so."

Again, a moment of thin-lipped silence. Ragnar's annoyance was plain as he broke it. "Your brother's guard is likewise prepared. Keep your messengers rested and ready. Our missing scouts indicate the karah has not been simply retreating. He will strike again, and we must be ready to reinforce wherever he does."

Bastor crossed his arms. "So you've still lost them, have you? An entire army, and their giants as well?"

Finally, anger stirred in the king's eyes. "You are in one of your moods. See to it one does not come over you while you're in command. I may have excused it in a jarl's heir, but it is unbecoming in a prince."

Bastor found himself looking at his brother. To his surprise, Young Ragnar returned the look. It had been a long time since the two shared any camaraderie, not since they were boys and Bastor taught him to hunt, forage, and fight. But against their father, it was an easy and natural alliance.

His younger brother spoke first. "Never fear, Father. Have we not always made you proud?"

"No. You have not." No fine words now; Ragnar's

temper had been stirred. Bastor marveled that it had been so simple.

Ambition grinds even a king's nerves down.

"This is a test for you, Prince Ragnar," their father continued. "Though Ragnarsglade is across the Whiterun, do not think it will protect you from the Syptens. Even now, they may have built rafts or ferries to cross. Guard our borders, and no matter the cost, do not let it fall."

The youngest son sat up slowly, smoke trailing from the pipe in his hand. Bastor could see his inebriation from his dilated pupils and loose posture, yet there was iron in his words as he spoke.

"I won't fail you, Father. I will hold."

Bastor kept his reservations private. His brother was not stupid, only a fool. He had not yet outgrown the youthful delusion of invincibility. Between that and his indulgences, the jarlheim would have to be blessed by all the Inscribed to survive a Sypten attack. For his people's sake, if not Young Ragnar's, he hoped it would.

But there was more implied in their father's words. As Ragnar remained the Jarl of Ragnarsglade, that placed Bastor as his heir apparent to both Baegard and the jarlheim. Yet he sought to test his younger son as if he stood to inherit.

He should have expected as much. After all, his father had tried to have Bastor killed.

He pushed down the blossoming rage. Vengeance was an icy blade. He would keep it sheathed until its time came, when the Seven Jarlheims no longer needed Ragnar.

Then, Father, I will strike so you won't rise, just as you taught me.

The king looked back to Bastor, then nodded to them both. "That is all. Do your duty."

With that, he returned to the other room.

Bastor stared after him. It was a curt farewell, but that did not come as a surprise. Theirs was not a family for tearful goodbyes. He looked to the divan to find his brother watching him. It unnerved him, that clarity even amidst his fog of intoxicants.

"Don't die, Brother," Young Ragnar said.

"Not buried yet, am I?"

For a wonder, both of them smiled at that. Yet his brother's merriment slipped away as quickly as it had come. "No," he sighed. "But this is war. More men, women, and children will die before it's through."

Bastor wondered then if he truly knew his brother. Most young men would leap at the chance to prove themselves in battle, to reach for eternal glory and an honored place among the ancestors and gods.

At least he has the sense to know better.

"Just make sure you're not one of them," Bastor said. "And our people, too."

As Young Ragnar nodded, Bastor turned away. He wondered if it would be the last time they saw each other. They both faced foes they were unsure they could vanquish.

But Bastor had to survive. To do otherwise would prove his father right in his opinions of his eldest son. And that would be the greatest failure of all.

He held himself high as he strode from the room, but deflated at once. His retinue still waited in the hall outside, with nothing better to do than fawn over him. Tove Of Petyr stood at their fore, and she immediately began babbling as soon as he emerged.

One battle over, he thought as he strode down the corridor. *But a war is fought on many fronts.*

Doing his best to ignore them, Bastor set about the final preparations to leave this all behind.

4. THE WAY HOME

"This is the matter of it: the home you left is never the same one you return to."

- Yofam Dragontooth, Slayer of the wyvern Vardraith, First Drang of the Iron Band

Bjorn had been watching for it. He peered over every crest, a fluttering in his chest like a flock of hens pecked to be released from their coop. His eyes had grown keener since leaving, approaching even Yonik's prodigious sight. So though light leeched from the day, he was the first to see it.

To start, the gray cliff of the Dawnshadow leaned overhead, glowing with orange evening light. Then came the high turrets of the manors, gleaming in bronze and silver. Finally, the walls, still standing here on the north side; a memory of the city's strength, and a reminder of what it could become once more.

"Oakharrow," Bjorn whispered. He reached up and stroked Clap's muzzle. "We're almost home, boy."

His horse nudged him back, as if to return the sentiment.

"Did you see it, Lord Heir?" Loridi appeared at his other side, the tall man leaning down so his braided blonde hair, grown long in the intervening months, brushed across Bjorn's shoulder. His eyes lit up, and he turned a grin on Bjorn. "Oakharrow at last! Thus does the exiled heir return, wreathed in fame and glory."

Bjorn managed a weak smile. "Fame" and "glory" were not exactly how he would describe his accomplishments. They had destroyed a pit of *khnuum*, robbing the Jotun of his dragonfire. He had met the King of Ice and received a mission from him that could save Enea from the invasion of giants. He knew the first steps he must take down the path and approached that initial crucial moment.

Yet for every victory, they had suffered an equal loss. The whittling away of the Hunters in the White. The massacre of Eildursprall and the gutting of the gothi order. And the final stroke of losing the Witterland Runestone to the King of Chieftains, whatever that loss meant.

Even if we succeed, what will be left?

Though he did not intend to, his gaze traveled to Tyra, who walked on Clap's other side. Her cheeks were flushed from the day's hike and the weeks spent in the sun, making her freckles stand out even more than before. Her eyes, summer green, seemed bright as they met his. She smiled, and he returned it, a quivering starting in his chest.

He did not fight only for an elusive future, once veiled in smoke and shadow. He fought for them: his friends, his clan, his family, if Aelthena and his father survived. He fought for Tyra. It was enough to persist in the face of impossible odds.

Yonik, who led their small party, turned and brought them to a halt, his mulish horse, the best they could recover from Eildursprall, hoofing the ground in protest. "We will stop here for the night," he said, ignoring his mount as he gestured to a hollow in the foothills of the Teeth. "And we must decide on our approach."

Bjorn felt the others look at him. He nodded, his throat suddenly dry. They had been discussing how to enter Oakharrow the entire journey south, yet had come to no sound conclusions. *We'll wait and see* had been the only thing he could say, and he said it often.

But the issue had rarely left his mind. Too much remained unknown. Which entrances did the Jotun watch, and which escaped his notice? Bjorn was no expert in Oakharrow's defenses, but as one of the jarl's sons, he had received a passing education in them. The most vulnerable point was the place where the Honeybrook streamed out from under the wall. Yet even with its flow weak with autumn, it would be difficult to travel up, and might still be watched, if the portcullis was not lowered as it should be.

He would not gamble with their lives. So Bjorn had sought answers the only way he could.

"I, for one, am ready for a hot meal," Loridi announced, taking the lead toward the hollow. "And if you're lucky, I'll tell a story or two to boot! Been saving a titillating tale about a milkmaid and her affair with a man she thought to be Djur, but... well, I won't spoil the surprise!"

"No fires," Yonik cautioned, ignoring the jester. Seskef followed after, though he moved at his own steady stride.

That left Tyra and Bjorn behind. As she glanced his way, a smile won free of him. Often, he marveled at the changes in her since they had left Eildursprall. Heim Numen lay in ashes along with the rest of the town. Yet even if it had remained, he thought some part of her had left behind the priesthood toward which she had oriented her life.

He could think of no other explanation for their nightly liaisons.

They had begun not two days after heading down from the mountains and into the main valley of Baegard. Bjorn had been lying in his bedroll, staring up at the shimmering sky above, painted by both the Blood and Sea Moons, when he heard her stir and approach. His thoughts turned from the horrors that lay behind and ahead, a different picture occurring to him: Tyra as he had accidentally glimpsed in the baths, unclothed and unaware.

She kneeled, then bent close to him and whispered next to his ear. "Are you awake?"

"Yes."

He had reached for her, though he did not know what he intended. So he was caught off guard when she grasped his hand in both of hers, then leaned closer. He was keenly aware of her breasts brushing against his chest. His throat squeezed shut, his breath coming quick.

"I'm tired of waiting." Her hands pulled his closer, cradling it so his finger brushed her throat. "How long would we have to wait?"

Even with his mind muddled, he understood. Waiting for the ashes to settle. For grief to fade. For pleasure not to seem like sacrilege.

By the heat blossoming through his chest, he was tired of waiting, too.

She pressed his hand against her chest. He pulled her head down to his with his free hand. Their lips touched.

They did not part for a long time.

Even if the others had not heard them quietly rustling about the blankets, they seemed to notice something had changed the next morning. Loridi teased them at every opportunity, while Yonik became quiet when it came up, his shadowed eyes having an air of consideration.

Like Tyra, Bjorn refused to feel ashamed. What they did was not immoral, nor did he regret it. She lit a fire within him he had never felt before. Her wit, her curiosity, her perseverance — never had he felt for a woman as he did for her.

And it was not without precedent. Embla had continued and deepened her relationship with Hoarfrost from all he had witnessed. The priestess had stayed with the Skyardi scout leader back in Eildursprall, the women joining in more ways than one. Some of the town's survivors had gone with the barbar tribe, while others remained behind to rebuild. Embla's intent had been to go with Hoarfrost as she looked after her people over the coming winter months, then prepared them for the future.

Before they had left, the Skyardi had stood before Bjorn and held his gaze with her icy eyes. Then she had extended her arm, and he had gripped it in the warrior's way.

"I will shield my people from the coming war," she had said. "But no matter the blood spilled between our nations, we are allies in this, Bjorn Borson. My warriors and I will stand with you when the time comes. Look for us upon Oakharrow's eastern slopes come winter's thaw."

Bjorn had nodded, emotion swelling within him. He wondered if he had ever met a braver and more loyal warrior. She could have remained hidden in the mountains and waited for the storm to pass, but instead threw herself into the thick of it. And Embla, prodigious with her own talents and tenacity, would stand by her.

Why could he and Tyra not do the same?

Yet with Oakharrow in view, Bjorn felt a different feeling rising. He did not want her to face the storm. He wished her to be as far from danger as possible, even if it put her on the other end of Enea. He wanted to protect her as he had failed to protect Keld, his brothers, and his mother. He needed her to be safe.

Tyra stepped closer. "It's hard to be back home," she said, guessing at the source of his somber mood.

Bjorn nodded. "We have to find a way in."

She took his hand. "We will. We've gotten this far, haven't we?"

He looked aside, gaze traveling to their appointed camp-site. "We'd best help the others. Don't want to give Loridi any more reasons to tease us."

Keenly aware of her gaze, Bjorn released her hand and pulled Clap after their companions. A lump sat in his throat that he could not swallow down.

This is the way it must be. The only way.

Their camp was mostly quiet. After telling his promised tale, in which the milkmaid's lover was revealed to be a barbar cowled in a stolen bearskin, even Loridi submitted to the general mood. Cricket chirps and bird calls filled the dusky sky as light faded beyond the western peaks of the Spine. They sat in a circle as they ate, avoiding each others' eyes and the questions swirling behind them.

"We'll venture closer tomorrow, then watch and wait," Yonik spoke into the silence. "Perhaps there's an opening we can take advantage of. The Teeth Gate, for one, or what's left of it; I doubt they've had time to repair it since we left."

"Patience." Seskef wiped at his brow; he was sweating despite the cool evening. "That's the way of the wise warrior."

Loridi stared at his partner. "Since when do you go around spouting sagacity? You're more a farmer than a soldier."

As the two bickered, Bjorn slipped away and found refuge in his bedroll. The others soon did the same. Tyra did not seek him out. He tried to decide if he was more relieved or disappointed.

The only way, he reminded himself, then pretended to sleep.

When his turn for the watch came, Bjorn relieved Yonik and sat on a fallen log. The mountains at his back, he stared into the gloom settled over the valley. Both moons chanced to be out again, casting the dark sky in a purple haze. Even without them, however, his vision had grown sharper over the past year, and especially in the last few months. The night appeared in layers of gray rather than the utter darkness that the Teeth had when first setting into them.

It was not the only change wrought upon him. A full beard sprouted along his face, already nearing as full as Yonik's own bush. His hair, already once trimmed, now fell well past his shoulders, and he had been meaning to ask Seskef to put it to the knife again. His body had grown resilient and strong, and even after a long day's hike, he suffered few aches and pains.

He had often pondered the mystery of his transformation across the leagues; now, it crept up on him during the long, dark wait. Perhaps he was merely filling out; he had only seen eighteen winters, after all, and still had room to grow. His frame was becoming much like his father's, tall and broad, if not as stout as Bor the Bear had been in his prime.

But this did not feel like ordinary growth, both in its speed and degree. To Bjorn, it had the sulphuric taste of sorcery. Yet the answers he came up with were unsavory, and with little recourse if they were true, he tried not to think too closely on the matter.

What will be, will be.

Once he judged it had been long enough, Bjorn rose and crept across the camp. Every noise seemed amplified in the quiet night, yet as Bjorn pulled on his heavy pack and took his sword belt in hand, the others did not stir. Barely breathing, moving with careful steps, he made away from the camp and down into the forest.

Once out of earshot, he exhaled. The first part was done. It was a risk leaving them without a watch, and guilt threaded through him for it, but it was the lesser of the dangers before them.

For him, the hardest part still lay ahead.

Despite Yonik's earlier words, Bjorn suspected he knew as well as Bjorn did that there would be no simple way into Oakharrow. They could wait a month without seeing a lapse in the watch. Oakharrow did not have a month, nor Baegard. Enea fell into deeper shadow with each passing day. To idle them away would be a vain attempt to put off the inevitable.

Bjorn had been a coward too many times before. He refused to act one now.

He knew his path forward. Torvald Geirson's rune-stones, the Four Shadows that would reveal the path through the rising Runewar, had shown that he must ally himself with the last individual he wished to. The same enemy that had stolen so much from him: his home, his family, his world.

He had to go to the Jotun.

Even in Eildursprall, some part of him had known what he would have to do. He knew where the Jotun was and how to reach him. It was just a matter of doing what needed to be done.

So he was doing it. He was giving himself up.

It was a risk, a towering one, but what decision these days was not? Bjorn saw no other way to reach the giant. The five of them could not battle their way into Oakharrow to meet the Jotun on their terms. If any of his allies remained in the city, Bjorn could not contact them. This was the only path left.

Still, he had sought to confirm it. Two nights before, in secrecy, he had looked upon the *vidasuum* runestone and used the Sight to glimpse the future. His path, though still murky, had revealed its next step, foolish though it seemed.

But he had seen what was to come. In this, at least, his doubts were silent. Bjorn would survive; the gods had willed it.

"I wondered if you would try this."

Bjorn whirled around, sword halfway drawn, and stared at the silhouette not ten paces from him. Only as he saw the man's eyes gleam with moonlight did he sheathe the blade. A part of Bjorn had expected this. Yonik's senses were far too keen by half to not notice his departure.

"I had to." Bjorn stared past the priest. Even in the darkness, he was reluctant to meet his gaze. "I won't risk the others."

Yonik advanced, stopping close enough for a hushed conversation. He had his gear with him as well, twin knives snug at his hips.

"That's not up to you." The gothi spoke gently but firmly. "Each man and woman gets to make their own decision."

"And I've made mine."

Silence filled the forest until Yonik's sigh broke it. "So you mean to give yourself up?"

A flicker of defiance rose in Bjorn as he stared the priest in the eye. "My path leads to the Jotun. There's only one way to reach him."

"No." Yonik shook his head, shaggy locks dancing about his face. "Do not confuse the goal for the path, nor prophecy for certainty. There are other ways, Bjorn, if we take the time to search for them."

42

Bjorn leaned closer, mere inches away, to hiss, "We don't have time. I know there are no guarantees. I know it seems like I'm throwing my life away. But I have seen this, Yonik. It's the only way."

The priest eyed him. "Was it when you snuck off? Don't think we hadn't noticed."

Bjorn grimaced. Of course, Yonik had. Little escaped the sharp-eyed gothi.

"Yes. I saw I would enter the walls." He hesitated, but there was little point in concealing the truth now. "I do not know how, only that I would survive."

Yonik sighed, then gripped Bjorn's shoulder. "Fine. If you have Seen it, then this is our way."

As swiftly as his hopes rose, they plummeted.

"No," Bjorn said quickly. "No, not *our* way. I must go alone. I cannot know what would befall you."

The man's generous eyebrows raised. "Even your visions cannot tell you everything, Stoneseer. It is a possibility, not a certainty. To make sure it comes to pass, you'll need someone watching your back."

For a moment, both stared at each other. Then Bjorn deflated with a sigh.

"Stubborn old wolf," he muttered as he turned away.

He heard the grin in the priest's reply. "Show me the way, bear cub, and pray the visions haven't led us astray."

5. THE WATCHER

"During every vigil, a warrior makes a choice: to protect his brothers or fail them. My men would sew their eyes open before sleeping at their posts."

- Yofam Dragontooth, Slayer of the wyvern Vardraith, First Drang of the Iron Band

Egil stood watch over the North Gate, but he only kept one eye on the darkness beyond the wall.

It was a moonless night, and the ever-present gloom over Oakharrow, hanging above like a swollen thundercloud, was a bitter taste on his tongue. There was little to hold Egil's attention, the trees becoming murky outlines even to his keen eyes.

The mountains look like resting giants.

He resisted the urge to scrub at his eyes. The thought was something Brother Yonik might have said. But poetry was best left to priests; a warrior sang with his sword.

The possibility for that sharp singing always lingered near. Many things had changed under the Jotun's rule, but the routine of the watch proved one of the most irksome. Every Baegardian on duty was paired with one of the giant's men, be they jotunman or mere barbar. Egil had no trouble staying awake with the savages nearby. Often, they openly watched him, grinning when he could not hide his discomfort. His suspicions were justified by talk of quarrels breaking out, and whether the Harrowman won or not, he always died in the end. Even so, Egil kept a dagger at the ready, remembering those frigid days fleeing the Woldagi from Jünsden.

I survived them once. I'll survive again.

His partner that night was a jotunman, and a big one at that, his generous gut covered by patchy fur. Like most others of his kind, he wore no shirt, but preferred to display his monstrous transformation, as prideful as if his fur were bangles of gold and silver. Several times that night, he had flashed his stubby tusks at Egil, taunting eyes glimmering in the torchlight.

Egil's look had drawn his partner's attention, whose name he had never bothered to learn. The jotunman grinned.

"Skinny boy," he grunted in his garbled voice. "Must want my cock to keep staring."

His laughter grated in Egil's ears, but he ignored him. Anything else would only encourage further gibes.

But this night, the barbar was not to be deterred. Sauntering closer, he loomed over Egil, a head taller and half and again as wide. "Go on — give it a taste. I keep watch for us both."

Fire spread through his chest, but Egil kept his expression impassive as he faced the bestial man. He could not ignore him this time. Things would only get worse if he failed to meet his challenge. Some battles could not be run from.

What a relief it was to take a stand.

"Noticed you beasts don't have women," Egil said softly. "Must get lonely. Lots of men sucked your cock, haven't they? Maybe tasted one or two yourself."

He had never had a gift for insults, but he judged that to be smart enough as the jotunman's smile turned to a scowl. The bestial man leaned down so their faces were inches apart. Egil had difficulty tracking his hand. His own had fallen to his knife's hilt, itching to draw.

"We have your women now, skinny boy. Later, I find me a sister or cousin of yours to rut. King Chief don't mind."

Thinking of his female cousins, he wondered if this savage could make good on the threat. The Jotun's networks had spread swiftly throughout the city, but his men were still brutes at their cores, all too flame-bent for subtlety. He doubted they could connect family lines beyond those who lived with each other. Then again, with people like his father cooperating with the giant, there was always the possibility.

Father wouldn't. Not our own kin. Though he had displayed little loyalty toward anyone else, Yaethun Brashurson had always looked out for his only son. He had to believe the same would hold true for the rest of their extended family.

Even if his life was at stake? Or mine?

The jotunman straightened and grinned at Egil's silence. "Ah... You coming 'round. Now, skinny boy. On your knees."

His knife had almost left its sheath when he caught sight of something in the corner of his eye. Stepping back to put some distance between them, Egil looked through a crenel at the shadowy tree line. Even in the darkness, he could pick out two figures emerging and coming toward the gate.

He frowned, wondering who would be mad enough to approach the gate at night. Once, he would have feared it was Syptens up to one of their tricks, but with enemies already inside Oakharrow's walls, anything that undermined the Jotun's dominion would likely benefit the jarlheim.

The jotunman opened his mouth to speak, but paused as he noticed Egil's gaze. Screwing up his piggish eyes, he stared into the gloom.

"Men," he barked. "Two of them. Friends of yours, skinny boy?" Without waiting for an answer, he reached for the great hornbow leaning against the wall and grinned. "Got a shaft for them they won't enjoy."

Egil reached for his own bow and nocked an arrow. He stared hard down at the approaching strangers, though he never lost sight of the brute next to him. Just out of bow range, the two figures stopped. Words, faint over the distance, came echoing up.

"Hail the wall! We seek an audience with the Jotun."

Egil narrowed his eyes. Not Syptens, then; more barbars, either scouts returning or others wishing to join Kuljash. He eased the tension on his bowstring.

The jotunman still seemed in a jovial mood. "Think you can meet with the King Chief, eh? Who the fuck are you?"

There was a pregnant pause before the same man answered. "I am Brother Yonik, a gothi to the Inscribed. I bring with me the heir to the Winter Mantle: Bjorn, Son of Bor."

Egil mouthed the names. *They're alive. They're here.* His heart pounded as he realized the bind they had put him in. Kuljash would crush them. Long had the giant sought Lord Bor's kin, killing all those he found, for those related to the ruling family were not so difficult to track down. He would not hesitate to execute both of them to better secure his power.

The jotunman screwed up his eyes, struggling to understand. "You... you're the jarl's heir?"

Egil turned to the jotunman. In a single motion, he drew, aimed, and loosed.

The arrow found its mark in the jotunman's neck.

The brute staggered and dropped his bow, hands scrabbling at the shaft. His eyes were wide as he stared at Egil. Blood dribbled from his lips. Egil tossed aside his bow and drew his sword, then stalked toward the barbar. Though the bestial man could make no more noise than gargling, he would not chance him making further racket.

His blade dipped, then came up dark. His fellow watchman slumped to the stone.

Egil looked up and down the wall. There was movement within the towers, shadows dancing in the firelight, but if anyone had noticed, they gave no sign of it. From one tower came raucous laughter; a gamble of knuckles in full swing, he guessed. The other was deathly silent; its occupants sleeping, if he had the Spinners' fortune.

Either way, he could not chance shouting, not the words he had to say. Egil sheathed his sword, picked up his bow, then took in hand a torch, which he waved overhead twice. Hoping they would understand his intentions, he turned for the nearby gatehouse.

A winch in the gatehouse cranked open the great wooden doors of the North Gate. It was not designed for one man to operate it, yet by bracing his shoulder against each spindle, one at a time, Egil eased it open. The gate rumbled; not a quiet sound, and one that the men in the other guardhouses should have heard. The watch used to have regular patrols along the walls that would have caught him, but the Jotun's men were far laxer. Through the murder holes in the stone floor, he saw the doors begin to part. A few turns in, and they were wide enough to admit a man.

Wiping the sweat from his brow, Egil hurried outside, bow on his shoulder and a torch in hand. Looking up the wall, he did not see any sign of barbars coming to check on things. Not wishing to push his luck, he hurried down to the gate to greet the foolish visitors.

The two were approaching; soon, they were close enough to recognize. Or at least, he recognized the priest. Upon seeing Bjorn Borson, Egil flinched. The jarl's heir had changed much since the winter before, almost enough to be a stranger to his eyes. Bjorn had always been tall, but now he had grown broad as well, both in the shoulders and chest. His face was even more startling: a beard every bit as thick and wild as Yonik's sprouted across his chin. Even his eyebrows seemed to have thickened, curling around the edges of his eyes. Yet those eyes, golden in the firelight, seemed even stranger. Gone was the cringing fear with which he had beheld everything before, Egil most of all. Now, his gaze was steady as he approached, burdened by a bulky pack that he shouldered with ease.

Egil's throat went strangely dry.

Yonik grinned as they came within whispering distance. "Egil Yaethunson. So you made it back. The Rook as well?"

Egil nodded, doubting he could have formed words if he had tried.

"Thank you, Egil." Bjorn spoke now, his voice soft; that, at least, had not changed. "We didn't expect to see a familiar face this night."

What did you expect? But Egil's tongue was still too thick and clumsy to move.

"The other watchman," Yonik continued, "we saw him fall. I'm guessing he was not loyal?"

49

Loyal. They assumed him to be their ally so easily. Still, they trusted, even after all they had experienced.

Halfwits, the both of them.

Anger finally helped Egil find his voice. "He was a jotunman. But we cannot talk here. Come."

He turned, belatedly realizing he should have given a warmer greeting, as between old comrades. But the night was moving too fast for pleasantries. He had killed one of Kuljash's men. It would be simple to determine he was responsible; they had been paired for duty, and no story could explain away the murder.

He'd made a fateful choice, and not only for himself. His father's plans would fall into ruin. Yet he did not regret it. He was tired of cowering before the Jotun. It was not how a warrior should behave.

Even Bjorn stood tall. If that coward could brave death this night, Egil could do no less.

He ushered them through the gate. It remained cracked open behind them, but there was nothing to be done about it. They had too little time to return to the gatehouse to close it.

"Keep watch and follow my lead," he muttered to the other two men. "Where I'm taking you won't make sense, but it's the only place you can go."

Egil turned and strode down the street, Bjorn and Yonik's footsteps crunching close behind.

6. DAUGHTER OF WAR

"When a warrior returns home, he wishes for a welcome kiss from his wife and an embrace from his bairns. Yet often, the glittering tip of a knife waits to peck him, for many whoresons prey on the headless house.

Home is not a gift — it's a battle prize. Its peace must be fought for."

- Yofam Dragontooth, Slayer of the wyvern Vardraith, First Drang of the Iron Band

Bjorn hurried after Egil with Yonik, stealing across the dark city like burglars on the prowl. In his mind's eye, enemies loomed from every shadow, waiting to leap out and strike. Yet above even his paranoia, one thought dominated all others.

He was home.

It had been nearly a year since he had left Oakharrow. A single year, yet the course of his life had drastically diverged. Once, he had trained to be the lawspeaker under Egil's father, to dispense judgment over the lives of men and women. Then he lost half his family, and the Harrowhall, and gained a duty he never wanted. A duty he soon abandoned for the hope of vengeance and peace.

Now what am I?

Even as the thought nagged at him, Bjorn knew better than to pay it heed. What or who he was did not matter now, only what he had to do.

Drawing from his thoughts, he studied the back of Egil's head. The scout was much the same as when they'd parted ways, just as abrupt and severe, but he also seemed somehow lessened. There was a fear in him that Bjorn found all too familiar. It leached into his eyes, his posture, the set of his teeth. He wondered at what atrocities Egil had witnessed playing out in their city. His scholar's courage flared so he could picture it: bodies falling from towers and blood flowing down the streets, filling in the cracks between the pavers. Repressing a shiver, Bjorn gripped his sword's hilt tighter and tried to push away the images.

"Where are we heading?" Yonik muttered to their guide.

Egil kept striding forward, giving no sign of hearing him. The gothi touched his shoulder. Egil jerked away from his touch and scowled at both Yonik and Bjorn.

"A safe place." The words lashed out like a cruel driver's whip, though the sentry kept them soft. "As safe as you two can get."

"And where is that?" the priest asked, patient as ever.

"There's no time to explain." Egil ran a hand through his hair. He had hair, now; Bjorn only then noticed his head was not shaved as it had been before. "Things have changed under the Jotun. We have new allies. Just follow me."

They remained silent after that. Bjorn tried to quiet his misgivings as they slunk through the dim streets. Often, they ducked into alleys to evade patrols, listening to the grumbling barbars until they passed. The Spinners' own fortune seemed with them that night, for they remained undetected. Dawn was not far off now, and if they were not headed for the Jotun directly, Bjorn knew they ought to be off the streets soon.

His misgivings grew as he recognized the district they were in: the Squalls, the heart of the Vurg clan, as much as any existed. By Yonik's frown, he noticed as well, though the priest made no objection.

Bjorn came astride Egil. "Tell me these new allies aren't Vurgs."

He had spoken familiarly to him, not as a jarl's heir to his warrior, but as old companions. Egil seemed to recoil from it, his shadowed eyes dancing with anger.

"Just follow, Lord Heir," the sentry grated, pointedly facing forward.

Bjorn wondered if they walked into a trap as he fell back. Egil's father had once been in line for the Winter Mantle. Perhaps he coveted it once more, and his son as well.

No. This is Egil we're talking about. He had never met a more stubborn individual. Even Annar would have been hard-pressed to compete. Surely, Egil remained loyal.

More loyal to you than to his father?

There was no more time for doubts. Egil turned them toward a nearby building, and Bjorn pulled up short to stare at it. It appeared to be a mead hall, rising higher than the other buildings around it and boasting a wide, long angled roof. Yet it was far from grand. Its roof was thatching rather than tiles, and the planks making up its walls were warped and weathered from poor treatment. From within, a chorus of muffled laughter rose. Firelight flickered through the cracks. It seemed the best place in the Vurg quarter for a common hall. Bjorn wondered if Skarl Thundson had plotted his rebellion here before he met his end at the end of a giant's blade.

Yonik stopped next to him to lean in close. "I question the wisdom of this even more than approaching the city without an army at our backs. But I will follow, Bjorn, with only one word of advice: the enemy of an enemy is not always your friend."

Bjorn flashed a brittle smile. "But sometimes they are. Hoarfrost was, and the Jotun must be. Why not another?"

The priest only sighed.

While they spoke, Egil approached the two men lingering outside the front door. No, not men, he realized as he and Yonik drew nearer, but women. They only rose as high as his shoulder, yet looked every bit as formidable as any huskarl. With broad shoulders and hard expressions, they wore mail and helms and bore arms as befit warriors. Before Hoarfrost, he might have been more surprised, but he knew now women could be as formidable as men. Volkur was said to be deadly with a spear in all the old stories, and tales of shieldmaidens who took after her were scattered throughout the histories and sagas Bjorn had read. Man or woman, they demanded his wary respect.

As Egil finished speaking, one warrioress knocked the butt of her spear against the door. "Let them know I call your head if it rolls," she said to the sentry. "Me spear needs new decoration." She shook her weapon and grinned as the bones hanging from the spearhead rattled against one another. They looked too small to be human; more likely, they came from dogs or wolves.

Or bairns.

Bjorn avoided both shieldmaidens' eyes as he passed between them.

The chamber within was illuminated by shifting orange light from several lit hearths. Stifling heat washed over

Bjorn along with the stench of the place: spoiled ale, sour piss, stale sweat. The source of the aromas, as well as the rough laughter and hushed words, sat or stood at the long tables lining the hall, at least two dozen people present. The firelight silhouetted most, but the features he glimpsed of the men and women were every bit as hard-bitten as the two shieldmaidens outside.

Conversations ceased as the room's occupants turned to look at them. With their backs to the flames, their eyes were cast in shadow. Bjorn kept his gaze on the far end of the room. Sweat dribbled down his back and face. He resisted the urge to wipe his forehead as he followed Egil forward.

Their destination was clear, for against the opposing wall burned two braziers positioned to either side of a large-backed chair. Armed and armored warriors stood next to them, while in the chair, a figure sprawled. Armaments leaned nearby: a spear, a seax, a round, nicked shield. The person filed a knife along their nails, trimming them with precise strokes that spoke of long familiarity with a blade. Their armor, chainmail falling midway down their thighs and peeking out from beneath their overtunic, looked carefully oiled, yet dulled from use. Their boots were dark and marked with scuffs and stains around the edges. Long, black hair fell across their face in braids, obscuring it from vision. As Bjorn's company neared, the figure looked up, and the curtain of hair parted.

Bjorn froze. Those glittering eyes — he knew them. Knew the hate smoldering within, the cruel humor, the promises of pain.

Those were the eyes of Skarl Thundson.

It cannot be. Back in Eildursprall, they had received report of Skarl the Savage's fate. Yet contrary evidence sat before him. Skarl Thundson had not died. He led the Vurgs still.

And Bjorn had willingly placed himself in his power.

He almost drew his sword. Their weapons had not been taken away, though the surrounding warriors left little chance of fighting their way out. Perhaps if he could have breathed in *khnuum* and accessed the Frenzy runestone, he would even those odds, but there was no time or opportunity for it.

Skarl smiled and brushed back his hair, revealing the other side of his head to be shaved. Only then did Bjorn realize his mistake. This was not, in fact, Skarl. Like the shieldmaidens standing guard, it was a woman with Skarl's features who sat in the chair.

"Egil Yaethunson!" she called merrily across the hall. "I knew you'd taken a likin' to me, but I never thought you'd visit this late!"

A few chortles sounded from the onlookers, the loudest coming from the warrioresses surrounding the throne. One of them, a towering woman with hair like fire, leered at Egil with a hungry look. Bjorn never thought to see Egil cowed, but there was a definite warble in the sentry's voice as he responded.

"We must proceed with our plans."

"Oh?" Far from put off by Egil's flat tone, the woman resembling Skarl only became merrier. "And does this have somethin' to do with those two? Don't be shy, loves — I'd like to know who the devils you are."

Bjorn wanted to flee. This was all moving too fast. Why would the sentry trust this woman who appeared to be related to the most brutal man to emerge from the Vurgs? A glance at Yonik showed he was not inclined to intervene, for a thoughtful look had stolen over him.

"Brother Yonik Of'Skoll, a gothi," Egil said, "and Lord Bjorn Borson, the true Heir of Oakharrow."

Silence filled the longhouse, only broken by the creaking of benches and stupefied murmurs.

The woman on the chair stared at Bjorn with her glimmering eyes. Though the irises were nearly as black as her hair, they almost seemed to burn from within.

"Bjorn Borson," she drawled. If the revelation impressed or surprised her, the warrioress failed to show it. "You're bigger than I'd heard. And hairier."

Bjorn felt himself flushing. The intensity of her gaze was difficult to bear, but he looked her in the eye as his father had long ago taught him. "Had to be. It was cold in the Teeth."

The woman threw back her head and howled with laughter, ale sloshing from her horn. The warriors remained silent except the female ones, who chuckled along with their leader.

"Handsome and clever!" the woman said when she calmed. "And here I'd heard you were a coward like your sister. Doesn't seem a coward, does he, Bodil?" This last she directed at the flame-haired warrioress, whose grin never wavered.

"Match him in the yard," the shieldmaiden replied. "Then we'll see."

"But he's our guest! And what offense could that comely face give?"

Bjorn tried to keep some shred of dignity as the women eyed him like a stallion they meant to take for a ride. But a thing they had said overrode his discomfort.

"My sister — why do you call her a coward?"

"Don't you know?" The Vurg woman screwed up her eyes at him. "Ah, guess not. Been awhile since you stopped back here. What a treat this is, eh, Bodil?"

"Tell me. Please." Bjorn wished the words came out less like pleading, but he could not help himself.

Egil twitched, but it was the woman who resembled Skarl who answered. "She fled Oakharrow, Lord Heir. Abandoned the city to that big bastard without a fight. Heard she's been playin' the lady over in Petyrsholm, though that was a while back. Gods only know where she's gallivantin' off to now."

Bjorn scarcely heard her. *She's alive. Aelthena's alive.* He shared a smile with Yonik before looking at Egil. He wondered why the scout had not told him; but then, they had had little time for talk since entering the city.

"I suppose you didn't know of her survival. It's touchin', really. Might make me weep." The warrioress loosed a wide yawn.

As Bjorn tried to orient his thoughts, Yonik spoke up. "Forgive us, lady warrior. We have only just arrived back in Oakharrow and find it much changed. Our companion has yet to apprise us of all that has happened. I'm afraid we do not even have the honor of your name."

The reminder brought Bjorn's mind reeling back to their fraught situation. He had a feeling Yonik's politeness would be cloying to this woman. Indeed, as she shifted forward, her smile had gained a sharper intent, like a dagger hid behind her lips in place of a tongue.

"'Lady warrior,' am I? I could get used to that! No one's ever called me a fuckin' lady before." She drained her horn and tossed it to the ground. "You don't know me yet, but you for damn sure know my father. Skarl Dragonskin jog your noggin?"

A chill ran down Bjorn's back, all thoughts of Aelthena disappearing. Skarl's daughter looked to have inherited much of her father's disposition as well as his bulk. Her shieldmaidens and other warriors filled the longhouse. They were utterly in her power.

Yonik showed none of Bjorn's fear as he spoke. "That is not your name, Daughter of Skarl. Not all of it."

The woman's laughter died at once. "No. Nor is it the name you should know, priest. It is Edda that the skalds will sing, that you gothi will catalogue in your histories and tell around festival fires. Edda Skarldaughter to start, but that is only the beginnin' of the names I will tear from the storytellers' tongues."

Edda Skarldaughter. It should not have shocked him that this warrioress would not call herself "Of Skarl," as was typical for women, yet it still came as a surprise. He'd never heard of such a patronymic; but then, he had never met such a woman, either.

Yonik bowed his head. "Your name is a gift, Edda Skarldaughter. But I hope you will grace us with more."

"What? Your lives?" Edda's smile was back. Bjorn preferred her without it. Like a wolf, she appeared more of a threat when she snarled.

Yonik seemed undeterred. "To start. Shelter would be welcome, but also aid in the battles to come."

Edda held out a hand, and a thrall hurried forth from the shadows to fill it with a fresh horn. She drank deeply. When she lowered the horn, froth lingered on her upper lip.

"You ask much and give little. I have half a mind to kill you both here and now. Or at least the boy," she amended, looking thoughtfully at Bjorn. "No need to shake my fist at the gods more than I already have."

"Gotten away with it so far," Bodil pointed out.

"And we'll break more of their laws in the days to come." Edda grinned at the flame-hair, then turned back to Bjorn. "Well, Lord Heir? Now's as good a time as any to show you're not the coward you're said to be."

Am I a coward still? He had changed much, to be sure, and had shown bravery on more than one occasion. He'd killed more men than he could count on his hands. Yet his old scholar's courage remained with him, the images it evoked never to be denied.

The flame-haired warrioress snorted. "He hesitates. That's answer enough, eh, Edda?"

In a flash of insight, Bjorn knew what he had to say. "Yes, I hesitate. I think over my response. Only a fool speaks without thinking."

"Or a warrior." Bodil still grinned, though her eyes had narrowed.

"Enough." Edda waved a lazy hand. "Answer, Bjorn Borson, if you mean to. Might be your last chance."

His heart thudded, but his voice did not waver. "This night, Brother Yonik and I approached Oakharrow's walls. We didn't know Egil would be on watch. We didn't know who would discover us or if they would slay us on the spot. But still, we came. Some might call that bravery; more would name it foolishness. I leave that to you. All I know is that a coward doesn't face down death if he can avoid it."

It was as fine a speech as he'd ever managed. Bjorn kept his posture upright and his chin up as he waited to see if it was enough to sway this martial woman.

Edda began to clap.

"Well said, well said! If you're not a warrior, perhaps you'll make a fine jester. Darby! Find them spots to curl up for the night, and food for their bellies." She turned her dark eyes on Egil. "For three, if I'm guessin' correct on what got these fugitives inside the wall."

Egil met her accusation with an icy stare. Bjorn had seen the other sentry fall and guessed the lawspeaker's son to be responsible. He wondered if the spilled blood weighed on Egil's conscience in the least.

Yonik bowed and thanked the Vurg leader, and Bjorn followed suit. Even Egil muttered a reluctant thanks before following Edda's thrall. He felt Skarldaughter's eyes on him as they disappeared into the dim recesses of the longhouse, burning like two coals that never extinguished.

Stoneseer, the King of Ice atop Yewung had named him. *The One with the Farthest Sight.* But just then, Bjorn could not see even a step ahead.

7. THE SCARAB'S COURT

The Huame's reign, pure and true
As the burning of the flame
With Desolation, all births anew
In justice and mercy's name

A cycle continued, eternity stayed
Life and death without end
The scarab scurries along before
The sweeping of the sand

- Words in the Sand, refrain 5;71-72

Sehdra did not sit comfortably on her throne.

In the days before her ascension, when she had prostrated herself before her brother or stood among the columns for the entirety of a morning, she had thought it to be as uncomfortable as she could be in an audience chamber. Yet the throne forced her into a yet more excruciating position. Sitting for endless hours was as painful as walking on her twisted leg. Now, she understood the hill of cushions on which her brother had sat, and with which she had nobly done away.

Power should bring pain, her mother had told her as a child. *Its pleasures are poison.* Yet Sehdra had never truly believed her. The bruises layering her mother's body, which she could do nothing to prevent, showed a visceral counterpoint.

Pain lay not in power, but the lack of it.

But now that she had a measure of authority, she found its taste as bitter as her mother promised. Sehdra had become a goddess. She wore the Ascendant Crown. With each new karah, a fresh crown was formed, but hers proved unique even among her line. Crown and mask had become one; what began on her skull crept down the cursed flesh of her face, then was secured in the back with a thin, silken strap. It was fashioned after her new insignia, the tusked scarab, so Wise Qa'a covered her face, while Red Bek protected her head.

The royal mask lay heavy upon her, and not only for its considerable weight. Like beetles to dung, her position attracted the attention of every enterprising Sypten among the armies. Suitors lined up outside her personal pavilion, the same tent as her brother had once occupied. It had still smelled of his excesses when she moved in, and she had not wanted to sleep in his bed. But with the Ibis and his mistress looking on, she had found it prudent not to protest.

Suitors were not her only sycophants. The nobility among the soldiers, the priests, even Vizier Zosar sought to worm their way into her good graces. All was chaos among the social hierarchy, and many sought to climb higher on the backs of others, though they might as easily fall.

Sehdra wondered if she should have found it flattering, all this attention. Some sought such adoration all their lives. But after years in the shadows, this moment in the sun was dazzling. Much of the time, Sehdra had to fight to keep her thoughts straight, wishing for just a moment to herself.

But nagging as her discomforts were, they were the least of her worries.

Though Sehdra burned incense, a practice Hephystus had begun before her, she always smelled her captor in the throne room. The giantess cast no shadow, yet always, Sehdra felt her looming just behind. Oyaoan pursued her even into her dreams, where the giantess often tore her limb from limb. There was nowhere Sehdra could go to escape.

"Divine One, if you please..."

She blinked, focusing on the man next to her. Zosar of White Aya had reversed his tune since her brother's demise. Before, he had treated her with derision; now, he was cloyingly servile. Nothing would change how she despised the man, nor would she forget his true character. Nevertheless, she allowed him to keep his position. In a better world, Teti would have occupied his place. Her old friend was far wiser and more skilled than the vizier could ever hope to be. But she would not subject Teti to more scrutiny than she already had. Zosar served as a convenient distraction, even if he made for an irritating one.

"Thank you, Vizier Zosar." Sehdra ignored the advisor's low bow and looked again upon the man standing before the throne. Nekau Baka was a general of the old order and maintained all its formalities. Still, she had seen enough of him in the past few weeks to detect the minute deepening of his furrowed brow and know he disapproved of her lapse in concentration.

Let him sit the throne, she thought. *Then he can judge if it is permissible.*

Her temper was short, but a lifetime spent biting her tongue had made her patience long. Sehdra dipped her head, just enough to be respectful, but not compromise the highness of her station.

"Please, general. I would appreciate if you started at the beginning."

It was not a request, and all in the room knew it. Nekau was the chief general, the leader and commander of all their armies, but she was the Holy Karah, a deity made flesh. Even more, he owed his rise from disgrace to her. He would brook no disrespect from his subordinates, and even less from himself.

Nekau Baka bowed deeply. "Of course, Divine One. Graybank, which Her Sanctity will recall is the outpost just north of the city Ragnarsglade, has been taken. As you commanded, any who surrendered have been spared and given collars."

Slavery had been the most merciful concession Sehdra could win for the war's victims. Between needing to remain undetected since their retreat to Qal-Nu and the impossibility of withdrawal from the war with the giantess driving it forward, none could be released lest they spread word of their movements. With the choice between slaughter or slavery, she had opted for the less permanent evil.

Sehdra's gaze slid over to Teti, off to the far side of Zosar. Though she took comfort in his presence, she would have sent him all the way back to Annax-Nu if he would permit it. Every moment he stayed with her, he was in danger. He was a hostage here even without chains.

She tore her eyes away before he could look up, an oath often repeated coming to mind. *I will free you, my friend. As soon as I myself am free.*

"Our forces have suffered, as Her Sanctity is aware," Nekau Baka continued, "but we remain sufficient for offensive action."

To Sehdra's mind, "suffered" was a mild way of putting

the fate that had befallen their forces. The elephant division had been devastated; only a score had survived the disastrous battle, and those the general had sent back to Annax-Nu to breed and repopulate. The surviving mercenaries had all but abandoned them; only a thousand remained of the eight thousand her brother had first gathered to his banner, and these the most desperate and destitute among them. Most were more vagabonds than soldiers from what she glimpsed from afar of their uncoordinated camps. The infantry had been reduced by half, six thousand remaining of the original host. The charioteers had fared better, only losing a fifth of their number, for they had been moving to the peripheries of the battle when the Hua-fire rose from the earth. Even the huame had lost two of Oyaoan's dozen.

Despite all, the People of Dust endured. The giantess did not call for the dissolution of their forces; to the contrary, she pushed them harder than ever, striving to blind the mountain savages as thoroughly as they could, taking outposts and villages and killing their scouts. And all her planning, it seemed, was coming to a head.

"If you would, general," Sehdra said aloud, "state your point plainly."

"Yes, Divine One. In my estimation, the Winter Holds are blind and separated. Should you wish to proceed, Ragnarsglade could be ours with a single forceful assault."

She hesitated. Though she knew it advanced Oyaoan's agenda to seize one of the savages' cities, the giantess had focused exclusively on Ragnarsglade since the disastrous battle at Petyrsholm. It seemed she sought more than a strategic advantage.

Why do you want this war? What is it you seek?

Another spoke up beside her. "Great Oyaoan is pleased with this news, general," the Ibis said, his bandied legs reminding Sehdra of the bird for which he was named as he sauntered forth. "She praises your performance, far superior to your predecessor's."

The general bowed at his words. Sehdra kept her expression carefully smooth. The giantess had not spoken, but none dared contradict the translator. More and more, the Ibis inserted himself, so that Sehdra wondered who truly led between the pair.

Yet in some ways, it did not matter. Their point was clear. The karah was a deity, but even gods had masters.

The Ibis paced before the throne. Sehdra stared at the bones woven into his back, which had the shape of the bird he had fashioned himself after. "Now," he continued, "Great Oyaoan commands that we press our advantage. We march for Ragnarsglade with the morning, general. All must be prepared to move at first light."

Again, Nekau Baka only bowed, though he knew as well as Sehdra that first light would come and go without their departure. But no one spoke contrary to the huamek, nor her translator. They simply hoped they could survive the consequences.

But there was a greater point that lay here. *We march.* Cold sweat trickled down her back. The war continued. The killing would start afresh.

And she could do nothing to stop it.

"What lies in Ragnarsglade? Why is she so bent on conquering it?"

Sehdra paced in her late brother's pavilion — *her* pavilion, a fact she had not yet grown used to. She was not given to pacing, given how any kind of walking shot agony up her twisted leg and into the base of her skull. But after days of sitting on the throne, walking had gained a strange allure.

Besides, I suppose power should be painful.

Teti shrugged. He had ordered the other servants out at her command, leaving only the two of them in the cavernous space. Considering at least some would be in Oyaoan's employ, she could trust no one but her oldest friend.

Sehdra's eyes roamed her quarters as her mind ground to a halt. Every piece of furniture was greater than those she had possessed before: the bed, the chairs, the table, the bathing tub. Once they returned to marching, they would each day have to be packed, then unpacked. For now, they provided her more modest accommodations than she might have attained within Qal-Nu. As the karah, it was within her power to commandeer one of the few remaining manors in the city. She had instead opted to remain with the army. Perhaps the nobles would see it as snubbing them, but Sehdra was too preoccupied to care. She had enough politicking without adding in more.

Continuing to pace, she chewed the good side of her bottom lip. "This differs from Petyrsholm; I can feel it. Then it was about crushing the Winter Holds in one fell blow. A strategic decision. But she overplayed her hand. Huame were not enough, nor Hua-fire, nor all our forces. We might have sieged them still, strained their will and supplies, and beaten them, but she did not order the attempt."

"Perhaps she was afraid," Teti offered quietly, his eyes following her. "The giants fled the battlefield. Even they are capable of fear."

"Maybe they are, but not she." Her leg was on fire; soon, she would have to relent and lie down, but not yet. "She saw something that changed her plans. It is a hint to what she truly wants."

What the giantess could want for was beyond Sehdra's imagination. Oyaoan had power, servants, adulation, fear.

Her every whim was satisfied. Suncoasters washed and groomed her, fed her and pleased her. They supplied her with the foul smoke and silvery substance that made her act so strangely. Yet she had likely had all of that even before she came north to Enea. How long had she languished before sailing across the sea?

Something had drawn her and the other huame here. And if Sehdra could figure out what it was, she might finally defy her.

The pavilion's entrance rippled, and a servant peeked her head in, her expression apologetic. Sehdra paused her pacing to stare at her. Perhaps the servant meant well by her intrusion, but she could just as likely be a spy. She could not allow herself to soften.

Even if it made her more like her brother than she cared to admit.

Teti hurried over to intercept the servant. After a few whispered sentences, he bowed to Sehdra, and with brief pardons, disappeared through the flaps after the woman. Sehdra limped over to a seat before an array of food. Flies had settled over it, but she only waved them away as she selected a slice of mango. It had a fermented taste even as it was still slightly sour. Their food stores dwindled, the supply caravans traveling along the Nu straining to provide for all their soldiers.

A few minutes passed before Teti reentered. Weariness had begun to claim Sehdra, yet she sat up straight as he strode toward her, his expression drawn.

"What is it? Is something wrong?"

"Nothing like that. Someone wishes to be presented before you, Sehdra. Someone who might be of use."

She stared up at him, trying to read his familiar face, but the emotion was foreign of late. Impossibly, he looked excited.

"Who?"

"His name is Seth. He looks to be little older than a boy, but he has already proven his resolve and loyalty. He is a Tusk of Bek, one of their martial disciples, and has served in this capacity in the Winter Hold of Oakharrow."

A glimmer of understanding finally came to her. "You cannot mean what I think you do. He survived?"

A slow smile spread across Teti's face. "He did. Not unscathed, as you will see, but well enough to continue service. He could be quite the valuable asset."

Sehdra knew it well. As a member of the royal family, she had been privy to enough conversations to glean the role Ha-Sypt had had in the fires at Oakharrow. The servants of Bek had often been used for perilous missions in the past, so it had been natural to do so in that instance. The specifics escaped her, though she had heard mention of using the more barbaric people of the mountains to enter the city. By all reports, the mission had succeeded, and the city had fallen into the barbarians' hands.

Or another giant's, if the rumors tell true.

But even beyond his dedication — or fanaticism, she supposed she should call it — that he had been away for so long meant he was unlikely to be an ear to Oyaoan. He might be untainted. Someone they could trust to serve her and not the giantess.

"Bring him in. We shall see if he is what we hope."

Teti bobbed his head, then swept toward the door. She tried not to fidget as she waited for him to reenter, the boy in tow.

Despite herself, Sehdra stared. Teti had undersold the boy's sacrifice. She could barely tell his age, for the skin on his face was waxen with healed burns. Eyes, misshapen from fire's touch, peered at her before he prostrated himself on the rugs just within the entrance. No hair grew on his scalp, for it was in much the same condition.

Now she knew how others must feel when looking upon her face. She tried to dismiss her horror.

If I hate being treated that way, so will he.

"Please, rise," she told him. The boy slowly obeyed, though he remained on his knees. Looking beyond his burns, she noticed his clothes, cut in a simple Winter Hold style, looked as if he had worn them for months on end. As a soiled stench permeated the air, she suspected that just might be the case.

"My apologies, Divine One," Teti said, noticing her twitching nose. "I believed you would wish to see him at once."

"I do. Please, Tusk Seth, rise. You need not kneel before me."

The boy once more obeyed, but she could see his hesitancy. Her order defied his way of seeing the world. She wondered if he actually believed her to be divine. Just then, it seemed distinctly possible.

"I understand you have suffered," she said. "Suffered in the name of our people and nation."

A long pause followed her words. Just as she wondered if he could speak at all, he murmured, "Faith is pain, Your Sanctity. Suffering in your service is a blessing. You honor me."

He started to bow again, but Teti's hand restrained him. "Once is enough," he chastised mildly.

Seth stood up, but he kept his head bowed, his eyes on Sehdra's feet.

She pursed her lips, wondering if he was too demure to be what she had hoped for. But no — his severe beliefs were exactly what would keep him pure and trustworthy. Even if they made her uncomfortable, she could not take them away.

They have seen him through his hardships. Let them be a comfort for as long as they can.

"I have many questions for you, Tusk," she said aloud. "But I think it would be kinder to us both to give you time to recuperate before asking them."

Another long pause. "As you wish, Your Sanctity."

She smiled. "I have only one I must ask now. Tusk Seth, please look at me."

Reluctantly, he did as she asked, meeting her eyes with the skittishness of a beaten dog. A part of her screamed at the injustice of his treatment, but she spoke over her objections.

"I will need your stout heart and mind in the coming days. You must keep my secrets and speak to no one else of them. Do you understand? Not even to the chanter of Bek, nor Great Oyaoan. Only Teti here, and myself."

He did not hesitate now. Seth fell to his knees again and prostrated himself before her. Sehdra had to fight back a smile at Teti's look of exasperation.

"It will be as you ask, Your Sanctity. May Bek take my tongue if I betray your confidence."

She winced, but did not speak against the oath. "Rise, Tusk Seth. Teti will see that you are fed, bathed, and clothed. I look forward to our future conversations."

The disciple rose, but he bowed his way out of the pavilion no matter how Teti urged him to do otherwise. Sehdra watched them go, then looked to her bathtub. Part of her wished to wash just from smelling the boy's odor.

Surely I have not grown that used to divinity.

Smiling, Sehdra selected another disappointing slice of mango.

8. TUSK

Mighty Bek, the Red Behemoth
Upon her Tusks, she relies
Sharp spears charge upon the rift
Defying storm-riven skies

- Words in the Sand, refrain 2;37

I am the Tusk.

Seth repeated the mantra as he scampered through the war camp. It was his shield as a soldier knocked into him and sneered. It was his blinders when slaves flinched at a glimpse of his burned face. It was his armor when even chanters avoided interaction.

I am the Tusk of Bek.

A Tusk had no need of beauty, or friendship, or love. A Tusk was an instrument of battle. Tusks were rare weapons, for they were built of the body. They were beloved of Bek, the Red Behemoth, Divine of Might and War. They were deadly, no matter their paltry appearance.

Seth believed this in his soul, but his malformed body

had frailer conviction. Agony walked with him ever since he burned down the black stone palace of the mountain savages. After the razing, he had waited in agony for the Divine to scoop him up in their hands and take him to his reward, to the Jackal's Delight.

But he had not been worthy of the afterlife. His mortal body healed, yet the pain stayed. In his cold cell, it was his only companion. Now, pain had become so familiar he wondered if he would feel anything in its absence. If all other emotion had been purged from his mind.

But this was not an obstacle, but a crucible. Faith was forged by pain. Duty only ended with death.

He had found the huamek of snow and rock, the one they called the Jotun, and served his purposes, just as the high chanter of Bek had commanded. But though his task was complete, when the opportunity came to flee his hanging, Seth took it. He wished to die, but he would not defy the gods' wishes. The only choice was to continue to serve.

So he fled, traveling across the wintry lands, though frost burned his poorly shod feet and hunger gnawed at his belly. Every night he spent shivering, curled in on himself, waiting for Hua's light to warm him back to life. Every night, he hoped he would not live to see the next day.

But he had, so Seth had pushed on. Wandering through the wilderness, he scavenged just enough to survive. He stole from the savages where he could, fled when they found him, foraged when he came upon the scarce vegetation he knew to be food. After he stole a fishing pole, he came as close to full as he had since his escape. The weather turned from cold to warm, and the nights grew easier to endure.

He pressed on south and came upon the first signs of abandoned Sypten camps. A hundred small signs pointed to them belonging to the People of Dust. Broken sandals and tools discarded. A tattered prayer shawl stamped into the mud. It was an army come to the Winter Holds, and that could mean only one thing.

Ha-Sypt had reignited the ancient wars once more.

Seth followed their trail of destruction first north, then back south when he saw they had not conquered the river city. The season turned again, and fear of the cold drove him faster. At last, he had arrived, stumbling onto the outskirts of the camp.

Yet his trials were not over. The sentries had been cruel in their questioning. They had shoved him, laughing as he gasped at their callous touch on his tender skin. Yet when his story could not be ignored, they had brought him to a chanter of Bek, who had swiftly sent him on to the karah herself.

During his travels, Seth's heart had grown cold even to the duty that had once set him aflame. But as he kneeled before his ruler and goddess, purpose once more filled his chest. He would give his life for Her Divinity, Sehdra the First, Holy Karah to the People of Dust. He would give it gladly. But that night as he walked through the camp, her orders weighed heavily on his mind.

I am the Tusk, he thought as he halted before a tent.

Seth was growing familiar with the pavilion, for he had stayed there the night before while waiting for the audience with Her Divinity. The chanter to whom it belonged, Amasis, was already looking directly at him with barely a flinch. Seth was grateful, unworthy as it was of him. This was a kind of companionship he knew and understood.

The priest's tent would have been simple to identify even without having already visited it. Dyed scarlet after Bek, it boasted elephant tusks erupting above the entrance, yellow-white ivory worth a fortune. None dared steal them, for the Red Behemoth was not known for mercy, nor were her followers. Bowing his head to the tusks, Seth ducked inside.

He paused at the sight that greeted him. Chanter Amasis stood over a kneeling soldier, holding a wide, shallow bowl filled with a viscous scarlet liquid — the blood of a slave, Seth assumed. Amasis tilted the bowl, allowing the blood to run down the shaven head of the soldier. It filled the creases of his armor, streamed down his shoulders and back, then dripped onto the stained rug under his knees.

Seth could not deny envying the man. Such a ritual was reserved for men of high importance, for the draining of blood left slaves weak for days afterward. It bestowed Bek's blessing, for the Divine was said to bathe in the blood of her enemies and thus become renewed. Men who underwent this baptism claimed a fraction of her power.

As soon as he recognized the contemptible thoughts, Seth drowned them out with his mantra. *I am the Tusk, the Tusk, the Tusk.* A weapon did not have feelings, least of all shameful ones against his betters. Seth bowed his head as he waited in the corner, trying to make of himself a shadow.

The soldier rose. Murmuring his thanks to the priest, he gave an offering of silver and turned around. Through his eyelashes, Seth was surprised to see it was none other than the chief general himself, Nekau Baka. The red veneer obscured the man's age, and his eyes looked bright as they stared at him. Seth bowed deeper, not straightening until the general had departed the tent, leaving a trail of bloody footprints behind.

"Tusk Seth," Amasis greeted him. "Your timing is well. All must be clean."

Seth obeyed at once. There was little warmth in the chanter's words, but little derision as well. They both knew their places.

When he had scrubbed away as much of the blood as he could from the rug and the tent flap, where Nekau's hand had left a mark, Seth returned to stand before the priest, head once more bowed. Amasis had moved to his writing desk. He did not look up for a long while as he scrawled glyphs onto parchment. Seth could have read them, if he wished, having been taught to read and write from a young age. His instructor, Shaper Ebana, had often explained why: *Words may be used as weapons, and the sharpest knife must know how best to wield them.*

Most assumed servants to be illiterate; such underestimation had served Seth well in the past. Now, however, he kept his eyes downcast. He would not betray his own order.

And if she commands it? What will you do then, Tusk?

Before that question, even his mantra flailed.

At length, the chanter paused and looked up. "Tusk Seth."

"Chanter Amasis." Seth bowed.

"You wish to speak."

"Yes, Father."

The chanter leaned back in his chair, quill twitching in his fingers. "Go on then, boy. I do not have all night."

"My apologies, Father." For a moment, though, Seth found the words stuck in his throat. He felt foolish bringing his burdens to one he was supposed to serve. Yet how could he serve when he did not know the way?

"I am lost, Father."

"Lost." Amasis's tone implied he should continue.

"I..." Seth paused. He could not confess the conflict on his mind lest it violate the one whose authority he questioned, but a different angle occurred to him. "Who is the highest among the Divine, Father?"

The chanter's eyebrows rose. "It is theology that bothers you, Tusk Seth?"

"Not directly, Father."

When it was clear no other explanation was forthcoming, Amasis frowned. A hand went up to stroke his facial hair, bound in a dark rope at his chin. "I will humor you, Tusk Seth, for the moment, since something has you truly troubled. Bright Hua is, of course, the highest among the Divine."

Seth had known the answer and feared it. Still, he pushed on. "And Hua's children — do they inherit his supremacy?"

This drew dangerously close to the heart of the matter, but Seth had to ask. Amasis shifted, but if he understood the significance of the question, he did not show it.

"They inherit authority, perhaps, for they enact the Bright Maker's will. But supremacy? That, perhaps, takes it too far."

With those words, Seth felt his chest ease. "Then their will does not supersede that of other Divine?"

He hoped he did not expose Her Divinity by asking the bald question, but this was the core of his troubles. This answer could finally put his mind to rest.

Amasis took his time in responding. His oil lamp, the sole source of light in the tent, cast flickering shadows across his face as the flame danced with his breath.

"No, it does not. But we mortals must take care when interfering in the affairs of deities. If it is possible, Tusk Seth, it is better to serve all rather than one."

Seth bowed his head. Though he usually accepted the judgment of the priests over his own, he had to draw his own conclusions in this. The Holy Karah had demanded his aid in a struggle against the huame. He could not refuse such a call without dishonoring a goddess herself.

Even if he struck against the children of a Divine, Seth finally knew he trod upon the right path.

"Thank you, Chanter Amasis, for your counsel."

The chanter frowned. "I trust it was helpful. Now go, fetch some water."

Seth bowed, then hurried about the task, his chest feeling lighter than it had since leaving Ha-Sypt. *I am her Tusk,* he thought with a rare smile.

9. LONG ODDS

"Never fight against long odds. They'll grow longer with each league marched, each ally lost, each mistake made. Don't toss blessed bones and pray. Plans fare better than prayers. No god has intervened for me yet, and I doubt any will."

- Highlord Carr Gunnarson, Fifth Arkjarl of Baegard

Looking back at the army marching through Petyrsholm's gates, Bastor had to grin.

They were as striking a host as they were diverse. Two and half thousand men, a full half of those still standing after the Battle of Dragons, traveled with him. Hailing from every jarlheim across Baegard, their assorted armor glinted dully like sunlight on a muddy river. They came from Aelford and Skjold, though their jarls had fallen and new leaders rose to the fore. From Petyrsholm and Greenwuud and Djurshand, though Petyr, Siward, and Hother remained ambivalent to Bastor's command. A spattering originated in Oakharrow, those few who had come with Asborn before it was taken, and even Ragnarsglade provided some, though Bastor trusted few of his fellow Gladesmen.

All of them looked to a half-Sypten bastard to lead.

The march bore even sweeter fruits, for while on the move, Bastor could evade his hangers-on. The ladies who accompanied the army, as ill-advised a decision as that was, trailed behind in their laden carriages. Bastor rode at the front, where he had only the other jarls, the jarls' widows, and his huskarls around.

As much as he could, he traded his cares for simple pleasures: the sun on his face, the wind through his hair, the rhythm of his mount pounding up the slope. He far preferred the company of his horse to any human. A tall black gelding gifted to him by his father, Bastor had unwisely named him, though it was customary for warriors not to, for war horses often fell in battle. Nevertheless, a majestic beast such as him deserved a matching name: so he became Nott, after the noble horse who carried Mostur Forgehammer into battle in the Inscribed Tales.

They had at least a week before they arrived, and he meant to leave every moment he could unspoiled from plotting and scheming. His mind, however, had different plans. He mulled over the battle ahead, remembering the little he had seen of the giant and his army before fleeing Oakharrow. There had not seemed many barbars under his command; the Jotun and his dragonfire had been the keys to winning the day. Hundreds perhaps, a thousand at most stood under his banner, and though they had the advantage of walls, Bastor would bet there were more than a few in Oakharrow chafing to throw off the giant's yoke. And they had faced down dragonfire and giants before in addition to bringing their own fair share of firesand. He could almost believe the odds were in their favor.

Yet even if he took back Oakharrow, many more fights lay ahead. Ha-Sypt had been beaten back, but only a fool would believe they had left the valley. Close to a dozen surtunar remained as well as plenty of sorcerous flames, to make no mention of the thousands of zealous warriors. If caught on an open battlefield, Baegard would be swiftly overwhelmed.

The Syptens knew this, and they did their best to keep Bastor's father blind. Most of the scouts sent south failed to return, and those who did provided little useful information. The karah was plotting something, but where he would strike next, Bastor doubted even the king could predict.

But Ha-Sypt was the known enemy. No Baegardian wished to have a Sypten ruler, and they would fight to their last breath to prevent it. One way or another, they would beat back the southerners and their mammoth allies. It was thoughts of Baegard's new king that plagued Bastor while he failed to sleep. Every day that his father remained in power solidified his position. Go too long, and even the jarls might grow used to being ruled.

He won't last long enough for that, Bastor promised himself again and again. *I'll make sure of it.*

Yet the evidence of the past undermined his resolve. How many opportunities had he had to kill Ragnar Torbenson? How many times had he wanted to put a knife in his father's back, yet stayed his hand? He was beginning to wonder if he ever would do as he vowed.

Making matters worse was how he failed to understand his father's recent decisions. He had given Bastor, a son he knew to be far from loyal, the command of half his forces. Not only that, but he had sent his least loyal subjects to support it. Alrik's son, Ingvar, a young man who had both his father's brashness as well as the recklessness of youth, had taken his father's title, and he seemed to like the king as little as Alrik had. Lady Sigrid of Skjold ruled in her late husband's place, and with all her knowledge of politics, she was even less well inclined toward King Ragnar. Siward was as loyal a man as they came, but he had been a jarl half his life and was independent of spirit. Though he had helped elect Ragnar, Bastor doubted he would continue to support the monarchy longer than he had to. Only Asborn Eirikson could be said to be a royalist, but he was so new to being a jarl and without sufficient men and power to back up his position that he would not pose much of an obstacle.

All my father's opponents gathered in one place. It was like Ragnar dared them to rebel. Like he gave them every chance for treachery to see if they would take it.

Bastor shook his head. That sounded all too much like one of his father's ploys. Rebellion would divide the nation; that was why the jarls had agreed to having a king in the first place. Perhaps this would smother the embers of insurrection rather than fan them into flame. If they did not take this chance, they likely never would.

And if we rebel, we doom us all.

Those were long odds for things to turn out well. But he had always been a gambler.

An approaching rider pulled Bastor from his thoughts. Expecting it to be a returning scout, he was surprised to find Asborn instead. The man's fiery hair contrasted poorly with his pale skin, yet the man's jaw had firmed over his time at Petyrsholm. He could almost believe him to be the jarl he claimed to be.

"Lord Asborn. How fares the ride?"

Asborn's brow wrinkled. "Well, Highness. I have a request of you, if I may. I wished to discuss your strategy for taking back my city."

My city. How swiftly arrogance seeped in.

"Of course! Come closer." Bastor waited for the man to bring his horse astride Nott. Both mounts strained to ascend the steep road, but Bastor's well-bred beast managed it easier. "The best plans are the simplest, I say," he continued. "Get in, cut off the giant's head, and deliver it to the king on a platter fit for Djur himself. What do you think of that?"

Asborn worked his jaw, plainly not missing the mockery in the words. "And how will we get in?" he asked stiffly.

"The gates, maybe. Iron and stone stand little chance against dragonfire, do they not?" Bastor reached out and clapped Asborn on the shoulder, rocking him in his saddle. "Cheer up, Jarl of Oakharrow! The sun shines and the birds sing. Here at the fore of our grand company, we can smell pine rather than the stink of our men. Leave the battles for when it's time to fight."

Asborn looked about to protest when he swiveled back. Hearing the approach of two horses, Bastor turned to more welcome visitors: Aelthena and Frey, wearing matching grim expressions.

A reunion if I've ever seen one.

"I will seek you later, Highness." Asborn turned his mount off to let the procession proceed past him.

Bastor scarcely noticed the jarl's departure, his attentions captured by the other two. Aelthena cast a lingering look after the man who stole her throne, and Frey watched her do so. Bastor did not bother hiding his smile, even as the former jarl's heir turned back to him with eyes narrowed. She had always understood him, from his faults down to his dubious quality. It was what he liked best about her.

That, and her irreverence. Though she no longer held any rank except by blood, and certainly no position, Aelthena consented to ride up with the other highborn leaders. No one could ever accuse the brash woman of being conventional, but ever since her jarlheim had been stolen from her, the Inscribed Laws seemed to mean little and less to her. It was a position Bastor found all too sympathetic.

Aelthena spoke first. "Why do I suspect you brought us on this war path for your own amusement more than anything else?"

"I admit, I was in need of jesters. And the dynamic between you three is... charming."

He winked at Frey, at which the guardian raised an eyebrow. Aelthena only shook her head.

"Regrettable, more like," she murmured. "But I didn't come to talk about Asborn."

Bastor did not have to stretch far to guess her intent. "You wish to know my plans for Oakharrow."

"What else?"

"Perhaps you dreamed of dresses, or jewelry, or cleaning, and cooking... What do women usually think of?"

"And here I was, going to thank you for not betraying me — again. But I'm not sure I will now."

"Nor should you," Frey added.

"Gratitude can go a long way." He paused, seeing if Aelthena would take the bait, then continued. "But I suppose some things are too expensive for even a prince's purse."

"Alabastor."

"Did I fail to point out my station?" When she again did not rise to his goad, he sighed. The leisure of the ride was quickly dissipating, and the reality of their situation settled back in. "Very well. A taste of power, and you become implacable as a wolverine! Ask your questions."

"Oakharrow. How do you mean to take it back?"

"Fire and iron — how else?"

"A direct assault on the walls, then."

"Gods, no! Do you take me for a fool? We'll go in the way I used before."

"By the Honeybrook?" Aelthena frowned. "I doubt the Jotun will have neglected the river portcullis. And any guards you bribed the first time will have forgotten their promises by now."

"Likely true. But all we need is a man inside, then we can orchestrate the same situation."

"But how do we get this man inside? And which man will go?" She looked around, caught Frey's eye, then glanced away. Bastor pursed his lips thoughtfully. The guardian would be a decent man for the job, but after his close brush with Ovvash during the raid on the Elkhorn, she seemed anxious for his safety.

That's love for you.

"Not him," Bastor said aloud. "The best man for the task is one who's done it before."

It took her a moment to understand. "You?" Aelthena hissed. "It cannot be you, you damn fool!"

Bastor grinned. Frey smiled as well, though his amusement seemed a barbed affair.

"How lucky I am to have you both," Bastor said. "Honesty is rarer than dragonfire to one of my stature."

"Your stature is precisely why we cannot risk your capture. Your father would be compelled to recover you, no matter the concession."

He was surprised to find he had to slow his breathing. Fire grew in his belly, and though it was not for his companions, he had to tread carefully not to burn them with it.

"I appreciate your confidence in my discretion. But if, by some ill favor of the Inscribed, I am captured, they'll never know I'm a prince."

"And if they already know?"

Bastor faced forward again, jaw tightening. Her counterpoints were all the sharper for knowing she was right.

"I wasn't made for this." He spoke without looking

around. There was almost a choke in his voice, and he had to clear his throat several times before continuing. "This finery. These formalities. Expectations."

"Nor was I for my circumstances. Bastor, I'm not even a jarl's heir anymore. I have nothing — no coin, no power. Your promises are my only currency."

He looked back at her, more surprised by her raw emotion than his own. Aelthena always stood tall, even when the world tried again and again to crush her. Yet just now, her posture sagged, and dark circles shadowed her eyes. Frey frowned toward her, but the guardian did not reach out in comfort. Even now, Bastor supposed they were too exposed for intimacy.

Only a moment passed before Aelthena drew herself upright again. "You may not be made for this, but you still must make best of the advantage. You're one heartbeat from the crown, one step away from our mutual enemy. It's the best position from which to claim vengeance."

Once more, Bastor imagined plunging a knife in his father's back. "I know," he whispered. "I know."

Hoofbeats came close from behind once more. In the few moments of reprieve, Bastor wrested back control of himself. Turning, he saw Asborn approaching with Lord Siward and the new Lord Ingvar Alrikson of Aelford in tow. The young man looked uncomfortable at being in the company of older jarls, but he put on a brave face.

"My fine lords." Bastor greeted them with a grin, though it felt more like a grimace. "To what do I owe the pleasure?"

"Highness, I heard tell of a war council." Siward's eyes flickered to Aelthena. "In which we are to discuss the assault on Oakharrow."

Bastor resisted the urge to glare at Asborn. No doubt his father's puppet had gone and tattled on Aelthena the first chance that he could. Now he had to humor the jarls the rest of the afternoon. The dynamics between himself and them remained too uncertain to be dismissive. After all, who had more power: one with a claim to the crown, or those with their own seats of power? It had been a long time since royalty reigned in Baegard, and none yet knew the rules. Thus far, they had settled for wary respect and deference, but there was no telling how long it would last.

"Yes, we must." Bastor motioned them forward. "Your pardons, Lady Aelthena."

"None needed, Highness." Aelthena was already pulling away, her usual stony mask settling back in. "Excuse me, m'lords."

Bastor watched her and Frey fall back, then the jarls take their place. If his experience with war councils was any indication, the pleasure of the day's ride had come to a decisive end.

10. A COLD HEART

"Wait till your breast grows cold to strike an enemy. A heart aflame casts light for leagues, and vengeance is best claimed in darkness."

- Yofam Dragontooth, Slayer of the wyvern Vardraith, First Drang of the Iron Band

Hunkered down in her shelter and afforded all the comforts of privilege, Aelthena could almost pretend she was still the jarl's heir.

The tent was not large, yet generous, given the circumstances. She had blankets aplenty to soften the ground and keep away the night's chill. A soapstone lamp with a supply of fuel allowed her to read and write into the night or hold private conferences. Food and drink were at her beck and call — though, with no servants, Frey was forced to fetch them. Her father, carted along with the army in a covered chariot, had been given his own tent, and he and Uljana were also well-provided for.

All was as it should be for a highborn. Yet for all the

lines of access kept open by Bastor's goodwill, the most good she could do was plot from the shadows.

Nothing I'm not used to.

Aelthena shook her head and squinted at the paper and its drying ink. She had been attempting to compose a missive to Siward, but her efforts once more floundered. She had almost swayed him to her point of view back in Petyrsholm. Given the time and opportunity, she felt certain she could do so again. But circumstances had changed drastically since then. He had ceded much power to protect his family. How could she expect him to defy a king and put them and his jarlheim in further danger?

The tent flap opened, pulling her from her thoughts. Frey peeked in, a mischievous smile playing on his lips. Aelthena pretended to scowl.

"What? Hoping to catch me undressed?"

The guardian put a finger to his lips, though his eyes still laughed. "Your guests have arrived, m'lady. Shall I admit them?"

"Oh. Yes, at once." Cheeks flushed, Aelthena set aside the writing box and parchment, then rose and smoothed her dress. After days of riding and only one change of clothes, it was already becoming stained, but the gloomy interior would hide much.

As her visitors trickled in, the tent quickly became cramped. She greeted each and gauged the warmth in their responses. Though it boded well that they had answered her summons, subtly delivered by Frey earlier that evening, it did not mean they would be amendable to her proposals.

Sigrid Of'Harald looked withdrawn and haggard as she spoke her welcome. Never cheery before, it was likely that now she was a widow, she would prove even less so. Still, Sigrid was a shrewd woman, and with no declared heir or children, she stood as the leader of her jarlheim's forces. If she aligned herself with Aelthena's cause, she would make for a potent ally.

Nanna Of'Alrik gave a friendlier greeting, though she, too, clearly suffered from her husband's death. Always big boned, she had become rounder of face and frame while her eyes seemed shrunken and hollow. Still, she put on an effortful smile as she embraced Aelthena, clinging a moment longer than was strictly polite before stepping away.

The last of the guests remained more of a mystery. Ingvar Alrikson, the new jarl of Aelford, was only eighteen winters old. He had his father's frame and bulk, yet a boyish face. His generous chin and sloped forehead were wrinkled with some inner turmoil. Aelthena guessed the transition to power after having just lost his father took its fair toll. Seeing the young man made her think of her own little brother, as they would be about the same age.

If he's survived.

Even if Bjorn endured, she could do nothing for him. With a breath, Aelthena returned to her present conundrum.

"Thank you all for coming. I know it would have been easier to ignore my invitation."

"And what are we here for?" Ingvar clearly meant the question to be a demand, but it came off as the whining of a petulant child.

"A fair question, m'lord," Aelthena said, every bit the gracious hostess. "As we must wake early to continue the march, I will cut straight to the point."

She looked each in the eye, measuring the strength of their belief in her. This was the moment she had waited for since she had learned the truth. Since she had gone to Petyrsholm and met her enemy face to face. Since she had been stripped of her title and birthright and pushed aside. She had not come this far to let the Spinners determine her fate. Aelthena forged her own path.

"Our king" — she could not help but sneer the word — "is not the man you believe him to be. He conspired against Oakharrow and had a hand in its downfall. He trafficked with the Jotun and Ha-Sypt. What is more, he had Lord Harald and Lord Alrik murdered, and would have killed me and my father as well, if he'd had his way."

Her accusations hung heavy in the air. Aelthena tried not to flit her gaze about the tent. She had to appear steady and certain, lest she undermine her bold statements. This would be difficult enough to swallow as it was.

Ingvar barked a laugh. "My father didn't love King Ragnar, but he never called him a traitor. I cannot believe it. No man would be so dishonorable."

"A moment, my son," Nanna breathed. Her eyes were wide and seeking. "Let us hear her out."

"And be included in her treason?" Despite his words, the young jarl seemed rooted in place. She could only hope her accusations rang truer to him than he cared to admit.

"Proof," Sigrid spoke sharply. "You wouldn't have said such things without proof."

"I will admit, I have less solid evidence than I would like. But I believe it is enough."

"Fine, then." Ingvar waved impatiently. "Go on, before all our heads are lopped off."

"I'll begin with how he murdered your husbands, Lady Sigrid and Lady Nanna, and your father, Lord Ingvar. We all know they were lost in the Battle of Dragons. But you may not know the circumstances under which they fell."

She turned to Sigrid, guilty for dredging up such pain, even as she knew its necessity. Her kin had fallen victim to treachery as well, and so she knew this was a wound better exposed than left to fester.

"Did you hear about Lord Harald's final moments?"

The Lady of Skjold gave a sharp nod. "Of course. I questioned every one of my soldiers."

"Then you know his killing wound?"

"Yes. A knife under his shield-arm."

Aelthena waited a breath, then looked at Ingvar, who frowned. "Lord Ingvar, how likely is a man to take such a wound in fair combat?"

His answer was soft and reluctant. "He wouldn't. Not unless he lost his shield. That's his protected side."

"But," Aelthena continued, "lifting your shield-arm would expose your side to a knife from behind, would it not?"

Ingvar remained silent. Almost, she could see the inevitable thoughts swirling inside his skull.

"It is possible." Sigrid narrowed her eyes, telling of deeper suspicions.

Aelthena turned to Nanna and Ingvar. "Now, of Lord Alrik — you were by your father's side when he fell, were you not, m'lord?"

"Yes." The word left the young man's lips in a whisper.

"And what wound felled him?"

"A cut to the back."

The words fell like an axe to a stump. Aelthena pushed the edge in deeper.

"Were you surrounded by Syptens?"

"No."

"Did your father turn and run?"

"No!"

Ingvar's face had transformed, youthful wrath dominating it now. Aelthena bowed her head. Even coming from one so young, the sight of it made her heart race and her palms sweat. She continued swiftly, lest his violence seek the wrong target.

"My second proof concerns the raid on the Elkhorn. Does it not seem strange that the stronghold of Petyrsholm was so easily infiltrated? But I have firmer suspicions than circumstance alone. Neither the gate to the castle nor the city was broken down, as you would expect from an invasion, nor were there signs of the walls being scaled. After the battle, however, the gates were found to be cracked open and the portcullises raised. Strange that warriors would overlook such crucial details, do you not think? Perhaps once it might occur, but twice?"

When the others remained silent but for Ingvar's furious breathing, she pressed on. "But you might wonder if thralls were behind the betrayal. After all, would they not help their former countrymen? But I have reason to believe them innocent. Prince Alabastor, who is also aware of this plot, inquired into this matter among the servants—"

"The prince?" Sigrid interjected. "If we cannot trust the king, how can we trust Alabastor Ragnarson? He has everything to gain from his father's triumph."

Aelthena held up her hands. "I know it must look that way, but this is one point on which you must trust me. Prince Alabastor is the last person who wants his father to succeed. He has sworn an oath to bring about just the opposite. I am confident he is dedicated to our cause."

If only she felt as certain as she sounded. Bastor seemed to hate his father, yet he had often served him. Still, he had done right by her of late, and she had not lied about his vow of vengeance. She had to believe in him or all this would be for naught.

Sigrid looked unconvinced, but she only made a slight gesture to continue.

"As I was saying," Aelthena started again, "the prince inquired among the thralls, for he is familiar with them. He received not only denials of their involvement, but explanations why they never would. It seems thralls are seen as either cowards or heretics by Syptens for not sacrificing their lives to fight against Baegard. They have little reason to help, for their countrymen will kill them as quickly as they will us. In fact, some thralls fell to Sypten swords in the invasion — further proof that what they say is true."

She paused to observe the response. Nanna looked sorrowful and weary above all else. Ingvar seemed as furious as before, tightening and loosening his fists as he stared at the tent wall. She doubted he had heard half of her words. Sigrid frowned, but her expression was thoughtful. She was the first to speak.

"What did you expect to come from telling us this, Aelthena?"

It was a leading question, one which must fully commit Aelthena to her conspiracy. Drawing in a breath, she tried holding her voice steady.

"I want you to help me set right the wrongs done to Baegard. We are the Seven Jarlheims; we were never meant to have a king. We must tear down the one who has set himself above us."

"Yes." The word would have come out in a growl, were Ingvar's voice pitched lower, yet his rage transformed it into something grating. "I'll cut him down just as he did my father!"

"Peace, my son." Nanna set a hand to his arm. The young jarl shrugged off, but he seemed somewhat chagrined.

Sigrid stared hard at Aelthena. Just as Aelthena feared the worst, she spoke again. "Is it true you killed one invader yourself?"

The question catching her off guard, Aelthena took a moment to reply. "Yes. They injured my guardian. I had no other choice."

The Lady of Skjold nodded. "Just one more reason to respect you. I must think on this, but I would hear more of what you have to say."

"As would my son and I," Nanna murmured, though Ingvar looked more like he wanted to pick a fight.

Aelthena gave them a small smile. Though this signaled a triumph, it did not make for a joyous occasion. Treachery and vengeance never could be.

"Another night, however," Sigrid continued, her eyes sliding over to the young jarl. "We would not wish to commit to rash action."

Ingvar sneered as he looked aside.

"Very well." Aelthena had hoped to say more, perhaps to even gain a verbal agreement, but she could see it was enough to swallow as things stood. "I will wait some time before issuing a second summons in case of unwanted watchers."

"Not too long," Nanna said with a valiant attempt at a smile.

They made their farewells, then her guests — or, with luck, fellow conspirators — left the tent. She still watched the rustling flap when Frey stepped in.

"Sounded like a success."

Aelthena grimaced. "I hope no one else overheard."

"Oh, no; I kept them away. That young jarl acts like a boar, but point his tusks in the right direction and he'll gut a few men before he falls."

"If we're not discovered before then."

Despite her words, she was beginning to think they might not be. Ragnar had placed all the people she was most likely to ally with together in Bastor's army, but his reasons still evaded her. To lure them into committing treason so he could move against them? To weaken their forces against the Jotun before he took them on himself?

She shook her head. There was no way of knowing. All she could do was build her house of bones and hope they did not tumble down on all their heads.

Frey stepped closer. His hands touched her waist and drew her against him so his face was inches from hers. She stared up into his eyes, only a glimmer of the blue-green visible by the lamp's flame.

"Best make good on what time we have," he suggested softly.

"You won't hear me object."

She brought her lips to his, wishing the moment would last, knowing it would slip away all too soon.

11. BOND OVER BLOOD

"Being kin don't mean being right, follow? Bond comes over blood when your friends have the truth of it."

- Erik the Fist to his band, the Red Berserkers

Egil watched the manor gate for a long while before slinking toward it.

The evening was gray with twilight. He had hidden for most of that afternoon, waiting for the spare crowds on the streets to disperse. Jotunmen and barbars patrolled, but Egil had been long enough among their ranks to know their routes. Still, there was always a risk of being caught. A warrior had to remain ever vigilant.

Egil glanced either way as he crossed the street and made for the gate. His father had risen high in the Jotun's court as he tried his best to become indispensable, but Egil knew Yaethun Brashurson was still kept under watch. Just then, he saw no sign of Kuljash's men, so he hurried the last steps and hailed the guard. Recognizing his houselord's heir, the guard cranked open the gate. Egil felt his gaze on his back as he crossed the inner courtyard.

Striding into the foyer, he ignored the staring servants, only addressing one to inquire after his father. As usual, it appeared Yaethun was cloistered away in his study. His empty belly rumbled, but Egil made straight for his father. Time was too pressing to delay.

Once admitted, Egil entered the study, but halted just inside the door. His father's study had always reached for opulence. The hickory desk was trimmed with silver, and gold statuettes stood atop it. A generous amount of books filled the shelves lining the walls, their bindings immaculately kept.

It was all for show. This was the grandest room in the manor, and it had been dearly bought. When Egil's grandfather had been the jarl, their family had been wealthy by any standards. Now, the best they could afford was this false gilding. That his father upheld it had always filled Egil with contempt, a feeling that had only intensified over the past year.

At his son's entrance, Yaethun Brashurson stood from his desk. Lawspeaker still in name, the chain of his office hung from his neck, rattling with the sudden movement.

"Egil!" he hissed, moving around the desk to stand before him. "What have you done?"

Egil tightened his jaw. "What I had to."

"What you *had* to do almost lost me my head! It may still cost everything we have worked so hard to gain! Killing one of the giant's pets is as grave an insult as you could have committed. I thought you had better sense than to strike before thinking." His father's scowl deepened. "It seems I was wrong."

Egil could not stop his lips from curling. He wished he

had not come. Yet this was his moment to say all he had needed to for months, years. Perhaps his entire life. He would not waste it.

"The time has come, Father. We must rise as one and fight back." He spoke the words with a calm befitting a warrior, almost as calmly as Vedgif Addarson might have said them. "The jarl's heir has returned."

Yaethun stared. "Bjorn Borson?"

"Yes."

"But you said he died in the mountains. That they would never survive."

"So I believed."

Egil thought of all the times he had underestimated Bjorn. Even his idiocy in approaching Oakharrow's walls had turned out to his benefit, if only by Egil's intervention. Still, it had not been a coward's choice. He himself could not have found the courage to do it. Perhaps Bjorn Borson was even brave enough to challenge the Jotun.

His father began to pace. Egil knew this routine and its implications: the schemes had started to sprout. If there was a way to turn the situation to his benefit, Yaethun would find it. Egil had to speak before he strayed too far down that path.

"You cannot always play both sides, Father. A man must make a stand."

Yaethun stopped and faced him. Egil tried hard not to clench his jaw. That disappointed look — how much of his life had he spent trying to avoid it?

"I thought," the lawspeaker said softly, "I raised my son to be cleverer than that. The first to stand is the first cut down. Remember Skarl Thundson? I would not blame you if you didn't. He and his name are nothing but a smudge on cobblestones now."

His father jabbed a finger at the window. Egil suspected what he indicated before he looked. In plain view outside the smoky glass lay the ruins of the old Harrowhall.

"Kuljash cannot be defied, Egil. He will kill all in his way. I don't know if I can protect you after what you have done, but if you remain unseen here—"

"No."

It almost came out as a growl. Egil's body felt like a fist, clenched and ready to swing. His father took a step back, eyes wide. Only then did Egil realize his hand rested on his sword's hilt. Air hissing between his teeth, he pried his fingers off and hung his hand by his side.

"No," Egil said again. "I won't hide under your wing. I won't scramble to make amends. I mean to stand with the rebellion, Father. Better to be cut down than cut myself short. I thought you had the courage to defy the Jotun, that this was more than your usual jockeying for power. I should have known better. It's like you said — you raised me to be cleverer than that."

He held his father's gaze, but he did not see the anger he expected. Instead, pity and disgust burned in those cold eyes.

"Go," his father hissed. "Give your life to the son of a man who stole your inheritance. But see to it you never return!"

Not trusting himself to speak, Egil turned away without another word. Exiting, he slammed the study door behind him. His feet stamped on the floorboards, defying his efforts to step softly. He had lost all sense of a warrior's control.

His father would not rat him out; that much loyalty, Egil believed, remained between them. But he could not say the same of his servants and household guard. His father might lose everything because of this visit.

Just then, Egil found it difficult to care.

The guard at the gate let him out, murmuring, "Inscribed watch over you, Master Egil."

He nodded his thanks, then crossed the street back to the alley from which he had first kept watch.

The Tangled Temple, where he had taken shelter with the others of the rebellion, was not far off. With darkness covering his trail, Egil opted for speed rather than stealth. He wished to be done with this ill-fated errand. Even still, he kept to side alleys where he could, trudging through mud, food leavings, and worse as he padded under windows. No one remained awake telling by the darkness behind the shutters.

As he reached the end of another alley, a squelch sounded behind him.

Egil spun while drawing his seax, but his assailant was already upon him. The man's rotten breath billowed over his face as he seized Egil's arms and forced them down. Snarling, Egil resisted, the tip of his blade inches from the man's belly.

Another called from behind the man in some barbar tongue. A pair on patrol. Egil's odds of survival plummeted further still.

The other man was proving the stronger, Egil's seax falling away rather than drawing nearer. Egil relented, ramming his head forward instead. Pain ratcheted through his skull as his forehead crunched into his assailant's nose. The man howled and loosed one hand to grab Egil around the throat. Stars blossomed in his vision, exploding in fresh constellations as the barbar shoved him back against the wall.

Again, his seax was locked down by his side, but his other hand was still free. Darkness edging in, Egil fumbled at his belt. He tugged as fingers closed about leather, a familiar weight falling into his hand. Gasping, his throat all but closed, he turned his wrist and shoved his arm forward with all his remaining strength.

A wheeze eked through the barbar's lips. The choking hand fell slack.

Air rushed down his throat; black spotted his vision. Shaking his head and blinking, Egil thrust his freed seax-hand into the man as well, striking thrice before working through his assailant's thick furs. Blood wetted his gloves.

The barbar stumbled back, then fell, unsheathing Egil's weapons for him.

The second man did not let Egil catch his breath. Howling, he leaped forward, an axe in one hand and a knife in the other. Egil skirted back, feet clumsy from lack of air. His heels bumped against the previous opponent's body, and just in time, he lifted his feet clear.

The second barbar was not so fortunate. Stumbling over his friend's body, he fought to gain his balance, but even the moment's distraction was too long. Egil surged forward, seax knocking aside the axe and knife digging into the man's shoulder. The barbar screamed, or tried to; a blade through the throat turned the sound to a gurgle.

Egil stepped back and watched the man convulse on the ground, then grow still. His lungs burned. His heart thundered. Even with his bruises and breathlessness, he was ready to keep fighting. Shaking his head, he tried clearing his eyes, but the spots remained.

Have to move. Other patrols nearby might have heard the clamor. Even though this pair had tried capturing him instead of immediately sticking him with a knife, he could not depend upon a stroke of fortune again.

Egil sheathed his seax, but kept his knife out. Looking

both ways out of the alley, he scampered forward. Strange as it was, a smile twitched on his lips.

He was not his father, to cower before anyone strong. He would fight to keep Oakharrow out of enemy hands. But for this night, two dead was enough.

12. WHERE YOUR HEAD RESTS

"For sage advice, heed nothing more than this: Keep your allies close, your adversaries closer, and your rival right under your bedcovers."

- Asger Fireside, a skald of Djurshand

B e wary," Yonik murmured in Bjorn's ear, not for the first time that day.

Bjorn looked up from his meal to see Bodil the Blaze coming their way. The flame-haired shieldmaiden wore her usual predatory smile, the look in her eyes like that of a hungry wolverine.

"My Lord Heir." She sat opposite of them at the long table and leaned across it. "How are you finding Edda's hospitality?"

There could be only one answer to that. "Good. Very good."

In truth, "good" would not have been how he described their two-day stay. When Bodil was not leering at him, or Edda had not summoned them for sessions similar to a lawspeaker's questioning of a criminal, the Vurg leader's warriors stared balefully at them from every part of the longhouse. He was not in chains, yet Bjorn could not help feeling like a prisoner all the same.

Bodil's grin widened. "I'm sure it could be better. More... comfortable."

"We couldn't ask for more," Bjorn answered quickly. What she implied made him think guiltily of Tyra, even though he had no intention of letting Bodil anywhere near his bedroll. Did Tyra resent him for leaving her behind? Or was she relieved not to throw her life away after his? Either way, he knew she was better off with Loridi and Seskef. They would watch over her.

The warrioress leaned away, her brow creasing. "Shame. Was wondering how hairy the rest of you is."

After a pregnant pause, Yonik spoke up. "Bodil, we wondered when we could meet our companions. I expected Elder Vedgif and Egil to come by now."

"Did you?" The Blaze's eyes peeled over to the gothi. "Well, we must all suffer disappointment."

Bjorn's doubts awoke anew. Had Egil set them up? Had he betrayed them? Questions plagued him during the long hours of the day and kept him up at night. He and the lawspeaker's son had always had an unspoken rivalry, at least on Bjorn's part, but he doubted Egil would be so petty as to settle it with their lives. Yet when the sentry did not return the first day, nor this one, his uncertainties dug in deeper roots.

A dangerous question edged onto his tongue. Only knowing his destiny did not end here gave him the courage to speak it.

"Is Edda keeping us here?"

The flame-haired warrioress turned back to him. "Far as I've seen, no one's keeping you anywhere but yourselves."

106

Her smile spread once more. "Maybe you should think on if there's a reason you're staying."

With a last lingering glance, Bodil rose and sauntered over to a knot of warriors, where she was greeted with the clinking of horns and cups.

Bjorn stared at the shieldmaiden's back. Had he entered the city only to cower within its walls? Did he pin his hopes on Vedgif so he would not have to act boldly himself? The questions lacked the bite they would have once possessed. He knew his mettle now. He was no coward.

Yonik leaned in close. "It was wise to wait, but I'm not sure we should delay much longer. We're blind here in Edda's fortress and cannot hope to make progress."

"How long should we wait, then?"

"Till tomorrow night. Then we'll find our own way through the city."

Bjorn whiled away the rest of the day, spending most of it pacing. When that grew tedious, he ate, drank, and dozed. During moments he thought no one watched him, he moved to a dark corner to study his runestones, eager to memorize them lest he need use them by memory alone. Yonik often sat with his legs crossed and his eyes closed, deep in meditation, or perhaps praying to the Inscribed. All around, Vurg warriors came and went, few speaking directly to them. Across the hall, Edda's dark eyes glistened from where she lounged in her chair. Bjorn caught her watching him on several occasions.

Their escape could not come soon enough.

That night, the monotony of their situation shifted. Bjorn had already crawled into his blankets when a *tap, tap, tap* came at the door. Sitting up, he watched as Edda's warrioresses opened it, then admitted two shadowed figures. As they swept their hoods back, Bjorn scrambled up and went to greet them, Yonik close behind.

"Vedgif Addarson."

The elder turned and met him with his usual flinty stare. He looked as eternal as he ever had, unyielding and hard as the Dawnshadow in winter. His head was still nearly shaved, and his pate shone where no hair grew.

"Lord Heir," he greeted him in his raspy baritone. Then, to Bjorn's surprise, Vedgif pounded a fist to his heart in a warrior's salute.

Egil did not echo the honor, but stood a step behind, gray eyes unblinking. He seemed to have gained fresh cuts and bruises on his face. Bjorn wondered what trouble he had found and who had caused it. Being old companions, he might have offered to heal his wounds, but he doubted the sentry would consent. And there was the matter of if he could risk the ritual within the confines of the longhouse, under Edda's prying eyes. Though the Vurgs were all but outlaws, it did not mean they would wish to break the Inscribed Laws where witchery was concerned.

After Yonik gave a hearty greeting, they all retreated to the farthest corner of the hall and bent their heads together to speak in hushed tones. Bjorn hoped they would not be overheard, though the contours of the place could make unintended words carry.

Yonik went first. "I'm hoping you have a plan for getting us out of here."

"Not yet." Vedgif frowned around the longhouse. "This is the safest place for you right now."

"The safest place?" Bjorn eyed the Vurg warriors with their sharp smiles and strange markings. "What about where you're staying?"

"The Tangled Temple isn't yet secure. We're likely under surveillance. Egil is risk enough to us as it is."

Bjorn hid his disappointment. The elder was rigid in his

thinking, but he knew his business. If Vedgif said this was the best place for them, he had to trust that.

Until Bodil the Blaze proves otherwise.

"What of the rest of this, ah..." Yonik waved a hand indistinctly, "rebellion?"

If Vedgif took offense at the gothi's hesitancy, he did not show it. "We've rallied a significant force from our own clan. The elders who remain support it, as do most of the Thurdjur highborn."

His gaze slid over to Egil. Bjorn wondered what that look meant, especially when the sentry grimaced. Was Yaethun Brashurson proving less than loyal? Having spent much time with the man, the lawspeaker having a change of heart would not have come as a surprise.

"From the Balturgs," the elder continued, "we have less support. Lady Kathsla remains besieged within Vigil Keep. Though we have had no recent communication, we believe she and her keepers continue to hold out; otherwise, Kuljash's men would have little reason to surround it. The Balturg elders are split in their opinions. Without their thane or the late Lord Eirik's widow to guide them, their spines are bent double."

Yonik leaned forward. "And what of the Vurgs? How did this union come about?"

"By accident. Edda Skarldaughter contacted me. Egil and I met with her representative, the warrioress Bodil."

He nodded to the far end of the room, where the flame-haired woman laughed raucously. Bjorn winced as she looked his way and pretended not to notice her leer.

"It took much talking, but it was plain in this, our interests are aligned. I accepted the risk and banded with them."

A fluttering began in Bjorn's belly. He did not look forward to fights, but with purpose burned into his mind and a less than comfortable present situation, he was eager to be on with it.

"When can we be ready?" he asked. "To take back the jarlheim?"

Egil stared at him, while the elder looked almost thoughtful. Yonik, on the other hand, seemed uneasy at the question.

"This isn't a matter to rush," the priest said quietly. "Before acting, it is best to know the will of the gods."

The will of the gods. Yonik rarely spoke in religious terms. Now that he had, Bjorn found himself resenting it. Was it the will of the gods that Oakharrow had been conquered? That his family had been slain and split apart? He did not know if Aelthena and his father remained alive, though the last reports to reach Eildursprall had said they were. The news in their travels south had spoken of a battle won at Petyrsholm, but every war came with casualties.

He met Yonik's eyes. "I didn't wait for the will of the gods when I entered Oakharrow. I saw a path, and I took it."

In the corner of Bjorn's eye, he saw Egil start and Vedgif wince. He ignored them both.

"Enea cannot afford delay. More giants come down from the north, if they've not already landed. And there are still the surtunar to reckon with. I must take back my home and find an accord with Kuljash if we're to have any hope of survival."

His words, which had grown steadily more impassioned, were met with silence. Yonik smoothed his expression, while Egil and Vedgif stared in open astonishment. Bjorn stiffened his jaw as it threatened to expose him. His visions contained truth; that had been proven time and time again. He had seen in the First Shadow runestone what must come to pass for Enea to survive the Runewar. If he showed his doubts now, how could any believe in him?

Egil finally spoke. "How do you know? All that — how do you know it's true?"

Bjorn met his eyes, wondering at the emotions smoldering behind them, brimming so it seemed they must spill over.

"*Seidar*. The rune magic. You saw me use it on the way to the Chasm. In Eildursprall, I learned to control it."

"Started to learn," Yonik corrected, but ruefully, as if even he struggled to believe it.

Egil chewed on that for a moment, then grimaced. His next words seemed pulled out like leeches off skin.

"Can others learn this magic?"

It was Bjorn's turn for astonishment. Egil could not mean what he thought he did. Before, the sentry had regarded anything Bjorn did with contempt. Just now, however, he seemed green with envy.

"That would not be wise," Yonik started, but Vedgif spoke over him.

"No. There's enough witchery in the world already." The elder scowled down at the table, but Bjorn knew it was intended for him.

Egil looked ready to protest, but a familiar warrior sauntered over to their table. Bodil the Blaze wore a grin, but the rest of her features were set as hard as stone.

"Enough talk for one day!" She clapped the elder and sentry on the shoulders. "Either you must drink and joke with us, or get back to your hidey-hole."

Their faces showed their resentment for the familiarity, yet neither Egil nor Vedgif said a word as they rose. They knew their precarious situation as well as Bjorn.

"We'll be back with more news," the elder said stiffly. "Until then, Lord Heir."

Again, Vedgif pressed a fist to his breast, then turned

toward the longhouse's door. Egil lingered a moment, then gave a curt nod before following him out.

The Blaze looked after them. "No fun, those two. Stones in bilgewater, as my Da used to say." She looked down at Bjorn, her gaze making him both hot and cold at once. "Your company, however, I could enjoy much, much more."

Yonik came to his rescue. With hastily made excuses, they retreated to their corner to sleep. Though Bjorn wrapped himself in his blankets, rest evaded him. The urgency of his mission had returned, setting his palms to sweating and his heart to beating.

Go, it thumped. *Go. Go.*

Yet he didn't know how. What path could he take to Kuljash to gain his aid? What path would not lead to his death?

Then, like the gods themselves placed it in his mind, the answer — so simple, so obvious — came to him.

Vedgif would not approve of it, nor Yonik. It promised peril, pain, and the possibility of madness. But it could also yield answers.

He set his hand upon his rucksack, where the Four Shadows were secured with his other runestones. The legacy of Torvald Geirson was the key. These stones were the cairns marking the path to a brighter future, and they contained the guidance Bjorn so desperately needed.

He was the Stoneseer. Understanding these prophecies was what he had been born to do.

Yet now was not the time to view the Second Shadow. He had to wait for the right opportunity, when he could See uninterrupted and undiscovered.

But soon, the next vision of the King of Ice would be his.

13. OVER THE HILL

ᚽ

*"This is my home, my motherland. Djur damn me if I
yield it to the likes of you!"*

*- Coppereye the Insurgent, First Drang to the Unchained
Thanes, to Thoros Wolfjaw, the Champion of Torvald
Geirson, the Last King of Baegard*

She had known it would soon arrive, known it might
be just over the next hill. Yet Aelthena was still
taken by surprise when the call came from ahead.
"Oakharrow! Oakharrow lies beyond the rise!"
Aelthena strained to see it. The day was misty with an
autumn drizzle, yet she brightened as she picked it out from
among the trees.

Oakharrow lay below. Her jarlheim. Her city.
Home.

She glanced at Frey and saw similar feelings shining in
his eyes, sharing in that look all they needed to.

Aelthena turned back to where her father rode. Unfit to
sit atop a horse, he was being carted in one of the covered

chariots such as the ladies of Baegard used to travel. She could just see his bearish outline hunched within, Uljana a dark smudge next to him.

Facing forward, she repressed a sigh. They might nearly be home, but her concerns weighed as heavily as ever. Things were much the same as before — which was to say, full of pitfalls and problems.

"Don't be so glum, my lady," Frey said. "At least we can begin the siege."

"What a show that will be."

The guardian only grinned. "You can never tell. Our wily prince may yet have something up his sleeve."

She could only hope he was right. Another war council would take place that night; then, she would learn more of Bastor's plans for the battle.

Or the lack of them.

They continued the march a while longer before the prince called for a halt. Though still leagues away from Oakharrow, caution bade them not to stray too close. The Jotun had had three seasons to lay traps aplenty for them; it would not pay to stumble into any before the battle began. Aelthena dismounted her white mare, which she had named Winterlily, and watched the scouts ride on ahead. Soon, they would know something of what obstacles lay between them and her home.

Leaving Frey to care for her horse, Aelthena went back to her father to help settle him. Either he had grown less volatile than before or she was growing more competent in assisting him, for when she offered her hand, Bor Kjellson meekly took it, leaning heavily on her as he labored to dismount the chariot. With every day, he seemed to age even further beyond his years.

"Look, Father," she said when he had his feet on solid ground. "We've made it back to Oakharrow. Back home."

She had not expected a response. Even at the best of times, the former jarl only stared at her with watery eyes that comprehended little. But now, he drew up to his full height and stared toward the distant city, almost like the man of her childhood.

"My son," he murmured. "I come, my son."

Aelthena flinched. *Your sons are gone!* she wanted to shout. *The eldest murdered, the youngest lost.* Did he think he came home to them? Were they still alive in his mind? And of his wife — did he remember Bestla Of Bor anymore?

Instead of asking, she sighed. "Come, Father. It's time to go."

Bor resisted her pull. Slowly, he turned toward her, his eyes catching and holding hers.

"I'm proud of you, Aelthena. Proud of all you've become."

Aelthena stared at her father. Each word had been slow and enunciated, yet she could scarcely believe them. How long had she yearned for such praise from him? How long had she strived for it, only to be denied it time and again? In that moment, she could almost fool herself into believing he was the man he had once been.

Bor continued to stare at her. Aelthena tried to speak, but her throat had closed up.

"Thank you, Father," she finally managed.

He nodded and looked back at Oakharrow. Then, as suddenly as he had bloomed, Bor Kjellson wilted. His shoulders slumped; his chest caved in; his head drooped like a flower on a bent stem. Aelthena kept looking into his eyes, desperate to see that spark of life again, but they had gone dull.

"Rats," he muttered. "Rats in the shadows..."

Disappointment washed through her, hot and fierce, but Aelthena had faced enough of it to quickly recover. Mindful of the warriors and highborn milling about her, she smoothed her expression. Uljana's gaze was upon her, so she looked at the thrall. In this, they shared an understanding. The loyal servant knew better than anyone else how precious these few moments of clarity were.

"Let's get him settled in," Aelthena murmured. She and Uljana each took an arm to lead the former jarl away.

───────────

Aelthena stifled her disdain as she waited for the war council to begin.

As the afternoon arrived, the rain relented, allowing an almost jovial atmosphere to emerge in the clearing where they had set up. She was forced to endure a feast as the agenda for the council was established. The retinue of high-born, mostly young women seeking to ensnare their new prince in marriage, milled about as if they had every right to be present. It was all Aelthena could do to hold her tongue and wait for Bastor to usher them away. She wondered aloud why he did not outright order them out, to which Frey wagered a guess.

"Perhaps he enjoys it. After all, he's spent most of his life as a social pariah and unfavored son. Must be nice to be admired for once."

She flashed him a cross look, though he likely had the right of it. Aelthena had seen Bastor angry before; his charm now was far from that. Still, it gave her no more patience until the prince finally turned the ensemble to the business of war.

Those who remained largely had her respect. Sigrid nodded at Aelthena, calmly composed before a knot of her drangi. Nanna stood near to her, Ingvar at her side. The young jarl was acting more raucous with his men than befitted his station, but with his mother's hand to guide him, Aelthena thought he might stay to the correct course.

Siward stood apart from the others, frowning before his silent warriors and failing to meet Aelthena's eye. Was it disdain, shame, or something else that kept him to his corner? From what she understood, he spent every spare moment with his family, who accompanied him on the campaign. Though the jarl had a hand in raising up their traitor king, Aelthena was reassured that he had not forgotten the threats to his daughter in the Elkhorn. There was still a chance of winning him over to her side.

Standing nearly alone but for a few keepers was the last of the notable attendees, Asborn. Aelthena avoided his gaze, even as she felt his eyes on her. Did he resent her, fear her? Or had her slight toward him fanned hatred into flame? She hardly knew her own feelings on the matter. They had shared too much to despise him entirely, yet his betrayal had been far more profound than hers.

At last, Bastor herded away the last of his sycophants and addressed them without preamble. "Tomorrow!" he boomed across the clearing. "Tomorrow, it begins. I will ride to Oakharrow and demand the Jotun's unconditional surrender. Who will join me?"

There was a breath of surprise. Sigrid broke it, speaking through clenched teeth.

"Highness, is it wise for you to be part of the delegation?"

"Wise? Gray gods, no! But neither was it wise to charge at giants and ignite their dragonfire." Bastor still wore a smile, but his gaze turned sharper. "If my father taught me one thing, it's that a task needing doing is best done yourself. I don't mean to let a title change that."

It was an admirable sentiment, if a foolish one. Though, considering it was one they shared, Aelthena hardly had grounds to criticize. Still, seeing an opening, she stepped forward, ignoring Frey's small sigh as she did so.

"I will go, Highness."

"Marvelous!" Bastor grinned at her. "A showing from Oakharrow's own is just what's needed."

Aelthena wished he had not phrased the sentiment so. Now, her former betrothed was obliged to respond. To do less would stain his honor.

"I will also go, Highness," Asborn said with a good degree less surety. "It is my duty as the jarl."

As if we needed the reminder. Despite the thought, she kept her expression smooth, even as Asborn turned his gaze on her. Though a quenchless fire burned in her breast, she could act frost-bent when need called for it.

"I'm sure it is." There was laughter in the prince's words. Aelthena hoped it was for Asborn and not her. "Any others?"

Young Ingvar stepped forward, chin raised and chest puffed out. "Let me go with, Highness."

Ingvar's mother stared worriedly at his back. Yet it had never been her way to speak against her late husband; she did not seem intent on beginning a practice of it with her son.

"I'll have you, Lord Ingvar, and be grateful for it." The gleam in Bastor's eyes spoke volumes to Aelthena, but the prince was tactful enough not to mock the youth aloud. "That's enough, then. Unless anyone else has something to say, drink and rest are in order."

Sigrid still looked mutinous, and Nanna uneasy, but none raised objections.

Bastor clapped once. "Good. Now, you'd best pick up a tankard or find your tents!"

Ingvar took the prince up on his offer at once, his huskarls joining in. Aelthena shook her head and turned away. Manly drinking was the last thing she needed this evening.

"Sure you don't want to join them?" Frey murmured at her elbow.

"Tempting as it is, I think I'll pass."

Grinning, the guardian held a low-hanging branch aside for her. She pressed through the thicket until they emerged on the other side. Once more, Oakharrow came into view, only the tallest rooftops visible at her present angle.

She didn't have high hopes for the upcoming delegation; in fact, they were as low as they could go. But tomorrow was the first step toward claiming back her home.

A step long overdue.

14. DAUNTLESS

The wyvern rose as tall as the cliffs, and her wings spread twice as long. Her jaws yawned wide as a city well, and her middle swelled and glowed, belly-forge burning with a red inferno.

But Yofam Vigoson stood dauntless before it. "Vardraith!" he called on high to the wyrm. "Suffer me your worst! Mine heart beats in my breast, untouched by fear's claws!"

Vardraith the Vain screeched, a sound like a thousand swords clashing, before unleashing her breath. The flames fell upon the warrior, and the ground grew black as coal. Yet when her breath ceased and the fires burned out, a man stood amidst the dark circle.

Not a single hair upon Vigoson's head was singed.

- *Myths of the Middle Land, by Alfin the Scribe*

A breeze tickled Bastor's face. Sucking in a deep breath, he released it with a contented sigh. It seemed the freshest air he had tasted since smoke had haunted the skies above Petyrsholm. Only a prince for a month, yet already he tired of it. The pageantry, the luxury, the fawning — it had turned as cloying as a season-old corpse. He had always been a scoundrel, a man living on the fringes of society, and though that life had scarcely contented him, a part of him wished to return to those days, like an elder longing for his youth.

Or a prisoner yearning for his cell.

With a wry grin, Bastor set his gaze back upon Oakharrow. At the early morning hour, the city's shadow reached far across the fields, though it stopped short of the tree line. A keen-eyed archer could pick off him and his company as soon as they touched the umbra. For his words to be heard, he would have to come well within their range.

But Bastor had never minded a bit of danger. Quite the opposite — nothing heated his blood like death's breath upon his neck.

Calling to his companions, he spurred toward their destination. Bastor smiled at Aelthena's outraged shout, but didn't turn back. Though she pretended to disdain thrills, he had seen her seek out enough of them to know she shared his appetite.

Nearly a dozen others rode with them. Frey, of course, dogged Aelthena's every step. Not to be outdone by the woman who had spurned him, Asborn, the so-called Jarl of Oakharrow, came a short way behind. Young Ingvar stared around them with a fresh-eyed gaze, though he tried to hide it. Eight huskarls completed the princely retinue.

Upon the wall, Bastor could just make out the glint of

sunlight on helms. Squinting, he tried to see if archers drew their bows and sighted them. This whole courtesy was likely a charade. What ground could they share with a giant, one who had taken their rightful land? Yet civility had its demands, and even bastards had to pay its dues.

When he decided they had come near enough, Bastor drew to a halt and leaned over to unstrap his shield. Drawing in a deep breath, he tilted back his head and bellowed, "I am Prince Alabastor Ragnarson, heir apparent to King Ragnar Torbenson! I come to demand of your master his complete surrender!"

He waited, listening for any distant echo of a reply. None came, either in word or arrow.

"If the Jotun does not comply," Bastor continued, "I'll be forced to make him! Already, we have driven back your Sypten allies, and a dozen giants stood among them. One poses little threat to me."

Again, he waited. Again, silence filled the still morning air.

"Now what, Highness?" Ingvar asked, a tremor in his voice that might have come from nerves or excitement.

"Perhaps we should wait farther back?" Aelthena noted drily.

As the young jarl frowned at her, Bastor shook his head. "We wait here until we have a reply, one way or another."

Skepticism shone in the others' faces, making a fresh grin win free of Bastor. They feared the arrow and its shadow falling from the sky. For him, death was an old companion.

In case they had not heard his first ultimatum, Bastor shouted it again, then had Ingvar do the same as his voice grew hoarse. The morning bled toward afternoon, and his party shifted restlessly behind. Even Bastor began to doubt.

Yet it took time to summon a city's leader. Perhaps the messengers moved slowly today.

His attention drifting, it took him a moment to notice the strange birds descending toward them.

"Shields up!" Bastor roared as he raised his own. Even as he spoke, four arrows fell to the ground ahead, dirt spitting up on impact. A fifth found a horse, the beast loosing a pitiful scream.

The sixth thudded into Bastor's shield.

With the force behind it, the arrow pierced halfway through the wood and jarred his arm to his shoulder. Bastor stared at the arrowhead. Had he held a weaker shield, it might have pierced through it and injured or killed him.

Bastor threw back his head and laughed.

When his mirth quieted, he turned back to the others' shocked faces. Aelthena and Frey only looked exasperated. Bastor couldn't help another chuckle.

"If he can walk, we'd best go," he told the guard with the injured horse. The arrow had taken it in the rump, so the huskarl now led it by the reins.

"Waste no time," Bastor added as he turned Nott away from Oakharrow. "Unless you'd like the next arrow to bite your arse!"

———

Upon returning to the encampment, Bastor's merriment drained away. He was back in the clearing where he held his war councils, once more staring at the faces of the highborn accompanying the campaign. The jarls, the jarls' wives, and even the hanger-ons all clamored for one thing, the mood like a second heartbeat thrumming in his chest.

War. War. War.

As much as Bastor lived for the thrill of battle, he hated war. War was a waste — of joy, of lives, of resources. Like a plague, it blighted everything it touched. Yet when giants and Syptens came to steal what was yours, what options were left?

Raising a hand, Bastor spoke into the tense silence that fell. "Yes. The Jotun delivered his message clear as a blue sky. He asks for war."

A cry went up, then was quickly silenced by Bastor's raised fist.

"But we won't throw ourselves against Oakharrow's walls. We saw how effective that proved for the Syptens at Petyrsholm. I won't give lives to gain so little."

"Then how are we to get inside?" Ingvar demanded. "They'll not be inviting us in soon!"

The young jarl's huskarls loosed raucous laughter. Bastor smiled indulgently, remembering all too well those carefree and foolish years of youth.

"No, they won't," he replied. "What we need is a way in unknown or overlooked by the Syptens. One I have used before in service to my father."

Muttering started up at that, the highborn no doubt wondering what he referred to. He pressed on before any could draw conclusions.

"The Honeybrook runs under the west wall. I have smuggled items under it before. As long as they have not lowered the portcullis or otherwise blocked the path, men could sneak in again."

Bastor glanced at Aelthena and Frey. They, at least, knew what illicit activities he had been up to in his past, yet they did not glare condemnation at him now.

Though the Inscribed know I deserve it.

Perhaps that lingering guilt was why the words formed

THE STONE OF IRON & OMEN

on his tongue. Or he chafed at a prince's bonds and already missed the thrill of balancing his life on a sword's edge.

Perhaps he missed being loathed instead of loved.

Bastor grinned. "What is more, as the man who knows the way, I will lead this infiltration."

15. THE VOLUNTEER

"In warriors, valor and vanity are edges of the same blade."

- Highlord Carr Gunnarson, Fifth Arkjarl of Baegard

As the clearing erupted with objections and a few sparse cheers, Frey sighed and shook his head. Once more, the scoundrel-turned-prince made a fool of himself, grinning like he'd won a prize in a contest. Around, his fawning subjects sought to persuade him to their point of view. Some were in favor of his proposed folly, leading a charge under Oakharrow's walls that would be fraught with peril. Others had more sense and tried to convince him to reconsider, unlikely as Frey saw that to be. Rare was the time he had seen Bastor remove his foot from a shite pile he had already stepped in.

Frey looked at the woman standing a step before him. She had remained silent thus far, no doubt waiting for the din to die down so she could set things aright, as she was always forced to. He could not help but admire her. Her carriage was perfect — regal, almost, and entirely unruffled by the unwelcome development. No matter what obstacles rose in her way, Aelthena circumvented them with a level head.

Even if her temper is more tumultuous.

She was stronger than any of these highborn men in the ways that counted. Unlike Bastor, she was clear-eyed in her goals as she worked toward them. Lady Sigrid was also admirable among the women present, but Aelthena was adaptable in a way she was not. She possessed all the qualities he could hope for in one he followed, all the qualities he commended. Though her poise was only one of many reasons he loved her.

As an opening presented itself, Aelthena stepped forward and raised her voice. "I fear I must agree with Lady Sigrid and Lady Nanna, Highness. It would present a significant risk to Baegard for you to lead the expedition, as I told you before."

The prince turned slowly toward her, as if reluctant to meet her gaze. "We must all take risks in war."

"But not unnecessary ones. Consider if the Jotun captured you. He would have a hostage that would lend him significant leverage when negotiating with your father. It would also guarantee him immunity from attack until you were recovered."

Bastor's lips twisted. Frey could imagine what he was thinking. Ragnar had risked his son's life many times before. By Frey's reckoning and Bastor's own account, he didn't much care for his half-Sypten heir. The king might even be relieved to have Bastor out of the way. Yet it did not negate the validity of Aelthena's point. All knew the value of a captured prince. The toll would be just as she said.

"What do you propose, then?" Bastor demanded. "That I send in men blind, who don't know the streets of Oakharrow or how to navigate them?"

His words struck Frey like the barrage of arrows from that afternoon. A realization shivered through him. Though it felt like pulling open scabs, though he knew a storm would awaken as soon as he spoke, Frey leaned close to Aelthena and whispered in her ear.

"I will go."

She jerked around to stare at him, eyes wide. Though the growing shadows should have dimmed their color, her emerald irises almost seemed to shine.

"I need you here," she hissed.

"You need me to go more."

"They'll kill you."

"Only if they catch me."

Frey smiled before her glare. After a breath, she turned away and faced the gathering at large. Most continued to yammer about the prince's declaration, but some had noticed their curious exchange.

Frey straightened and kept his silence. She was his leader and his lady; he did as she commanded. But in this, he was in the right. She would come around to it in the end. She was too practical not to.

Noticing the prince's gaze, Frey shrugged. Bastor looked amused, but in that bitter way of his, like he had an inclination to drown in mead.

Again.

"I suspect we'll settle our infiltrators before long," the prince said. "Now, we must plan our siege. If the gods smile upon us, it won't be a long one."

Frey suppressed a chuckle. He did not intend to let the gods have a say.

16. THE FIRST TREMBLING STEP

"Every battle begins with a single step. Every war ends in silence."

- Lion Ankhu, Paragon of Pawura's Sorrow in the 171ˢᵗ Flood of Gazabe

The river tossed Sehdra's raft about like a toddler given a Duaat board.

Occasionally, she had spent time on water before. Some of her brightest childhood memories had taken place during the leisurely cruises her parents had brought her and Hephystus along on the calm stretches of the River Nu. In those rare moments, Sehdra almost imagined their family was happy. Her father, while never warm, had not laid a hand on her mother during those times, and her mother had smiled and laughed, murmuring the names of the places as they passed by. *Your inheritance*, she would say, though they both knew her brother was first in line for the Ascendant Crown. It was almost as if, even then, her mother had known that Physt would be the architect of his own end.

But memories would not keep her dry, nor whole. Clinging to Teti's arm, Sehdra tried not to look like a frightened girl as the river pitched the raft back and forth, always seeming on the verge of crashing into the gray rocks rising from the surface at regular intervals. The Whiterun was nothing like the Nu she had experienced, running as frothy white as its name suggested. Rapids were unavoidable; though scouts had traveled along the river for leagues in either direction, this poor ford was supposed to be their best option for crossing to reach the jarlheim on the opposite shore. Thus had Oyaoan ordered ferries to be built, and the People of Dust had complied with their usual efficiency, completing the task in a handful of days.

Efficiency, however, rarely lent itself to comfort. Being the karah, Sehdra had a vessel to herself, sharing it only with her servants and carts. It was far from luxurious; made up of twenty logs lashed together with hemp, they were barely trimmed and rough with bark beneath her sandaled feet. Being too anxious to sit, she stood throughout the voyage, and her twisted leg twinged with every rock they were pulled over. Increasingly, she was forced to lean on Teti to remain upright.

Yet, for all its drawbacks, the river crossing lent her something rare: a moment for candid conversation.

"Speak to me, old friend," she said, just loud enough for Teti to hear over the rush of the water. "What progress have you made on our plots?"

"Much, I think." Given a servant's leeway, Teti was freer than her to travel around their camps and facilitate their plots. "Nekau and Raneb are willing to meet you in private."

Her chest loosened, if only a fraction. "That is welcome news."

"Yet I must warn you, Divine One: the chief general was most reluctant. He repeated several times that he would make no promises, nor hear any word against Great Oyaoan."

She grimaced. Having the general on their side would matter greatly in the days ahead. Without the support of the military, they could not hope to prevail against Oyaoan in a rebellion. Yet that Nekau Baka relented to meeting with her at all was a positive start.

"And Amon?" Sehdra queried.

Teti frowned. He had never trusted her brother's general, and his distrust had only deepened with the man's fall from grace. Amon Baka was far from her first choice as well, yet if Nekau resisted her plots, she would be unwise not to pursue other options.

"The general will also meet with you," he admitted. "This very night, if you are willing."

Her heart pattered. It was one thing to arrange meetings; actually convening with Amon would be a tangible step toward treason — and death, if they were caught.

"I am," she said, hoping the river hid the tremor in her words. "Will you arrange it if we reach the shore?"

"Of course. And I believe you mean *when* we reach the shore."

They shared a smile, though Sehdra's was brief, her thoughts turning down a different avenue. "And how goes the... other plan?"

Teti gave her a long look. Even knowing him as she did, she could not unearth everything behind those eyes.

"It is in place," he said, so quietly the river almost drowned out his words. "Whenever you feel in danger, my contacts can spirit you away."

She frowned off downriver. Part of her hated making such plans. If she did not stay to contend with the giantess, what hope did her subjects have of freeing themselves from Oyaoan's tyranny? Yet she had been prudent for too long to be foolhardy now. With Oyaoan in power, escape could become necessary at any moment.

"Good," she murmured. "We shall leave it there." For good, she hoped. But in the court of power, hopes were often confounded.

The ferry jolted, and Sehdra flung both arms around Teti to stay upright. Though willowy in stature, her friend remained as steady as ever.

Sehdra drew in a mouthful of air, then released it.

In drips and trickles, the trauma of the river crossing had faded from her mind. Having changed into dry clothes and with solid ground beneath her feet, Sehdra felt more herself again. Behind her, the crossings continued, and would until darkness halted them for the day. Teti stood a couple of paces away, where he would keep watch with Amon's personal guard, monitoring each other as much as looking for spies.

The breath had not calmed her. Nothing seemed likely to. All she could do now was to be like a lioness and face her fears.

Smoothing her grimace, Sehdra strode into Amon's quarters.

Amon Baka was leaning over a map of the Winter Holds and other unfurled scrolls. Captains stood at either elbow. At her entrance, the general looked up, then immediately dismissed the others. Both men bowed deeply and murmured pardons to her before departing. Even with the giantess coming out of the shadows, her position still commanded respect. She found a small satisfaction in that.

The general eyed her for a moment before following his men's lead and bowing. "Your Divinity. I am pleased you came."

"You seem pleased."

He made a poor attempt at a smile. "My apologies, Divine One. I struggle to show appropriate appreciation these days."

Little wonder why. Under Hephystus, Amon had been the chief general, leader of all Ha-Sypt's forces. But his fortunes had largely fallen with his monarch's. The defeat at Petyrsholm had led Oyaoan to reinstate Nekau as the chief general. Though he kept Amon on as a subordinate, Amon's reach was diminished compared to the other generals, now commanding only a quarter of the soldiers he had before. Barely older than thirty floods and his military career was all but finished.

"May I offer you a seat?"

"I will stand." She could not say why, but pride demanded she remain upright. Her leg spasmed, as if to remind her of her foolishness.

Ignoring it, Sehdra stepped further within, pretending to observe the surroundings as she watched the man on the opposite side of the table. "Despite the rumors I am spreading about this meeting, pleasure and appreciation are my last concerns."

Amon's eyebrows raised. "I apologize, Divine One. I do not follow."

"It will be said that I came here to claim satisfaction." Sehdra almost succeeded in saying it casually, but a warble at the end of the sentence betrayed her. She had far too little experience with such affairs to appear cavalier, as much as she might wish otherwise.

The general stared at her for a moment before comprehension lifted his features. "Ah. I see."

"A necessary cover for my being here." Sands, but she sounded as if she were trying to excuse poor behavior. Even as the karah, she struggled not to revert to Sehdra the Scarab, hiding in the shadows. "I assume, with your reputation, that will not bother you."

"Of course not, Divine One."

Something in the way he said it awoke her doubt. Sehdra studied him from the corner of her eye. Even if she had not known he was experienced with women from Physt's lascivious gifts, she would have assumed it. His jaw was strong and peppered with dark stubble. His eyes were both warm and hard, and his teeth were bright and even. More attractive still was the confidence that emanated from him, even now in his defeat, as sure in his actions as a leopard prowling a grove. And there was something else undefinable, almost an earthen scent, that wafted lightly about the tent.

It was not modesty that made him hesitant. Was it worry about becoming entangled with another karah, and the further damage it might do to him? Or was the idea of their coupling so repulsive? She pushed down the thought, even as her hand betrayed her by reaching up to adjust her mask.

"Then, shall we...?" Amon smiled and raised an eyebrow.

Lowering her hand, Sehdra drew up as straight as her twisted leg allowed. "My servant keeps watch outside this tent for any prying ears, as does your guard. I hope we may speak frankly. We both have much to gain from a partnership, you and I."

His amusement drained away. "Some may gain more than others."

"Perhaps." She wondered how he thought the scales

balanced. "Both, however, would benefit from greater freedom."

The words drew dangerously close to sedition. If he was not inclined to it, Sehdra was placing herself in a fatal position. Yet Oyaoan had punished Amon and shown him no loyalty. Surely, a man such as him balked at being pushed aside.

The general regarded her for a long moment. "Freedom, in my experience, is dearly paid for."

"We have already paid for it."

"And it will draw further blood if pursued."

She could tell he understood what she implied. Sweat beaded behind her mask and trickled down her face.

Amon sighed, then reached for a goblet and drained it. Only then did Sehdra notice the uncorked jug behind him, the scent of wine, the flush touched upon his cheeks.

Setting down the empty cup, he looked up with watery eyes. "Why me? Nekau is the chief general now. He commands all our forces, while I have barely five hundred under my banner."

"Greater power brings greater scrutiny. Our work is best done in the dark."

"And you are not watched?" Amon laughed, a harsh edge to it. "Your man cannot stop others from seeing through your lies. I doubt any will believe them."

Again, he jabbed at her so callously. Even as the karah, she had not won his respect. Anger flushed through her. Who was he to deny her if she wished to have him? He was her subject, and she, his goddess.

But I am not a goddess, am I?

As quickly as it had come, the fury escaped in a long exhale. That line of reasoning belonged to her brother and her father, and most of her ancestors before them. It had led them to war, death, and ruin. Led them to shun and dismiss their deformed daughters.

But she knew the truth. No divinity came with the Ascendant Crown. To believe in lies would make her no better than them. Worse still, it would bring all her people, perhaps all of Enea, to ruin.

Amon watched her, a corner of his lips curled. Though the war continued within, Sehdra made a mask of her face, as survival had long ago necessitated she learn to do.

"You know the risks and the rewards," she said. "Should you wish to accept, send for me discreetly."

She turned to leave. A shuffle from behind warned her of Amon's approach.

"Divine One, please wait. Forgive my boorish behavior. I understand and agree with you. I desire freedom above all else, and the greatest freedom comes with being chief general."

There they were: his terms. Sehdra did not turn back for several long moments. When she did, she spoke over a shoulder rather than deign to face him.

"Very well. It will be yours, provided you do not make it a permanent habit to overindulge in wine."

From the corner of her eye, she caught his grin. "We can both hope."

"Do not be idle, Amon Baka. When next I visit, I expect you to have made progress."

"Progress, Divine One?"

Sehdra turned back enough to catch and hold his gaze. "I seek to learn what she desires. Her, and the others of her kind. Why they came to this land at all. When I discover this, we must be decisive in our actions. You and your men must be ready."

The general hesitated, then gave a sharp nod. "I will make certain it is so."

It was all she could ask for. With one last look, Sehdra swept from his tent.

17. PRIDE

If I have learned one truth in my studies, it is this: pride has slain far more men than steel.

- Confessions, by Alfjin the Scribe

Riders, Gertrud! Riders have come through the north gate!"

Gertrud started and looked up. Eydis stood at the entrance to the back of the manor, hands propped on her hips, her round face red from running. She had just come from the kitchens judging by the splatters down her apron.

"Riders from the north?" Gertrud repeated.

"Have you lost your wits? You know what it means!"

For a moment, she failed to grasp her friend's meaning. Long hours of toil had dulled her mind, a necessity to survive the tedium. Gertrud shook her head of its cobwebs, and finally, the words sunk in.

At long last, the day had arrived. A slow smile split her face. "He's returned."

"Yes, silly woman!" Despite her tone, Eydis barked a laugh. "But will you greet him in those?"

Gertrud looked down. She wore her undyed linens, stained and rank from washing clothes in cattle urine. Long ago, she had grown used to the stench herself, but others were not so inured to it. Already, she could imagine her son's nose wrinkling, his lips curling. He would refuse even to touch her.

She stood at once. "I must wash!"

"Of course you must, and change as well! Come, come — I shall hurry you along."

Abandoning the laundry, Gertrud ran for the river while her friend fetched her festival-day best. Scrubbing until her skin was red, she rose from the river and ran unclothed up the bank. Mud squeezed between her toes, and the wind was chill on her damp skin, but she noticed it no more than she did the stares of the other servants and thralls as she ran for the house.

With her son's return, the days would brighten from their gloom. Her life would press forward once more rather than circle in the same endless loop. He was her joy, her pride, her purpose. She had given all for him and still, she would give more.

Eydis clucked her tongue at seeing Gertrud's state, but she nevertheless helped wash the mud off her feet and bundle her up in her clothes. Her ears pounded as if the horses already rode up the drive to the manor stables. Gertrud hurried, lacing up the dress, then turning inside to stare into a mirror, though servants using them was frowned upon. Today, she did not care.

Swiftly, she braided her hair and wove flowers through it; dandelions, though little better than weeds, were all she had. Finishing, she stared at the woman in the bright reflection. Once, she had been reckoned the beauty among the

Lynx Manor staff. Her golden, silken hair and fine features had caught the eye of her son's father. Now, decades later, she was no longer in the bloom of youth, yet she still turned heads when out of her laundering linens.

Satisfied, Gertrud restrained herself to a walk and went to stare out one of the front manor windows. Her breath caught as she saw him. Her chest swelled with pride. There he rode at the head of his small host through Ragnarsglade, head held high, all the adulation of the city heaped upon him. Swiftly, he would arrive at Lynx Manor where she waited.

His inheritance. His home.

When he reached the front doors, Gertrud was already waiting. She stifled her smile, mindful of his past irritation at her exuberance, and waited for him to approach and acknowledge her.

Her son left his horse to be stabled by one of his men, then strode toward the manor. There was a slight unsteadiness to his gait; no doubt the ride had been strenuous even for a man of his hale nature. Gertrud could not help but stare at him until his eyes slid over to hers. His lips curled into a smile as he stopped several paces away from her.

"Mother."

"Ragnar." She longed to throw her arms around him and draw him near, as she had not been allowed to do since he was half her height. But a servant's life was one of restraint, and the years had taught even flighty Gertrud the lesson.

Ragnar narrowed his eyes. She thought he most looked like a jarl's son like that, haughty and above the common rabble. But if the talk around town was true, he was more than even that now. Far, far more.

"Come," he said curtly. "Bring fresh mead to Father's study at once."

Gertrud bobbed her head and hurried on her son's heels

to do as he bade. She had fed, clothed, and cared for him all his childhood. It was only fitting she do the same for him as a man.

By the time she returned with a small cask of honey-wine, Ragnar had already kicked off his muddy boots and laid back on the divan occupying the center of the study, a pipe trailing sweet-smelling smoke. Repressing a wince at the fresh stains on the rugs and the effort required to scrub out, Gertrud poured her son a horn of mead and stood at the foot of the divan.

Ragnar waved a lazy hand, already seeming lethargic from the smoke. "Sit, Mother, sit. My father's not here to make you stand like a common servant."

Gertrud sat gingerly in one of the high-backed chairs positioned next to the divan. Folding her hands in her lap, she quieted the questions stirring in her head and waited for her son to speak. Talk too much or too soon and she risked being sent away.

The young man gazed at her. Remembering the glimpse of herself in the mirror, she was pleased with how much his eyes were like hers, bright and green as a spring meadow.

"Well?" he said at last. "Are you not going to offer your praise?"

Gertrud's chest tightened, but she smiled. "You always have my praise, my son."

"Not 'my son'. I believe you mean 'my prince'."

"Yes, my prince."

As Ragnar smiled, she returned it. Her son, a prince. Her mother — ancestors keep her soul — would have never believed what Gertrud had made of her life. *Whore!* her mother had screamed after learning Gertrud was pregnant with the jarl's get. *You'll be nothing but his whore!*

She was no whore, however it had begun. She was the mother of a prince.

"That is not all, though." Ragnar sucked down smoke, then coughed it up before continuing hoarsely. "Father has all but assured me I am his true heir, not that bastard brother of mine who claims the title."

Gertrud's breath caught. "Can it be true?"

"I say it is!" her son snapped. "Why else would he send me here? He means me to first inherit Ragnarsglade, then the kingdom. This is where I'll prove I am worthy. Then, someday, perhaps someday soon, you will be mother to a king."

Mother to a king. She had not dared imagine having her son be a prince. A king was too far to stretch her imagination.

"I am so proud of you, my prince."

As soon as the words left her mouth, Gertrud cringed, expecting a reprimand. Instead, Ragnar grinned and sat up.

"How could you not be?"

Draining the horn, he held it out. Gertrud refilled it. Her son settled back in the divan again, sitting up but slouching. The elation left his face as he stared into the dark hearth opposite him. The sunbeams filtering in through the windows cast shadows on half his face.

"Just so long as those damned Syptens don't spoil things. I imagine the rumors have made their way here, how they've been spotted just beyond the Whiterun. 'Tis why we took the long way around, coming down from the north."

"Syptens so close?" Gertrud realized she was gnawing her bottom lip and forced herself to stop. "Should you not send for your father? Our men remain with him, do they not?"

Ragnar leaned forward so swiftly mead sloshed out of his horn. "Do not presume to tell me how to rule!" he hissed. "I don't need Father's help in handling them. If I beg for him to save me from ghosts the moment I arrive, how shall he ever know he can trust me? No, Mother. I will deal with this on my own, in my own way."

Gertrud remained silent, but her doubts did not. The southern devils were very much real, not monsters from the stories she had told him as a child. Determined and regal as her son might be, she feared ignoring them would be a mistake. But she knew no way to say it that he would heed.

"They cannot cross the river." Ragnar leaned back, staring out the eastern windows, beyond which the river lay out of sight. "The Whiterun is too swollen this time of year and too wide, and we collapsed the bridge up by Graybank and cut the ferry lines. They'd have to build their own, and they are welcome to the attempt!"

He barked a laugh and took another long draw on his pipe before speaking again.

"I will handle this. I must. Alabastor wouldn't believe me capable of it. He thinks I'm good for nothing but drinking, smoking, and fucking. But what does he know? He's known far more for being a drunk than I am! The half-breed bastard."

Her son drained the horn and held it out again. Gertrud refilled it.

"Leave the cask," he ordered with a dismissive wave. "And send that pretty thrall to me. What was her name, something barbaric... Takit?"

Her throat tightened. Takhat was her name. Among both the thralls and servants, she was the most beautiful, even in a roughspun dress. Gertrud knew her son's appetites and weaknesses. Though she hated for him to indulge in them, she had never been able to refuse his requests.

"I will send her in, my prince."

Ragnar grinned. "It is good to be home, Mother."

Gertrud turned away to hide her expression. "I am glad to hear it, Prince Ragnar," she murmured. "Very glad."

18. IN THE DARK

I

His words grow more worrying with each day. Torvald says it feels like he is searching through the darkness, trying to grasp something that he cannot put words to. He says night is falling upon the kingdom, and he is not wrong — the jarls grow impatient with their ailing king as Coppereye's insurgency continues.

"The world writhes," he says.

I often have the urge to slap sense into him. Yet I do not touch him, but only listen. He scarcely notices the kindness, trapped by his black visions.

He is lost to me, I think, for good.

- The diary of Siva Of Torvald, Wife of King Torvald Geirson, Matron of the Harrowhall, the Last Queen of Baegard

Night had long since fallen when the last of the reveling warriors slumped into their corners. Only when their snoring filled the hall did Bjorn rise from his bedroll.

Moving as silently as he could, he dug into his pack. Even more than keeping watch for stirring Vurgs, he eyed Yonik, wondering if he detected the glow of the man's silvern eyes or only imagined it. But no; he was asleep, as were the others in the longhouse.

After days spent under constant watch, Bjorn finally had a moment to himself.

It did not take long to find what he sought. Withdrawing the carefully wrapped package, Bjorn pulled apart the cloth and lifted the stones free. In the darkness, it was difficult to differentiate the Four Shadows from one another, the task made trickier by the way they muddled his thoughts, pulling at his mind even without *khnuum's* influence. Tucking his waterskin under his arm, he took them in hand along with one other stone, then ventured near the dying embers of the least occupied fireplace. He winced with each creak of the boards beneath his feet, yet no one roused that he could tell.

Kneeling before the flames and trying not to knock the feet of the sleeping men stretched toward the heat, Bjorn placed a stone among the coals. The flecks of silver in the drascale ore soon glowed as it absorbed the heat. He tried not to fidget as he waited. The men and women around him made small noises as they slumbered on.

When he could endure it no longer, Bjorn unstoppered his waterskin and tilted a small stream onto the ore. Steam billowed up from it. He leaned in close to breathe it in, wincing only a little at the rotten stench, then relaxing as the heady rush of *khnuum* filtered through his body.

The time had come. He knew his task. He would not cower from it as he might have in the past. Fear no longer commanded him.

It was not prudent. It went against Yonik's counsel. But it was the right thing to do.

Yonik's not the Stoneseer. I must follow my own counsel.

A hand closed around his arm and tugged. Bjorn whipped around to see his captor was a Vurg with a tangled, black beard and squinting eyes.

"Whaddya up to?" the warrior rumbled. His eyes darted to the steaming stone. "Dousin' me fire, eh?"

"No, nothing like that. I'm just—"

"Maybe makin' it dark to take a stab at me, eh? Trynna flee, are you?" The Vurg's voice steadily grew louder with each word, and his scowl more pronounced.

"Please, this is a misunderstanding—"

Shouts from outside the longhouse doors made both of them stop and turn.

Thumps sounded against the outer walls. The Vurg warrior cursed under his breath. Bjorn noticed the man's other hand feeling around him; seeking a weapon, no doubt. Fear clenched tight around his heart, heightened by the influence of the *khnuum*-steam.

He didn't know what was happening outside: if it was a quarrel between warriors, or enemies come to kill them, or mere raucous roughhousing. But he could not stand idly by and find out.

Wrenching away from the man's grasp, Bjorn clutched Torvald Geirson's runestones to his chest and scrambled to his feet. The Vurg roared and lunged after him, and Bjorn went tumbling as the warrior caught his feet. Kicking and clinging to the bench before him, he won free and continued his dash across the longhouse.

"The damned heir!" the warrior roared, "he's up to somethin'!"

Bjorn didn't stop as the chamber came alive. Reaching his pack, he stashed away the Four Shadows, then grappled for his sword and shield. Only as he took them in hand did he hesitate. He could not fight all of Edda's huskarls; what was more, this was all rooted in a misunderstanding. Sucking in a breath, Bjorn freed his hands, then slowly stood with them upraised and empty.

Edda had emerged from the room beyond her throne. Her baleful gaze fell upon him, her black hair tangled into braids. In her hands she clutched a spear and a shield.

He did not need the Sight to know what her judgment would be.

Before either could speak, however, the doors to the longhouse burst open. Dark shapes flooded in.

"An attack!" Edda shouted. She spared Bjorn one last glance before rushing forward. "Get up, you lazy louts! Fight for your gods-damned lives!"

Bjorn stared at the invaders as they engaged the rising Vurg warriors. Even by the scant light of the banked fires, he could tell they were barbars, and many of them jotun-men, judging by their size and hairy appearance. In moments, the longhouse filled with the clashing of weapons and the screams of the injured and dying.

Yonik appeared next to him, eyes alive and long knives in hand. "We fight with them!" the gothi said before sprinting toward the melee.

It was enough to decide Bjorn's course. Kneeling, he picked up his weapons when a thought occurred to him. His head was still muddled by *khnuum*. Ordinarily, that would hamper him. But there was a way he could turn it to his advantage.

But can I master it? Or will it master me?

Repressing his doubts, Bjorn plunged a hand into his pack and rustled through it until he pulled out a bag of jangling stones. Ripping it open, he parsed through them until he found the one he sought. Bjorn let the others drop as he held it up. The lines of the rune burned into his eyes, then drove in deeper. The longhouse fell away around him, the shadowy Hall of Doors replacing it. Ignoring the endless portals down the misty corridor to either side, he stared at the door before him, into whose face the same rune was carved.

Gramur. Frenzy. Teeth bared in a snarl, Bjorn wrenched the door open.

Red painted his eyes. His senses sharpened. The thoughts that constantly plagued him melted away like mist before sunlight. Next that he knew, Bjorn was flying across the longhouse, grinning and screaming until his voice broke. Men and women thronged together, each struggling to gain the upper hand.

Bjorn threw himself into the thick of it.

The boss of his shield bashed into faces. The rim turned aside weapons. His sword wove in and out of their armor and flesh, the drascale edge deadly sharp. Blood sprayed across his face, yet Bjorn laughed. His hilarity only grew as an axe cut a shallow wound into his arm.

They couldn't put him down; they could barely touch him. In this moment, in this pitched battle, he was immortal, and all would soon know it.

A jotunman emerged from the fray and barreled toward him. Bjorn met his charge with his shield, but all his fury wasn't enough to stop the man. They both went down hard, tumbling over a bench. Bjorn whipped back up to his knees to smack the rim of his shield on the barbar's head. The beast-man was stunned, but only for a moment. Recovering, he roared and thrust his seax at Bjorn again.

Bjorn greeted him with the kiss of his sword. Stabbing through his throat, he felt the bones of the barbar's neck splinter, the impact jolting up his arm.

Withdrawing his blade and surging to his feet, Bjorn

saw three more enemies fighting a woman with a spear and shield. Bjorn charged, barking a laugh as he cut into the side of the first barbar. Only then did the other two take notice. As the first man fell back, clutching at his wound, the woman jabbed her spear at a second assailant, while the third turned to meet Bjorn's charge. Bjorn grinned at the jotunman's wide eyes. Even these beasts were beginning to fear him.

Bjorn feinted a strike so that the barbar flinched away. Leading with his shield, he turned aside his adversary's axe and worked his sword through his gut. He spared one moment to watch the terror turn to agony before kicking him away.

Spinning, Bjorn made to cut down the last enemy, but halted as he saw the woman with the spear knock him down and stab him through. She looked up, her dark eyes meeting his, and nodded.

Bjorn twitched, ready to strike. Vaguely, he recognized her, yet it hardly seemed an impediment. They had been allies of convenience. Now that their common enemy was gone, she would be the next to fall.

Some distant part of his mind screamed in protest. *Don't! That's Edda! Edda Skarldaughter, remember?*

His scowl deepened. Skarl the Savage had been his enemy; his daughter must be the same. He took a step forward. The woman's brow furrowed.

"Bjorn!"

The voice made him pause and turn. Yonik approached him, hands empty and raised. The priest looked pained, though Bjorn could not see any wounds beneath the blood splattered over his furs.

Perhaps I could help with that.

The thought startled Bjorn back to awareness. The Hall of Doors reemerged before his eyes. With invisible hands,

149

he shoved the Frenzy door closed. As *seidar* faded, exhaustion swept in.

His legs buckled. His head fell. His knees hit the floor.

Yonik was beside him the next moment, holding Bjorn up by his shoulders and murmuring in his ear. "Are you returned?"

Bjorn nodded. His head ached and felt as heavy as a sack of grain, but it was far better than the horror of contemplating violence against a friend.

"You should stand if you can," the priest continued. "I fear we must give some explanations."

Even in his wearied state, Bjorn could imagine what he meant. His memories were always hazy after the Frenzy rune consumed him, seen as if through a pink mist, but he could still recall that final look on their hostess's face.

She had seen his intentions in that moment. That he had nearly slain her.

Though the effort felt beyond him, Bjorn rose to his feet, only remaining upright by the gothi steadying him. Edda stood in the same spot staring at him. He raised his gaze to meet hers. The Vurg chief's eyes may as well have been pieces of coal for all he could read in them.

Yonik spoke first. "I must apologize for the Lord Heir. He—"

"—is a Djur-burned berserker."

Bjorn would have been startled had he had the energy for it. Instead, he only stared dully at Edda.

"I'd heard the tales," she continued. "Yet I never believed them. Even my father lost to his battle-rage was nothin' compared to you, Bjorn Borson."

Yonik squeezed his arm. Belatedly, Bjorn realized he must give some response.

"I suppose I am," he murmured.

"What else could it be called? Though you have the

height of a warrior, I thought you too skinny and mild-mannered." Edda cocked her head, a small smile softening her features. "But I've misjudged you. I doubt any of my champions, Bodil included, could have stood up to you."

Bjorn bowed his head. Even in his muddled state, he recognized the compliment. "You honor me, Edda Skarl-daughter."

"But for all your martial prowess," the Vurg leader continued, "you cannot stay. The Jotun knows you're here, or maybe he tires of me. Either way, you must find a different hole to hide in."

"We have another place," Yonik asserted. "We'll go there at once."

Bodil the Blaze stepped up next to her chief. She looked to have been in the thick of the fight from the amount of blood saturating her armor. "Are you certain, Lord Edda? Better he has warriors to fight by him than to fight alone."

"He'll not be alone. Our Thurdjur friends will look after him." Edda smiled. "Is that not where you mean to go?"

Yonik answered once more. "It is."

"But are we not fiercer fighters?" Bodil insisted.

"Of course! None would be so foolish as to suggest otherwise. But just now, stealth serves us better than strength."

Edda gave her champion a look that brooked no further argument. The big woman stepped back, disgruntled but obedient. Bjorn could scarcely summon the energy to be grateful.

We're free. We're going to Egil and the others. Edda seemed genuine in her desire to be their ally. Still, it would be a relief to be free of her watchful gaze.

"With your permission, Edda Skarldaughter, we will take our leave." Yonik betrayed not a hint of urgency in his voice, but Bjorn could feel it in his tight grip on his arm.

"Of course." Edda tossed her black braids over her shoulder. "And when the time comes, Lord Heir, I look forward to fightin' by your side again."

Bjorn could only nod as Yonik turned him toward their packs.

19. REACHING

Some men fear magic. Others crave it. The wise avoid even its mention. Seidar brings power, but every ritual requires sacrifice. The Inscribed Laws compel me to believe the spirit is too dear a price to pay.

- Counsel on the Inscribed Beliefs, by Mother Vigilance

Egil bolted upright, seax in hand, before he recognized what had awoken him.

Voices — familiar ones. He stared around the shrouded interior of the Tangled Temple until he spotted three cloaked figures by the barred double doors, their heads bent together. It was not a particularly alarming sight; a score of men occupied the temple and often engaged in missions after dark, and rare was the moment when the nave was completely quiet. Yet Egil suspected these were newcomers to their insurgency, ones he knew well.

Rising from his furs, Egil walked barefoot across the wood floor to the group. He confirmed his conjectures as he came close: Bjorn and Yonik had taken leave of Edda Skarldaughter's hospitality. The man keeping watch, a former guardian named Menith Karlson, spoke with them. By his deference, he also recognized the exiled Heir of Oakharrow.

He took in the pair's grisly appearance as he neared. Blood splattered their cloaks and faces, some of it their own, judging from their cuts and tears. Though they seemed exhausted, neither looked to have suffered serious harm.

"Egil," Bjorn greeted him, almost sounding relieved.

Egil stifled the startling swirl of emotions that rose at the greeting. "The Vurgs were attacked."

"Yes." Yonik crossed his arms. "Though we're still not sure why."

"Skarldaughter lose many warriors?"

"Fewer than the Jotun did."

The priest glanced at Bjorn, and Egil followed his gaze. The heir cast his eyes downward. Egil frowned while Menith chattered the explanation.

"The Lord Heir was like a berserker of old, he was! Least, from the way the gothi tells it. 'Tis why Feral Edda let them go free!"

Egil could only stare. He remembered how the heir had been toward the end of the fight down in Chasm Valley. Even then, he'd fought as if sprites of fire possessed him.

But a berserker?

"How?" The question came out as a demand.

Bjorn finally met his gaze, honey-hued eyes seeming to glimmer golden in the moonlight. "*Seidar.* Rune magic. There is a runestone that invokes Frenzy. It can turn even a coward into a warrior."

Egil kept his gaze hard on Bjorn. His magic had always made him uneasy, though not as much as it unsettled Vedgif. It seemed he had only waded further into its mires since the Hunters in the White had gone their separate ways.

A coward into a warrior.

Egil had little fear in battle; he did not need such a crutch. But if it could gift Bjorn with such prowess, what could a proper warrior do with it?

He turned to Yonik. "Can others do this? Look upon this runestone and become a berserker?"

The priest hesitated. "Those with the talent, yes. But few possess it."

The implications were clear: *You do not.* Egil scowled. He did not like being underestimated, even when he did not know if he desired such a thing. Magic was forbidden by the Inscribed Laws. There was no telling what horrors its influence might inflict upon his spirit.

"But this is a discussion for another time," Yonik continued. "Seeing takes its toll, and Bjorn has paid a heavy one. He needs food and rest. Where is Vedgif?"

"Of course! Thousand pardons, Brother Yonik, m'lord. Follow me; I'll show you where to wash up and get a bite to eat, though I suppose you know the ways better than I. As for the elder, he's out at the moment. I'll send him your way as soon as he's back in."

Egil let the trio go, watching as they processed down the center aisle to where a kitchen had been improvised next to a hearth. Thoughts swirled through his head, murky and undefined. With no other purpose, he returned to his bedroll, though he had a feeling he would claim little more sleep.

Egil awoke in the predawn dark, staring up at the gnarled ceiling of the Tangled Temple. One notion filled his head, one he could not dismiss.

I have to try.

Perhaps witchery was frowned upon by the Inscribed and Baegardians. Perhaps it would lead him to greater sins and tarnish his soul. But they were in the thick of a war; several, in fact, if all he had heard in the Jotun's court was true. Berserkers had long been renowned in the sagas and songs. Was not Djur himself claimed to be the foremost among their ranks when the battle-rage seized him?

It was not dishonorable to yearn for power. Even if that power was born of magic.

Unable to fall back asleep, he rose to tend to the fire, then scarfed down a bowl of soured milk soup. There was little else to do but pace until the heir and the priest stirred in the nave's corner.

Egil restrained himself until Bjorn sat up and rubbed at his eyes, then strode over to stand over the heir.

"Let me try it."

He tightened his jaw as both men looked at him with sleepy surprise. Egil refused to let his own doubts show.

"The Sight?" Bjorn guessed.

Egil nodded.

"That's not a good idea." Yonik stretched and yawned before rising to his feet. Though he was not a young man and had only just awoken, his movements were as smooth as if he had already warmed up his muscles in the yard. "Even if you possess the talent, it takes time and practice to be of any use."

He learned it, Egil wanted to say. *How could I not?* But he thought better of speaking the words aloud. As tolerant as Bjorn was, that slight might be a step too far.

"There are risks," Bjorn added, rising as well, though with a good deal more stiffness. "Many of them. Even if you don't succumb to the magic, you'll not be able to control yourself. I... I almost killed Edda before Yonik stopped me."

The gothi grimaced, by which Egil gathered it must be

true. But it mattered little in his case. Egil had always been his own master. Magic would not change that.

"This is war," he said flatly. "We have to take risks."

By the gothi's raised eyebrow, Egil had not fooled him with platitudes.

Bjorn sighed. "If you're open to it, I suppose we could try. Yonik?"

"Very well," the priest relented. "I cannot stop you. But this cannot be our first priority. We must speak with Vedgif and discuss what comes next."

Egil gave a grudging agreement. He could wait as long as needed; his resolve would not erode. Besides, he had questions of his own he needed the elder to answer.

Vedgif stood by the altar. His head was not so cleanly shaven as it once had been, and partially healed wounds marred his scalp, yet his eyes remained as hard as ever. He stood erect as he awaited their approach.

"Lord Heir," the elder said, pounding a fist to his chest in a warrior's salute.

"Elder Vedgif," Bjorn responded.

"I heard of the attack. Neither of you are harmed?"

"Nothing that won't heal."

The veteran nodded. Egil wondered if he would be so sanguine about it had he known Bjorn had used magic to stay alive.

"If you can forgive me cutting the pleasantries short," Yonik spoke up, "we should turn our attention to more immediate concerns. How safe are we here? Or rather, how long can we depend on being safe?"

Vedgif's brow creased as he thought. "Not long. We only moved here after a raid at our old hideout, an Oakheart mead hall, a week past. This was why I did not wish you two to come here; there is much to be done still to secure it.

Even with our precautions, it won't be long before they find this place; days, a week at most."

"Then we'll make the most of it." The gothi turned to Bjorn. "What do you need?"

"Time." The heir cast a wary glance at Vedgif. "And a secluded space."

Egil could guess what that meant. *More witchery.* For the elder's sake, he let it remain unspoken. Yet another question had to be asked.

"Why did you come here?" Egil demanded. "Why risk everything to enter Oakharrow? We don't have the forces to retake it, not yet. We have no way to drive out the Jotun himself."

Once, Bjorn would have flinched at the inquiry. Now, he met Egil's eyes with a steady gaze.

"To make an ally. Not for this war, but for the war to come. The one... foreseen."

As Bjorn paused, Egil sensed hidden depths in those words. Had the heir glimpsed more with his magic, this *seidar*? Did he know which battles would be fought and the players on each side? Once more, the power of the rune magic showed its face and roused Egil's envy.

Yonik broke the silence. "We can use my old hut for a Seeing. Set it up while I speak with Vedgif a moment longer."

Bjorn nodded, bowing to the priest's orders as if he were his acolyte. As he turned to leave, Egil spoke up.

"Let me go with you."

The heir and the gothi exchanged a look. Vedgif stared off to one side, not bothering to hide his scowl.

"Very well," Yonik relented. "But teaching you cannot be our focus, Egil."

"I know."

Perhaps this thirst for magic was only a distraction. Perhaps he only sought to learn it for his vanity. Whatever its source, Egil felt compelled to know as much of it as he could.

He waited for Bjorn to grab his pack, then they set out together from the temple's back door. Egil followed the heir across the muddy courtyard to one of the round hovels set along the back of the compound. Bjorn had to put his shoulder to the door to shove it open, the hinges having grown stiff with disuse. As the door swung in, a cloud of dust puffed up. The heir coughed, then grinned back at Egil as if in a shared joke. Egil looked aside. Once more, he felt oddly warm under Bjorn's gaze.

"Can you believe Yonik lived in this for years?" the heir commented as he stepped inside, then bent before the hut's cold hearth.

Egil helped gather and stack wood, some still stashed away from before the priest left. He tried not to feel awkward as he bent around Bjorn to place it.

"They're not supposed to care about worldly things," Egil replied after a long pause.

"But they're still men and women. Comfort must count for something." Bjorn shook his head. "He's an odd man. The gods built him differently, I think."

There was nothing to say to that. On that point, he and the heir entirely agreed.

Soon, a fire burned in the hearth. It did not take long for the hut to grow uncomfortably hot. With the heat of the day oncoming, it would become unbearable soon. Egil voiced no complaint. A warrior did not show weakness if he could help it. Besides, the discomfort would be well worth the price of what he learned here.

When the initial flames settled down, Bjorn placed a stone among the coals. Egil wondered if this was a runestone, then saw by its rough-hewn edges it appeared to be little more than a common rock.

"What is it?"

Bjorn glanced up. "Drascale ore. It contains *khnuum*."

"'Nume'?"

Bjorn smiled. "An Old Djurian word, I think. The steam from *khnuum* is necessary for the Sight. Think of it like the spark that allows the magic to catch flame."

Egil said nothing, letting his silence draw out an explanation.

"Once the ore is hot, we'll remove it from the fire and pour water over it." Bjorn indicated an iron pot he had filled from his waterskin. "Breathe in the steam, then we can look upon a rune to open a door."

"A door?"

Bjorn was patient as he continued to explain. Egil tried to follow, but the ritual bewildered him. Somehow, he was supposed to see a "Hall of Doors," where he would open a door — not with his hands, but with his mind. But he was only supposed to crack it open instead of open it fully, lest he invite some kind of danger.

Egil caught himself rubbing his temples. Bjorn smiled.

"It will make more sense once we go through it. If you are capable of *seidar*, that is."

Capable. That and more was what Egil had always striven to be. He refused to be found wanting.

Soon, Bjorn removed the ore from the flames, then poured the boiled water over it. The rock hissed, and steam flooded the hut. For a moment, Egil held his breath, apprehensive of this steam that could cause magic, but his eagerness soon overcame it. He sucked in the heavy air and felt it settle in his lungs.

"Be wary." Bjorn's voice had fallen low. "*Khnuum* can warp your thoughts, make you believe things are there that are not. Make you do things you never would otherwise."

An inkling tickled the back of Egil's mind, but once more, he held his tongue.

"You may remember the incident with the keepers. When I... hurt one."

How could he forget it? Egil had often heard the other Hunters in the White discuss it. Though Bjorn had never admitted as much, they had guessed it was one reason the heir had departed Oakharrow so swiftly. It was yet one more thing about their strange heir that had kept Egil at a distance. Now, he wondered if the same madness would claim him.

But he knew himself. Rare was the moment Egil lost control. He would not do so now.

Though his head grew light, Egil clenched his fists to keep himself grounded in his body. "What now?" he asked through gritted teeth.

Unlike himself, Bjorn appeared relaxed, far more than he usually was. He had a confidence here that Egil lacked.

"Now we test if you're a *Volur*, a seer. Look upon the rune etched into this stone."

Bjorn held out his hand, and Egil looked down at the smooth rock nestled in his palm. Lines were carved into it, jagged and harsh, yet done with what seemed exquisite intentionality.

"What now?"

"Observe each part of the rune as well as the whole. Form it in your mind's eye and focus on it."

Egil did as instructed. He traced the rune with his gaze, then closed his eyes and imagined it in burning lines. When he was sure he had the complete picture, he held the rune in mind for several long moments.

Nothing more happened.

161

"Aren't I supposed to see a door?" Egil demanded.

"Perhaps not. I didn't see the Hall of Doors my first several times. Though I saw visions..."

Egil cracked open an eye. Bjorn was withdrawing something from his pack, a bundle of what appeared to be more runestones. The heir winced as he looked upon them, then selected one and tucked the rest away.

"What are you doing?"

Bjorn glanced up, a nervous flicker to his eyes. "I must See for myself. To know the path forward."

A feeling stirred in Egil's gut that had nothing to do with his own ritual. "We should wait for the gothi."

"That's not necessary." A smile flashed on Bjorn's lips, as if to reassure. "As you seem resistant to *khnuum*, you'll be enough. If I struggle to wake up, cut my arm deep enough to startle me."

Egil could only stare. Bjorn had never seemed sly before, but the situation had the stink of a setup. Still, Bjorn belonged to the ruling family of their clan. Egil was nothing if not a loyal Thurdjur.

"Fine."

"Thank you, Egil. Believe me when I say this is for the best."

Before Egil could respond, the heir bent his head to the runestone cupped in his hands. Then he began to shake.

Egil leaped around the fire and caught Bjorn as he tumbled sideways. His eyes rolled up inside his head so only the whites showed. His mouth hung open, and a bit of froth appeared at the edges.

"Bjorn!" Egil roared. *"Bjorn!"*

The door to the hut burst open to reveal Yonik. "What is he—? The damned fool!"

The gothi shoved Egil aside to cradle Bjorn's head. Egil

stood, hand on his knife. For once, he was uncertain what to do.

"What's happening?" he demanded, voice cracking.

Yonik answered without looking up. "He's trying to see the path forward. Even if it means his death."

20. THE SECOND SHADOW

Once, the fault is mine.
Twice, the fault is thine.

- A Baegardian children's rhyme

He was tossed from dream to dream.

Bjorn tried to swim against the current, to stay above it, but all his efforts came to naught. For all his *seidar*, he had no power here. He was a sapling in a flood, bent back so far as to snap in two.

For the moment, at least, he remained whole.

This was nothing like the First Shadow. Then, Torvald Geirson had guided his Seeing, the visions flowing from one another like the changing light of dawn and dusk. Now, it was like when he had been twelve winters old and caught in the swell of the Whiterun's rapids.

Annar had saved him then. No one would stop him from drowning now.

But he could not succumb. His kin, his friends, his people — they needed the knowledge of this rune. The King of Ice had dedicated his centuries-long existence to attaining these glimpses of the future. Would Bjorn let them all down now?

The challenge was too great for him to match, yet he tried all the same. Striving with every fraction of will, Bjorn surged toward the far end of the tempest. Wind lashed him. Rain pounded like nails into his eyes and face. He could no longer see, but only reached, reached—

Abruptly, the storm ceased. He had crested the surface. Bjorn opened his eyes.

He stood on empty ground, the waters drained away. Before him, a stone slab stabbed into the ground, dirt spilled around it, as if a massive hand had placed it there. A crack ran down its middle. Upon its face were carved thousands of runes.

Trapped in a ghostly body, Bjorn drifted closer, pulled toward it like it possessed a current of its own. As he approached, the runes glowed red, brighter with each inch neared. Soon, the light grew blinding, and he cringed away.

Then a figure took shape above the cracked slab, its body formed of a radiant mist. The phantom grew until it towered over Bjorn. He trembled, knowing he could no more fight it than these visions.

Without warning, the red specter dove toward him. Its misty body obscured the stormy sky. Bjorn threw up his arms and closed his eyes, but the vision was unavoidable.

Cutting through the rushing wind, he heard words spoken by a familiar voice.

Reach. Reach for the runes. The Beast slumbers in buried minds.

Torvald Geirson. Though the King of Ice had perished atop Yewung, some part of him apparently lingered in these stones.

Bjorn had no time to think on it, for the red mist

collapsed about him. He felt it like moisture on skin, tasted its coppery tang as if it filmed his tongue.

Blood, blood falling everywhere—

The mist blew away, unveiling a new scene. An individual sat crumpled in a chair, head bent to their cupped hands. At first, Bjorn thought them to be a man; then the surrounding details added context. The rug at their feet was barely large enough to accommodate them. The braziers to either side were more like candles.

This was no man, but a giant.

Its features came into starker detail, and Bjorn realized this was not the kind of giant he expected. It did not match the jotunar he had seen in the First Shadow, but had leathery skin, large, flapping ears, and a trunk falling from its face. A surtun, then: a fire giant from the sun-stricken lands far to the south.

The giant paid Bjorn no mind, even as he was pulled toward it, entirely preoccupied by whatever it so greedily consumed. The substance shimmered in the firelight, and some trickled through the giant's large fingers. Bjorn stared, seeing something about it as familiar, though he couldn't remember what.

Silver, the King of Ice once more whispered. *From silver blooms gold. Their light and life, their strength and flaw.*

The giant jerked its head up and stared directly at Bjorn. It should have filled him with fear, but Bjorn found himself standing upright. Once more, he possessed a body, but it was unlike any he'd known before. He was growing taller and broader, swelling in muscle and bone. Soon, he rose higher than the surtun, though it now stood and faced him with a huge, curved sword in hand. He found a weapon in his own, a sword so long it would have spanned the whole of the Baegardian Valley.

Bjorn looked up and beyond the giant's chair. It was not

alone; a dozen more surtunar and half a dozen jotunar stood behind it. All rushed toward Bjorn, weapons raised, voices trumpeting, footsteps merging into a rumbling thunder that grew louder with every moment.

But he had no fear. He had become a match for them all.

Bjorn bellowed as he swung his mountainous sword. As he did, Torvald's whisper rose once more in his mind, still audible despite the din.

Men. All begin mortal. This weapon is sheathed within you.

Bjorn's sword carved through the giants, splintering tusk and bone, iron and hide. As it cut down the last of them, Bjorn found his grip on the sword slipping. It spun away from him, dissolving into red mist that multiplied and formed into a tall wall.

Bjorn looked up at it. As details emerged, it appeared as a vast, immeasurable cliff of scales.

I have seen this before.

A brisk breeze puffed against his right side. Bjorn turned to see blue mist had appeared in a similar towering bulwark. This texture was more like the hairy hide of the jotunar.

I have seen all of this.

Bjorn craned back his head. Though there was no end to the walls enclosing him, he had a feeling that far above, two faces as large as the moons looked down on him.

This did not feel like the rest of the vision. This was not a dream or memory. The beings that beheld him felt as if they saw him *now*, in this moment. And they felt very much real.

All the fear lacking when he faced the giants returned a hundredfold. Bjorn collapsed to his knees as the King of Ice murmured once more.

Gods. Inscribed and Divine, beyond our reach. Yet they watch; they listen; they touch upon this world.

The walls began to tilt, great slabs of them crumbling away. Bjorn could only stare up as they fell toward him. If he was to be buried beneath their consideration, he knew it to be his fate. It was inescapable, inevitable.

A boulder bludgeoned him, knocking him on his back. A second crushed his chest, a third his legs. Bjorn tried to scream, but he lacked the breath.

The boulder that caved in his head came as a mercy.

———

His arm burned. His head ached. A buzzing, like that of a hornet nest, filled his ears.

"Bjorn... Bjorn..."

He wanted to slink away: away from the pain, away from those wasps of memory. But they kept stinging, always stinging. He could not forget.

"He's awake... Come, Bjorn... Come back..."

Bjorn peeled open his gummy eyes.

The world was dark, yet by the fresh air against his skin, he guessed he was no longer in the hut. The tall rafters slowly came into view, signaling someone had moved him into the nave of the Tangled Temple. Judging by the shrouded atmosphere, night had fallen; he had been unconscious for at least half a day.

Two figures leaned over him, illuminated by firelight. He recognized Yonik first, the shaggy-haired priest too distinctive to forget. More surprising was that Egil kneeled next to him, face creased in what could only be concern.

Working the little moisture left to him around his mouth, Bjorn tried to speak. "What happened?"

Yonik exchanged a glance with Egil. Beyond the pair,

Bjorn glimpsed others standing in vigil. Vedgif was at the front of them, wearing a more pronounced scowl even than usual.

"What do you remember?" the gothi asked, each word hesitant.

Bjorn stared at the temple ceiling as he sorted through his memories. The visions had been clear when caught in the throes of them, but already, they faded. Panic pressed sharp claws into his chest. Desperately, he tried to recapture them as they fled.

"There was a stone slab, etched with runes... the Witterland Runestone, I think. The runes glowed red, then something rose from it: a sprite, or maybe a demon... It rushed at me, then the scene changed."

Bjorn paused, realizing how mad he must sound. But the remembered visions were asserting themselves stronger now.

"Then there was a giant in a chair, a fire giant, who was eating... *khnuum*."

The epiphany poured through him, cold and shocking as the waters of the Honeybrook in winter. Somehow, he weathered it and pressed on.

"It was eating, then it looked at me, and I... grew. I became like a giant myself with a sword to match. When I saw beyond the seated surtun, there were more of them, surtunar and jotunar both. But I wasn't afraid; I was greater than any of them. I swung my sword, and I cut them down — but something even greater rose."

Bjorn stuttered to a halt. He could see them again: the strange cliffs towering over him, the murky moon-faces far above, the colossal consideration. Even their memory flooded him with fear. Had they been gods? He could imagine their names: the wall of scales could have been Nuvvog, and the other of fur, Djur. They had seemed so present, so real, yet wrapped up in the rest of the visions, how could he truly know?

Bjorn pressed the heels of his hands into his throbbing eyes. Though he had lain unconscious for a long while, already, he tired again. Hunger and thirst assaulted him as well. He could not make sense of all he had seen, even when everything depended upon it.

Hands touched his shoulders. Gently but firmly, they pressed him down.

"Rest, Bjorn," Yonik's voice said from far away. "We'll talk more later."

If the priest said more, Bjorn heard nothing of it; sleep already trundled him in its folds.

21. UNSPOKEN

ᚺ

In my experience, in both life and scholarship, that which remains unspoken is more poignant than speech.

- *Confessions,* by Alfjin the Scribe

The sun was setting when Frey and his company prepared to leave. Aelthena kept her arms at her side as she walked toward the two dozen men through the war camp. The urge to cross her arms was strong, as if she could hold herself together. It was all she could do to resist.

She was used to Frey being her second shadow wherever she went, used to him watching out for her well-being, and not only as a guardian would a highborn. His presence was a comfort; his absence, an ache. Now, he threw himself into the heart of danger.

The damned noble fool.

Aelthena couldn't help a little smile. No matter how she resented his reckless courage, she also had to admire it.

Frey noticed her approach and turned with a rueful

grin. The other men glanced at them, but most returned to donning their armor, securing their weapons, and readying for the coming infiltration. Only two remained staring: Sven Arvidson, a keeper accompanying the mission, and Asborn. As the proclaimed Jarl of Oakharrow, her former betrothed considered it his duty to oversee the operation, though he was not so deluded as to go with.

Aelthena ignored the men and focused on Frey. Bastor had placed him in charge of the mission as the company's drang, yet the duty seemed to weigh lightly on the guardian. Even now, he sauntered as if he had not a care in the world. Standing before him, she longed to hold his hands and press her lips to his, ached for him to hold her as he had the night before. But even if Asborn had not yet been present, it would have been too great a risk. They could not be openly affectionate lest her former betrothed retaliate in a more vengeful way. Already, they took too many risks.

So she stood there, tongue-tied, wishing she could voice the thought filling her head.

I love you.

Only words, as simple as any other, yet somehow impossible to speak. She had thought them all the night before as they lay together in the dark, skin still sticky where they touched one another, his arms pressed under her breasts. But instead of speaking, they had lain in silence. A gulf yawned between them, filled with all the morrow held.

Aelthena met Frey's bright eyes and startled. As well as she knew those eyes, they held something new in them now, a mirror to her own mind. She looked aside. She wanted to make him say that which she could not, but she would not force it lest he fail to return.

No — he will return. He must.

Firming her jaw, Aelthena raised her gaze again, determined to say something. But with the challenge before him, what words could she say that would not fall flat?

Frey opened his mouth as if to speak, but he, too, was mute. It made her smile and told her all she needed to know.

"Don't mind me," a third voice broke in. "You need not interrupt your gawking for your prince."

Aelthena whirled to see Bastor standing next to them, an amused squint to his eyes. Though he loved teasing them, he fell short of jovial now. Little wonder why; with how avidly he had wished to go on this desperate expedition, she suspected the source of his melancholy. Still, she could dredge up scant sympathy. He was far too cavalier about speaking of her and Frey's relationship, even when he knew the consequences.

"What do you want, Highness?" she asked, giving the title a sardonic twist.

Bastor grinned. "Only to ensure the leader of our mission understands what he must do and when."

"I understand, Prince," Frey spoke before Aelthena could snap back a reply. "Trust me: with my life depending on it, I'm not liable to forget the details."

"I suppose. But try to enter before the signal, and you're liable to end up as feathered as a sparrow."

"All the more reason to stick to the plan."

"He knows," Aelthena intervened. "Wait for the diversion to make for the river. Then, in two days' time, he'll take the North Gate, and we'll take back my city."

Her fists clenched at her sides. The thought of recovering Oakharrow from the Jotun was the only thought that kept her from begging Frey not to go. Not that he would listen. He was just as eager to liberate the jarlheim with his family still trapped inside.

Bastor barked a laugh. "Look at me, fretting like a cook

over his kitchen! Fine, Frey Igorson, fine; I'll leave you to do your job, and I'll do mine."

"As it should be, Highness." A corner of Frey's lips tweaked. "Staying at the back of our forces, you mean?"

The prince winced, but his smile endured. "Best return, guardian, else I'll miss your needling. May Djur shelter you, and Volkur guide your blade."

Frey put a fist to his heart and bowed as the prince meandered off. It left the two of them alone once more. The sounds of the other preparations at the far end of the camp echoed across the meadow. Aelthena looked at the darkening walls of her home and wondered what Frey would find within.

"Aelthena."

Her name drew her gaze back to him. Again, unspoken words sat heavy on her tongue, but she chose lighter ones.

"Don't die, alright?"

Frey grinned. By the twinkle in his eyes, he knew what she meant.

"I've survived this long," he replied. "What's a couple days more?"

Aelthena forced a smile. Two days; that was all she had to wait. Then she could say all she should have before.

22. UNDER FIRE & STONE

Nothing fires a man like a woman's love.

- Common Baegardian saying

Don't die.

Frey shook his head as he led his party through the gloomy forest. Aelthena's parting words were simple on the face of it, but they echoed with hidden depths, feelings he had not dared to voice. He did not fear the love itself, nor a life spent with Aelthena; those were blisses he only yearned for. It was that death loomed over their days, waiting to rip the dreams from his chest and make mockery of the happiness to which he drew so near.

A low-hanging branch nearly clobbered him, bringing Frey back to the moment. *Plenty to fear now, Frey Igorson, without inventing your own.*

Straightening, he glanced at the sky above the city to his left. Night had long ago fallen, and only the faint prickle of stars and the city's faint glow lifted the darkness. Even the moons hid, having risen and set earlier in the evening. It was as good a chance as they would get, though they would still need the Spinners' fortune to succeed.

Next to Frey walked another complication to the mission. Sven Arvidson strode rather than slunk, reeking with his desire to command. A wiry man with a wispy black beard and a balding pate, he seemed a competent enough warrior, showing little in the way of nerves and speaking sense more often than not. But he was a keeper and Asborn's man. Worse still, he sought to undermine Frey's leadership at every turn. One ill-timed order might send the company into disarray and doom them all.

Frey knew he ought to nip it in the bud, just as his mother had always instructed when he helped in the garden. *Let something grow,* she'd scolded whenever Frey grew lax, *and it'll be harder get rid of it later.*

He had never learned the lesson for gardening. Failing to apply it now might have far worse consequences.

Ahead, Frey heard a new sound arise: the rushing of a river. As if on cue, Sven spoke up.

"Eyes up, men. Once we reach the river, we'll follow it to the end of the forest, then wait for the prince."

The other warriors in the company glanced at Frey, but Frey only smiled. The keeper was determined to prove he was in charge, that much was clear. Another man might have challenged him for the dubious honor, but there was no time for it. Besides, Frey had seen fractured leadership kill as often as poor counsel. Until the man made a call that would get them killed, Frey had no intentions of counter-manding him.

That did not ward against nasty thoughts as he watched the man take the lead. *Self-important bastard.*

They reached the river, then walked beside it, following it upstream to the city waiting above. At the edge of the tree line, Sven called for a halt. Frey stopped with the rest and waited.

A man sidled up next to Frey. "You the drang, or is the keeper?"

In the darkness, Frey could not identify him, nor did he recognize his voice. Many in their company had been unfamiliar to him, hailing from the other jarlheims. This man had wild, dark hair and a lisp to his speech. Judging by his accent, he likely originated from one of the Aelford clans.

Frey clapped the man on the shoulder. "We both are, according to him."

"Sounds a good way to get us killed."

"I won't let it go that far."

The warrior only grunted and ambled away.

Frey hunched against the tree, his shield resting next to him, and stared at the sky above the city. Time stretched on, taut as drying hides, until it seemed the moment must snap.

But if there was one thing Frey had developed a talent for as a guardian, it was patience. Before Nuvvog's Rage had descended upon the Harrowhall, he had filled his time with little more than standing around or monitoring the corridors. He only rued that he could not crack jokes now and make the others laugh, silence being the more prudent course.

Besides, I doubt anyone is in a jesting mood.

A hiss sounded off to their left. Frey snapped his gaze up in time to see the darkness blossom into flame.

Wincing, he squinted at the blaze that defied the night. A roar accompanied it, booming in a clap that rustled the surrounding leaves. A hot wind blew on Frey's face, leaving a bitter taste on his tongue. As soon as the eruption came, it fell apart. Streaks of embers and sparks fell toward the city below.

Given another moment, the sight might have been

exhilarating. As it was, it only meant the time for action had arrived.

"Come on, men!" Frey beckoned into the deafening silence, speaking before Sven had a chance to. "Up the Honeybrook!"

Their company charged up the hillside, even the keeper obeying. Keeping close together, they burst from the trees and out into the open. Frey gripped his shield tightly and kept his hand on his seax's hilt as he ran, holding his weapons belt in place. They seemed a rattling herd to his ears, their gear impossible to keep silent.

The sky split open again, and fire rained down from the heavens. Frey grinned as he sucked down air. Surely, no one would look their way, not with this show worthy of the gods.

The gray walls towered overhead as they drew closer. Frey could see the opening under the wall where he, Aelthena, and the others had snuck out of the city long months before. Hoping Bastor's supposition would not be wrong, he made for the gap.

A shout from above nearly sent him sprawling to the ground.

"Press on!" Frey shouted. A sentry had spotted them, his head poking through a crenel, and there was little point in keeping quiet now. He pushed his burning legs on, heaving in air as the gap grew ever closer.

Movement atop the wall warned him a moment before the arrows fell.

Frey threw up his shield. At once, arrows thudded into and through it. Splinters of wood shot into his face, and three arrowheads glinted menacingly as another eruption came from above. Those three sharp points could have taken his life had he reacted a moment later.

He only ran faster. Around and behind, men shouted and shrieked as arrows missed or found their targets. A part of him yearned to turn back and help the fallen, but they all knew what they had volunteered for. This was the mission. They had to succeed, no matter how many lives were lost.

Frey ran on.

A fourth arrow fell upon his shield, then a fifth, but none tasted his flesh. At last, Frey reached the opening under the wall. Letting his shield fall, he looked up, only for his stomach to plummet.

The portcullis was lowered.

Frey stared at it for several long moments, despair freezing his mind. As others ran up behind him to hunch under cover of the wall, it thawed again.

I'm the drang. Past time I acted like it.

"Sven," he snapped as the keeper, who had survived the arrow storm, came panting up next to him, "check the portcullis."

The man eyed him, but surprised him by failing to utter a protest. As Sven waded in, the last of the survivors arrived and began muttering among themselves. Frey did not meet their eyes, watching Sven's progress instead. From the corner of his eye, he noted about half of the company had been lost. A smile tugged at his lips, but he forced it back down.

Already, you're failing them.

The keeper had to swim the last stretch to reach the portcullis, a nigh impossible task as the bank slipped away to the full current. Frey watched his bald pate bob up and down as he listened to the warriors' disquiet and the shouts from the defenders above.

At last, Sven swam back. Before he had even surfaced, he spoke hoarsely, "Open! Looks closed, but it's only halfway down. If we can pull ourselves beyond it..."

As swiftly as it had died, hope surged in his chest again.

"Search for the rope," Frey barked at the company. "Should be somewhere here along the bank."

The men reacted at once, doubts dissipating. Frey slipped into the shallows to follow his own command, barely catching his balance as mud sucked at his boots. The river was icy cold, and as he plunged a hand in, his fingers quickly grew numb. Still, he searched under the murky surface. All seemed mud and pebble. Doubts rose again. What if the rope had frayed? What if the barbars had cut it away?

Then something corded resisted his pull.

Frey grinned as he yanked the rope above the surface of the water. Seeing the discovery, his company crowded behind him. Frey gave them a proper look now. Arrows bristled from every shield. At least one man had a snapped shaft sticking from his flesh. That any remained under that killing rain was a gods-given miracle.

"I'll go first," Frey called back. "Use the rope to pull yourself up against the current. When you reach the other side, be ready to fight."

The men nodded, while Sven added, "Quick, now!"

Unsure now if he was glad that the keeper had survived, Frey broke off the arrows from his shield, then slung it across his back to set both hands to the rope. It was slick with algae and mud. He hoped the past year had not moldered it enough to snap.

Too late to second-guess now.

Sucking in a breath, he threw himself into the river. The current swept his legs out behind him, leaving Frey to pull himself forward by his arms. It was as good a time as any to swim up current; the Honeybrook was at its lowest, and winter had not yet made its waters deathly cold. Yet it was still chill enough to tighten his chest and compress the little air in his lungs.

He hauled himself forward, hand over hand, fighting for every pace gained. Reach, heave; reach, heave. Water beat and clawed and bit at him. His lungs burned. He visualized what awaited him and wondered how his wearied muscles could be up to the task.

Breathe. Have to breathe!

But the surface was too far above. If he tried to rise to it, he would have to release the rope and be swept back under. Panic setting in, Frey scrabbled at the rope, hauling himself faster, fearing it wouldn't be fast enough.

His hand knocked against a peg, rough and hard.

Guess I've reached the end of my rope.

Frey pulled his legs forward to bunch them under him, then sunk his boots into the marshy riverbed and heaved himself up. Blessed air rushed down his throat, but he had no time to enjoy it.

The sound of men shouting filled his ears. The darkness ahead of him heaved with bodies. Steel and iron clashed against shields.

Frey ripped his shield off his back and held it ahead as he stumbled from the river. Blinking his vision clear of droplets, he unsheathed his sword with a muddy glove, then surged up the bank.

The impact of the arrows rocked him back. His arm burned; one had penetrated the wood and nicked him. Around the shield's rim, Frey glimpsed at least three warriors standing on the ridge above, waiting for Frey to come closer.

Wouldn't want to disappoint.

He charged up the slope, slipping but keeping upright. Two men attacked as one. Settling his feet, Frey caught the axe of the leftmost man on his shield and kept the one to the right away with a swing of his sword. The axeman yanked back, tilting Frey's shield down and exposing his body. Snarling, Frey kicked from under the shield, catching the barbar in the knee and sending him stumbling away.

The third man hefted a hammer and closed in from the front, while the rightmost barbar howled and attacked his flank. Sword blurring, shield lashing, Frey met their strikes and turned them aside. His shield splintered under blows from the hammer, his arm aching down to the bone. Slashing once, then twice, the man to his right went down, hands flapping over his split belly.

Then Frey saw the archers.

He looked up as all four drew and took aim at him. Cursing, he whirled to put the rising axeman and hammer wielder between them. The barbars had their backs to their allies and could not see the danger. Grinning at Frey's retreat, they hefted their weapons and sprang forward.

A thrumming filled the air. The barbars both halted mid-step, eyes wide and mouths ajar. As Frey watched, the warriors slumped to their knees, revealing the arrows sprouting from their backs.

He did not waste the moment, for already, the archers nocked another round. Battered shield raised, Frey charged at them. At any moment, he expected an arrow to split through and end his foolhardy mission.

The round loosed; arrows thudded into the wood or shot past him. None even slowed him.

Panicked yells rose as he barreled into the leftmost archer.

The man collapsed under the blow with a wheezing protest, the iron boss gouging into him. Hoping it was enough to incapacitate, Frey turned from him to face the other three men. The archers had drawn seaxes and fanned out around him. His determined resistance had made them cautious; a good thing, for his breathing had grown ragged, and his muscles were heavy, as if filled with iron. Frey wasn't sure how many more he could kill.

Four, with any luck.

The man he'd knocked over proved resilient, rising and drawing his own seax. Blood leaked from the barbar's nose, and he moved as if sporting a broken rib, but it only seemed to fan his fury. Frey feinted an attack to make the man flinch back, then postured toward the rightmost enemy. None over-committed, seeming content to delay. Likely, they awaited the arrival of reinforcements.

Frey smiled. A coppery taste filtered between his teeth. Evidently, he had bitten his tongue, for it swelled in his mouth. Fear rose and choked him. His breathing came quick. One blow, one misstep, one hesitation, and his life would come to a swift, unremarkable end.

"For Lord Asborn!"

The yell was almost as surprising as seeing who sprinted past to charge at the barbars. Sven Arvidson engaged the two men at the right end, spraying river water with every movement.

Perhaps he's not so bad, after all.

With a fresh grin, Frey struck at the injured archer. The shield boss met the man's seax, then overcame his resistance and barreled into his arm. The man howled and stumbled back, arm cradled to his chest.

The next adversary was not so easily deterred, coming at him with a barrage of blows. It was all Frey could do to keep up his defense. His sword chipped and slipped in his slick glove. His shield grew ragged, a quarter of it soon shaved off with no prospect of salvation.

From the corner of his eye, Frey saw the wounded man rise yet again, seax in his good hand. With an agonized cry, he charged.

Frey swung his sword in an arc before him, trying to

gain space to breathe. His legs threatened to give way. He had scarcely stopped moving since pulling free of the icy river, and he'd been stiff and half-drowned to start. Enemies closed in on either side. Frey looked for aid, but none seemed forthcoming. Sven had his own pair of barbars to deal with.

Another yell came from the river.

As the barbars startled and looked toward the newly emerging man, Frey took his chance. Stabbing forward, he caught the uninjured barbar with a cut to his sword-arm. Roaring, the man stumbled back and fumbled for his weapon with his other hand.

Frey turned on the remaining man, relying on sheer brutality as skill eroded with his strength. Putting his shoulder into it, he barreled into the barbar for a third time. The man tried striking around the shield, but the flat of the blade merely bounced off Frey's shoulder.

Bearing them both to the ground, Frey jabbed his blade into the man's side. The steel slid in until the barbar stiffened, then went limp beneath him.

Lurching to his feet, Frey raised his shield, ready to meet a charge. As he took in the scene, he let it fall with a sigh. Another of his men had emerged from the river. Together with the other, they made quick work of those remaining. Sven had held his own and seemed in fine form as he dealt the final blow to his opponents.

Frey fell to one knee and gulped down air. He wiped at his face with a sleeve, to little avail. Blood, mud, and sweat were smeared across him from his hair to his feet. He had to blink rapidly just to see.

What Aelthena would say if she saw me now.

Soon, the enemy was dealt with, and Frey's reduced company gathered around as the stragglers rose from the river. When the eleventh man confirmed he was the last,

Frey repressed a grimace, rose to his feet, and looked toward the inner city.

"Best leave now — the fighting will have drawn others. Come!"

The men obeyed. Even Keeper Sven fell in line as they hustled toward the dark streets among the shanty buildings. It was the beginning of a long night, a hunt for whoever remained of their allies. Rest still lay hours away, if they found shelter at all. Frey only kept moving by holding tight to his reasons for coming.

This was his home, and his kin were in danger. He had left them unprotected for far too long. And Aelthena was counting on him. He would hate to disappoint her most of all.

Love-sodden fool.

Sighing, Frey continued forward, always keeping his eyes to the shadows.

23. PRAY

In times of hardship, I commend this prayer:

> *Lerye, Sister of Life, hear my plea*
> *Hear me in my time of need*
> *Preserve my daughters close to me*
> *Keep them hale and full of glee*
>
> *Yusala, Sister of Love, hear my cry*
> *Hear me as the world spins by*
> *Protect my kin both far and nigh*
> *Keep them warm, jocund, and spry*
>
> *Skirsala, Sister of the Hearth, hear my moan*
> *Hear me in the dark of gloam*
> *Shelter my sons as they roam*
> *Keep them 'til they return home*

- Counsel on the Inscribed Beliefs, by Mother Vigilance

L erye, Sister of Life, hear my plea..."

Gertrud bowed forward until her forehead rested on the hard stone. Smoke from the dandelions and mint burning upon the altar hit the back of her throat. She swallowed, not wishing to cough and dishonor the Inscribed during her prayers.

"Shelter my son... keep him home. He knows not your will. Guide him to your path..."

They were faithless words, unworthy of a devoted mother. Ragnar Ragnarson had shown himself to be every bit as ruthless as his father in the week since his return. Dissenters complaining of the unharvested crops burning in fields and the reports of Syptens on the march were met with sentences of treason and sedition. Most were sent to the stocks to be harassed by angry mobs, who were pleased to have targets upon which to vent their own frustrations. The most vocal protestor had been given a swifter punishment. His body still hung from the gallows when Gertrud last dared to look.

She pressed her head so hard against the altar it felt it must cut her flesh. Ruthlessness, she could admit, was needed in a warrior and a leader. But cunning, which his father had never lacked for, seemed worryingly absent now.

Her son was clever; of that, she had no doubt. Yet day after day, he dulled his mind with smoke and mead and distracted himself with servant girls in his chambers and in his father's study. During his brief moments of sobriety, his mood was so foul that mercy was a distant dream, and cruelty rose in its absence, as did a stubborn denial of any warning signs that he trod the wrong course.

Gertrud wanted to help him, to show him the grave mistakes he made. When she implied he might be overindulging in pleasures, Ragnar had raised his hand as if to backhand her. But even with his head muddled, he had refrained. He respected her as his mother, and so she knew he was not beyond redemption. This hope sent her often to the manor chapel, as it had now. And so she prayed.

"Volkur, Daughter of War... Protect my son and his soldiers from our enemies. Save his life, so he may serve you. Djur, Father of All..."

Gertrud paused mid-sentence, struck by a thought. Djur could not save her son. She doubted even wily Nuvvog could pierce the cloud surrounding his mind.

"Please..." she whispered, but the small chapel felt achingly empty. She yearned to feel the presence of the Inscribed, as she often had throughout her life, but they did not come. She was alone.

The gods had abandoned Ragnarsglade. Only she remained between Ragnar and the precipice toward which he carried them all.

Dragging herself to her feet, Gertrud staggered from the chapel. She knew where she had to go. What she had to do.

Like a soldier marching to his death, she went to her son.

Gertrud raised a hand to the door, then hesitated. Muffled noises emanated from the king's study. Though she suspected what they portended, still, she listened.

First came the low rumble of her son's voice, then the high-pitched laughter of a young woman. Gertrud breathed a sigh of relief. For the moment, they were not engaged in their usual ungodly behavior. Still, her chest remained tight as she knocked.

The response came at once. "I told you before: leave us be!"

Gertrud forced out the words, unable to help her voice becoming high and wheedling. "It's me, Ragnar. Your mother."

Her son's reply was too muffled to hear. The boards creaked with footsteps, and a moment later, the door swung open to a half-naked woman.

Gertrud averted her eyes. She knew her: Brenna, one of the serving girls. Brenna seemed to possess no shame in what she did, for she stood bare-breasted with her chin raised high. Evidently, she had embraced her new role as Ragnar's concubine when the thrall girl, Takhat, had proved less than enthusiastic.

Well did Gertrud know the path Brenna had set down. She understood why she acted as she did. But along with pity burned resentment. This girl was complicit in her son's downfall. None here was innocent.

Myself included.

"Move aside," Gertrud said shortly as she stepped past Brenna and into the room. It reeked of smoke and sour ale and a musk she tried not to identify. Empty bottles and kegs lay spilled about the floor along with various garments.

Her son sprawled amidst the wreckage on a stained divan. His shirt was also missing, revealing black tattoos in savage designs upon his chest. She had not seen those before and wondered when he had acquired them. His stare was vacant as it fell upon her, but his mood seemed no less foul for that.

"Well?" he demanded as the silence stretched on. "What was so urgent you needed to barge in, Mother?"

Gertrud swallowed down the reprimands welling up inside her. "I'm worried, Ragnar. Worried for you."

"Worried!" Her son barked a laugh, and the serving girl tittered with him. "When are you *not* worried! Always pecking at me like a hen at a chick." Abruptly, he sat up, his gaze sharpening. "But chickens don't taunt lynxes unless they have a death wish."

Her heart felt it must snap in two at his threat, yet Gertrud tried not to let him see the hurt. In men such as him, it would only serve as encouragement.

"When you began punishing scouts," she said as calmly as she could, "they stopped bringing you their full reports. But I heard them speaking to one another as they ate. Syptens have been seen, Ragnar, on this side of the Whiterun. Too many to be a scouting party."

Ragnar's scowl deepened. His eyes were hooded and bloodshot. She wondered if he truly heard anything she said. If anything could make a difference now.

"I will tell you once more, Mother." His voice was a rumble, low and threatening. "I won't hear anymore of ghosts. The bridges have been burned, the ferry lines cut. Those damned devils will never cross the Whiterun. Don't mention your fears to me again. I wouldn't have you force my hand."

Gertrud could not hide her quivering now, though her greater fear was not for herself. She had endured beatings before. Her son dying would be a far deeper injury.

Ragnar smiled, teeth stained dark with ale. "Is that all?"

She was still searching for the right response when a noise sounded from outside the manor.

Gertrud stiffened, listening. It sounded like the blowing of a horn, but that could not be. The horns upon the wall only blew when there was reason for alarm, like a fire.

Or an attack.

"Ragnar," she whispered, but he was already bolting to his feet and almost tumbling over in the process.

"What is it?" he demanded. "What's happening?"

Brenna screeched and covered herself with her arms. Mindless and overwrought, she scurried this way and that, like a panicked sow in the yard. Gertrud searched deep within her for the calm necessary for any servant to long survive. She buried her panic, just as she had buried her emotions all her life.

Bending, she retrieved the serving girl's blouse and tossed it in her direction. Brenna caught it, but only stared at it, as if unsure what to do.

"Dress," Gertrud snapped, then turned to Ragnar. "My son, go put on your armor. I believe the war has found us."

Gertrud turned away from her son's gape and strode for the door. She would help him prepare and sober up, then march him out the door. Ragnar needed to make a showing, now most of all. She had made him the son of a jarl, and that came with responsibilities as well as privileges.

She could not protect him now. All she could do was pray.

24. TEARS OF SALT

They wept as they warred in the mud
Tears falling with the sharp iron thuds

But the dead do not weep
These words, we must keep:
Shed tears of salt over blood

- The Saga of Skaldi, translated by Alfjin the
  Scribe

Once more, Sehdra watched a battle unfold from atop a hill.

Ragnarsglade stood a little way distant, yet on the open plains, it remained clearly visible. Teti stood silent by her side, both of them shaded beneath a tent. The sun was the most perilous thing they faced, while Sehdra's soldiers slaughtered hundreds below.

No — not my soldiers. This is Oyaoan's doing.

Her gaze drifted to the giantess. She stood outside of the

pavilion and in the light, her translator by her side. Her face, never pleasant, was furrowed into a deep scowl, yet it did not seem from displeasure. There was something in the way she leaned forward, in how she clenched her great fists, in how her trunk lashed from side to side and set the jewelry upon her tusks dancing, that spoke of eagerness. Of claiming something long anticipated.

Oyaoan was to blame for the atrocities committed this day. Sehdra had tried swaying the giantess from this course, but her subtle protests had gone ignored. Neither Oyaoan nor the Ibis wished to consider any other course. They were bent on dominating the Winter Holds, though they spilled rivers of the blood to do it.

Yet Sehdra was the Holy Karah, the living goddess of Ha-Sypt. The acts of her people were laid at her feet, even when it was not fair. Life had never been fair; she had known from the day she was born with cursed flesh.

Sehdra looked back to the battle, not wishing to witness it, yet knowing she must. Ragnarsglade had none of Petyr-sholm's doughty defense. Its walls were of wood rather than stone, and they burned swiftly as artillery flung Hua-fire upon them. The city, if it could be called such, had caught flame as well, filling the sky with smoke and turning the sun red — red as Bek, it seemed to Sehdra.

The Baegardians put up as stout a defense as could be expected. With desperate bravery, they faced down numbers twenty times their own and fought among their walls of shields until Sypten infantry bore them down. They brought their own Hua-fire to bear, but seemed to have precious little of it, judging by the paltry explosions flung at her people. The flames claimed perhaps three hundred, far too few to stem the tide.

Yet the previous battle had struck fear not only in

Sehdra's soldiers, but the huame. No longer did they carry Hua-fire upon them, or even so much as touch it; this task had transferred to humans for the first time. By how long it took the giantess to take this course and how reluctant Oyaoan still seemed to embrace it, Sehdra judged this had been a difficult decision. Why that would be, when Hua-fire posed such a threat to them, was a mystery to consider after the battle.

As the walls of Ragnarsglade fell and the flames died down, Sypten warriors rushed in. Though they had no elephants for the charge, enough charioteers and foot soldiers remained for a swift penetration. Like a river breaching a dam, the People of Dust flooded through the streets, sweeping away the paltry defenses in their wake. Holdsmen were divided into groups, and some began to surrender, seeing the fruitlessness of further fighting.

Sehdra did not have to watch much longer. Within half a day, all resistance had been squashed. Swords were sheathed, and chains and collars were brought out. Thus did a Winter Hold become hers.

Or rather, Oyaoan's.

She sighed, her shoulders bowing, victory an acrid taste on her tongue.

Not long after the armies moved into Ragnarsglade, Sehdra received a summons.

Oyaoan, the Ibis, and the other huame had gone down to the city some time prior. Before their presence, Sehdra expected any remaining resistance would be extinguished. It was one thing to fight foreign soldiers, another thing entirely to stand against such indomitable foes. Sehdra had been asked to remain behind — *For your safety,* the Ibis had said with a smirk.

To her shame, the order had come as a relief. Even knowing she was in some way to blame for all those butchered that day, she could not help but hate coming any closer to the desolation.

But that had always been a vain hope.

With Teti walking beside her palanquin, Sehdra's procession followed the Suncoaster messenger through the blackened streets. It was like traveling through Gazabe's Blight, the afterlife of the damned. She had avoided the sight following previous battles, but now the atrocities crowded close around. The flames had spared few buildings, most reduced to blackened skeletons, their bones clawing at the sky. Drifting among the ruins were ghosts, people faded by ash and soot, awaiting their inescapable fates.

Screams rose from among the smoldering buildings. Through watering eyes, Sehdra glimpsed a few of the ongoing tragedies. Families crying over the dead. Soldiers forcing bindings onto women and children. A mother pleading on her knees to save her family, while the Zakowan sellsword standing over her slapped her across the face.

Sehdra had thought she had grown numb to it all. Yet at this woman's beating, her mind thawed. Leaning toward one of her guards, she pointed at the soldier. "Warn that mercenary against further violence. These people are not to be harmed."

"At once, Divine One." The guard bowed and hurried off toward the scene.

Sehdra stared until the offender looked up and saw her. Only once he bowed and groveled did she order the palanquin to carry on.

Teti stepped in close. "You cannot save them all, Divine One."

"I cannot save any of them, Teti, not truly. Our customs will not be so easily broken. It is their right to claim slaves from the prisoners, as I must also do."

"They will be treated well under your care. A slave's life need not be miserable."

Sehdra smiled at him. If anyone knew that, it was Teti. Though he had been castrated to be made into a palace servant, he had never lost his resilience.

"I will make sure it is so," she murmured.

Her throat was raw and her head ached from the smoke by the time they reached their destination. Sehdra lifted her gaze to stare at the citadel set in the center of Ragnarsglade. It stood atop a stout hill, a gravel path running up to its entrance. Unlike the rest of the city, this manor was made primarily of stone. Positioned apart from the common buildings, it alone defied the fires, untouched but for a few sooty smears. The fortress had not yet fallen either, it seemed. A few archers peeked out of arrowslits, waiting for the People of Dust to mount an assault. The stout double doors stood, no doubt barred from the inside. It would cost scores of soldiers to claim, yet the Baegardians could not hold out for long.

Not with Hua's power on our side.

Oyaoan stood just outside of bow range staring up at the citadel. Now that the city had burned down, she stood as the next tallest thing around. Sehdra's eye was drawn to her repeatedly, anxious to know why the giantess had brought her here.

The Ibis came from around the huamek. Walking with that bobbing gait of his, he grinned and stopped before her palanquin to sketch a mocking bow. "Divine One, Great Oyaoan thanks you for coming."

Sehdra dismounted her palanquin in silence, not speaking until she stood before the man. "It is good to experience our conquest up close. Though I see it is not yet complete."

"No, Divine One. The final token is yet to fall." The Suncoaster looked up at the citadel. "But I do not think it will take long."

"I am glad to be present to witness it."

It was a guess at her purpose being here. By the Ibis's grin, the implication had not escaped him.

"The Divine willing, it shall be so. But it is on a different matter that Great Oyaoan wishes to speak."

A snake seemed to slither down Sehdra's spine. "I would be honored to discuss whatever Hua's Child wishes."

At last, Sehdra had a sneaking suspicion she knew what this invitation was about. Why else would Oyaoan bring her here, to the center of her triumph, if not for intimidation?

She suspects. She knows.

By Teti's restless shifting, he had surmised the same as she: this would be a dangerous visit. But he had the sense to stifle his fear and grow still.

The giantess moved, turning to stare at Sehdra with those black eyes, small in her massive head. Only decades of practice enabled Sehdra to keep her expression smooth. Behind her mask, though, her cursed flesh twitched, unable to be fully controlled.

Oyaoan rumbled in her strange, guttural tongue. The Ibis cocked his head like a bird, then spoke as she finished.

"Great Oyaoan understands you have been growing close to the disgraced general Amon Baka."

The skin on her arms erupted into gooseflesh. Sehdra swallowed, trying to recover her voice. "I would not say close. But as the Great One once told me, it is wise to sow seeds where one may."

The Suncoaster narrowed his eyes even as he smiled. "So you believe his career is not yet at an end. Curious, since he served your faithless predecessor."

Sehdra endeavored to keep her face blank, her breathing even. *In, out. In, out.* Her thoughts calmed enough to parse through them.

"I had hoped to keep this matter private," she said, enunciating each word. "But I would not wish to make Great Oyaoan uneasy. Amon Baka has qualities other than his generalship. These are what I take advantage of in the privacy of his pavilion."

For a moment, the Ibis only stared. Then he loosed a laugh and looked back at the giantess. Oyaoan was implacable in her stare. Sehdra could only meet it for moments before looking back at the translator.

"Even a goddess has carnal needs, I see! Very well, very well. But what of your visit to the high chanter, Raneb Nautjer? Even for you, Divine One, that would be a scandalous affair."

Silent curses ran through her head. Sehdra had hoped to draw the priest into her conspiracy as she had Amon, but Raneb had been too distant to even make the attempt. Yet it seemed even that much she would be forced to pay for. Still, before the blatant disrespect, Sehdra felt her composure rebuilding.

"I may be a goddess, Ibis, but I also seek solace in the spiritual. Qa'a served as my Inspiration during my mortal life; even now, he and his chanter guide my path."

The Suncoaster grinned. "As you say, Divine One. It seems you are gathering many councilors to you in these times. Zosar, Amon, Raneb... People you trust."

With the words, he snapped his fingers before her face. Despite herself, Sehdra flinched.

"I am sure you will not mind, then," the translator continued, "if Great Oyaoan borrows your slave on occasion. Teti, I believe his name is?"

Sehdra thought she had been afraid before. Now, she knew true fear. *Not Teti. Anyone else, please, just not him.* She might have fallen to her knees before the Ibis then and there if she thought it would preserve his life. She did not dare look at him lest the words break free.

But in the end, she knew it would not matter. Oyaoan and her servant might chain her, but she would not step into the manacles herself.

"It would g-gladden me to have Teti serve Great Oyaoan." She swallowed, hoping the stutter had not betrayed the lie as she faced her friend. The compassion in his eyes almost broke her. "Teti, if you would serve the huamek in any capacity she requires..."

"Of course, Divine One." He bowed, all evidence of concern hidden from his body. Of the two of them, Sehdra had always believed Teti the braver, and now he showed it.

The Ibis watched the exchange with pursed lips, then shrugged and waved her away, as if she were his servant. "Stay or leave as you wish, Divine One. It might be a show yet."

With that, the translator ambled off toward where Sehdra noticed the chief general Nekau oversaw the siege.

Sehdra did not move after him. Thoughts spun through her head, so swift as to be dizzying. Oyaoan and the Ibis suspected her plots. With each step forward, she fell deeper into their quicksand trap.

But she was not buried yet. Stopping now would not save Teti. She had to press forward and strike at the heart of Oyaoan's plans. She had to take back her home.

Somehow.

Teti moved close to her side. "I am still here, Divine One. Do not surrender to fear."

She wanted to embrace him. Instead, she contented herself with looking him in the eye. "I never will."

25. THE NECESSITY OF SACRIFICE

M

Unto the Children, surrender their due
An offering of Silver and sand
Born of Divine, sacraments shall accrue
The gift of the gods to the land

- Words in the Sand, refrain 5;96

S eth waited three breaths, then peered around the edge of the tent.

He could barely see by the evening's dying glow. It had taken him days to track down his quarry, painstaking hours spent watching any of the giantess's servants he could locate across the ruined city and the war camp outside of it. They had nearly caught him a half dozen times, and he had even been threatened by a pursuing soldier.

But a Tusk of Bek could not be foiled for long.

The wagon was heavily guarded. From his vantage point, far enough away to remain unnoticed, he saw two dozen soldiers standing or pacing around it. Another twenty milled about the peripheries, ensuring no one passed close by without permission.

Seth had been following some of those allowed near. Four guards escorted a Suncoaster clad in a red feathered robe. This was a favored servant of the giantess; a priestess, he guessed her to be, of their foreign perversion of the Divine. Seth had tailed her for the past two days, hoping she would lead him to what the Holy Karah desired.

The red-robed servant was swiftly admitted by the guards, then escorted to the wagon. In the dim light, Seth could not quite make out the activities occurring around the wagon, only that the servant's arrival had caused a stir. No torches were visible anywhere nearby. Instinct born of experience evoked a tingling in his spine, telling him this was a portentous sign, yet Seth had been trained better than to leap to conclusions.

Belatedly, he saw the coverings on the wagon had been removed, and something metallic beneath caught the glint of the fading sunlight. The servant stepped up to this metal object. Moments later, a substance flowed out. It shone almost as if it contained light itself, yet moved like sand. All those around it seemed wary, as if they handled fire itself.

Seth had seen its like before. He knew the name the mountain savages had given it.

Khnuum.

Slowly, carefully, he backed away. He knew enough now to understand. This was the source of Hua-fire. The source, in great part, of the giantess's might.

Seth slinked away into the dusk.

"How heavily guarded?"

Seth bowed his head deeper. His goddess's displeasure

was plain in the question. He hoped he had not done something to bring it down upon himself. Running through his actions, he searched for what misstep had led him astray. He had given her proper respect by prostrating himself at her feet. It was, however, growing late, as he had gone at once to report to the Holy Karah. Yet was it not as she had commanded? Only the pleasure he took in her scent, spicy and sweet at once, could he account as a sinful thought, and one he could not easily control.

"I counted forty men surrounding the wagon, Divine One," he spoke aloud. "More may have been out of view."

"Tusk Seth. Please look at me."

He always struggled with these commands of familiarity, but he did his best to obey, lifting his head enough to see her eyes, though he kept his gaze upon her feet.

The Holy Karah's lips twisted to one side, away from the mask melding scarab and elephant together. "Understand I am not frustrated with you. I only wish it were easier to reach her Hua-fire."

"Yes, Divine One."

He did not say they would need a small army to fight off the Suncoaster guards. It was plain the goddess already knew that.

Her servant, always at her side, spoke up. "It is a problem to consider another time, Divine One. Just now, it is enough to know where it is located."

"We cannot always delay, Teti. Soon, we must act."

"I understand, Sehdra Karah. But act too quickly, and we will bring down her wrath before we can respond."

Seth bristled at the servant's audacity. Who was he to tell the Holy Karah what she must do? That she seemed to value Teti's words only made it more infuriating.

"Very well." The goddess sighed. "I thank you, Tusk Seth, for finding it. Now, we must focus not on what

Oyaoan has, but what she has come here to claim. Can you uncover this for me as well?"

"Yes, Divine One. At once."

He rose from his knees and backed toward the flap, the way memorized upon his entrance so he did not have to look. Only when he felt the fabric of the tent against his legs did he rise, turn, and leave.

Though out of the Divine's presence and past the guards standing at the entrance to her tent, Seth straightened only a little before fading out of the way of a passing group of charioteers. As if unaware of passing their goddess's tent, the noblemen laughed raucously, spirits sloshing from the jug they passed between them. Had his gaze not risked drawing their eyes, he would have glared his hatred at them. But a Tusk did not indulge such base emotions. He was a servant of the Divine, no matter how he must debase himself to do it.

So he continued on, head bowed, meeting the gaze of no one. Yet, as Seth made for Bek's pavilion, a sudden smile came upon him. His goddess had entrusted him with yet another vital task, one to which only he was suited. It would not be easy, nor did he know how to accomplish it.

But he knew this: even if it cost his life, he would see it through.

Bek, grant me the strength to do your will. I am your servant. I am the Tusk to gore your enemies. All I am, I dedicate to your service.

His eyes closed, his jaw working through tasteless food, Seth circled the words in his head. He was unworthy of being granted anything by a god, he well knew, but prayer was a reminder to humble himself before those he served.

Bek, show me the path to do your will—

"Tusk Seth."

He flinched. He was not used to being noticed, much less addressed. Though he slept in the tent of Bek, he spent little time there otherwise, only long enough to take a spare meal before venturing out to serve his goddess. What brief moments he was there and awake, Chanter Amasis saw fit to ignore him before he went out, as he had this morning. Seth understood. They each had their duties; there was no time to waste on idle talk.

As it was just after daybreak, Seth was still hunched over his slab of emmer bread and cup of sweet beer. Slowly, he looked up to see the Holy Karah's servant peering inside the tent flaps. It spoke to how deeply he had been in his prayers that he had not noticed his approach. But then, with many footsteps crunching on the ground outside and the grumbling of the groggy men starting up, he had grown used to ignoring most sounds outside the tent.

Seth did not speak as he stood. Even as a royal servant to the Holy Karah, Teti held no authority over him. He owed him no gesture of fealty and thus gave him none.

Teti smiled. He looked kindly, but Seth could not trust it. Smiles were rare among the Tusks of Bek, and for good reason. Faith was pain. Pleasure had no place in service.

Though Seth extended no invitation, the servant stepped inside and let the tent flaps fall closed behind him. "My apologies for disturbing you so early. This errand is better done when prying eyes are less keen."

Seth's shoulders tensed. This man appeared beside the Holy Karah during Seth's every visit, but it did not mean he was loyal.

"Nothing to undermine Her Sanctity," Teti rushed to say, perhaps having seen something in Seth's face. "This is in service to her."

He let his shoulders fall, though Seth still spoke no word. *Silence is a sieve; the truth filters through it.* So it was written in the Words in the Sand; so Seth believed.

As intended, Teti broke the long pause himself, his voice low. "I understand you have located where the stores of Hua-fire are kept."

That insight was no surprise; the servant had been present when Seth told the Holy Karah of it. His mind turned over all the possible ways Teti might intend to betray his mistress.

"Sehdra Karah was well pleased by this, as you saw yourself," the servant continued. "It is a substantial source of our adversary's might. But just as it brings the huamek power, so might it grant us the same."

There it was: the servant's traitorous angle. He wanted power — not for the Holy Karah, but for himself. Seth wondered if he should cut his lying tongue out or bring him before his goddess so she might see her justice done.

Teti, who had been slowly nearing, took a step back, eyes widening. Seth stilled his thoughts. It would not do for the servant to see violence before it was needed, just as White Aya counseled in the scriptures.

"Tusk Seth, please. You are suspicious, and I cannot fault you for it. While all I do serves Her Sanctity, this is one matter I wish to conceal from her. Not to bring her harm, but to protect her from it."

When Seth still did not react — much as he burned to do so — the servant continued. "You have only just met her, but I have stood by Sehdra Karah's side since before her ascension. Half her life, I have watched over her and seen her grow into a woman. I know her gentleness, her compassion, her love for her people. You must have seen it, too."

On this point, they could agree. The goodness of the Holy Karah radiated from her every action and movement.

She knew suffering as he did. She extended grace toward him when he deserved none.

His lips began lifting before Seth squelched the feeling down. No — thoughts of her would not seduce him. Not when one so close might plot against her.

Teti gave him a small smile. He had not neared again. To one trained in death, as Seth had been, his fear was like a perfume filling the tent.

"She would not wish any harm to come to me," the servant continued. "Nor to you. She does not see the necessity of sacrifice; at least, not in those she should. But pain is often imperative in service, as I trust you know."

Faith is pain. Yes, Seth knew this. His burned flesh reminded him with every movement. Something in the thought finally compelled him to speak.

"You wish me to secure a measure of this fire."

"No, no, not you. I would not take you from the tasks set to you by Sehdra Karah."

Seth gave a slight nod. That, also, was something he could approve of. He had made the offer as a test.

"Tell me of its location," Teti continued, "and anything you know of how to reach it. Others are better positioned to handle its acquisition, should it be possible."

For a long stretch, Seth considered the request. Until now, Teti had given him no reason to distrust him. Now that he took a moment to consider things, the servant was already in a position to harm the Holy Karah if that were his intention. Perhaps all he said was true. Perhaps this was another way he could serve his goddess.

Seth nodded. "I will tell you."

A relieved laugh won free of the man. "Good, good. For a moment, I thought you would sooner kill me than speak."

For once, Seth did not repress his smile.

26. BANE OF GIANTS

"I fear what awaits me in shadows. There, I see beasts both tender and terrifying."

- Torvald Geirson, the Last King of Baegard, two weeks before his disappearance

E gil remained by Bjorn's side as much as he could.
It had been a full day since the jarl's heir had made his foolhardy mistake. In that time, the sky had rained fire, a concussive blast of air thundering over the city. Egil's heart skipped at the sound, remembering the first time he had heard it, yet he did not venture out after the men Vedgif sent to investigate.

The source was plain: Nuvvog's Rage had returned to Oakharrow. Why this would happen now remained a mystery, for the scouts had returned with little to report.

So Egil returned to his self-appointed station by Bjorn's side. The heir awoke in fits and starts, doing little more than eating, drinking, and hobbling outside to relieve himself before falling back asleep. Whatever ritual he had subjected himself to had taken an exacting toll, but Yonik said he would survive.

Still, Egil returned to Bjorn's side again and again, watching over him like a hen over her eggs. He had settled the heir into his bedroll, then brought him food and watered ale whenever he awoke. Though Egil tried not to hover, he was drawn back to Bjorn like a boat to an eddy.

From whence had this loyalty grown? The question plagued him all the long hours. When Egil joined the Hunters in the White, he had done so not only at his father's behest to monitor Bjorn, but to prove himself the best of Oakharrow's warriors. There had been no thought of service owed to his jarl, nor of upholding the jarlheim's honor. Even now, he was not sure it was by lofty ideals he acted. There were a hundred ways to rationalize it: that Bjorn was an important seer, that he was the jarl's true heir, that he was a potent fighter, that he could stoke the resistance in Oakharrow.

But those were not the true reason. Something else drew him to Bjorn, a thing unmentionable. A shadow denied, yet dogging his every step. Egil dared not look closer, but he no longer dismissed its existence. He had denied himself too long in service to his father to continue.

"Egil?"

Startling from his thoughts, Egil looked around. Bjorn had sat up, eyes crusted and bleary. A beard, almost entirely absent when leaving Oakharrow, blossomed across his chin in a thick tangle. It made him seem older and unkempt, and somehow suited him.

Egil looked away, swallowing. "Hungry?" he grunted.

"And thirsty, if you don't mind. I'll be strong enough to get it myself next time."

Egil held up a hand to forestall further excuses and went to fetch the meal. In an attempt to avoid drawing attention, their den of rebels went without fire as often as they could, so the food comprised cold salted mutton and stale rye bread. It was more than some had in the city these days. With the Jotun in charge and the Sypten threat to the south, industry had ground nearly to a halt. Only Vedgif's position as a Thurdjur elder and the clan backing the resistance kept them in sufficient supply.

Once Bjorn had scarfed down the meal and drained a waterskin, he laid back, blinking slowly as if his mind was still in a fog. Egil crouched near him. Menith watched the door, so he had a few minutes to spare.

"Lord Heir—"

"Please, just Bjorn." Bjorn smiled, a bit of life returning to his eyes. "We're close enough for that, at least."

A lump lodged in Egil's throat, but he spoke around it. "You were speaking of what you saw before you fell unconscious. Of your... visions."

It was still difficult to swallow, the existence of magic. The gods and their influence had always seemed distant before, appearing only in storms and floods or during foul harvests. But ever since Nuvvog breathed upon the Harrowhall, the Inscribed exerted their presence over Enea stronger than Egil had believed possible. Bjorn's magic — the Sight, as he and the priest called it — was the most unexpected of these ways.

Despite his hesitancy, a part of him yearned for it. And though he had shown little aptitude thus far, Egil had never been one to give up at the first failure.

Bjorn blinked. His gaze had turned distant for a moment. "Yes. They almost seem like dreams now... Can you remember what I said?"

Egil recounted the scenes as best he could. The Witterland Runestone with glowing runes that spawned a red mist. The fire giant consuming silver sand. Bjorn becoming a giant himself and cutting through both jotunar and surtunar. The walls of scales and fur.

"I don't understand," Egil finished. "Does it mean anything?"

Bjorn lifted his gaze, which had fallen to the planked floor. "I think it's our future — a possible one, at least. There's a lot I haven't told you. What I learned in Eildursprall. Whom we met atop Yewung."

Egil hid his surprise. He had known Bjorn and the others were headed for the gothi town, but why ascend Yewung? It seemed an impossible task, for the mountain cleaved the sky itself. Surely, mortals were not meant to set foot upon it.

Yet Bjorn did many things others did not dare.

"Tell me," Egil murmured.

"I'm not sure you'll believe me."

"Even after what I've seen from you?"

"Even then."

Egil sat cross-legged before Bjorn and leaned forward, closer than he usually dared. "I take that as a challenge."

Bjorn laughed weakly as he sat up. "Have it your way."

As the heir explained all he had seen and done since their parting at the Jotun's destroyed war camp, Egil tried to believe him. Much of it stretched his imagination, none more than the King of Ice appearing and gifting Bjorn runestones before fading back into myth. He focused on the little he could understand.

"The Witterland Runestone. The Jotun sent his men to steal it. Now, it's appeared in your vision. Is it a weapon?"

"One of magic, I think. Though what the red mist means..." Bjorn frowned toward the altar, lost in thought.

"These runestones, the Four Shadows," Egil pressed. "They truly tell the future?"

"One future, I think. It's more of a path: the best path to victory, whatever that looks like."

"And each Shadow shows a length of that journey?"

"The primary pieces of it, yes."

Egil crossed his arms. "Then we must take back the Witterland Runestone. If it's a weapon, we cannot allow the Jotun to have it."

The heir's amber eyes darted up to Egil's, then away. "It's not that simple."

"Why not?"

"The First Shadow... I haven't told you what I saw and heard in it." Bjorn's mouth puckered like he'd sipped sour milk. "We must ally ourselves with the giant. Or I must, at least."

Egil stared at him, watching the heir wither beneath his gaze. He did not temper his feelings.

"You cannot be serious," he said flatly.

Bjorn shrugged. "It was what Torvald showed me, what he foresaw. How could I not believe it?"

"It's madness. You don't know Kuljash. You haven't seen him or heard him speak. He's ruthless, Bjorn. There can be no alliance with giants. They trade in power, and we cannot match theirs."

He cut off the bitter words and looked aside. Bjorn did not deserve his anger. It was meant for the giant who had stolen their home and killed so many of their clansmen. The one who had fractured loyalties between sons and fathers.

"I understand." Bjorn spoke the words as gently as a snowfall. "But I also know what we face. The threat to Enea is greater than one giant. The Runewar sweeps the land and spares none."

Egil looked back, his curiosity sparked. "The Runewar?"

"It's what the King of Ice called it. He'd seen it coming for a long time."

Bjorn frowned, seeming to suffer a sudden memory. Instead of inquiring into it, Egil mulled over his words. *The Runewar.* It was a chilling name in what it implied. That this would be a conflict won not by steel and blood, but seers and sorcery. A thing for which Egil had no talent.

The heir spoke again. "More giants come, both from the north and south. I assume they know more about this conflict than we know. If we are to survive, we will need the Witterland Runestone and its weapon. Do you truly believe we can seize it from the Jotun, from Kuljash? Can we kill even one giant?"

Before the challenge, Egil hardened his will. "Better to try than lay down and die."

Bjorn cast him a wistful smile. Egil stared at his twisted lips, his gaze lingering until he forced himself to turn away.

"There is the question of the third vision," Bjorn said. "When I became greater even than the giants. It must be metaphorical, yet I cannot understand how."

"Magic," Egil muttered. "How can anyone understand it?"

Bjorn loosed a low chuckle. "True. Yet we have to try."

It was a knot beyond Egil's pallid imagination to untie, yet he made the attempt all the same. "Perhaps it has something to do with how you become a berserker, with the Frenzy runestone."

The heir stiffened. "What makes you say that?"

"It's the only piece of magic you've mentioned that seems useful in battle."

"Close to true." Bjorn's gaze grew distant. "Though every tool can harm, depending on its use."

Egil waited, hoping he would clarify what he meant. Yet as the heir spoke again, his thoughts seemed to follow a different thread. "Perhaps with the gods..."

"What about the gods?"

Bjorn startled, his eyes darting up to Egil's. "I... I'm not sure."

A chill ran through Egil. He had witnessed the Mad Jarl's spells before. This moment had been too similar for comfort. Searching for a distraction, he asked, "What does it mean that the fire giant was eating silver sand?"

Bjorn's eyes widened. He sat up straighter in his bedroll. "It's *khnuum.*"

"What?"

"*Khnuum.*" Whatever the word meant seemed to excite the heir, judging by the brightness in his eyes. "It was what made the Chasm-fog dangerous back at the Jotun's old war camp. It's in drascale ore and is necessary for magic. It's also what causes dragonfire."

Khnuum. Egil worked the word silently around his mouth. "What does it mean? Is it Old Djurian?"

"I don't know." A smile split Bjorn's face, almost child-like in its exuberance. "But I think it's what the giants have come for."

Egil tightened his arms against his chest. "I don't understand."

"But I finally do, Egil. They didn't come just to conquer us, though they must believe it necessary. They came for *khnuum!* They need it for their magic, yes, but also for sustenance. Perhaps even to survive."

"How do you know that? The visions?"

"Yes. It's something Torvald said of it: *Their light and life, their strength and flaw.* I think he meant that just as *khnuum* gives power, so it also extracts a price. For them, it's their very lives."

Before Egil could respond, three knocks came at the Tangled Temple's front doors.

In a moment, he stood with his sword drawn. "Stay here," he hissed at Bjorn, then stalked silently across the nave toward the door. As he neared, it rattled under a fist again. Egil tensed, ready to spring forward.

A voice called through. "Elder Vedgif! I am Frey Igorson, a guardian of the late Harrowhall and in service to Lady Aelthena Of'Bor. I bear urgent news for the rebellion!"

Egil stared at the warped wood. Behind him, the Tangled Temple came alive as others gathered at his back.

"I know Frey!" Menith grinned as he came abreast of Egil, his beard spreading wide. "That's his voice, alright. Didn't think the bastard survived!"

"Open the door," Vedgif ordered at Egil's back.

Egil moved forward to obey, though he kept his sword bared. Heaving on the heavy bar, he lifted it enough to open one door, then stared out at the small crowd of men beyond it. One man stood in front, arms crossed over his chest. His blonde hair was sweat-slicked against his skull, and mud and blood caked his leathers and chainmail. Yet his eyes were bright and his smile wide as he looked first at Egil, then those beyond him.

Though he did not know the guardian beyond his reputation, the man's words awoke a fire in Egil. At long last, Oakharrow would rise. And he meant to fight at the fore.

27. SEEDS

"Fomenting insurrection is akin to a farmer tending their fields: one must sow the seeds and pray they will grow."

- Lion Teos, leader of the failed Second Yeshept Uprising

Stepping inside the temple, Frey surveyed the ragtag group of rebels with a smile.

He had a smile for every occasion. The one that rose now was far from his most pleasant. Vedgif Addarson had gathered his men, yet they numbered no more than two dozen — far fewer than Frey had hoped to find when the Thurdjur elders sent him here. It had been nearly a full day since they had fought their way into the city, and he and his men had barely had a bite to eat or a wink of sleep.

Yet, when facing impossible odds with the hopes of a prince, a lover, and all of Baegard riding on his shoulders, what else could he do but laugh?

After clasping arms with Menith Karlson, the surviving guardian a welcome sight, Frey turned to Vedgif. "A fine group they look, elder. Is this all your men?"

"More will come to the call." Vedgif's gruff voice was hard, and his expression betrayed no doubt. Frey wished he could feel as certain.

"Good," he replied cheerily. "With what we're set to do, I think we'll need them."

The elder eyed him for a long moment. "How did you and your men enter?"

Frey pretended not to notice his suspicion. "A watery and bloody way. You can hardly have missed the diversion that helped us, the way Prince Alabastor lit up the sky. As for the means, we had knowledge of a smuggling route up the Honeybrook, a rope buried in the mud. The true stroke of fortune was that the river gate was raised. I assume you had something to do with it?"

In what seemed a rare occasion, judging from the severity of the lines on his face, Elder Vedgif smiled.

"No, that was the barbars' own doing. I've kept a watch on it in case retreat became necessary. At first, I expected it to close any day, but the enemy appears to have overlooked it."

"Overlooked it?" Frey shook his head. "Any warrior worth his steel could hardly miss such an opening."

"Barbars are not used to manning cities and walls, and these are less principled than most. Perhaps the Jotun would have seen it, but he rarely wanders the city, Djur be thanked."

"And the Spinners as well, with that stroke of fortune."

A third voice broke in. "Perhaps it was not luck, but the will of the Inscribed, Frey Igorson. Though that would depend on your reason for being here."

Frey turned to the man who had spoken. He had a grizzled face with more hair than skin showing. Gleaming eyes peered out from the mess. Without the accouterments of his station, it took a moment for Frey to place him.

"Brother Yonik. I'm heartened you survived as well."

The gothi smiled, but his eyes remained steady and unblinking, his question hanging thick in the crowded temple.

"Suppose it's best to cut the bandage off." Frey flashed a bracing smile. "Prince Alabastor has commanded me and my men to take the North Gate this night, so we might allow the army a way in."

Silence greeted his words.

"That will be difficult," Vedgif said at length. "They have doubled the watch and heightened their caution since an earlier incident. Your diversion will have worsened it."

Frey followed the elder's gaze to the pinch-faced young man who had first opened the door. *Egil Yaethunson.* He remembered him leaving with the Hunters in the White and being caught up with the first instance of Nuvvog's Rage. He also remembered who his father was. Did these men know the lawspeaker's role in bringing all of this about?

And the apple never falls far from the tree.

But that was a battle for another time. "No matter how many men that boar sends, we'll take it." Frey spoke with certainty, as if that might make it true.

From the corner of his eye, he saw Sven Arvidson nodding vigorously at the declaration. Frey barely refrained from rolling his eyes.

"But can we hold it?" Yonik murmured.

It was a concern of Frey's as well, but he tried not to let it show. "We only need to do so until the prince arrives."

"Who is this Alabastor?" Vedgif narrowed his eyes to slits. "Lord Ragnar's natural son?"

Bastard, more like. "Yes," Egil said aloud. "Though it's 'king' and 'prince' within their earshot."

The veteran gave a wordless grunt.

"The prince means to take the city?"

The voice came from behind the others, deep-noted yet strained. Frey tensed as the men parted, revealing a tall young man nearly as hairy as the priest. Though big, his shoulders were somewhat bowed, and his frame had yet to fully fill out. But it was the eyes, so light a brown as to almost be golden, that told him who he was.

"Bjorn Borson. Lord Heir," he added a moment later, putting a fist to his heart and bowing. When Frey rose, he wore a grin. Already, he could see Aelthena's expression when she reunited with the brother she had assumed to be lost to the snows of the Teeth.

"Frey Igorson, Guardian of the Harrowhall." Bjorn returned the smile, if with less enthusiasm. "Though with you being here, I must wonder if I am still the jarl's heir."

Frey opened his mouth to answer, then paused. "I suppose not, with Lord Bor no longer being the jarl. However—"

"My father is alive?"

Bjorn swayed, his expression dazed. The sentry, Egil, was by his side before he could totter over, holding him up with a devotion Frey recognized.

Well, isn't the world full of surprises.

Frey only grinned. "He is. Alive and well, as much as any of us just now. And so is your sister."

"My sister..." The young man's eyes grew misty. "Aelthena?"

"Yes." Frey's throat went tight. "I'd say I've kept her safe, but she's protected me just as much of the time."

Bjorn looked lost for words. Despite the joyous news, a frown started to claim his face before smoothing away. The heir's eyes found him, and the way he stared at Frey, it was like they were the only two in the room, no other warriors bearing witness to the reunion.

"Please, Guardian Frey, continue to protect her and

Lord Bor. By the law, Aelthena is still my father's successor, for I renounced my claim when I went into exile. I am the jarl's heir no longer."

Frey stared at him, as did everyone in the temple. Somehow, it evoked a smile from the young man. So incongruous was the expression it seemed Bjorn must be becoming as sprite-touched as his father.

No, never that. That disease claiming her brother would kill Aelthena. Yet the thought refused to be entirely quieted.

Frey cleared his throat. "At the moment, Lor— ah, Bjorn, your family has been deposed. Lord Asborn has been declared Oakharrow's jarl by King Ragnar's decree."

For a moment, silence claimed the temple, all the way up to the rafters. But it was not long before discontented mumbling started up.

"Perhaps," Brother Yonik said over the hum, "we should leave matters of succession for after we retake the city. At the moment, only the Jotun reigns."

It seemed the nudge Elder Vedgif had needed. "The gothi is right," the veteran said. "You spoke of taking the North Gate, Guardian Frey. Tonight?"

Glad to stand on more certain ground, Frey hastened to answer. "Yes, if possible. The sooner we do it, the less time the damned giant has to figure out what we're up to."

The veteran nodded, seeming undeterred by the timeline. "I'll send out the call. Be ready when we are."

Aren't I supposed to say that? But, as usual, Frey only smiled in answer. All that mattered was the mission's success. If it took inflating this prickly man's ego to do it, he wasn't above humility.

Though, as his gaze lingered on the former heir and his distant expression, Frey wondered if he still had the full picture of what was occurring here.

28. THE WAIT

"Answer the door with a knife drawn when greeting unexpected guests. Hospitality is a virtue best saved for peaceful times."

- *Highlord Carr Gunnarson, Fifth Arkjarl of Baegard*

Bastor had done little in the past two days but watch the gray walls of Oakharrow. This night proved no exception.

The jarls and drangi argued in the clearing behind him, worrying over tactics and gates and formations. He ignored them, preferring his own thoughts. Everything he needed to know lay spread out in the city below.

Sometimes he stood, sometimes he paced. Always, his eyes drifted to the jarlheim rising from the evening gloom. He had issued the order for the men to prepare hours before in case Frey acted before light entirely leaked from the sky. His armor, cleaned and polished to shining, hung heavy from his frame, but it was a comforting weight. An omen of what was to come.

Let it be here already.

It seemed he had hardly done anything but wait since becoming a prince. Wait for the highborn ladies to leave him be. Wait for his gaggle of bootlickers to lap his shoes clean. Wait for the battle to begin. Now, the man he waited on might be dead.

That would make for a long wait, indeed.

He was no prince in his heart. He would have sought the seedy mead halls in lowborn districts even without his father's orders. A man could not change his nature, and all knew the nature of bastards, himself best of all.

Bastor grinned toward the walls. His one consolation was that his scouts' reports placed Frey and his men as having wormed their way into the city. If they had survived on the other side, however, was a different matter. Bastor had a difficult time believing Frey would die easily, but war had taken better men.

And worse ones.

Aelthena seemed anxious as well during the few moments Bastor had seen her between meetings. Though she tried to hide it, he could see it in the way she curled her arms about her middle, or how she constantly glanced over her shoulder. Did she fear a knife in the back, or hope to see the man who had once stood there? Seeing her in such a state, Bastor wondered if he should have refused Frey in leading the company. But he had been the right man for the job, better even than Bastor himself, as much as he hated to admit it. War called for sacrifices, and time and lives were the currencies he spent.

Bastor forced himself to root in place. Spread throughout the camp were his warriors, over two thousand strong, all armed and waiting. He heard their impatience in nervous laughter, in the creaking of steel and leather, in the incessant sharpening and oiling of blades, the tightening of already tight straps.

The anthem of war that no skald can capture.

Bastor roused from his thoughts as figures neared. The first drang of his personal guard, a veteran known as Kare Lone-Ear on account of a notably missing body part, intercepted them from where he had stood a dozen paces ahead. Bastor watched the ensuing discussion with disinterest. Most likely, it was another report come in with the same status as before: no change.

After a minute, Lone-Ear left the group to approach Bastor. "Prince, you might wish to speak with these three. Sentry found them lurking at the edges of the camp. Thought they might be Jotun spies, but with what they're saying..."

"By all means, bring them over."

He didn't have high hopes for the diversion, but just then, anything would serve. The drang returned with the three newcomers in tow. Though they were filthy enough to be barbars, their features tended toward Baegardian, as did their clothes. Their mannerisms, too, failed to fit the mold of the wildfolk.

Converts to the giant's cause?

Curiosity piqued, Bastor beckoned them closer. Two men and one young woman, the first man was tall and blonde and wore a nervous smile as he glanced at his surroundings. The other man was wide as well as tall; where his companion smiled, he frowned. The woman — more a girl, on second glance — had a pretty, freckled face set amid strawberry hair, which spilled down in curls from under her hood.

"Prince," Lone-Ear said, pointing at each of the three, "these are Loridi Kelnorson, Seskef Gulbrandson, and

Acolyte Tyra. They claim to be recent companions of Bjorn Borson, the former Heir of Oakharrow."

"Yes, I know who Bjorn is." Bastor looked from one anxious face to the next. All met his gaze, even the girl, though with varying degrees of certainty. "You say recent. Where has Bjorn gone then, if he was with you three before?"

The strangers exchanged looks. "Your Princeship," said the blonde man, Loridi, "if I may call you so, we're not precisely sure. We hoped you could tell us."

"Highness," the stout man, Seskef, intervened, "we believe the Lord Heir left with the priest, Brother Yonik. But we do not know where they went."

"It was in the middle of the night." The girl, Tyra, sounded close to tears. "When I awoke, he..."

Bastor held up a hand. Despite their evident distress, a smile tugged at his lips.

"Save the rest. There's someone who should hear this story. Lone-Ear! Come on. We've a tent to visit."

29. COALS & CINDERS

Skaldi said unto the quarreling pair:

Beware! Two paths you may take
Old flames fade to coals
Old hate smolders in cinders

- The Saga of Skaldi, translated by Alfjin the
* Scribe*

Aelthena smoothed back her father's thinning hair as her vision blurred.

She was not given to weeping. Even as a child, her mother had marveled at her lack of tears. Most often, she had held onto anger rather than sorrow. Shouting had suited her better than wailing.

But all that seemed to change with Frey's departure.

Blessedly, her father did not protest her touch. He had been calm all evening, doing little more than staring out the open flap of his small tent. Uljana stood in one corner, intently watching father and daughter, though she pretended not to. Aelthena wondered at her constancy, but only briefly. It was hardly her greatest concern.

Outside, the camp bustled with activity. Bastor had given orders to be prepared and wait, and men went about their tasks with a nervous air. The building of catapults occupied the bulk of the soldiers' attention. Overseen by experienced artillerists, a dozen had already been erected with another set under construction.

Aelthena would have to venture out into the tumult eventually. With only Uljana remaining as a servant, she had to be content with making do for herself. At another time, it would have been liberating, if in an odd sort of way. She did not have to wait for others to bring her food, but fetched it from the highborn mess herself. She did not subject herself to others' hands while bathing, as much as bathing could happen in a war camp. No one set out her clothes or attended to them but her.

She had been served all her life. Only now that she was free of it did she realize what a burden that had been. Still, she lived on Bastor's charity, and the coming siege and her worries robbed the experience of any joy it might have held.

"Can we win this battle, Father?" she murmured, running a hand through his graying locks. "Can Frey do what he claimed?"

She had heard the reports of Frey entering through the smuggling route and knew the barbars had not shot him down before Oakharrow's walls. But once inside, what had become of him? Had barbars swarmed him and his men? Had he been taken before the Jotun and cut down like Skarl Thundson?

The old jarl grunted, a small, soft sound. Aelthena realized she had tightened her hand on his shoulder. With an effort, she relaxed her grip.

Here I am, pining after a man, just as I vowed never to do.

Her childhood had afforded ample opportunity to be contemptuous of how most girls were around boys. Seeing the simpering fools they became, Aelthena had been determined to never be like them. Even if she had to drive away all men, as her mother had warned she would, she thought it a fair trade to keep sight of herself.

She had maintained that same attitude with Asborn, to his dismay. Yet with Frey, it had lapsed of its own accord. Though he protected her, he never sought to reduce her. He yielded to her commands, but stood firm when he believed himself in the right. They were not adversaries vying for control, but allies bolstering one another.

Perhaps she did not need that fight anymore. Frey helped her keep sight of who she was.

But he was gone, and only now did she realize he had taken a part of her with him. Frey had been the wolf at her back, ever watchful, ever warding. He was her strength when she was weak. Aelthena wielded authority, but she would have faltered many times without him propping her up.

And now, he could be dead.

No. Don't think like that. He's alive. He must be.

She did not dare look too closely at that logic. Faith, a little used faculty of hers, had become her only levy against the dark waters of despair. For now, it would have to hold.

"He will return," she muttered, as much to her father as herself. When he did, she would tell him all she had withheld. Tell him what he was to her.

"Coals..."

Aelthena started at the low rumble. "What did you say, Father?"

The old jarl hummed for a moment. Uljana edged

forward, like a mother toward a toddler about to fall. Bor coughed and shook his head free of Aelthena's hand, then spoke louder.

"Coals? Or cinders?"

A chill prickled her nape, like at an ice sprite's touch. It sounded like a reference to the old Djurian saying about lost love and buried hatred. She forced out the breath she had been holding. It was just a fragment of memory surfaced, no more. Unattached and bearing no meaning.

The flap of the tent swept open, revealing Asborn standing in the entrance.

Aelthena stared, heart hammering, and not the way it used to when they were alone in his chambers. Her old betrothed was clad in gilded armor, gleaming once more, though its shine was blunted by nicks and old dents from the previous battle. Sword and seax were belted at his hip, and a shield lined with bronze hung from his left shoulder. His helm was tucked under an arm, revealing his stony expression in full. Hair touched by fire was cropped short about his face. Lines crinkled his brow, as they always had when he was worried. Aelthena wondered what afflicted him now, but she kept such thoughts from touching her voice.

"Asborn. What are you doing here?"

The corners of his eyes pinched. Belatedly, she realized she had left off his title once more, but her pride refused to let her amend the mistake.

"Mistress Aelthena. I thought we might have a word." His tone was softer than expected, but still plenty brusque. Armed as he was and with their colored history, her shoulders only eased a little. There was no Frey to protect her now.

But she did not need him. This she could handle on her own.

"Of course," she replied. "But let us leave my father in peace. Shall we go to my tent?"

Asborn gave his answer by turning on his heel and striding out. Aelthena glanced at Uljana before following. The thrall watched her go with wide eyes, only moving to the former jarl as the flap fell closed.

"Come," Asborn said, already moving away. "I could be called away at any moment."

If only it were now. She tailed him, dread icy in her limbs.

Her temporary home was next to her father's, so it was not a far walk. Asborn stepped in, pulling aside the flap with more force than necessary. Aelthena ducked after him, taking a moment to strap up the flap so it would remain open; an unnecessary precaution, she hoped. Asborn's eyes followed her as she moved to stand opposite of him. For a moment, only the distant sounds of the waiting horses, soldiers, and creaking artillery filled the tent.

"I just want to talk." His words came out in a croak. Asborn cleared his throat before speaking again, a feverish light seeming to fill his eyes. "With the battle coming, I wanted to... clear the air."

A bitter smile tried twisting its way free, but Aelthena suppressed it. Though the start was promising, danger still hung thick in the stifling air.

"What is there to talk about?" she said softly. "Truly, Asborn. What can either of us say?"

"That we're sorry. Sorry for the way things turned out."

She stared, more shocked than if he had struck her. "Are you sorry?"

"Can't you see I am?" He looked aside and raked one gloved hand through his hair, mussing it. "Gods, Aelthena, it's all a ruin. Things moved so fast, and these wars... Just, if I die today—"

"You won't die." The reply came instinctively. One never said otherwise to a man riding to war.

"If I do," Asborn insisted, "I don't want to die wondering." His eyes flitted back to hers, wide and hungry. "Are you sorry as well?"

She pursed her lips. It did not take her long to settle her mind. "What would I be sorry for, Asborn? After all you've done, how could I be sorry?"

His expression twisted. In two strides, he'd crossed the tent and loomed over her.

"For breaking your vow, to start!" he hissed. "For coupling with your guard like a common whore!"

Aelthena did not give an inch of ground. She stared up into his furious eyes and let all her own loathing show.

"No, Asborn," she said, her control solid ice before his paltry flames. "There's only one thing I regret: not ending what we had sooner."

His face flushed. His jaw clenched. His hands fluttered at his sides. Did they itch for weapons, or to wrap around her throat? Eirik Bloodaxe's violence ran through his son's veins; it was all too plain to see.

He could kill her. Here and now, he could strike her down, and try as she might, Aelthena would be unable to stop him. But she did not yield. She refused to give him what he wanted. She would not deny the truth, her truth. To herself, she would be loyal to the very end.

The moment stretched. Cracks appeared in her resolve. Asborn, too, seemed to waver, the flush fading and an exhalation wheezing from his lips. Seeing a way out, Aelthena dug deep within herself and dredged up the old feelings she had once harbored for Asborn.

"I'm sorry; I spoke in anger. In truth, there is something I wish I could take back: hurting you. It was never my intention, Asborn. And I'm sorry it happened this way."

It was all she could concede. Perhaps she broke a promise, but Asborn had sided with Ragnar and raised him as king, even when he knew him to be a snake. He had stolen her jarlheim from her. A broken heart would mend; insurrection could never be forgiven.

But they had been honest words. Aelthena had thrown the first stone. It was only right that she own up to the fault, no matter how slight or unintentional.

Asborn looked from one eye to the other, as if hoping to see more than what she had said. He opened his mouth to speak, then hesitated.

A figure darkened the entrance.

Aelthena whipped around, pulse racing faster than before. For a moment, she thought it was Frey returned; but no, the man standing there was too large.

Bastor.

The prince wore a grin as he entered. Yet, as his eyes darted over the scene, his expression swiftly morphed.

"Lord Asborn, step back from Lady Aelthena."

Feelings crossed and knotted inside her. Bastor's face was shadowed, yet the threat was plain in his voice. Asborn must have heard it as well, for he obeyed at once. "Highness, I—"

Bastor silenced him with a look. His armor was dark where Asborn's was bright, and his size made for all the more intimidating sight.

The prince glanced at Aelthena. "Is everything well here?"

"Well enough." Somehow, she felt reluctant to share the complete truth. "We were talking."

"As she says," Asborn hurried to add. "I just wished to have a word."

Bastor ignored the proclaimed jarl for a long moment as

he stared at Aelthena. When he turned to Asborn, his scowl deepened.

"Your men need you, Lord Asborn. Tend to them now."

Asborn hesitated. For a moment, his left hand rested on his sword's pommel. Yet good sense prevailed. As he moved to obey, his hand fell away.

"Mistress," he murmured to Aelthena as he passed.

The prince watched the proclaimed jarl exit, then stepped farther in. "And I was bringing cheery news. Though I suppose it remains unspoiled."

She peeled her gaze from the tent flap, still rustling from Asborn's departure. "News?"

"Best to drink from the source, as they say."

At her curious look, Bastor only swept open the entrance once more. A trio of figures, two men and a woman, stooped inside her tent, the space only just large enough to fit them all. In the gloom, their faces were hard to recognize, though the two men seemed vaguely familiar. All three bowed upon their entrance with varying degrees of flourish.

"Who are they, Bastor?" she murmured.

The prince grinned, his mood already seeming to recover. "If they speak true, they are former companions of your brother, Bjorn."

Bjorn. How long had she longed to hear someone speak his name? To hear news of him had seemed too much to hope. It had been so long since he entered the snow-cloaked Teeth on his foolhardy mission. Between barbars, giants, and the elements, she had long feared the worse.

Yet here were three of his comrades. The reminder helped her place the two men. She had seen them among Bjorn's company — the Hunters in the White, as she had deemed them on a whim.

"Your names." Her throat had gone dry, and she had to swallow before continuing. "Please, I would know them."

The tall blonde fellow bowed again. "Loridi Kelnorson, m'lady. This here is Seskef Gulbrandson and Tyra."

"Acolyte Tyra, m'lady." The young woman's cheeks turned as red as her hair. She bobbed her head once more, eyes darting between her and Bastor.

Bastor crossed his arms. "No need to be nervous, acolyte. Her frown is worse than her bite."

Aelthena barely heard him. "You were with my brother," she said to the newcomers. "Tell me — where is he now?"

The two men exchanged looks. Tyra lowered her eyes. Fear gripped Aelthena's heart and squeezed it hard.

"Just now, we don't know," answered the stout man, Seskef. "We'd hoped he had found his way into this camp."

"We saw Baegardian banners flying and thought he must have seen the same," said the tall man, Loridi. "But it doesn't seem he came here."

"When were you last with him?"

Loridi winced. "A week ago, m'lady, or thereabouts."

A week. Far sooner than she had thought possible. The fear eased its grip, but did not entirely dissipate.

"As we said to the prince" — Seskef bowed slightly to Bastor again — "the priest Yonik Of'Skoll went with him, from all we could tell. They left in the night the same day we glimpsed Oakharrow."

She narrowed her eyes. "You were approaching Oakharrow?"

"Yes, m'lady," Loridi broke in. "The Lord Heir had a vision that he must go there. And... well, I think he meant to speak with the Jotun, somehow." The lanky man scratched at his matted hair before letting off at a look from Seskef. "The details were murky on how he was going to do that, though."

J.D.L. ROSELL

Aelthena could scarcely draw a breath. She thought of Bjorn as she had seen him in Vigil Keep after he had attacked the keepers who guarded the Sypten prisoner, sprite-touched and unreasonable in his convictions. Now, he claimed to have visions. Would he believe them so deeply that he tried entering Oakharrow despite the obvious madness of the attempt? She feared it was a glimpse into his future, if not his present.

"Thousand pardons, m'lady," Tyra murmured. "I know how this must sound, but Bjorn did have true visions. He was named the Stoneseer by..." She moistened her lips. "That is, he was a seer, and was trained in the Sight by Mother Sign, one of the Silvers of Heim Numen. I was an acolyte there, before..."

"Before what?" Aelthena's throat tightened along with her chest.

"The jotunmen came. They burned down Eildursprall and killed all they came across. Some survived, but... I fear our order numbers few now."

Tyra's eyes shone, and the two men's faces creased with grief. It seemed too genuine to be faked. Aelthena crossed her arms, wishing it would ease the pressure welling up inside her.

"You say my brother had true visions, that he was a seer. How could you know this?"

The girl wiped her eyes with a sleeve. "The Silvers knew rune magic. Though it has long been forbidden to use, we guarded its power, knowing it must one day be wielded again. Mother Sign taught him the secret of it. And he... saved me."

As Aelthena watched the acolyte try to hold back tears, she realized how Tyra was involved in all this. *They were fond of each other, perhaps even lovers.* Though gothi were forbidden such intimacy, her own past cleared her of delusions that they did not occur, and made her question if it was right for them to be prohibited in the first place.

She stepped forward and gently gripped Tyra's arms, eyes prickling with heat. Tyra's luminous green eyes slowly met hers.

"Wherever he is, I will find him." Aelthena glanced at the other two men. "I swear it, by all the gods above and below."

The two men looked at her with fresh admiration, and hope shone in the girl's face. They seemed to know the vow was not lightly made.

Aelthena pressed Tyra's arms, then released her and stepped back. Bastor still watched with twisted lips, yet even he did not seem immune to the pathos.

"Since it seems their story was true, I leave them to your care," he said. "Mind they keep out of trouble and keep you safe."

The reminder of Asborn's visit cleared her misty vision. "Take back my city and I promise to be nothing but trouble."

The prince laughed and rolled his shoulders. "I'd expect nothing less. Back to the watch, now."

With a nod, he passed by Bjorn's companions and left into the shrouded evening.

Rising from hasty bows, the three looked at Aelthena. For a moment, she was at a loss for what to do. Yet it had never taken her long to form her next plan.

"You have had a long journey. First, we must find you food and shelter. Then I would hear what my brother has been up to all this time."

The trio exchanged significant looks. Aelthena wondered just what had occurred, and if she could trust that they would divulge everything. But it did not take long for Loridi to bow once more.

"It would be our honor, m'lady. Though I must warn that you may not believe the story we have to tell."

Aelthena smiled. "I'll be the judge of that. Every detail, Loridi Kelnorson. No matter how unsavory."

As the men cringed and Tyra flushed anew, she guessed that, true or not, the tale would at least be a riveting one.

30. TO THE END

"When death closed in, the gods drew near. It is only by their grace that I vanquished the dread wyrm."

- Yofam Dragontooth, Slayer of the wyvern Vardraith, First Drang of the Iron Band

The end was nigh.

Neither prophecy nor experience brought Gertrud to the conclusion, but the fear. The corridors were rank with it, and it filled the soldiers' eyes as they hurried by. With each man who had died defending the doors against the southern invaders over the past four days, the fear had risen higher, like floodwater seeking to overwhelm a dike. That same fear lodged in her heart, yet she refused to show it. For her son's sake, Gertrud buried it deep and remained strong.

It was all she could do for him now.

Ragnar had relinquished his habits of wine, smoke, and women, but she almost wished he would return to them. When he was not screaming at his men to fight harder, he brooded in the darkest corner he could find. His barely masked terror was the hardest of all to bear.

Gertrud comforted him at every opportunity. When he ranted, she listened. When he grew violent, she endured his blows without complaint. The bruises on her flesh were no worse than the burdens he had to bear. The fate of the jarl-heim was on his shoulders, and it quickly crushed him.

But it was all for naught. As Gertrud peered out a narrow window to see the approaching Sypten herald, she knew the final blow would soon fall.

"Jarl!" the herald cried, his Djurian only lightly accented. "Her Sanctity, the Holy Karah, demands your complete and total surrender. Continued resistance is futile!"

Gertrud glanced at her son. Ragnar stared out of the window next to hers. He gnawed at his nails, as had once been his childhood habit, though it had been years since she had seen him surrender to it. Blood trickled from his cuticles. He did not speak into the pause, but only stared down, eyes shining with unspilled tears.

"Should you open the doors and lay down your weapons," the herald continued, "the Holy Karah shall be merciful. Your men and women will become her servants, their lives spared to be dedicated to her sacred purpose. None need die."

Her son's eyes darted over to Gertrud's. The anger was gone from them, but the fear was harder to bear.

Pulling his bloody fingers from his mouth, Ragnar yelled back, "And what of my life?"

The herald squinted at his window. Men up and down the hall shifted and glanced at their leader. Cowardice was plain in his words and cracking voice. Any will to fight must soon wither before such a display.

"The life of the jarl shall also be spared," the herald

called up. "You shall be the Holy Karah's privileged guest until you are ransomed by your father and king."

One soldier, a lined veteran whom Gertrud understood to be one of her son's drangi, stepped close. "You cannot trust a Sypten's word, Highness. They will slaughter us down to the last babe whether or not we open those doors. We must fight and win our way into Volkur's favor! Let us earn our battle-glory and die as warriors should, to drink with our ancestors in their eternal halls."

Ragnar spun toward the man. He lacked the girth of a warrior, but he had always had his father's height, so he looked down on the veteran. Fear seemed to make his rage burn all the higher, his spare frame trembling.

"There is no glory here!" he hissed. "There would barely be a battle! Will you find glory in burning alive? In striking at smoke? They have Nuvvog's Breath at their whim and a thousand times our number. We cannot win! But maybe, *maybe* we can survive."

As quickly as it had arisen, his anger petered out. Ragnar turned from the drang back to his mother. Gertrud's heart broke at the look in those eyes. Though he hated to be touched before his soldiers, she could not help drifting closer.

"Your father will ransom you," she murmured. "You are his heir. You are valuable to them. The karah will spare your life, if only for the coin."

The drang looked at her with open disdain, but Gertrud ignored him. She was a woman, meant to dwell among the sprites of earth and ice come her final rest. Even if they killed every one of them and deprived these men of their deathly inheritance, it was worth the chance to save her son.

Ragnar drank of her belief like a thirsty dog at a puddle. "How do you know, Mother? How do you know they will spare me?"

She reveled in being acknowledged so before his men. Daring a step closer, she murmured, "We cannot know. But it is the chance we have. You can face this, Ragnar. You are your father's son."

His lips, always so sensitive, quivered, and his posture wilted. Her son stared out the window, eyes haunted by the task before him.

"Jarl!" the herald cried again. "What is your answer? Be swift, before Her Sanctity calls for the torches!"

"Wait!" He pressed against the window, desperate to be heard. "Wait. We'll unbar the doors. Do it!" he snapped at the drang at his shoulder, who opened his mouth to protest.

For a moment, the veteran looked liable to disobey. Then his years seemed to catch up with him all at once.

"Yes, m'lord," the man muttered, turning and tromping down the hall.

Gertrud watched him go, anxious that he might disobey. Her son's eyes drew her gaze back.

"Will you come with me?" His words came out as little more than a whisper. "When I go out?"

She reached forward and gripped his arms tightly. "Of course. I will walk with you the whole way."

And she would. Only in defense of her son did Gertrud find courage, but it was enough to carry her to the very end.

31. HIDDEN

Deep through dirt and root and stone
The faithful delve and mine
What sacrifice is not duly owed
To the Children of the Divine?

- Words in the Sand, refrain 5;97

Seth had never thought himself especially skilled. Before his mother gave him to the priests, he was told she had said, *Make of him what you can. The red moon was full the night he came; perhaps Bek has claimed him.* He did not remember this, being not one flood old then and just weaned from his mother's milk, but the priests had told him it often enough that it became his past, the only one he had.

And it was true: Bek's fire blazed within him. As he grew up in the temple, his unruly behavior thoroughly tried the shapers. Ever did Seth challenge, and question, and defy. Switches broke upon his back, but his will remained intact.

It was the candle flame that did him in, his hand held over until the flesh burned. He could not stand the fire for more than a minute. From then on, he believed the priests when they spoke. No longer did he challenge them when they said he was thoroughly lacking in ability, that he must humble himself and pray for some redeeming quality that he might win his way into Gazabe's Delight. Forged in burned flesh, their word became his law.

Yet in this new stage of his life, Seth learned he had at least one talent: being invisible in plain sight.

Night made his task simpler as he flitted from one husk of a building to the next. His skin was dark, and he wore clothes to match. Only by the light of the smoldering fires throughout Ragnarsglade could he be seen if those he followed looked back. Though, arrogant as they were, they never did.

The dozen Suncoasters rode upon chariots through the streets as if they owned them. Seth's fury at how brazenly they defied his mistress's will awoke for a moment before he tamped it down. Anger would not serve him here. All insults to the Holy Karah would be repaid by completing his mission.

How he knew this was the right group to tail was by the one who led these foreign soldiers. The Ibis, he called himself, likening himself as a Divine and not a man with a name. The bow-legged Suncoaster did not drive himself, but rode behind another, his gaze set on the road ahead, barely blinking with his intensity. Clearly, he had a mission and was eager to see it to fruition. That they went under cover of darkness only reinforced what the Divine One had claimed.

This would reveal the Great One's purpose in coming to the Middle Lands. The Ibis would lead Seth to what the giants sought.

The desolation, dark as the Jackal's Blight, carried on for a league, then ended in the ashen mounds that were all that remained of the walls. There, the Ibis did what Seth knew had been inevitable: he spurred the chariots to a faster clip. All Seth could do was watch as the Suncoasters sped through the fallen gate and out of sight.

When the rumble of hoofbeats and wheels faded, Seth stood from his spot behind a charred wall and strode over to where the company had departed. The plains beyond the city had largely been spared, brushfires efficiently extinguished through the combined efforts of hundreds of soldiers. Seth watched the fading torchlight of the Ibis and his soldiers as they rode down the road west of Ragnarsglade.

He could not follow them this night. But neither would he fail his goddess.

Seth waited until the following evening for the Ibis to return.

As he heard the crescendoing sound of the chariots, he rose from his hiding spot and peered around the broken wall. He had sat within the ashen shell of a house, a place so filthy and inhospitable not even those few vagrants who eluded the soldiers took shelter in it. A minute later, the Ibis rode through, still readily identifiable by the white tusks interwoven into his bared torso. The giantess's translator dismounted his chariot and strode down the rubble-strewn street with six warriors in tow.

A day's ride, there and back. Seth chewed on a mouthful of dried mutton, wincing as his tender skin pulled. Where the Ibis had gone and what he had done remained a mystery. But if this place he had visited was important, as Seth suspected, he would soon return to it.

He laid down in that same spot, only the cold ashes for a blanket. Though he spent as much of the night shivering as sleeping, Seth quieted his complaints as they arose. Faith was pain; he knew the lesson well. That his pain served a purpose was all he asked for.

Though patrols left in the morning, none had the Ibis with them, so Seth slunk away to secure a mount. Given the karah's authority, granted by her seal on a ring he kept tied around his neck, he returned to his post, hiding the horse behind the tallest remaining wall he could find. Lacking a chariot, he would have to ride atop it as the mountain savages did. Though he had never attempted it before, Seth had often found himself in situations where he had to learn quickly. This was just one more test placed before him by the Divine. Soot soon covered him again, but he did not bother brushing it off.

Faith is pain.

His vigil did not bear fruit that night, nor the next day. Breaking from his watch only to relieve himself, Seth slowly depleted his food and water stores. Soon, he worried he would not have enough for the inevitable journey. If nothing happened that night, he would have to leave his post to resupply and risk missing his opportunity.

His fears proved unfounded. As the sunlight turned golden and streamed over the burned city, the Ibis reappeared. This time, the translator led a much larger retinue. Two dozen Suncoasters rode chariots, while another dozen drove carts. Behind these, soldiers brought forth a score of slaves. The mountain savages stumbled as the Suncoasters prodded them with spears, keeping them moving despite their deprivations. Seth thought of the time he had masqueraded as a Winter Hold slave and bared his teeth.

Yet his goddess had condemned these people to their fate. He had to drown the pity in his heart and harden himself to their pain.

Once they reached the gate, the company set off at an ambling pace. Seth waited for the last of the slaves to trail through before rising and attending to his horse. The beast whinnied, perhaps sensing Seth's inexperience, yet he still dragged himself atop it. His burns screamed as he scraped them on its rough coat. Seth only breathed through the pain, sat up straight, and clumsily propelled his horse down the hill.

Only as he approached the ruined gate did Seth realize guards had been posted there. His gut clenched, but he did not let his fear show. It was one advantage of his injuries: expression had burned away with the rest. His hope lay in that these were Syptens, not Suncoasters, though they stared at Seth just as hard as his horse clopped up to them. The beast only halted before their lowered spears, skittering a step back before dancing in place.

"On whose authority do you ride out?" one sentry challenged.

One hand tight on the horse's mane, keenly aware it might buck him off at any moment, Seth freed his other to dig into his shirt and pull out the karah's ring, hanging from a cord pilfered from the city wreckage.

"The highest authority," he rasped.

Frown deepening, the guard raised his hand. Seth gritted his teeth, but there was no avoiding it. Slipping the makeshift necklace off his neck, he dangled the ring toward the guard, though he kept a tight grip on the cord. His horse made it no easier, for it never ceased to move.

The guard caught the ring in his hand and cradled it, staring at it for a long moment before releasing it again.

"The tusked scarab. Very well — go with the Divine's blessing."

Seth nodded to both guards before pressing his heels into his mount's flanks. The horse skirted backward before it went forward, to the mocking grins of the guards.

I am a Tusk.

Smoothing away his embarrassment with the refrain, he focused on the road ahead. The Ibis's company had nearly moved out of sight, yet he could not risk coming closer. One glance back would be sufficient to see him following. Once darkness fell, he could move closer since he did not bear a torch of his own. It would be difficult going if they left the road, perilous even if they did not, but he had no other choice. He had to follow.

A league passed, then two. Night came at last. With careful urgings, Seth moved his mount closer, keeping the glow of the party in sight. Judging by how long it had taken the Ibis to return the last time, it was likely they had several more leagues left to travel, perhaps as much as a dozen. The first time they had ridden swiftly atop their horses; now, their pace was much slower. Seth's horse stepped unsteadily on the uneven, dark road, but though he stumbled twice, neither was enough to lame it.

The night stretched long. Seth's eyes burned with keeping them wide open, peering into the shadows to not let his horse misstep. He considered walking, but without knowing what he would find at the end of the trip, it was best to save his strength. Only as the moons, each half-full, rose into the sky did his eyes find relief. Their combined light cast the world in a purple haze just bright enough to see by.

At last, the sky lightened again, and dawn shone at his back. Trees had cropped up around them, and the land steadily rose toward the mountains a score of leagues ahead. Still, the Ibis and his followers did not stop, but continued on through the morning. The road became rougher as they ventured farther from Ragnarsglade. Seth wore a perpetual scowl, wondering what could draw the huamek's servant out so far.

Soon, the day brightened too much for Seth to believe he could go unobserved and keep them in sight. He fell even farther back until the company was no longer visible. His heart pounded at the thought of losing track of them, but being discovered would ruin the entire venture. The karah deserved better service than that.

Though he kept a careful watch, he was still caught off-guard when the company reappeared before him.

Breath catching, Seth slid off his mount and tied it to a branch before slowly approaching. The Ibis had halted at an opening in the woods, judging by the brightening canopy ahead. Yet the light there was gray, as if shining through a thin fog. Coming closer, a distinct scent filled the air. Seth flared his nostrils as he breathed in. The aroma was bitter and rotten.

Like spoiled eggs. Like the Great One's odor. Like the stench of a faraway place where Seth had once dwelled.

But they were only suspicions until he confirmed them. Seth continued forward at a crouch, keeping every step slow and methodical. He glimpsed guards ringing the perimeter of the opening. Beyond them, the slaves were being prodded forward. The weeping of a woman turned to screams as a guard attempted to beat the pitiful sorrow from her. Though he tried not to feel her pain, he could not deny a sliver of it came through.

Faith is pain.

He did not let it distract him from his mission, but slid ever closer. Now, he could see the Ibis standing before his carts, hands clasped behind his back. He seemed to stare down at the clearing as if it fell away into a ravine.

Closer still, Seth saw what deadened the light: mist or smoke billowed up from the ground, spreading its sulfurous scent through the surrounding forest. Seth knew what he would see next as he turned his gaze to the mist's source. Knew it, yet he still had to confirm.

He waited behind a tree as the slaves were forced down the slope and out of sight. Minutes passed. The Suncoaster soldiers shifted, clearly uncomfortable. The Ibis, barely in Seth's view, remained as complacent as if he watched a herd of antelope.

At last, the slaves reemerged — or some of them did. One immediately collapsed upon reaching the top, and the cauldron they carried tumbled to the ground, spilling out its contents. Seth held his breath as he stared at the substance. It appeared like sand but for shimmering silver in the sunlight. It was just as Seth expected it would be.

Khnuum, the northern huamek and his savages had called it. *Silver,* it was named by the Words in the Sand. Whatever its name, Seth knew what it was.

The source of Hua's fire.

He retreated, his pulse quickened, his burns irritated. Seth forced himself to move slowly. He appeared to have gone undetected. Hissing out a sigh of relief, he reached his horse and freed it, then struggled atop it and pressed his heels in deeply.

His goddess needed to know at once. His chest swelled with the thought that he would tell her.

Seth all but flew back to Ragnarsglade.

32. SINS OF THE CHILDREN

The sins of the parents
Stain the soul of the child
Once one has fallen aberrant
Their progeny, forever defiled

- Words in the Sand, refrain 15;33

Sehdra sighed as she laid back on her bed, her twisted leg relaxing for the first time that day.

It had been a slog of a day. After half a week spent sieging the jarl's manor, the Winter Holds prince had finally yielded. In the end, all it had taken was a promise to spare their lives, one all too easily broken.

But Sehdra would not willingly go back on her word. Her herald had spoken truly as far as she was concerned. The king's son, as she understood this Ragnar Ragnarson to be, was a valuable hostage. They could claim a king's ransom for him — quite literally, as Teti had pointed out with a smile.

She was surprised that her actions, bold as they were, had

not been impeded, but Oyaoan and the Ibis had turned their attention elsewhere. These past few days, she had seen little of either, though what could be more pressing than taking over the last bastion in the city was beyond her. It had to do with Oyaoan's purpose behind this conquest, whatever it was; she was sure of it. But Seth had been absent as long as the Ibis had. She could only hope his prying had not been discovered.

For both our sakes.

Voices rose at the entrance to her tent, startling her from her reveries. Sehdra's eyes fluttered open. The war camp outside the conquered city was never truly silent, even at night, yet a disturbance directly outside her door was unusual. She wondered if now, in the heart of darkness, Oyaoan meant to mete out her punishment.

Her leg seizing, Sehdra sat up with a wince. Teti, not yet lying down for the night, looked over at her, a sympathetic smile twisting his narrow lips.

"Shall I check, Divine One?"

She was too weary to tell him off for his formality. "Please. But be careful."

Bobbing his head, he strode from the tent. Sehdra listened to his muffled voice, then the response of whoever else stood out there beyond her guards. Preparing for the worst, she picked up the royal mask and secured it. Her nightgown was sheerer than preferred, yet depending on who had come, the suggestion of nudity could play to her advantage. Few would dare look lecherously upon the karah lest their eyes be gouged out for their insolence. Against those who would, she had few defenses besides.

Just as she had extracted herself from her heavy quilts, Teti reentered. His expression struck a jolt through her.

"Who is it?"

"Seth, Divine One. He has returned with urgent news."

She composed herself as the disciple would expect: a goddess, not a weary, quite mortal woman. "Admit him."

With an eyebrow quirked at her revealing robe, Teti moved to obey. Calling outside, he held open the pavilion flap so the youth could duck inside.

As soon as he stepped foot within, Seth prostrated himself on the rug, forehead pressed to the dirty fabric. Sehdra repressed a sigh and walked closer.

"Rise, Tusk Seth. I wish to know what you have learned." Ordinarily, she would have spoken more informally with one in whom she placed such confidences, but familiarity would only make the devout youth uncomfortable.

"Your Sanctity." Seth rose, but only to his knees. His eyes alighted briefly on her, then darted back down. She regretted her choice of dress now. The last thing she wished to inflict on the poor, burned youth was more discomfort. Hastily, she took a seat and crossed her arms and her legs. She did not ask him to fully rise, assuming he preferred supplication.

"Forgive my absence, Divine One. I have been following the one called the Ibis." His head rose slightly, just enough to glimpse his eyes. "I know what he and the Great One have sought."

Sehdra's breath caught. "Please," she forced out. "Tell me all."

The youth gave a meticulous report, detailing his efforts to follow the Ibis's party, which went as far as sleeping in the mud and riding a horse bareback in the Baegardian fashion. She could not tell if her wonder or horror was greater. Had this discipline been trained into him or grown from his nature? She suspected it was not gentleness that could fashion such a weapon, but whips and harsh words. But when he was the tool she needed, could she truly regret the methods that forged him?

"On the fourth evening," he continued, "I succeeded in following the Ibis's company. He brought a dozen carts and twenty slaves along with forty men. I waited until they were nearly out of sight, then trailed behind them. As night fell, I ventured closer. I do not believe I was discovered."

She tried to imagine such a ride. Flying through the darkness, nothing but the moons and stars lighting your way... It sounded like a treacherous journey, to say the least.

"What did you find, Tusk Seth?" she asked softly.

He bowed to her question, but only continued his report as if she had not interrupted. "Come dawn the next day, Divine One, the Ibis and his company halted. I dismounted and approached on foot. They stood in a clearing set amid a forest of tall pine trees. Foul-smelling mist filled the air. I know this smell, Divine One; I have smelled it before. But I went closer to confirm."

Her words fell to a whisper. "What did you see?"

"A pit, Divine One. The northern giant and his servants, to whom I was sent in the mountains called the Teeth, called the substance in the pit *khnuum*. It is the source of Hua-fire."

Some part of her had wondered, suspected even, as soon as he began describing his discovery. Yet the implications still stole her breath away. Gulping down air, Sehdra focused her spinning mind.

"What does this substance look like, *khnuum*?"

"Like ash fallen from stars, Divine One. I believe it is the same 'silver' referenced in the Words in the Sand, for it resembles it. It glitters in sunlight, shifts in one's hands like sand. It is dangerous. A single spark can ignite it."

Seth's jaw spasmed. Sehdra wondered if the memory of

how he had gained his burns had arisen in that moment to haunt him.

Teti leaned in close to murmur in her ear. "This *khnuum* must be within the canisters cast by the huame's servants. I suppose the devices contain something that produces a spark upon impact."

Sehdra nodded. It was only the first of her suspicions. But as much as she trusted Seth, she did not wish to give voice to the rest with him present.

"Thank you, Tusk Seth. Your karah acknowledges and appreciates your courage and persistence. Please, take what time you need to care for your needs. I will send for you when I require you next."

"My needs are nothing, Divine One. Faith is pain."

Giving another forehead-to-earth bow, Seth rose halfway and backed out of the tent. Sehdra watched him disappear through the flap. She wondered if his faith would compel him to obey his karah, or instead find some other way to serve her.

She looked up at Teti, who seemed deep in thought. "In some ways, he frightens me."

"Hm?" Teti blinked down at her. "Ah, you mean the youth? He does possess a certain... intensity."

"Zealotry, more like. I believe he would do anything to serve me, though I have done nothing to deserve it." Sehdra shook her head. "But never mind that. We have learned more important things this night."

"It seems so. The giantess has been seeking more of her weapon. Somehow, she knew she would find it here."

"Yes."

Had she known it by inference? Their onetime conspirator, Ragnar Torbenson, had possessed it; it stood to reason that his territory would be the source of the weapon. Yet Oyaoan and the Ibis had displayed an almost preternatural sense of knowledge. As if they could anticipate the moves of those around them with startling clarity.

As if by sorcery.

The thought evoked a memory. "It's not just a weapon, Teti. At least, I don't think. Silvery sand... I have seen Oyaoan with *khnuum* before. In her tent, once, when she was eating it."

Teti frowned. "Are you certain? It seems an unlikely substance to consume."

"I am." Elation surprised her with its spread, lightening her body and untwisting her leg for a moment. "We know what she wants, Teti. What she needs. What she has sacrificed so much to gain. If we can take it for ourselves, take it away from her..."

Her words trailed off, the feeling fading. How could they deprive Oyaoan of anything she set her sights to? She still had her Suncoaster servants and the other huame in addition to her own formidable strength. Likely, she could even command the People of Dust, too, if Sehdra spoke against her. The giantess held all the pieces, her side of the Duaat board stacked.

Yet Sehdra knew her secret. She knew what Oyaoan wanted. That knowledge was not power, but it was the promise of it.

For now, it was enough.

Sehdra had not yet left her tent when Teti brought her the morning's news.

"Executions," she repeated. "Including the king's heir?"

"Yes, Divine One."

Sehdra collapsed in a chair and rubbed at her temples, fingers working under the mask she had just secured in place. Her head ached from constantly inhaling smoke and moving about on her withered leg, and the news did not improve the situation. But time waited for no woman; giants, even less so.

"Help me up. It seems our morning's course has been decided for us."

Delaying only for her palanquin to be readied to carry her across the ravaged city, she and Teti soon found Oyaoan. The giantess was not one to hide even if she could have. She stood in the street before the manor, now emptied of its inhabitants. The usual crowd of Suncoasters surrounded her, and two other huame hovered nearby, glowering from on high as Sehdra's small company approached. She avoided their dark eyes, hoping today would not be when she met her brother's fate. Though these days, it only seemed a matter of time.

It was not the giantess that drew Sehdra's eye now, but the constructions rising before her: two pyres, stacked high with wood salvaged from the city, posts erupting from their centers. Sehdra dismounted and, ignoring the spasm up the right side of her body, limped over to the small knot of people milling about before them.

"Great One," she called above the Suncoaster babbling. "I wish to speak with you."

The giantess's enormous head turned toward her. Her leathery trunk curled around itself, an agitated gesture not unlike a cat's flicking tail. Sehdra stiffened under that black-eyed gaze, but she did not slow.

The Ibis materialized from the crowd, two rows of bright teeth on full display. "Divine One! Great Oyaoan expected you this morn."

Sehdra kept her gaze on the giantess. "I have had news, Great One, that our prisoners are to be executed. I hope this is not true."

The giantess, as usual, gave no sign of hearing her. She had not even rumbled in that guttural language of her people before her translator answered.

"It is quite true, Divine One. Why should it not be? Great Oyaoan knows one must eradicate one's enemies, lest they return to stab you in the back. Would we leave King Ragnar's son alive when killing him would strike a mighty blow?"

It took a colossal effort not to shift her gaze to the Ibis. Still, Sehdra persisted.

"Great One, there may be elements to this decision that you have not fully considered. The prince is far more valuable alive. Killing him might harm the king, but it would also rally his people to fight harder against us. Keeping him alive as a hostage or for ransom gains us much more, and our enemies less."

She meant to press the point, but the giantess shifted to face her, throat vibrating with deep notes.

"Great Oyaoan has considered all paths, Divine One, and knows where each leads." The Ibis stepped closer, close enough for her to smell the Suncoaster spices in his sweat. "Killing Prince Ragnar leads your People of Dust down the most fruitful path."

For whom? she wanted to ask. But she already knew that answer. The huame only acted to benefit themselves, no matter the cost to others. Sehdra knew Oyaoan's motivations now. She had a frame into which she could fit her actions and decisions. It was only a matter of time and effort before she figured out the giantess's plans.

"Besides," the translator continued, "this is your people's way, is it not? 'The sins of the parents stain the soul of the child' — have I not read this in your Words of Sand?"

Sehdra looked aside from his mocking smile. It was true the Divine had decreed this, conveyed through diviners to be written into scrolls. Yet she could not help but contemplate the blasphemous counterpoint.

Should any be held responsible for the actions of another?

Oyaoan, seeming to tire of the silence, turned her baleful gaze away and left, each step a minor quake. The other two giants with her followed. Sehdra saw little point in remaining behind and turned away.

The Ibis spoke, drawing her up short.

"Who is the burned boy that visited your tent last night, Divine One? I would not suppose you had an appetite for cripples as well as pariahs."

She halted, head spinning, not daring to look at the translator. Sehdra desperately wanted to consult with Teti, but their collusion would put her friend in further danger than his position already did.

"Burned boy?" she said with careful disinterest. "I do not—"

"Pardons, Divine One," Teti interrupted, drawing both their gazes. "I can explain. He is a disciple to a chanter — the chanter of Red Bek. He brought an invitation to the Holy Karah to worship with him, should Her Divinity wish it, to bless this war we are so righteously winning. I beg your forgiveness for not telling you, Divine One, but you were resting, and I did not wish to disturb you."

"That is alright, Teti." The spinning of her thoughts slowed. There was no knowing if the story would convince the wily translator, but it sounded plausible on its face. She would have to be even more cautious when conferring with Seth in the future, if she could at all. Perhaps she would have to go to him; a prayer to Bek would be a valid excuse.

"A disciple." The Ibis smiled, but his narrowed eyes made it seem more like a grimace. "Perhaps I shall also seek consolation from Red Bek soon."

With that, the translator swept a mocking bow, then sauntered back to the other Suncoasters, who carried on constructing the pyres. Sehdra wondered idly if it would be better to wait to have the man killed or to do it sooner. Without the Ibis, could Oyaoan make her will known?

Not yet. The hiding cobra takes the last bite.

Patience would lead her to victory; impatience, to ruin. Show Oyaoan that her side of the board was not so empty as it seemed, and the huame might take it upon themselves to end her game altogether, inconveniences be damned.

But that knowledge would not lessen the sting from watching the bodies burn.

PART II
IRON

"For every one of us, living in this world means waiting for
our end."

— Seamus Heaney, *Beowulf: A New Verse Translation*

33. IN THE GODS' HANDS

"My path will seem folly to those who do not travel it. But I am a ship in voyage, sailing through the mist. Only standing at my prow can you see as I do."

- Torvald Geirson, the Last King of Baegard, three days before his disappearance

With one eye on the backs of the other occupants of the Tangled Temple, Bjorn slipped the Four Shadows into his satchel and tied it shut. From all he could tell, he had packed without his companions knowing. The gods knew Frey had brought plenty to occupy their attention. With the plan set to take the North Gate that very night, their sleepy lair had turned into a buzzing hive. Vedgif had gone out to rustle up more men from their hiding holes across Oakharrow. Frey and his handful of warriors rested, having not slept the previous night, or ate and planned for the raid. Egil usually joined them, as did Yonik, though both came back often to check on Bjorn.

Pleading weakness, Bjorn had retreated to his bedroll. It was not entirely a pretense. His limbs still dragged, his head felt stuffed full of wool, and his eyes were sluggish in their sockets. Knowledge such as he had gained came at a cost, one he was lucky not to have paid for with his life.

But he could not delay. If the rebellion succeeded and the North Gate was taken, Prince Alabastor's warriors would flood the city. With dragonfire in their hands, even the Jotun himself might not stand before them. That very night, Oakharrow could fall.

His home might soon be freed.

Opposing emotions clashed in his chest, provoking a grimace. A large part of him could not help but be over-joyed at the prospect. His people had been under the giant's foot for over half a year already. They were tired, afraid, and starving, and winter was just around the corner. If the Jotun was driven out — or, if he stretched his imagination to its limits, killed — they would at last be free of tyranny.

Then Aelthena would lead them to better days.

News that his sister and father were alive had shaken him to his core. He had hardly dared think of them, much less believe they had both survived. Yet here came a guardian of the Harrowhall claiming not only that they lived, but were camped with the army right outside Oakhar-row's walls. As Frey had been serving and protecting Aelthena since fleeing the city, Bjorn had no reason not to believe him.

His home and his kin were headed for liberation, so long as their mission at the North Gate succeeded. Bjorn felt a calling to assist them, to make sure they won the wall and held it.

But he served a greater purpose.

To win the war — not this small part of it, but the entire Runewar — Bjorn had to make an ally of Kuljash. Torvald's visions had told him so, and considering all the King of Ice had known, who was Bjorn to say otherwise? That meant he needed to reach the giant before Oakharrow fell. Should the Jotun lose the city, Bjorn doubted he would have another opportunity for contact.

Bjorn heaved himself to his feet. Evening had bled away, leaving Djur's star-dusted cloak to darken the sky. Time was short. No matter how fragile he felt, he had to leave.

He walked as quietly as he could to the temple's back door. With his sword and seax belted at his hip, his bag in hand, and his traveling armor donned, he hardly looked as if he were only stepping outside for a moment. Yet he hoped if anyone glanced his way, they would only think him readied for the night's assault.

Only at the door did Bjorn pause and glance behind. Yonik had his back to him. Egil had gone out to fetch other allies for the upcoming battle. He longed to see both their faces one last time. Only the gods knew if he would ever see them again. Torvald Geirson had foretold that Bjorn must go to the Jotun, but a vision did not guarantee that any particular event must come to pass, much less turn out the way Bjorn hoped.

Frey, who faced the priest, glanced up at Bjorn. His brow furrowed a little, and his eyes darted over his person, no doubt noting every detail of his preparation. Knowing he had lingered too long already, Bjorn nodded to the guardian and turned away. The door squealed shut behind.

Outside, the air was cool. A hint of winter laced the city's usual fragrance. Repressing a shiver, Bjorn strode for the exit from the yard, legs wobbling. He wondered if he even had the strength to reach his destination.

But his path called. He could not falter.

The door protested as it opened. "Bjorn."

He stopped short with a sigh. "Yonik," he said without turning around.

"You're going to him. To the Jotun."

It was not a question. Likely, Yonik had suspected this was Bjorn's plan as soon as he muttered what he had seen in the Second Shadow, perhaps even since he had led them to Oakharrow's walls, expecting to be admitted despite all evidence to the contrary.

Bjorn finally looked back, gazing at the priest by moonlight. With both red Skoll and blue Lavaethun in the sky, a purple pall limned his frame.

"You know I must. This is my last chance. Enea's last chance."

"How can you be sure?"

"You know how. Torvald saw it. *I* saw it. How can you doubt his visions now?"

"I'm not saying they don't hold truth. But truth looks different depending on the angle. Seeing the paths the future might take doesn't make you infallible, Bjorn. Even prophets may err."

Prophet. Bjorn choked down a laugh. Once, he had followed the gothi with near blind devotion. He had led men to their deaths among the Teeth for a dream of vengeance. But Yonik had been fierce then, unfazed by any amount of danger. Now, the priest seemed lost among the darkness.

For the first time, Bjorn saw he was afraid.

"I am no prophet, old wolf," he murmured. "Perhaps Torvald was, but not I. That doesn't change what I must do. No, I don't see the full length of our path, but it is the only one visible. We cannot know what fate awaits us at its end; should we not still follow it? Fear never stopped you before."

Yonik flinched. Then, strangely, he smiled.

"Long has it been since I feared for myself. Any hope for

joy died with my dear bairns and wife, and fear thrives on hope. No — I dread what may happen to you, Bjorn. You, and all those across Enea whom we still might save."

The words landed like a blow from an unseen axe. Bjorn's weakness multiplied, and he swayed on his feet. Yonik was there at once, steadying him with a hand to his arm.

"Bjorn?"

"I'm fine." He gripped the priest back. "When you stare at one thing too long, it becomes all you can see. You're as selfless as always, Yonik. Still, I think this is our one opportunity. If we cannot reach the Jotun and ally with him tonight, I don't think we ever will. The future is one set of crossroads after another, each choice determining those ahead. A river, once dammed, never flows in the same place."

Yonik's eyes drooped at the corners, yet he still nodded. "Very well. If you're certain this is the best course, I will follow you."

"Follow me?" All this time, Bjorn had been trying to convince his wanton mentor to let him go. It seemed the priest had been wavering in a different decision. "You didn't appear in the Second Shadow. I don't know what fate awaits you."

Yonik's lips twisted into a wry smile. "I'm not worried for myself, Bjorn, remember? Come; they'll wonder where we've gone soon. Especially Egil, whenever he returns."

At mention of the sentry, Bjorn winced. He could easily imagine Egil's look of betrayal. But war had many casualties. Friendships were the least among them.

"Then let's go."

Walking the streets of Oakharrow came with an odd nostalgia. Bjorn kept his head bent as he and Yonik wove in and out of alleys, avoiding patrols and their torchlight. But every once in a while, he looked up to gauge their surroundings, and memories snuck up on him.

He glimpsed the baker's shop where his mother had bought him and Aelthena sweetmoons, the pastry crumbly and sticky. Then there was the clothier who had stitched the first cloak featuring Bjorn's own kill of a wolf. He walked along streets where he had run away squealing from Yof as his brother bellowed playfully after him.

But those places lived only in his mind, for time had changed and twisted them. The bakery was boarded up; the clothier's shop, burned. His kin was slain and his home destroyed, even its rubble ruled by his enemy.

He could not live in the past; it was naught but ashes. Only the bleak future remained.

The distance to the Harrowhall was short from the Tangled Temple, and though the threat of discovery stretched the journey, it was not long before the ruins of his home came into sight. Yonik motioned them into an alcove from which they watched those standing guard before it. A pavilion, large enough for a giant, was raised behind it inside the remains of the Harrowhall's atrium. Bjorn clenched his fists, anger spiking through him. It took several moments to master it.

"Ten jotunmen at the entrance," the priest murmured. "More next to the tent. I wonder if Kuljash sleeps where he rules."

"If he sleeps at all."

Yonik looked back with a raised eyebrow. Only then did Bjorn realize bitterness had seeped into his voice. This task was hard to swallow now that it came to doing it. He had thought the weight of Enea's needs had snuffed out his own desires.

It will be. It must.

"We won't be able to sneak past." Bjorn murmured.

"Likely true."

"Then there's only one choice."

Yonik glanced back, eyes gleaming as moonlight caught on them. Slowly, he nodded. "Lead, and I will follow."

Those were words he had never thought to hear from the maverick priest. Bjorn shook his head, then slowly, painfully eased past him and into the open. There was no turning back now. Their fates were in the hands of the Inscribed.

The jotunmen did not immediately see them. Only as Bjorn forced himself forward did he catch their eyes. Their howls froze the blood in his veins. The scent of smoke and burned stone curled in Bjorn's nostrils as they rushed toward them.

Djur, protect me. Protect us all.

The barbars approached with weapons drawn. Yonik held up his empty hands, and Bjorn followed suit. By their frenzied gazes, he thought they would cut them down all the same.

But they drew up short, their steel not yet falling. One barked in their tongue, and the others crossed the final distance. Rough hands seized Bjorn. His weapons belt was ripped away, his sword and his seax going with it. As they dragged off his pack, Bjorn felt the urge to cling to it. Fears flitted through his mind. What if they had a seer among them, one who could peer into the Four Shadows? What if he gave Kuljash weapons he could use to destroy Baegard instead of save it?

But he knew what the giant wanted, knew the threat they faced. So he let the barbars rough him up, stripping him of all his protections and leaving him as vulnerable as a babe left out in the snow.

"We must meet with Kuljash," Yonik was saying. "We have information he will greatly desire."

The jotunmen laughed in the priest's face. "No go to Jotun," one grunted in broken Djurian. "To cell!"

Bjorn heaved a sigh. He knew the end of this path, but there promised to be many switchbacks in it. He stumbled along as his captor shoved him toward where the dungeons had caved in, to be a prisoner in the ruins of his home.

34. MEN OF WAR

"We men of war walk a different path. In each battle, we are born again. In each peace, we slowly die."

- Highlord Carr Gunnarson, Fifth Arkjarl of Baegard

Egil looked for Bjorn as soon as he entered the Tangled Temple.

His errand had proceeded smoother than expected. The patrols made themselves visible by the torches they held, and he knew Oakharrow's roads well enough to avoid them. His reception at his destination, too, had been unexpectedly warm. Edda Skarldaughter had all but leaped at his request, as had Bodil the Blaze standing at her shoulder. With such women, he supposed he should not have been surprised.

Not immediately seeing the former heir in the nave, Egil turned to Frey. The guardian's furrowed brow gave him pause. Frey had more often smiled, despite all the hardship he and his men had endured to sneak into the city, yet there was no trace of one now.

He looked at Vedgif, but there had never been hope of finding out anything from the veteran. As usual, the elder was stony-faced and unaffected. The priest, Yonik, might have yielded more results, but he, too, appeared to be absent.

His gut twisted. Egil shoved away hasty conclusions. Perhaps Bjorn and Yonik had stepped outside for a breath of fresh air; gods knew it was foul in the temple after being occupied by so many men for weeks on end. Yet a glance at their bedrolls showed them to be empty of belongings.

Refusing to speculate, Egil strode toward Frey and Vedgif and blurted, "Where are Lord Heir Bjorn and Brother Yonik?"

Vedgif's brow creased. "Gone."

"Gone?" Fire welled up in him, spreading from his gut through his chest. "What do you mean, gone?"

"They left, Egil." Frey spoke almost gently. "Took their packs and left. I know rumors had gone 'round about Bjorn's lack of courage, but this—"

Egil found himself inches away from Frey's face, words pushing out between clenched teeth.

"Don't say he's a coward! He's not. He's braver than you'll ever know!"

"Egil Yaethunson."

Vedgif's cold address dampened the sudden rage. Egil stepped away from the guardian, breathing hard. He could not quite unclench his fists. It might have been easier if Frey had despised him; instead, Egil only saw sympathetic understanding. He looked aside, face burning.

"Cut this idiocy, warrior, and give report," the elder snapped. "What did Edda Skarldaughter say?"

Shutting out his wrath felt like closing a door against a blizzard. Still, Egil forced his thoughts straight. "She said yes. Eagerly."

Vedgif's frown deepened.

"Can she be relied upon, this Edda? She is a Vurg, after all." Frey seemed determined to ignore the incident. For that, at least, Egil was grateful.

"Yes," Egil answered before the elder could, even managing to look the guardian in the eye. "In this, she can. She likes to fight."

Frey shrugged. "Very well. Our fate may very well be in their hands." He rolled his shoulders, then looked around the Tangled Temple. "I see no reason to delay. Shall we be off?"

Vedgif turned to the other men. "Gather your arms! We leave at once."

Though the others burst into action, for a long moment, Egil could not make himself move. His body seemed infected by a vitriolic sprite, leaving his limbs shaky in its wake.

He left. Left for the Jotun. Left me.

He did not need anyone to tell him outright. Part of him had known it as soon as he stepped through the door and saw Bjorn and Yonik missing.

But now was not the time for dwelling. Clenching his teeth until his jaw ached, Egil went to fetch his gear.

Darkness slid across his skin like oil on water. Egil kept his eyes wide and his head turning as he and the other warriors stalked through the streets.

They had only just exited the Tangled Temple when they came upon their first patrol. Egil's swift arrow had stopped the hornblower before he could sound a warning. The others died with only a few wails. These days, such sounds were hardly cause for alarm. The Djur-damned barbars had their way often enough with the populace to make them as familiar as a raven's squawk. Vedgif had ordered that they move swiftly, relying upon speed rather than stealth. When seizing a gate to admit an army, there were few other recourses.

Egil had an arrow nocked and ready to draw as he jogged at the fore of the company. His heart hammered from more than the encroaching shadows and the enemies possibly hidden among them. His inner turbulence had grown as he took his first life of the night, and many more were yet to be claimed.

The wall came into view before the second patrol appeared. They were too close to the wall; this fight would alert even those sentries idly playing games in the watch-towers. After what he had pulled to admit Bjorn and Yonik, they would no longer neglect vigilance.

Egil set his feet, tensed his bowstring, and waited for Vedgif's command. The elder had his sword bared and stood in the middle of the street scowling toward the enemy. The barbars, four in all, were laughing among themselves, voices harsh in the night's quiet.

"Now," the veteran called softly.

Egil aimed, drew, and loosed. Next to him, four other archers did the same. Arrows hummed toward the pool of light. Three barbars jerked as shafts sprouted from their body. Two cried out and stumbled, while the third — Egil's target — collapsed to the ground.

He readied another shot. Around him, the other rebels sprinted forward, ready to finish the lingering enemies. The sole barbar still standing fled before the onslaught, shrieking a warning toward the wall as he went. He had not gone two dozen paces before Egil's arrow knocked him to the ground, the missile taking him in the middle of his back.

But the damage had been done. Cries sounded from the

wall. Shadowy figures streamed from the nearest towers. There were more of them than when Egil had manned the wall, perhaps two dozen at a glance. Fewer than their own numbers, but more than they could swiftly sweep.

Egil drew his sword and bared his teeth. The more foes, the better. He had not come for an easy fight.

35. HOLD THE GATE

"Much of a siege comes down to who holds the walls."

- Highlord Carr Gunnarson, Fifth Arkjarl of Baegard

As his careful plans erupted into pandemonium, Frey sighed and joined the fight.

He should have expected nothing else. The patrols had been too frequent, their enemy's wariness too great. From what he had gathered, several incidents had cropped up over the past week, conflicts between the Jotun's men and other forces across the city, to make no mention of Frey's own infiltration. That an army camped outside their walls made the situation even more fraught. Oakharrow's occupiers had long expected a fight.

He only hoped they had not prepared for a mad rush from within the walls.

He sprinted toward the closest stairs. His shield and sword should have felt light, but the privations and pressures of the past two days made them heavy. Still, as the battle-thrill settled into his blood, he ran as swiftly as if he took part in one of his boyhood races. No greater glory awaited the man who met their foes first, yet still, he strained to edge out the man next to him.

One of war's many ironies.

Seven barbars stood atop the wall, bows raised and ready to loose. Frey held his shield up, obscuring them from view and leaving the rest to the gods. Two arrows thudded into his decrepit shield, the same as he had entered the city with, but neither split through.

"Spinners be thanked," Frey wheezed as he pressed on.

Sven Arvidson was the first to reach the wall. With a cracked yell, the keeper swung at the barbar guarding the bottom of the stairs. The mountain man, clad in heavy furs that looked to be from a massive wolverine, met Sven's swing with his shield, then kicked him back. Asborn's man stumbled, nearly losing his footing, but he soon recovered and charged again.

A moment later, Frey was there to aid him. As the barbar snarled and chopped at the keeper, Frey dipped around to stab their adversary between the ribs. The man went down, spluttering blood into his tangled beard.

Frey pulled his blade free in time to face a second barbar. This one lashed at him with a makeshift mace that was tipped with a misshapen lump of iron. Frey took the blow on his shield.

The tortured wood finally shattered.

"Volkur's tits!" Frey fell back, arm and broken remnants of the shield cradled to his chest. His forearm seared with pain, and his hand hung limp. Panic seized hold, but the barbar bearing down on him proved a greater concern.

Focusing through spotted vision, Frey deflected the next blow with his sword, the blade catching the cudgel on the shaft. The next, he narrowly dodged. With each abrupt movement, agony ratcheted up his arm, and darkness blotted his vision. He wondered how long he could continue to stand, much less fight.

The barbar wound up for another swing. Before he could loose it, a blade darted in and severed his hand.

Frey stepped back, releasing a shaky breath as Egil cut down the howling barbar. The sentry's sword sliced through his thigh, and when the brutish man fell to one knee, Egil chopped into his neck. The screams stopped as the lice-ridden head rolled across the stones.

"Much obliged," Frey gasped, but Egil had already spun away.

Suspecting he would do more harm than good by continuing, Frey retreated to lean against a building among the shadows. The archers atop the wall had their eyes set on other targets, so for the moment, he was as safe as he could be amid a battle.

Gritting his teeth, he examined his arm. It had an unnatural bend to it now. Midway through his forearm, the flesh bulged upward like he had grown an extra elbow. His gorge rose, and only with a colossal effort did Frey swallow it back down.

His arm was useless, but that did not mean he had to be. Gritting his teeth, Frey tried tucking his limp hand into his surcoat. His knees went weak as fire enveloped his arm. Barely clinging to consciousness, he sheathed his sword and made a second effort. At last, the broken arm stayed.

Have to take the wall. Have to open the gate. Aelthena'll kill me if I don't.

With a weary grin, Frey blinked open his eyes and studied the wall. The winch would lie within the gatehouse above the gate. Trained in the defenses of the city as a guardian, he knew one winch would operate the gate while the other raised the portcullis. With any luck, the barbars had not dropped the portcullis; it would take precious time to raise and require strength Frey did not have even at full health. Even for the gate, made of heavy oak and reinforced with iron, he doubted he would be sufficient.

"Guardian."

He had noticed other men streaming past him, but failed to see the one who stopped. Frey turned to blink at Vedgif Addarson, sword bloodied and shield unbroken. Truly, he was a veteran of many battles, for the blood spraying and the screams filling the air behind him only seemed to make him grow calmer.

"I can fight." Frey wondered if it was true even as he made the claim. Still, he levered himself upright and, after a moment's swaying, steadied on his feet.

The elder looked him up and down, then nodded. "We will take the stairs to the south, then come around the gate-house from the opposite side."

Without waiting for a response, Vedgif took off at a lope. "Djur preserve me," Frey muttered under his breath as he stumbled after him.

At any moment, he expected arrows to rain down on his head and pin him to the ground, yet a glance up showed the archers had more pressing targets. His fellow rebels had gained the wall, Egil at their fore. The sentry seemed frost-bent most of the time, but now his true nature emerged. Gripping his sword with both hands, he cut through the barbars, his cropped blonde hair dyed scarlet, his features every bit as savage as their enemies. It seemed there was no accounting for people's appetites.

Vedgif had already gained the stairs and doggedly ascended them. Frey hissed out a pained exhalation with each step he took up, his tortured body screaming. The pain in his forearm had blossomed into an inferno, one that spread into his skull and down his spine. He wondered if he would ever fully recover.

First, you have to survive.

With the barbars' attention occupied by the assault, their way to the gatehouse was clear. The door even lay open. Frey knew a sentry would have been flogged for such an oversight during a drill, but barbars received no such training.

Vedgif pushed inside, shield and sword raised. By torches burning in the brackets along the walls, Frey looked around the gatehouse, only breathing once he saw it to be empty of enemies. A table was tucked into a corner, four chairs scattered about it. Oil barrels occupied another corner. They had yet to be heated, judging by the banked hearth nearby. A rack of weapons, mostly empty, stood along the wall facing the city. Two winches lay on the opposite wall, and murder holes, used to pour hot oil over or shoot arrows at those below, riddled the middle of the floor.

"Bar the doors." The elder discarded his gear even as he gave the command.

Frey could not help but laugh as he awkwardly sheathed his sword, a simple task now made difficult by his condition. Even closing a door seemed beyond reach just then. But as Vedgif shot him a look, he stifled his amusement and turned back to the door. Shoving it closed with his good shoulder, Frey leveraged his body weight to slam down the bar into the lock.

"Hopefully, we won't need more men in here." He punctuated the words with a smile. "Doubt I'll be able to open this as easily."

Vedgif did not spare him a second glance. His own door closed and barred, the elder moved to stand before the two winches. Each rose two-thirds of their height, long spindles coming off of a pulley a stride around. Chains were wrapped around one, while ropes as thick as Frey's arms were on the other.

"The portcullis is raised," Frey noted with relief. The latch, which could be struck to release it, was still upright. The winch with ropes had no such latch; the doors had to be cranked both open and closed.

The elder gave him another studying look, then set his hands to the spindles of the gate's winch. "Come help me."

The words he had been dreading Vedgif would say. Still, Frey tottered over and set his body against one of the upright spindles, his good hand to the shaft. They two, an aging man and a cripple, were all Oakharrow had at the moment. He could only hope the gods were smiling on them that day.

Though the signs haven't been fair.

"Push!" Vedgif grunted, and Frey heaved. His shattered arm awoke with fresh protests. He barely stifled a whimper as he heaved against the winch. For a moment, they made no progress; then a bare inch gave way.

"Again!" the elder wheezed, and when their second effort faltered, "Again!"

Through the murder holes below, they watched their slow progress. Inch by inch, the gates parted, first enough for a man to slide in sideways, then for one to stride in straight on. Pain filled Frey's world, but somehow, he found the strength to press on. He wondered if it was only so he would not disappoint the old veteran. Vedgif seemed to possess Skoll's own stamina. Though he panted and dripped sweat, he never faltered or slowed the rhythm.

The door Frey had closed rattled on its hinges.

He startled so badly he almost lost his grip. Frey stared dumbly at the door, hoping he had imagined it. Though hallucinations would signal their own issues.

"Open door!" a guttural call came from the other side, dispelling all such notions. "Or I do!"

"Again!" Vedgif never relented, pushing hard at the

winch. It almost seemed the veteran had not even heard their enemy's threat.

But what else could they do? Their salvation lay in opening the gate. Only then could Bastor lead their armies in and sweep the invaders from the city. Though, now that it came to it, the aid seemed likely to come too late.

Especially when Frey could not give the signal for the prince to charge.

There was nothing he could do about any of it. All Frey could do was shove down his pain, heave at the winch, and pray.

The door shook on its hinges. The bar rattled. For the moment, both held.

Frey laughed, wiped the sweat from his forehead, and hauled at the winch again.

36. SECRETS OF THE STONE

Long have I studied the face of this stone. Long have I traced its lines, once finely cut, now eroding to ruin. Were I given to flights of fancies, I might believe something more lay beneath the words I translate. Some latent magic of our forefathers of which only they knew.

Yet a scholar must not submit to imagination, but leash it. If seidar lives in the Witterland Runestone, I will only extract it through steady study and rigorous application. True knowledge is a secret known to many, but understood by few.

- Commentary on the Witterland Runestone, by Alfjin the Scribe

Footsteps crunched. Pebbles cascaded down to the floor. Shadows danced along the walls.

Bjorn raised his head. His cell had long ago lost his attention. Little more than a crumbling hole in the ground, it had been decrepit even before the Harrowhall's desolation. The dirt floor, filmed with years of lazily scraped excrement, produced a miasma that hung rank in the stifling air. He was forced to breathe through his mouth just to endure it. The walls, formed of stone, had largely caved in so that the cell was exceedingly cramped. The only thing that appeared intact were the bars keeping him inside, and those barely held on.

Stuck in their moldering cage, all they could do was listen to the rumble of battle rise higher. Bjorn wondered if the rebels had seized the gate and admitted the army outside yet. He wondered if his friends were still alive.

Or if I left them to die.

Before the approaching visitors, Bjorn had to banish his doubts. He and Yonik had their own problems to solve.

"Ready yourself," the priest muttered as he stood. He had been placed in the same cell as Bjorn, for other prisoners filled the few intact cells. He appeared unbowed by their circumstances, enduring them with his usual tenacity. Bjorn wished he felt the same. All the same, he would endure and do what he must.

Two of their gaolers appeared before their cell. Bjorn slowly stood. Both were jotunmen, made fiercer by the fire-spawned shadows upon their faces.

"Come," the one bearing the torch snarled. "You see King of Chieftains."

His companion opened the cell with a worn iron key Bjorn recognized. Once, he had carried a ring of them for Lawspeaker Yaethun when visiting the dungeons. As the door swung open, the torchbearer strode off, while the second jotunman gripped Bjorn by the shoulder and shoved him forward.

Only two. Either their appearance failed to intimidate their captors, or their unexpected surrender made them believe they would not flee now. A safe assumption in this case, though a bold one.

Bjorn scrambled up the incline, then dusted himself off and looked around. Amid the ruins of the Harrowhall, placed here the Hall of Tapestries had once been, now rose the Jotun's colossal tent. The walls were formed from half-tanned hides sewn together and looked to be buttressed from beneath by beams and broken columns from the original construction.

"Move!" one of their guards grunted, shoving Bjorn forward.

Bjorn lowered his gaze and kept his eyes on his feet as he picked his way over the rubble. Step by step, they were herded toward the Jotun's tent. Something they had said seemed to have gained them an audience, after all.

Even as the prospect of standing before the giant filled him with dread, Bjorn drew up straight. This was his chance. He was not the man his brothers had been; not calculating and clever like Annar, nor brash and boisterous like Yof. He lacked the raw ambition and savagery of his father.

But he was a Son of Bor. The Bear's blood ran through his veins.

He held his head high as they walked the length of his family's desecrated halls. The dark stone alternated being brightened by smears of ash or darkened with scorch marks. Broken rock crunched beneath every footfall. Bjorn recalled the majesty of his home before all this happened, but had to push the memories away before melancholy sunk in its fangs.

They entered beneath the wide opening into the great tent, stepping between two leering jotunmen. He looked across the peoples gathered within, down the length of pebble-strewn stone, to the wooden throne erected next to the Oakstone. The petrified wood had melted and burned down to a shapeless lump, a shadow of its former glory.

His resolve quavered as he met the black eyes of the Jotun.

For all he had heard and thought of the giant, for all he had seen him in dreams, beholding Kuljash in the flesh still inspired awe and terror in equal measures. He looked far larger and savager even than he had in Bjorn's vivid imagination. Shaggy brown fur, tangled and matted, covered his face, arms, and chest. Tusks, yellowed and threaded through with minute fractures, extended from next to a wide mouth. He wore pieces of armor, but far from a full regalia, composed of pauldrons and lamellar of a black iron that had the shine of Harrowsteel. A skirt of barely cured pelts covered his upper legs, while his feet, as hairy and bulky as the rest of him, were bare as they rested on the rubble. Even seated, an elbow leaning on one arm of his great wooden platform, the giant was at least three times Bjorn's height, if not more.

Bjorn swallowed, then swallowed again, unable to rid his throat of the lump lodged in it. His bladder strained. His legs shook.

Remember your purpose, he told himself. *You are the Stoneseer, the One with the Farthest Sight. Your fate begins here.*

Only as jeers arose from the rest of the tent did Bjorn notice they were not alone with the Jotun and his men. Many of those in the audience appeared to be barbars. The eight standing nearest the dais were more ornately decorated than any Bjorn had seen before, with glittering jewelry of silver and uncut gems, and colorful headdresses and clothes. The chieftains who had joined Kuljash's war, he guessed.

Not all hailed from the mountains; more than a few of those gathered were Baegardian. Several he recognized as Vurg, both by the yellow in their clothes and their dark eyes and hair. One or two appeared to be Balturg, while one lone Thurdjur stood near Kuljash's feet. This man, he knew all too well.

As Bjorn's gaze fell upon Yaethun Brashurson, the former lawspeaker met it. He had never been cheery, but his expression was the dourest Bjorn had yet seen. Gone was the smug superiority, the brimming ambition. Now, he seemed a sad, old man, bent by all he had seen and done, his bright eyes dulled. Perhaps it was what he had brought his city to that bowed him so. Perhaps it was the betrayal of his son.

He should have hated his former mentor. Bjorn found he could only pity him.

Something closer to the Jotun drew his eye. Leaning beside the giant's massive chair was a stone Bjorn had spent countless hours thinking of since first encountering it in Heim Numen's library. Next to the Jotun, it seemed a small slab, though Bjorn knew it rose two and a half paces tall. In his vision, its runes had glowed red, but here and now, it seemed little more than ordinary stone. Still, as Bjorn gazed upon the Witterland Runestone, something moved in the recesses of his mind. Almost, it felt like the rattling of doors, all struggling to burst open.

Bjorn shifted his gaze back to his captor. While he had been taking in his surroundings, Kuljash had not blinked as he beheld him and Yonik. Bjorn found his back buckling under the weight of that gaze. He itched to speak, but scarcely knew where to begin.

Yonik stepped into the gap he left. Clearing his throat, he spoke with only the slightest tremble. "Chief Kuljash, you honor us—"

The gothi broke off with a gasp as the torchbearer backhanded him across the face. "The King of Chieftains speak first!" the barbar bellowed, spittle flying from his lips.

Yonik straightened and wiped a trickle of blood from his mouth, but gave no response. Bjorn pressed his own lips tightly together. It seemed all they could do was wait.

When Kuljash shifted, Bjorn flinched. Every movement reminded him of the strength within the giant's enormous body.

"Speak!"

The word boomed from the giant's mouth, guttural and garbled, but clear enough to understand. Bjorn looked at Yonik, and the priest nodded back at him. Blood trickled from his lips, which were curved in what was supposed to be a reassuring smile.

Bjorn sucked in a breath, faced forward, and met the Jotun's eyes.

"Thank you for the audience, King of Chieftains. I am Bjorn Borson, son of the jarl, Bor Kjellson. The Heir of Oakharrow."

The crowd jeered at the proclamation, but Bjorn did not cringe. It was not a wholly accurate declaration on several fronts, but Kuljash seemed to only respect power. He had to hope his position made at least some impact on the giant. Why else, after all, had they been brought before him?

"I have sought you out, Chief Kuljash, of my own free will," he said as the court quieted. "I submitted myself to your guards without violence. You must wonder why I would do this."

Bjorn paused to let the giant respond, but Kuljash showed no such inclination. As his captors grunted to either side and discontented muttering spread, he hurried on.

"I have seen a vision, King of Chieftains. A foretelling of the future by the most powerful seer of our age. In this vision" — he spoke louder as the crowd began mumbling again — "I was shown that an unexpected alliance must be forged. It is the path for my people's survival, and the path for Enea to come through the rising war. It is the only way you survive, Chief Kuljash."

Outrage spread like fire over spilled oil. Bjorn waited for a blow from the guard. Despite himself, his jaw trembled.

No attack came.

The giant shifted in his seat, and silence fell at once. All those at court seemed acutely attuned to the Jotun's moods. But before Kuljash could speak, hurried footsteps came closer from outside. Bjorn turned to see a barbar stumble in, streaked with sweat and his eyes wide.

"Thousand pardon, King Chief," the man babbled in accented Djurian. "North Gate is took! Army come now!"

The court erupted, first with confusion, then resolving into panic as the truth set in. Bjorn grimaced. He had known this was coming. His time was up too soon. Still, a part of him rejoiced. Oakharrow might soon belong to his people once again.

But at what cost?

The Jotun did not react for a long moment. Then he slammed his feet down and ascended to his full, towering height. The ground rumbled with his movements, and everyone present quailed before him. The giant's head nearly brushed the pavilion ceiling, dozens of feet high.

"Out!" the giant bellowed. "Out, all! No flames! Men, come!"

His court rushed to obey. Yonik pulled Bjorn to the side and out of the stampede's path as jotunmen pushed their way in. One man threw a torch into a bucket by the entrance to douse it, and other warriors around the tent rushed to do the same.

As the pavilion fell into darkness, Bjorn's skin crawled. Only his heightened vision allowed him to see vague impressions of what occurred. The jotunmen seemed to have better vision in the dark than he, for they moved swiftly and surely through the gloom.

Bjorn leaned close to Yonik. "Can you see what they're doing?"

"A little. They approach Kuljash. He has some sort of black iron bowl open before him. Each man dips his hand in, then puts it to his mouth. They shudder at whatever they taste. One is retching it back up."

"I can hear that." Bjorn's own stomach twisted at the sound, and he had to swallow bile back down.

"The others move to stand before the Witterland Runestone. Then they — Djur preserve us."

"What? What is it?"

But the tumult filling the pavilion gave him the answer. The men, not quiet before, were growing animalistic and furious. Raucous, uncontrolled laughter burst loose from some that rang with eerie familiarity. Figures streaked down the fur carpet and raced outside, gleaming eyes wide with ecstasy, teeth bared in bloodthirsty grins.

He knew the truth then. This was what the prophecy carved into the Witterland Runestone had meant. These were the Warriors of the Stone.

"Berserkers," Bjorn whispered. "He's made berserkers."

37. THE CROWN OR THE BLADE

*"Nothing makes a man come alive like spilling blood.
Even if it's his own."*
   *- Yofam Dragontooth, Slayer of the wyvern Vardraith,
First Drang of the Iron Band*

What's taking him so long?" Bastor breathed. "Always reckoned the man competent, but now..."

He had been muttering to himself, but Kare Lone-Ear, who stood a few feet away, took it upon himself to answer. "There's still time for Frey Igorson. Look, sire — they fight on the wall."

Bastor squinted toward the shrouded city. They stood half a league distant, far enough that in the low light, it was difficult to make out much of anything. Only the flickers of shadows against the torchlight told of movement atop the walls.

"Seems your old eyes are sharper than mine. What else do you see? Is that Djur-burned gate open yet?"

"The portcullis is raised. The gate — yes, the doors are opening."

"Then shite on the signal!"

All morose lethargy sloughed off. Bastor slapped at his armor, ensuring it was secure, then strode toward his horse.

"We fight!" he roared across the encampment. "Up in your saddles! Pull on your boots! It's about Djur-burned time!"

Drangi sprang into action, rallying the warriors under their command into the approximation of formations. Those who had horses leaped into the saddles and drew their weapons. Archers strung their bows and tightened the straps on their quivers. Artillerists hustled to hook up catapults to mules to haul them within range of the city. Others carefully handled the few iron barrels of firesand they had left, readying them for transport by cart.

Bastor slammed his helm onto his head, pulled the straps tight, and hauled himself onto Nott. Taking his shield in hand, he grinned toward the distant walls. He felt like a beast woken from its winter slumber, ravenous and revitalized. This was where he belonged — in the saddle, off to war. He was no pampered prince to be fawned over, no coward leader to command from the back. This was his fate, the length of his lifethread. He had been born to defy the Spinners, to spit in Ovvash's eye, to sneer at the sprites that would bear him to an early grave.

This was life, and he devoured it whole.

"With me!" he hollered, then took off down the hill.

Despite his urgency, Bastor kept his gelding to a trot, allowing Lone-Ear and the rest of his cavalry to catch up. A trot was also necessary for his horse's sake. In the darkness, it would be all too easy to break a leg.

Twisting around, he glimpsed by torchlight the three jarls trailing at the back. Ingvar looked at once thrilled and terrified. Asborn had better reign of his emotions, though his stiffness showed them plainly. Only Siward was relaxed in the saddle, though his frown left no doubts to what he thought about riding into battle once more.

Bastor turned back. He would spare no more thoughts for them. How the jarls carried themselves was their choice.

With his men at last formed up, Bastor coaxed Nott to a canter. A charge would break any initial resistance, then he could fight to Frey and the rebels within. The warriors on foot would come in afterward to hold and sweep the streets of any lingering enemies.

And if the giant is there, fighting with them?

It would likely spell a swift end for their cavalry if so. Yet Bastor had killed giants before. Jotunar would fall the same as surtunar.

With two hundred horsemen riding with him, Bastor pressed in his heels. His gelding flew down the slope. The distance was eaten by the steed's long stride, and the walls quickly neared. Bastor squinted against the wind's bite at the figures atop the wall. More seemed barbar than Baegardian, but the fighting carried on. The gate was fully open now, and the portcullis raised, just as Lone-Ear had said.

Bastor had his shield at the ready, but no arrows rained down on them even as they closed within a hundred paces of the gate. Nott surged up the slope to the road, then picked up speed again as they crossed the final distance to the city. Hooves pounded behind him, his warriors close on his heels. Enemies seethed on the other side, seeming to just be arriving at the battle. They filled the street for as far as he could see; hundreds of them, perhaps thousands. Bastor switched the reins to his shield hand and drew his axe with the other. Its polished edge, wide and sharp, gleamed with angry torchlight.

The walls rose around him, then above. The sharp ends

of the portcullis flashed overhead, then he was through the gate.

The enemy swarmed all around him. Bastor loosed a wild laugh.

His first stroke split a barbar's head in two. His fierce horse screamed and kicked through the men ahead of them. Weapons bristled and dipped toward them. A pained whinny told of sharp ends finding their way under Nott's armor. Bastor lashed around him, blade finding flesh wherever it dipped. Blood and mud spat into the air.

The mass of enemies was breaking apart, men fleeing for side streets to avoid being trampled or cut down, but there was still plenty more to fight through before he could turn back for another charge. Still, once the rest of the cavalry followed, the barbars would be swept away like nightsoil in a river. He just had to keep pressing forward.

A spear dipped toward him. Bastor tried chopping it out of the way, but it went too low. Nott loosed a pitiful nicker, then went down.

Bastor flew from the saddle. Crashing among barbars, he sent them sprawling as they cushioned his fall. Weapons clanged against his armor, but the finely wrought steel kept most at bay. Bastor barely felt the pain of those that found flesh. He rose, roaring and swinging.

"Shite on your mothers' graves!" he bellowed as he caved in a man's nose with the rim of his shield. "I liked that gods-damned horse!"

He cut down man after man, yet he was surrounded. Enemies with sharp weapons and killing eyes charged forward, and he barely rebuffed their attacks. All it would take was one well-aimed strike, and he would be through.

A torrent of horsemen broke through, sweeping away enemies beneath hooves and steel. They split around him and his fallen horse, making a small island amid the stampede.

"Yes!" Bastor cried as he met the attacks of the three foes remaining near him. These mountain men, too, were attempting to fall back, eyes wide and staring. Their defense had been broken; their spirits swiftly followed. All it would take was a final blow, and his forces would claim the day.

The rattling of metal and the screams of both horse and man put an end to that dream.

Bastor risked a glance back toward the gate. The portcullis had fallen on one of his mounted men, splattering gore under the gatehouse. The rest of the cavalry scattered from it, unable to get in.

The bulk of his army was shut out.

Curses sprang to his tongue, but movement from one of his opponents drew his attention back around. Bastor deflected and countered. A hand went flying. The man stumbled back, staring at the leaking stump his arm had become, mouth working. The other two exchanged glances. Neither made a move toward him.

Heaving in a breath, Bastor thought through his options. With the portcullis closed, the odds weighed heavily against him. Though the barbars feared his warriors, the handful of cavalry that had made it into the city would not be near enough to rout the sea of the Jotun's fighters. And the giant himself might yet show up.

The gatehouse! Get to the gods-damned gatehouse!

He wondered if the portcullis falling closed meant Frey was dead. But he could not worry about that now.

Bastor turned to break for the gatehouse. Before he had gone three steps, the pounding of feet spun him back around.

Bestial men charged up the road, axes and swords and

wickeder weapons in hand. They looked to have once been human, but some vile witchery had twisted them into snarling monsters fit for a child's nightmare. Hair as thick and twisted as fur spread down their arms, backs, and chests. What looked like overgrown teeth shot out from the corners of their mouths. Bastor stood well over six feet tall, but some of these men rose even higher, and with broader shoulders to match.

The two barbars he had been facing backed clear away. It seemed he was not the only one they feared.

With nowhere to go and nowhere to run, Bastor faced them. Some of his cavalry charged toward these newcomers, but four of the beast-men split off to make toward Bastor. They leered at him, bloodshot eyes full of thirst and madness.

"Come on!" Bastor banged his axe against his shield. Maybe they were stronger than him, with greater reach and numbers. Maybe he had little hope of victory. But he had always preferred to die to a blade than beneath the weight of a crown.

"Come on, then!"

38. FIRE WITH FIRE

A kingdom. My husband left me a kingdom. A burden I never wished to carry.

I have no more sons to aid me. A day does not pass without rebellion, small or large, or an incursion by our enemies.

I only wished to be queen, not king, as I am now in all but name. I do not wish to argue with jarls over taxes and wars and injustices. The corridors and kitchens of the Harrowhall were enough to content me, as was the care of my children, before the Spinners stole them away.

Yet duty does not follow desire. I will try to reign, Torvald. Try to keep our homeland from tearing itself apart. But with each day that passes, my love, I will curse your memory.

- The diary of Siva Of Torvald, Wife of King Torvald Geirson, Matron of the Harrowhall, the Last Queen of Baegard

Aelthena ground her teeth as she stared at the North Gate, watching Bastor and the other men ride down the hill to the city. Even carrying torches, they appeared dark blobs in the night. The camp was swiftly emptying as warriors on foot hustled after the cavalry.

All the men went to fight, while she, once more, waited before her tent.

At least this time, I don't stand alone. Loridi, Seskef, and Tyra stood close around her, the men assigned to be her protectors in Frey's absence. Their presence brought a measure of reassurance, but none knew if the night would be won or lost. Before that uncertainty, there could be little comfort.

In the time before the battle began, they had divulged their travels to her, as unbelievable a tale as it was. At length, they spoke of rune magic and her brother's mastery of it. Each word deepened Aelthena's fear. The entire story smacked of the madness Bjorn had shown before he had departed for the Teeth, even if the three before her did not seem to share it.

But her brother's sanity was not her highest concern just then. Those she cared for might already be dead. Half a league distant, all Aelthena could see was vague fighting by the gate. The Baegardian army still thronged outside the city walls. That could not be good; what reason could they have to remain without? If the North Gate remained open, they would be filtering inside quickly.

The thought gave her purpose. She set off with a long stride.

"M'lady?" Loridi spoke at her back. A glance showed him and the other two to be tailing her. "Ah, where might you be off to?"

"Something's wrong," she said without slowing. "I mean to find out what."

"How do you know?" Tyra's voice fell to a whisper. Aelthena wondered if it was from worry for Bjorn. If he had made it inside, it was possible he fought alongside the rebels.

"The men sit outside the walls when they should be inside them," she finally responded.

"The gate might be blocked," Seskef murmured. "Or closed."

Aelthena nodded. "You have mounts?"

"Yes, m'lady," Loridi answered.

"Good. Saddle them. We ride for the artillery line."

Loridi sputtered protests, but Seskef hushed him. Aelthena smiled. It was good that a man who called himself "Lord Sword," as he had informed her not long after introductions, had the sensible "Skiff" to keep watch over him. And Tyra, quiet though she was, had the touch for keeping both of them in line.

Where's the one to keep you in line?

But she did not need leashing. Something was wrong; of that, she was certain. She would not stand idly by while there was a chance of setting things right.

Though the grooms appeared baffled by her request, they recognized her and obeyed at once. Aelthena held her tongue while their horses were saddled, watching Clap, Bjorn's horse, dance with matching impatience. When at last they were ready, she mounted Winterlily, spread her riding dress over the white mare's back, and mouthed a silent prayer.

Protect them, Djur, Volkur, Skoll. Protect Frey, and Bastor, and my little brother.

"Come!" she called over her shoulder, setting Winterlily off at a trot.

297

Riding by moonlight, they ate the distance between them and the army amassed under Oakharrow's walls. As they neared, it became clear that pandemonium had erupted. Aelthena squinted into the darkness toward the gate. It could have been a trick of light, but she thought she saw something metallic gleaming where the open doors should have been.

The portcullis.

She understood at once. The gate had been opened enough for a charge, but the portcullis had shut before most of the men made it through. Judging by the number of those left behind, the few within would be chopped down along with the rebels who took the gate in a short order.

Fear squeezed her lungs as she rode toward the back lines of the siege. There, the catapults were lined up, looking to have only just been loaded. The artillerists seemed hesitant to release, perhaps heeding Bastor's prior orders to damage the city as little as possible.

Aelthena barely slowed her mount before sliding to the ground. The artillerists stared as she and her companions approached, no doubt wondering what a highborn lady was doing on the battlefield. She did not let that undermine her composure.

"What is happening?" she demanded of the closest warrior, a bald man with a braided mustache that hung past his chin.

The artillerist scratched at one fuzzy cheek, perhaps trying to decide if he should report to her or not. Under her glare, he swiftly made his choice.

"The prince led the charge inside, but the portcullis cut off most of the cavalry and left out the rest of the warriors. Reckon they're trapped in there with the enemy now."

Aelthena grimaced. Of course Bastor had led the charge; he had always been as reckless as a newborn pup.

Yet, complicated as the man was, he was her advocate and ally, and he was attempting to liberate her city. She had to at least try to help him.

"How long has it been?" she asked.

"A quarter-hour, no more."

Long enough. Aelthena looked across the artillery. What could help Bastor now? Her gaze settled on the wagon, set midway through the line, and the barrels stacked atop it.

"Dragonfire," she murmured, then spoke louder. "Dragonfire can save them. Ignite a load of firesand above the city, as you did before."

"Hold now, mistress. I reckon I ought to take my orders from a drang or jarl — or better yet, the prince himself."

Aelthena took a step closer, barely a foot from the man now. He did not rise high, and she found she looked down on him, if slightly. It was enough to steel her voice.

"The prince cannot give orders right now. Do you wish to be the one responsible for him perishing? Or would you rather save him?"

The man's hand twisted through his mustache as his eyes flickered up and down the line. Apparently, their drang was nowhere to be seen, and Asborn, Ingvar, and Siward had gone with the charge. The artillerist grimaced.

"Mistress, if you can find a jarl who—"

Aelthena turned away, her patience spent. "Loridi! Seskef!"

"M'lady?" The men stiffened at her tone.

"Please help this artillerist load a barrel of firesand. Clearly, he does not understand his duties."

"Here, now," the man growled.

Aelthena turned back to see his hand had fallen to his seax. Up and down the line, the artillerists tensed. Some reached for weapons, but none yet drew.

Loridi and Seskef stood at her shoulders, neither

299

backing away. A part of her quailed at the threat of violence, memories of previous fights for survival flitting through her mind. But the doubts were small enough to quash.

She forced a smile. "Either you shoot that firesand, or I will. Which would you prefer to tell Prince Bastor you chose once we rescue him?"

The artillerist's eyes flickered between her and the men at her back. With a snarl, he pulled his hand away from his weapon and turned.

"Ove! Kensley! Change out your load — we're giving 'em a show!"

39. LAID BARE

"Every warrior knows one thing: the face of death scours you clean, strips you down to the man you truly are."

- Highlord Carr Gunnarson, Fifth Arkjarl of Baegard

Egil cut down another barbar and stumbled back against the door.

His enemies crowded the wall ahead, yet they hesitated, giving him a moment to breathe. The bodies of their brethren littered the stones before and behind them. Egil had fought with other rebels at the start, but one by one, the barbars had killed them as the reinforcements became too many.

Now he stood alone, his back to the barred guardhouse door.

He bared his teeth at the barbars, buying a moment more. His sword felt as heavy as an anvil. Any grace had long since been replaced by sluggish lurches, like those of a boy new to the yard.

But Egil had always known when and where to strike. His training had not yet failed him.

He would die here, rich in battle-glory. He had felled a dozen enemies and aimed to kill a dozen more. His ancestors would welcome him to their mead halls with cheers and claps on the back. He would be a hero. Valor lay not in success, but in daring to reach for it.

This was the end he had been destined for. He had sought it when he went east into the Teeth. He yearned to prove his mettle, to earn a name beyond Egil Yaethunson, a reputation beyond the scion of a treacherous, wheedling man, born of a line too weak to shoulder the Winter Mantle.

Now, however, as death reared ahead, a part of him wished for a different fate. He remembered Bjorn and their late camaraderie. Remembered the flush stirring through him when he gazed into his amber eyes.

He did not want to die anymore. But it did not look like he had another choice.

Prince Bastor's army was stuck outside the wall. The prince himself, if Egil guessed his identity correctly, was surrounded in the street below, his lifethread to be snipped as soon as Egil's. Frey must have stormed the guardhouse and opened the gate, but it had not been long afterward that the portcullis fell shut. The guardian, too, was likely dead, and unable to open the door at his back.

The rebellion had been squashed, the invasion repelled. All that remained within his grasp was a glorious last stand.

The barbars found their courage again. A pair stepped over the bodies of the fallen, edging closer. One stumbled, his foot catching on a limb.

Egil burst forward. Stabbing forth with his hand-and-a-half blade, he nicked the clumsy man on the throat before pivoting and parrying the thrust from his comrade. The first barbar stumbled back, eyes wide, a hand clutched to his bloody throat. His feet tangled with another body, and he went down hard.

The second barbar bellowed at his comrade's fall. Pressing the shaft of his axe against Egil's sword, the man brought his shield up to slam it into his side. Pain split up his ribs as Egil banged against the door.

Focusing through it, he slid his blade free of the axe, sidestepped the inevitable blow, and brought his sword back around. It clanged against the man's upraised shield before he dipped it under, scoring his leg. The man's balance lurched, and his follow-up strike went wild. Even weary, Egil easily dodged the blow and slashed at his exposed side.

The barbar, hampered by two wounds, tottered back, but two more already stepped around him. Egil did not dare pause. To leave room for thought would allow despair to seep in. He would not yield. He would fight and kill for as long as he stood.

Then the world burst into flames.

Next that he knew, Egil was on his knees. His ears rung as if giant hands had clapped over his head. His vision had gone blurry, but already, it grew steadier. Shaking his head, he stumbled to his feet and leaned back against the guard-house door. With eyes dotted with black stars, he saw the barbars staggering about in much the same state. Sucking in a breath, he coughed on a mouthful of smoke and ash that had a fouler taste underlying them.

Rotten eggs.

A memory filled his mind. Steam had filled the hut, reeking of that same stench. Bjorn's face loomed from it, like a moon illuminated by the banked fire. The runestone lay in his hand, the lines upon it writhing like a tangle of worms.

Egil narrowed his eyes. Instead of the vision coming into focus, another replaced it. Now, it was as if he stood within the Jotun's hall again, as he had many times while by his father's side, staring toward the giant upon his makeshift chair. Only his gaze was not drawn to Kuljash, but to the weathered slab leaning next to him.

The Witterland Runestone.

For a moment, its face glowed bright, each rune outlined in red. Then a door appeared before his eyes.

The Hall of Doors. Egil remembered Bjorn speaking of this place. He had not been able to see it before. Now, of all times, it seemed it had finally come.

He reached for the door. In that place, he had no body, yet his will made the heavy wood shudder. The rune etched into its face burned red. Fear, sharp with unfamiliarity, threaded through him as he imagined what lay beyond.

But the Spinners had all but cut his thread. No worse fate could await him there.

Egil wrenched the door open.

The world reappeared, cast in bright pinks and dark scarlets. His body felt light, agile, strong. Doubt and exhaustion melted away. Pain was replaced by the swell of power.

He was a creature beyond humanity now: immortal, implacable. Death stalking the shadows.

The barbars before him backed away. Their eyes shone with knowledge of what he had become. He was Djur's cloak sweeping across the sky, the falling darkness. Inevitable as the world's end.

In silence, Egil raised his sword and started forward.

40. FRIENDS & FOES

"War makes meaningless the words 'friends' and 'enemies'.
All that remains is who fights by you, and who against."

- Lion Teos, leader of the failed Second Yeshept Uprising

Frey parried the blow with a final burst of strength.

A dozen wounds bled across his body. Agony was his reality now. His buoyant spirit, which had borne him through many harrowing times, had finally deflated.

The men before him closed in, leering with killing intent. He was outnumbered, outlasted. He would not survive another assault.

After he and Vedgif had opened the North Gate, the battle had seemed all but won. But it was not long before barbars broke down one of the doors. Frey and the elder had fought hard to defend the winches, but with only two of them, and one of them aged and the other injured, they were soon driven back. Frey had watched a man strike the latch and drop the portcullis, helpless to stop it. He had listened to the ghastly screams of men and horses dying below.

Though the fight looked lost and their enemy endless, still, they fought on. Frey had managed to put down two of his opponents, more from being underestimated as an invalid than from any prowess of his own. But the barbar he faced now was more patient, content to let Frey wear himself out by blocking his attacks. Two more, one of them a massive bestial man, worked at the gate's winch. Soon it would be closed, extinguishing any chance of rescue.

He would die here in this guardhouse, he knew now. He would never see Aelthena or his kin again.

Then the tower grew bright, and the stones trembled.

As the floor shook him off balance, Frey fell against the wall behind him, sending another flare of pain up from his broken arm. A whimper broke free that he was too damn tired to bite back.

Staggering upright, he squinted at his enemies. By the flash of light from without, he could tell dragonfire once more filled the sky. He wondered where its embers would fall, if they would melt this tower as they had the Harrowhall.

But it did not matter. Death loomed around him, be it from flames, fists, or steel.

The ever-stubborn Vedgif recovered before Frey did. Rising, he swung his sword and kept his two foes at bay. Another rose before Frey, a hatchet clutched in each hand and blood between his teeth. If it was the man's own or another's, Frey did not know, nor did he much care. It was just a matter of time before one of those hatchets found a home in his skull.

The moment's distraction cost Frey. As the barbar lazily struck, Frey barely managed to block. The follow-up blow nicked his good arm. Once, the pain might have fueled on his determination, but now it drowned it. Frey gasped, leaned back against the wall, and prayed the man would give him a moment to breathe.

But the gods had abandoned him all that day. They would not listen now.

The din echoing in through the open door grew louder. A hope for rescue? No — he knew better than to expect that. The dragonfire had not hit the gate; he would have felt if it had and likely died for the close audience. More likely, barbars were competing for the pleasure of chopping him and the elder into pieces. He could almost picture it: all of them sitting at a long festival table, Frey and Vedgif's bodies dismembered, pink red muscle hanging from white bones. He would not put it past the bastards to enjoy human flesh.

The barbar's axes fell again. Frey threw his sword up in a desperate parry. Yet even with his focus on staying alive, he saw from the corner of his eye the warrior at the opposite door fly back, a spear sticking from his middle.

At his comrade's dying cry, the axe-wielding barbar left off the attack and turned. A figure ducked through the door-way, a woman as large as any Frey had seen. Her hair was the color of fresh flames, and her smile was pink with blood. Her armor, covering her from neck to feet, was dented, scuffed, and filthy with gore. She seemed like Volkur herself, descended to play at war among mere mortals.

"Good," the shieldmaiden declared as she pried the spear from the limp barbar. "I needed a few more to kill."

Frey's foe howled and charged at the warrioress, and both men at the winch joined him. She showed no fear as she whipped the spear around. It moved in a blur as she cut one, knocked another, and skewered the third in the leg. As the spear was wrenched from her grasp, she drew axe and seax from her belt and met the attacks from the two men who still stood. The third, the axe-wielder Frey had fought, cursed and retreated, staring at the length of wood erupting from his thigh.

Frey slumped down the wall and watched the flame-haired fighter kill one barbar, then the other. Drenched in their blood, she grinned and stalked toward the man on the ground. He had not pulled the spear out, perhaps fearing the pain, so she was able to grasp the length of wood from safely out of striking range.

"Here," the shieldmaiden cooed. "Let me help."

She jerked the spear free. The man screamed, a mewling, pitiful sound. The warrioress put a swift end to it as she plunged the spear into his chest.

Frey flinched as the woman's gaze found him. Tilting her head, the shieldmaiden studied him. Her braids, wet with sweat and blood, swayed to one side. She seemed unimpressed by what she saw, for a moment later she shrugged, she pulled her spear free, and turned toward Vedgif and his opponents. The elder had received several wounds and sagged against the wall, but his determination had not broken, nor had his shield dipped.

Would she kill Vedgif as well as the barbars? By her look and accent, she was Balturg, though she was savage enough to be from the mountains. Even if she did hail from Oakharrow, too many Baegardians had betrayed the jarlheims to be certain of any loyalty.

Better fight on, then.

Frey struggled to his feet. The effort was almost beyond him, but the brief rest had returned a little strength to his limbs. His splintered arm howled as movement rekindled the pain. Frey gasped and tried blinking away the stars in his eyes.

When his vision cleared, Frey discovered a second woman stood in the doorway, staring at him. She, too, wore armor as if born to it. Her hair was raven-dark, as were her eyes; a Vurg, plainly. Though tall for a woman, she stood no higher than Frey. He found little reassurance in it, for her spear and shield were both painted dark from recent combat.

A sudden suspicion filled him. He croaked out what he thought to be her name.

"Edda Skarldaughter." Frey tried to muster a friendly smile, but all he could manage was a grimace.

The woman pursed her lips. "Leave this one alive, too, Bodil. I suspect he'll look fine when he's washed off and patched up."

They were reassuring words, on the whole. Still, Frey wasn't sure he liked the implications.

He cleared his throat. "The portcullis and the gate — we must raise them."

"So we will." The Vurg leader raised a generous eyebrow. "Or are you telling me to do it alone?"

"Not alone, Lord Edda." The red-haired warrioress, Bodil, had finished helping Vedgif dispatch the remaining barbars and strode toward the Vurg leader. "I will help."

"Then we'll take the portcullis. You two, on the gate."

Frey exchanged a wearied look with Vedgif, but there was little else to be done. Staggering across the guardhouse, he looped an arm around a spindle and hauled on the winch.

41. A GOOD DEATH

"The honorable warrior does not hope to live, for that way lies cowardice. All he looks for is a good death."

- Yofam Dragontooth, Slayer of the wyvern Vardraith, First Drang of the Iron Band

The beast-men roared, and Bastor bellowed back as he took the first swing.

His axe sliced through the air in as mighty a blow as he'd ever summoned. Yet as it met a spiked cudgel, it stopped short, for the man — if he could still be called a man — proved the stronger.

The malformed barbar shoved back the axe and kicked forward. A hastily raised shield kept his ribs intact for the moment, but Bastor was hard-pressed as the other beast-men struck. An axe chopped into his shield, taking off a sizable chunk. A third smashed iron-shod fists against it, cracking the wood and sending pain rippling up his shoulder.

The last barbar could not be blocked, only avoided. The

largest among them, he swung a long-handled hammer with a steel head that had to weigh two stones. Bastor danced back from the first blow and deflected the backswing by knocking its haft.

By all rights, facing stronger and quicker opponents, he should have already been dead. But the beast-men, equally eager to spill his blood, kept getting in one another's way. The one with the spiked cudgel and shield snarled as the man wearing iron gauntlets tripped him. Another with tusks that twisted in front of his mouth and carrying an axe and a seax hissed at the large one with the warhammer as he stepped to the front.

Coordinated, it would take but a single charge to take Bastor down. Their chaos he could use to his advantage.

Going low, he hit the elephantine hammer up and away from him and hooked his axe around the brute's ankle. A mistake — though he tried tugging his leg out, the blade cutting into his skin, the enormous man did not so much as budge.

A grunt was his only warning.

The hammer shaft crashed onto Bastor's back. Only his armor prevented him from suffering more than a bruise.

Retreating, Bastor barely raised his shield in time as two iron gauntlets hurtled toward him. This beast-man moved with a limp, yet he was just as quick and brawny as his comrades. Bastor's shield cracked again, worryingly so. He doubted it could take many more hits.

He struck around his shield with his axe, but his blade stuck. Too late, he saw why, as the beast-man caught it in one impervious hand and yanked it away. The brute grinned as he tossed the weapon aside, then made a grab. Bastor struck with his shield, the boss knocking into his foe's chest. An ordinary man's chest would have caved in; this beast merely let out a pained grunt.

It did not stop the beast-man from grabbing Bastor with both hands, dragging him in close, and slamming his forehead forward.

Bastor reeled. His back met hard earth. The world pitched violently around him. Blinking through sweat and blood streaming down from beneath his helmet, he raised his shield and tried reorienting himself. The beast-man was already on him again, one hand yanking aside his shield, the other pounding on his ribs. Even through armor, the blow felt as if it cracked bone.

The sky erupted with fire and light.

Already on the ground, Bastor braced himself as a fiery wind pummeled down. *Dragonfire.* A catapult must have sent a load flying as a distraction. With a silent thanks to that enterprising artillerist, he surged back to his feet. The battle-maddened beast-men had devolved into confusion, brawling with each other instead of attacking him. Bastor lunged for his axe and struck one with his back turned to him. The blade bit in deep, just shy of the spine.

The brute howled and spun, his shield leading. Bastor threw himself to one side and came back to his feet as the barbar bore down on him. Every breath was laced with sulfuric smoke now, its haze spreading across the city. His vision spun as if he had spent the night drinking.

Bastor blocked the cudgel once, twice. The shield trembled, close to breaking, and his arm screamed under each impact. Moving to the offensive, he swung his axe and struck two quick blows, but neither injury slowed his opponent. The barbar kicked under his shield, and Bastor's leg folded under the blow, sending him to one knee.

The brute loomed over him. Bastor knew he should have felt fear. But a fresh feeling rose within him, one muted by the overwhelming odds. Rage, an ever-burning coal, burst back into flame, spreading through his limbs and dampening his pain and terror.

The cudgel smashed down. Bastor's shield splintered apart.

He rose all the same.

Bastor struck at the barbar's head once, twice, thrice with what remained of his shield, little more than the steel boss and lingering splinters. The beast-man stumbled back, face a bloody ruin. Bastor didn't relent, chopping now with his axe. The blade bit into flesh, again and again, until it found his opponent's neck.

The brute sank to his knees, eyes vague, blinking slowly. A hand pressed to the blood welling out of his neck. At last, his mind caught up with his body, and he collapsed.

Bastor laughed, the sound shrill and wild to his ears. He held up his ruined shield and bloody axe as the other beast-men finally broke off their struggles to face him. There was no fear in their eyes, but a wariness had grown. They knew now he was as much a predator as they were.

The world had turned pink. A pall cast by the dragon-fire? Bastor scarcely cared.

With a roar, he charged. The warhammer swung; he dodged. The gauntlets punched; he took the hits with a grin. His axe and boss met seax and axe, but he slammed his helmeted head into the bluff chin. The beast-man wielding the weapons kneed him in the gut, but Bastor felt nothing from it.

Something sent him flying to the ground.

The hammer. Bastor struggled to rise, demanded it of his body. Slowly, it complied.

Too slowly.

He barely saw the gauntlet before the beast-man bashed in his face. Black dotting his vision, Bastor swung his axe, but the haft hit on something before the edge could find its mark. A second blow, then a third. His helmet only covered so much, and it could not save him from this.

A good death.

It was all he could have hoped for, all he could have gained. Fury ebbed, and pain crawled back in to claim him. He closed his eyes. A blow erupted into his side, shattering bone.

The end was coming,

Then came a yell: the yell of a man. Squinting through swollen eyes, Bastor saw one of his men strike at a beast-man and throw up his shield against another. Kare Lone-Ear — his stubborn drang was trying to save him.

The beast-man with the axe struck Lone-Ear once in the leg, then dug his seax into his shoulder. The veteran traded him the blow, burying his sword in his belly, but he was already sinking to his knees.

Bastor wished he had been a less loyal man. For his bravery, his only reward would be death.

Soar with the sprites, my friend.

Witnessing the drang's last stand awoke a last surge of resolve. Taking advantage of his gauntleted opponent's distraction, Bastor heaved himself up and chopped at him. The beast-man reacted too slowly. His iron gloves clattered and fell away from the haft of the axe, the head lodged in his belly. He collapsed, eyes wide with misbelief.

Strength fleeing, Bastor sank back to his knees. Only a shadow falling over him compelled him to raise his head. The largest of the beast-men stood over him, his warhammer raised, metal head glittering in the firelight.

Bastor watched it. He would meet his death with open eyes. Ovvash's embrace would welcome him like an old friend, and he would step into it gladly.

The ground shook.

The brute looked up, hammer hesitating. Then, with a high shriek, he ran the other way.

Hooves pounded the cobblestones all about him. Bastor watched as silhouetted horsemen formed a ring around where he had fallen. Men dismounted to kneel by his body, shouting words he could not make out. Still, he knew these were his soldiers, come to save their prince.

Somehow, he did not welcome the rescue. An acute disappointment wended through his heavy limbs. A sigh hissed out through his tortured lips. He had thought it was all over — the striving, the killing, the pain. He had thought he had done his part and could finally be at peace.

Instead, once more, he endured.

Bastor closed his eyes and collapsed onto his side, mercy shushing him to silence.

42. THE SECOND BATTLE

Battles are fought on two planes: one of flesh, and one of strategy. To win a war, you must triumph in both.
  - Sieging the Winter Holds, by Paser Baka, chief general to Holy Karah Khufu

Bjorn smiled as he watched the North Gate, far below, be overrun by the invading army.

He and the rest of the Jotun's party had paused atop the Dawnshadow to witness this final blow. Not long after the jotunman berserkers had torn from the giant's hall, Kuljash had given orders to evacuate. It was as if, even as he sent his men out to fight, he knew the battle was lost.

Maybe he did know. With the giant's knowledge of *seidar*, none could say what Kuljash did or did not know, Bjorn least of all.

He watched the cavalry pour through the streets, running down barbars or scattering them into side alleys. Though it was difficult to distinguish one person from another, Bjorn knew those on horseback were Baegardian, and the riders were clearly part of the victors.

It seemed a strange echo that he should watch Oakharrow be liberated from the same vantage point he had watched the Harrowhall burn. Perhaps he should not celebrate the victory, yet he could not help it. Though it endangered his task, a task with ramifications for all of Enea, a deeper part of him still rejoiced.

His home was retaken. Oakharrow was freed from tyranny. His sister could rule once more.

Officially, she was no longer the jarl's heir, nor was he. But Aelthena had never been one to take a blow lying down. One way or another, she would find her way back to the Winter Mantle. She would become the jarl, as she always should have. Even Annar would have had difficulty competing with her, in Bjorn's estimation.

The Jotun roared, and all thoughts fled before it.

It was like the snarl of a greatbear, only deafeningly loud, shaking his skeleton like a barbar bonewoman rattling her cup of knuckles. Bjorn covered his ears, fearing he would go deaf so near the din. Beside him, Yonik did the same.

As the ululation ended, Bjorn looked up at the giant. He had wondered why the Jotun did not challenge the Baegardian warriors at first. Once he saw Kuljash's reaction to Nuvvog's Breath, he wondered no longer. Though it seemed impossible for such a creature to feel fear, Bjorn would have sworn it was terror that passed over that craggy face as flames filled the sky.

Kuljash stared toward the North Gate, and Bjorn followed his gaze. Situated high above, they could see down into the city. Signs of resistance looked to be few and far between. The battle was all but won, and his captor knew it.

What comes next? Not even the King of Ice had known, at least from what Bjorn had seen thus far. He had to figure out the rest for himself.

The giant looked down at Bjorn. Like a shirt on a splinter, his black-eyed gaze snagged him. Those eyes were fathomless, like staring into a lightless winter cave, never knowing what creatures might lie within its depths. The mammoth creature curled his lips, somewhere between a beast's grimace and a man's smile.

"Come," Kuljash growled, the word rumbling in Bjorn's chest.

Turning, the giant walked away, the earth trembling with each step. The jotunmen and barbar chieftains that accompanied them, no more than five hundred in total, parted before their leader, moving aside the laden wagons that contained all they carried from Oakharrow: plundered riches, poor possessions, barrels which could only be filled with *khnuum*, and the Witterland Runestone. None looked hopeful about their future prospects.

Into the Teeth as winter sets in. Despite fear still shivering through him, Bjorn cast Yonik a bemused look. Back to the mountains they went, to where this entire venture began.

The priest seemed less amused. His generous brow was creased, his lips lost amidst the bush of his beard.

A jotunman shoved Bjorn, causing him to stumble forward. His and Yonik's hands were bound, giving no illusion to their status among the group. Yet he kept his head high as they marched up the slope.

He trod destiny's path now. He would see it to its end. Perhaps prophets could make mistakes, but he was not wrong in this. He had seen what needed doing, and he meant to do it.

This task took a scholar's courage to accomplish, and that was one kind of bravery Bjorn had always had in ample supply.

43. LOVE & LOSS

ᚾ

Many nights, as I lie awake in my cold bed, I wonder what I could have done to save my sons. If the right words would have stopped them from marching off to war. If the smallest action might have preserved them.

I torture myself without relent, without intent, even as I know the truth. The strength of a mother's love is only surpassed by a son's pride.

- The diary of Siva Of Torvald, Wife of King Torvald Geirson, Matron of the Harrowhall, the Last Queen of Baegard

She said she would spare me. She said she would..."

Gertrud cradled her son's head against her bosom, her heart splintering a little more, even though it felt as if it could break no further. She had not held him like this since he was nine, embracing him without worrying what the world would think.

Ragnar had not protested as she gathered him close. He was beyond caring what the Sypten guards outside their cage thought of him, beyond any shame of being observed by the populace streaming around their post in what had once been the central green of Ragnarsglade.

His people had been enslaved. Those who resisted among his men, like the brave drang in the manor, had been put to the sword. The deceitful karah, that crippled snake who lied from behind her grotesque mask, had tricked him.

Of course, her son sobbed. He had every reason to weep. He needed her now as he never had before. Gertrud meant to be there for him until the very end.

"Hush, my son, hush... We will join the gods soon."

He had mocked and decried her placations to start. Now, she hoped they brought him the comfort they did her.

Ragnar lifted his head, eyes red-rimmed and bloodshot. "I'm sorry, Mother. Sorry for it all. You're the only one who's loved me, you know that? And I never showed it back. Father... he never loved me, never loved anyone. Damn him! He gives me his name, but I don't want it. I don't want any of it. Better I die than inherit his legacy!"

She tried to quiet him again with soothing words, but he only ranted on.

"Do you know what he did? Know all the crimes he's committed? He sold Oakharrow to that giant from the north, the Jotun. He bargained with the rest of Baegard with Ha-Sypt, then went back once he had what he wanted. I tried telling him not to, but when did he listen to me? Did he ever listen?"

Fresh tears spilled down his face for a time. As he quieted and went limp, she mulled over his accusations. Of course, his father was capable of it all. She had never been under any delusions about who he was. But great men made great decisions, be they for evil or good. Could she regret bearing his son when it had brought Young Ragnar so much opportunity?

Yet here, in the end, the gods had passed their judgment. She was a servant who had climbed too high. Her son would pay for her hubris as much as his father's.

At least the Inscribed had not abandoned her, as she feared they would. She felt them crowding nearer with each passing minute. When she closed her eyes, their breath fell on her cheeks: one side warm, the other cool. As her hands smoothed back her son's hair, the shiver of scales appeared beneath her palm instead, or the brush of matted fur.

Some doubted the existence of the gods, or believed them too mighty to concern themselves with mortal affairs. Gertrud knew better. And here, in the hours before she joined them, her faith received its proof.

I am ready, she prayed as she looked up at the sky through the bars. *Take me. Take my son. We are ready to join you.*

Like other young men, Ragnar had likely always dreamed of joining the sprites of fire and air, where warriors ascended to their eternal halls of valor to drink and fight for eternity. But if the spirits of earth and ice took them both, it seemed a better fate to Gertrud. She would never be separated from her son again. They would be together under Ovvash's care. Her heart would be full, and his vices of smoke, women, and drink would go unfulfilled.

I am ready. Take me home.

A key jangled in a lock.

Gertrud opened her eyes to the cage door swinging open. Ragnar still lay across her. A semblance of pride must have returned to him, for he sat upright as the guards entered and snarled at their captors. If only he were given a sword, he could prove himself worthy of ascension. But that was not to be. These savages from the south would rob him of his proper death, to be buried like a woman or child.

Gertrud was roughly lifted as well. Once they were unshackled from the bars, she and Ragnar shuffled from the cage. Daylight knifed into her eyes. After spending all the long day under its touch, her skin had become reddened and tender, and her head pounded. Still, as her gods pressed close, her chapped lips curled upward.

I am ready.

"Mother... they mean to burn us. Burn us alive."

She opened her eyes. Her stumbling feet had borne her to the plaza before Lynx Manor. There, wood was stacked in two great piles, harvested from the ruins of the surrounding city. Pillars rose from amid the pyramids, rope coiled around their bases.

Gertrud closed her eyes again. So Nuvvog meant to claim them. It was just as well. The Trickster God had pulled a foul antic on them, his breath having helped the southerners in taking their city. Yet any god's attention was better than their absence.

"Release me, damn you! I won't go up there! You'll have to kill me first!"

Alarm roused her back to awareness. Gertrud watched in horror as Ragnar struggled against his guards. One punched him in the stomach, doubling him over. Another knocked him across the face.

"Stop! Don't hurt him!" she screeched. Death was one thing, prolonging the torture of life quite another. Unable to stand it, she wriggled, hoping to escape and aid him.

A slap sent her reeling, an angry Sypten word following it. Its intention was plain even without knowing the meaning.

Her vision swimming, Gertrud raised her head and saw her son had ceased to fight. A sword rested against his neck.

Even now, he feared death too much to throw himself upon it.

After several moments, the guard removed the blade, and his companions shoved Ragnar onto the first pyre.

Gertrud resigned herself to being hauled up the second stack of wood. The guards flanking her cursed as they slipped on the timber, its surface slippery with oil. Eventually, all three made it to the top. Turning her around, they pressed her back to the pillar, then wound the rope painfully tight about her. Gertrud paid it little heed. Her gaze lingered on her son, who was being similarly bound.

Ragnar's head fell her way. One eye had swollen shut, yet it was the despair writ across his face that struck her deepest. She mustered a smile, hoping to reassure him, even when she knew it could do no good.

He will die here; both of us will. Die upon the ruins of our home.

When they were both secured to their poles, she looked to the torchbearers standing at the edges of the pyres, waiting for them to end this agony. Instead, a middle-aged woman stepped forward. Her brilliant golden robe with a white sun emblazoned upon it marked her as a priestess. The woman turned her back on the condemned and began to speak.

As she went on in the Sypten tongue, Gertrud raised her gaze to where the woman faced. Consumed by her son's plight, she had scarcely noticed the giantess and the Sypten ruler atop the scaffolding. Resplendent as the queen was in black and red, the figure towering overhead was more awe-inspiring still. Gertrud had glimpsed the giantess from afar, both from the manor and her cage, but only then did she understand just how domineering Oyaoan was. Her legs would have buckled had the ropes not held her upright.

The priestess finished her speech and turned back to

the pyres. Her dark eyes rested on Gertrud for a moment, then she held up her hands toward Ragnar. Gertrud's pulse went faster still as the torchbearers advanced on her son.

"No, no, *no*! Don't make me watch him burn! Please, *please*, spare him—"

A guard barked something at her. Fearing to bring further pain to Ragnar, Gertrud bit her lip until she tasted blood and held back her pleading. She looked back to the giantess, but Oyaoan appeared riveted upon her son. Her expression was too strange and unfamiliar to truly know what she thought, but she could not imagine it as anything but hateful.

The karah's gaze drew her eyes down. Wearing the blended mask of a black beetle and a red elephant, her face was also difficult to read. Yet she was human and a woman. Gertrud thought she saw a softness there: regret, though perhaps that went too far.

Her gaze went back to her son. Her reticence only lasted until the first torch dipped to light the oil-soaked wood.

"Mercy, Queen, mercy!" Gertrud screeched at the Sypten monarch. She knew no mercy lay in the giantess's heart; this duplicitous woman was her only chance. "Please, pity him! Have you no pity in your heart? Do you not know he is valuable to you? He could be ransomed to his father — his father is the king now, King Ragnar. Or he could tell you of Baegard, things you cannot know! He will give you anything, anything, only spare his life!"

She never saw the blow. Gertrud slumped in her bonds, head throbbing from where the guard had hit her. "Mercy," she whispered.

The crackle of flames brought her back to life once more.

"Ragnar!" She screamed his name across the gap

between them. Orange tongues lapped at the pyre, at his feet. "Ragnar!"

Her son shrieked as well. "Mother!" He squirmed to escape the heat. "Mother, please!"

"Ragnar! I'm sorry, I'm so—"

A sob choked her throat as the flames reached his legs. She wished she could die then. Wished the guard would finish her before she had to witness her son burning alive. Before she burned herself.

"*Ragnar!*"

Another blow came, then merciful darkness claimed her.

44. RISE

"No more can we wait for the proper moment; they have oppressed us for too long. We must rise, lest doubt crush our courage."

- Lion Teos, leader of the failed Second Yeshept Uprising

Sehdra stood and spoke with every scrap of authority she had left.

"*Halt!*"

The torchbearers paused, halfway bent to touch their brands to the second pyre, and looked up at her. Everyone faced her now. The young man's screams had already ceased, so his blackened corpse failed to claim any attention before this unexpected development.

"Divine One," Teti whispered in her ear, "please do not!"

Sehdra ignored him. Her twisted leg twinged. Her cursed flesh flushed hot beneath the royal mask. Worst of all to bear was the weighty gaze of Oyaoan. The space between her shoulders itched, expecting a massive hand to fall and squash her, just as the giantess had her brother.

Yet she stood firm. In this moment, she had to stand. She knew Oyaoan's secret. It gave her enough strength in this moment to defy her.

"Douse your torches," Sehdra told the men at the pyre, then looked at the guard who had knocked the woman unconscious. "You. Cut her down."

Muttering arose from the soldiers and Suncoasters, who had gathered to watch their enemies burn. The stink of flesh and oil still filled the air as the king's late son burned to a skeleton. Her throat itched from breathing in the foul smoke. The heat from the pyre billowed out on the crisp day to waft against Sehdra's skin, a reminder that she herself walked through fire.

The chanter to Hua, who had presided over the executions, shuffled closer, brow creased and hands wringing like she strangled an invisible cat. "Divine One, I pray I do not speak out of turn. But is the mother not guilty of the sins of the son?"

Sehdra imagined herself as White Aya with a cobra's flat gaze as she stared down the chanter. "I have heard it said children bear the sins of their parents, not the other way around. What is more, Chanter Iset, this woman can be of use to us. She has lived in the king's manor, shared his bed. She knows his ways, his lands, his secrets. Gertrud, paramour of Ragnar Torbenson, is a valuable tool. Just as a farmer would be foolish to throw away a sharp scythe, so would I be to toss her aside."

The priestess's eyes flickered up to the giantess, whose shadow fell across the scaffolding. Sehdra resisted the urge to see if, even now, death fell upon her. When no one shifted, Iset bowed deeply, then shuffled aside, her expression as dour as before.

Sehdra looked back at the guard, who had set foot on the pyre, but still hesitated. As her eyes fell on him, the man sprang to obey. In moments, his knife had freed the sense-less woman, and he caught her before she tumbled to the wood.

"Bring her to my quarters and instruct my servants to care for her. Should she wake before I return, tell her we will speak, and that she is to rest easy until then." Sehdra pursed her lips. The woman's son had just died. How could she rest easy ever again? "If she is overly distressed, have my healer administer to her a tonic for rest."

The guard bowed his head, and a torchbearer, having extinguished his flame, helped him move the limp woman off the plaza.

The drama seeming at an end, the gathered dispersed with many furtive glances and bowed heads. Sehdra watched them leave, doing her best to ignore Teti's fear and disapproval all but radiating from behind her shoulder.

The Ibis sidled into view, his smile even more predatory than usual. "How magnanimous of you, Divine One, to spare the unworthy woman's life. Surely, such benevolence is becoming of you."

The itching feeling expanded across her back. Unable to help herself, Sehdra glanced up at Oyaoan. The huamek was looking at her, but with no more hostility than any other time. After a moment, the giantess raised her gaze, turned, and walked away. Each step shook the scaffolding with worrying tremors, though the structure held.

"As mercy seems the fashion this day," the Suncoaster continued as the rumble of his mistress's steps faded, "I suppose Great Oyaoan shall spare some of her own. All the more because this was not... unanticipated."

Sehdra stared at him. Her limbs felt as if they had turned to stone. It perplexed her that her actions had not angered Oyaoan and the Ibis, but the answer he proposed was too implausible to believe. If they had prophetic powers, how could she ever outmaneuver them?

Yet it made a certain sense. The giantess made strategic decisions as if seeing how they would play out for weeks down the road, if not seasons and years. Sehdra had assumed it was because of an intuition and intelligence cultivated over centuries. This explanation, improbable as it first seemed, accounted for it better yet.

Only a lifelong practice in discipline kept her expression smooth. "I would hate to disappoint you, Ibis."

The translator laughed, the white tusks in his flesh rippling up his stomach. "I do not think you will disappoint us in the end."

With that, the bow-legged man departed in the same direction as his mistress.

Only when he was out of earshot did Teti lean in close. "Divine One, if you will pardon me, this was damned unwise."

Sehdra looked at him, a smile winning free of her. "Perhaps. But, however small a victory it was, it *was* a victory."

"One worth the price?"

"Only time shall tell, my dear Teti."

45. THE FIRST TASTE

"The first taste of victory sours, for more battles wait just over the next rise."

- Highlord Carr Gunnarson, Fifth Arkjarl of Baegard

Aelthena entered the North Gate as close behind the army as she dared. Dawn's glow over the mountains to their left only just lifted the gloom over the city, but it could not lighten the deathly pall.

The first portent of what awaited her came as she passed under the gatehouse. The sounds of the men within it echoed down through the murder holes, but it was the blood, grown viscous since it had spilled, dripping lazily down made her flinch. She grimaced as a globule fell on her gloved hand and tried to shake it off.

This is the least of what's coming, she reminded herself.

Winterlily skittered beneath her, leery of venturing further in. She was no battle-trained warhorse, but a well-bred mare, and never meant for such a scene. Aelthena had no choice but to be merciless, pressing in her heels and compelling her on, though she scarcely wished to go herself.

As she beheld what had become her city, she brought her horse to a halt and stared.

The stench struck her first, thick with blood, urine, and nightsoil. Aelthena swallowed back bile and took in all those who had fallen. Bodies were everywhere: hacked apart, stomped to pulp, stabbed and slashed and savaged. Most wore barbar trappings, but many were her fellow Baegardians. Sons and fathers, their lives given to the slaughter.

Mouth filled with the battle's perfume, Aelthena knew this was the relish of triumph. But until she knew those she loved were alive, its savor was too bitter to swallow.

She glanced over at those traveling with her. Loridi, whose face was usually lined with laughter, looked pale and serious. Riding behind him, Tyra had her eyes squeezed shut, all but burying her head in the tall man's back. Seskef stared grimly about them, sorrow lining his brow. Noticing Aelthena's gaze, the stout man pointed at the ground.

"Jotunmen."

Aelthena saw what he meant at once. Among the dead were men so twisted they hardly seemed human any longer. Coarse hair, ranging from bark brown to black to dirty blonde, layered their skin and faces. Tusks jutted from the corners of many of their mouths. Even with the gore layering their bodies turning her stomach, she could not pull her gaze away for many long moments.

"They look like him," she murmured, then raised her voice to be heard over the din. "They look like the Jotun."

Loridi jerked around, and Seskef frowned. It seemed a revelation to them, though surely, that was why these beings were named "jotunmen."

Tyra raised her head to stare at Aelthena, eyebrows drawn. "Made in their image," she muttered, as if to herself.

Aelthena had no time to wonder at the girl's words, for a knot of men amid the street drew her gaze. Her breathing grown more shallow still, she made for the group. Part of her was convinced she would see Frey or her brother at their center. She needed to see their faces. Even if they were dead or dying, it was better to know than to endure the uncertainty.

But neither Frey nor Bjorn lay there. Instead, Aelthena glimpsed another familiar face over the crowding figures. His skin had lost its haleness and grown sallow. His eyes were closed. Bruises and cuts were visible across his body where blood did not paint it.

She whispered his name, for a moment unable to speak louder. "Bastor..."

Her prince — her friend — had fallen. Yet, telling from the urgency of the surrounding men, he still clung to life.

Loridi edged up next to Aelthena. "They got Prince Alabastor? The gods have a cruel sense of humor, they do."

"Long have we known that," Tyra murmured.

"He's still alive." Aelthena spoke with more confidence than she had a right to. "Let's pray Volkur is merciful this day."

Seskef came up on her other side. "He killed those two jotunmen, or had a hand in it."

Aelthena saw the evidence of it then, bestial men cut down by the rips of an axe. Bastor was a sizable man, but these creatures were larger still. To have killed one would have been a feat; two seemed unimaginable. Torn between looking in on the prince and fearing what she would find, she remained there, Winterlily shifting nervously beneath her, her brothers' companions doing the same to either side.

Loridi's cry roused her from her stupor. "Ho! Unless Nuvvog tricks my eyes, I believe Egil stands yonder!"

For a moment, the name was meaningless. Then ice threaded through Aelthena's veins.

Slowly, she looked around. She picked out the lawspeaker's son at once. The battle had turned his tuft of blonde hair pink and black from the battle, and his face was made harsh by a scowl. He looked to have been in the thick of things, for there was hardly an inch of his armor uncovered by carnage. His sword, still unsheathed, hung at his side.

Ignoring her companions' words, Aelthena led her mare through the crowd toward the man. The lawspeaker's son saw her coming. He did not lower his gaze as she dismounted and stood before him. She scarcely noticed the filth filming the pavers.

"Egil Yaethunson, where is my brother?"

Egil flinched; a sign of guilt, to her mind. Aelthena's hands bunched tighter. She hoped Loridi and Seskef would fight on her behalf if it became necessary. What was their relationship with the former Hunter in the White? The order to strike tipped her tongue.

She swallowed it down and spat out instead, "Where is he, traitor-son? What have you done with Bjorn?"

"I..." The lawspeaker's son tensed his jaw and looked aside.

Loridi slid to the ground next to her and angled his body between them. "M'lady, there must be a misunderstanding. Egil was nothing but loyal to Bjorn and the company. We parted friends, all of us, or comrades at least."

"I misunderstand nothing." She took a step closer. It brought his bared sword within striking distance, but she refused to be cowed. "I know what his father has done. I know his schemes, his treachery. Have you been in contact with him, traitor-son? Have you spoken to Yaethun Brashurson?"

The young man lowered his eyes. Had she not known better, she would have thought there was a tremble to his lower lip. When he spoke, however, his voice was steady.

"Yes, I have."

"Why shouldn't he?" Loridi protested. "A son must speak with his father, no? What crimes has Lawspeaker Yaethun committed?"

Aelthena ignored him. "Your father deserves far worse than death for what he has done," she said to Egil. "He betrayed all Thurdjurs, all of Oakharrow, all of Baegard. Ovvash's hells, he betrayed Enea! Without his aid, the Jotun never could have gained a foothold within the city. The battle today happened because of him. All this death, because of *him*."

She stepped closer. From the corner of her eye, she saw Egil's hand twitch. Still, she pressed on.

"One who consorts with scabs, and especially the son of one, is likely the same. A traitor."

At that, life stirred back into the young man's eyes. "I'm no traitor."

"No? Then why consort with your father?"

Egil hesitated, then something within him seemed to break free.

"You don't understand what happened here. I broke contact with him as soon as I could. I joined the rebellion. Look around! Who do you think won the wall? Your prince fell in the street! I fought alone, and I cut down all in my way."

Aelthena forced a smile. "He's your prince as well, traitor-son."

Despite her gibe, the passion of Egil's claims made her

wonder. Candor seemed to fill them; desperation, too, and also prickly affront.

He believes them. Which either meant he told the truth, or he was sprite-touched in some way.

"Bjorn," the sentry said, bringing her back to the moment. Egil seemed to struggle to say his name somehow. "He... left before the battle."

"Left?"

Egil grimaced and looked aside. "He had a vision. Thought he must ally with Kuljash for the good of all."

A vision. She longed to spit the bitter taste from her mouth. Every mention of her brother was followed by a whisper of magic of late, and she tired of hearing it. But it was the implication in Egil's words that threatened to snap the leash on her temper.

"Are you telling me," she said in a low voice, "that Bjorn went to the Jotun? Willingly?"

"It seemed his intention."

A dozen different curses sprang to her mind. But before she could utter any of them, someone spoke from behind.

"Why am I not surprised to find you here, stirring up trouble before the dust of battle has settled?"

Aelthena was whirling around before he had finished speaking. Frey stood there: battered and bruised, but alive. All sour thoughts slipped away at the sight of him. She wanted to embrace him, the consequences be damned, but his arm tucked into a makeshift sling gave her pause.

"You're hurt."

He seemed to try for his usual roguish smile, but it came out as a grimace. "It's nothing. Just a bone snapped in two, 'tis all."

Aelthena was tempted to roll her eyes. Instead, she gripped his good arm. "I'm just glad you're alive."

"As am I."

Staring into his eyes, she wished they were alone together and far away from all of this. But peril still threatened them. Clearing her throat, she stepped back and turned to look at Egil. The sentry was already ambling away. She stared at his back, eyes narrowed, wondering if he could possibly be on their side.

"He fought with us, you know." Frey had not released her arm. Even with his hand in a thick leather glove, his touch was gentle. "What's more, he fought like a Djur-bred devil. Never seen a man wield a blade like that."

Aelthena gave him a sharp look. "I could have said the same for you. Is he so skilled?"

"More than skilled." Frey nodded toward the wall. "From what I hear, he killed a score of the bastards, most on his own and outnumbered."

Awe threatened to grow in her. She squashed it back down. "It doesn't matter. Skill with a blade doesn't mean there's any goodness in your heart."

"Oh, I wouldn't say that about Egil. I have a feeling he's gentler than you think. The way he was with your brother—"

"Bjorn." Her focus turned, all other matters paling in comparison. "You saw him?"

"Yes. Sorry, I should have mentioned it before. He was staying with the rebels, but slipped out before the battle."

As swiftly as hope had arisen, dread smothered it. "He deserted?"

Frey shrugged and winced, the movement seeming to pain him. "Not exactly. Truthfully, I don't understand it myself. Egil could tell us more. Those two had their heads bent together since the moment I arrived. The sentry seemed to watch over your brother, protect him. Bjorn was weak from witchery, as I understood it. Something the priest got him up to, no doubt. Had something to do with a vision, I think."

That Nuvvog-cursed vision. Head spinning, she finally gave voice to the fear needling her. "Did he seem... sane?"

His wince told her much. "He wasn't raving, if that's what you mean. But I think he believed in things I'm not sure are real."

Her breathing came quick. Sprite-touched. It had come upon him so early in life, much earlier than it had for their father. And there was nothing she could do to protect him.

I'm sorry, little squirrel.

But even as she was forced to accept the damning evidence, she refused to surrender him. If he had gone to the Jotun, then she knew from whom she had to win him back.

"But that," Frey said, bringing her attention back to him, "I fear, is a conversation that will have to wait."

Aelthena followed Frey's gaze to an individual riding toward them. Even if he had not been atop a horse, his golden armor would have made Asborn stand out in the crowd. Though it was scratched and dented where it had not been before, he looked far cleaner than many of the warriors. Apparently, he had not been one of those who had made it inside the gate before the portcullis fell. Yet his expression was just as hard as any who had been in the thick of the fight.

Her stomach tightened as she waited for the Jarl of Oakharrow to approach. Her only consolation was that his sword remained sheathed at his side.

"Mistress Aelthena." Asborn spoke with a slight sneer. If he was as exhausted as the others, he did not show it, but sat straight in the saddle, chin held high.

"Asborn."

His scowl deepened. "I am not your betrothed any

longer. You will address me as 'lord' or 'lord jarl,' especially within the bounds of my city."

With each word, he drove the knife in deeper. But it was a wound Aelthena was used to bearing.

"Very well, *my lord*." She put enough emphasis on the title to leave no doubt to her feelings.

"Aelthena..." Frey breathed, soft enough that Asborn could not hear the warning.

"With Prince Alabastor gravely injured," Asborn continued, ignoring her tone, "and the armies occupying my jarlheim, I am in charge. You are not to give any orders to my men — especially the artillerists."

She did not hide her curling lips. "Gods forbid I do anything to save lives."

"I will have your word on it, mistress. Do not make me take more drastic measures."

You struck the first blow, she wanted to throw back at him, but she held her tongue. Not only was it unwise to say, she was not altogether sure it was true.

Asborn smiled. "Now then, come with me. My mother will wish to see you. If I must disappoint her with news of your refusal, you must also bear her ire."

Aelthena stood firm. "I'm sorry, Lord Jarl. But I must find my brother at once. I'm sure Lady Kathsla will understand that family comes before duty."

The false jarl's face flushed in a way she had only seen caused by embarrassment before the wars began. Now, anger seemed the only thing capable of raising his blood.

"Fine, he hissed. "But you will come to Vigil Keep once he is located. Do not delay, Aelthena."

Asborn turned his horse and clopped back the way he had come. Headed for his keep, no doubt.

Let him rot within it.

As soon as he was out of sight, Frey took her arm. "While we look for your brother, I'll explain all I can."

"Please do."

Aelthena looked around at the others. With nods, they followed behind. She kept that much authority, at least. A good thing — she knew she would need it and more to win the battles ahead.

Particularly if the Jotun had her brother.

46. A SON'S SHAME

Shame is a sickness shared among kin. Where it finds fertile soil, it grows and spreads so it infects the entire line.

- Counsel on the Inscribed Beliefs, by Mother Vigilance

Egil watched as his home's front gate squealed open. He stood in the middle of the street before it. Though he had slept until late that morning, exhaustion pooled inside him, making his limbs heavy and his eyelids droop. He forced himself to stand tall, regardless. He was clad in aqua clothes befitting a Thurdjur highborn, lent to him by the council of elders for the occasion. He had bathed and scrubbed away the blood and grime of battle at Elder Vedgif's home the day before. Though he would have preferred to come here straightaway, it had been important to the council that he appear as the proper heir to his house, not a gore-splattered conqueror. He came to uphold the Harrow Law rather than break it.

Yet the battle memories still loomed behind his eyes, the

feeling of invincibility largest of all. Without it, he was not sure he could bear what was to come.

At last, the man he had both awaited and dreaded seeing came through the gate. Yaethun Brashurson had always given the impression of being in control of his fate. He had maintained his facade even as he endeavored to take back his father's mantle and exact long-awaited vengeance. None could suspect a polite man of deposition.

But that composure was cracking, revealing the man beneath. Fear had dominated Egil's father since the Jotun's arrival. Now, it was a mountain blizzard scouring all other sentiment away. Egil could scarcely look at the man whining to the guards who hauled him along. The contrast between this man and the one he had once believed him to be shredded his memories to ribbons.

One thing had not changed in his father, however, as evinced by his immediate surrender: Yaethun Brashurson did not fight a losing battle.

Egil's scowl deepened, disguising all that hid behind it. Vedgif, who stood next to him, shifted a fraction.

"Steady," he murmured. "Hold the line."

They were a drang's words, yet held as much comfort as the elder had ever offered. Egil nodded to him, grateful he did not stand alone.

The guards brought the former lawspeaker before them. Egil met his father's stare and stiffened his jaw. Yaethun's lips curled in a sneer. All the man had to say shone in his eyes.

Egil looked aside first. He had expected disappointment, betrayal, even shame from his father. But the vitriol, pure and undiluted, was too much to withstand.

"So, my son." His father's words dripped with acid. "You deny your own blood and kin once again. And you claim to have honor!"

Egil only glared back. There was no reasoning with madness.

"You think me a snake, don't you?" Yaethun continued. "A serpent slithering his way to the chair? It's *my* fucking chair! *My* mantle! It does not belong to that slobbering, thieving halfwit! It was my birthright — and it would have been yours!"

Before his father's raving, Egil found his own anger freezing. He stood motionless, his heart the only thing moving, thumping wildly in his chest.

Yaethun jerked his head back toward their family manor. "Oh, you think you're content with this, don't you? Content to rob your own father! They'll never give you a scrap of it, not a silver, copper, or stone. Those conniving cublings will take everything that was your due, just as their father took your grandsire's throne. You'll inherit nothing, Egil No-Son. I disown you! You won't have my name, my position, my honor. Nothing, *nothing* will you have from me!"

Vedgif stepped forward. The elder did not bother hiding his disgust. "Take him to the Balturg keep," he told the huskarls holding Egil's father. "And gag him."

Before the men could comply, Egil leaned in close, arresting their movement. His father stared into his eyes and flinched.

"Better to be a pauper," Egil said quietly, "than a traitor."

He walked past, ignoring his father's cries as they became muffled by a gag. He strode up to the two guards waiting at the open manor gate; Colden and Hemming, their names were. The men had both long served his father, and Egil had dueled them throughout his childhood until he bested both in the yard.

The guards exchanged a glance, then Colden cleared his throat. "Master — that is, houselord."

Egil nodded, not letting show how the title chilled him. *Houselord.* This was his estate, now. His father's lands belonged to him.

Only then did it feel like a betrayal. Even if it had been the only choice he could make.

"Have two men ready to leave within the hour," he told them. "We go to Vigil Keep."

They knocked their fists to their chests as Egil strode past.

Guilt lingered the next day when Yaethun was brought into Vigil Keep's chair-room.

Egil attended with many other notables of Oakharrow. Lord Asborn sat atop his castle's throne, scowling down at the prisoner and his rattling chains. At the jarl's side stood his bent mother, Lady Kathsla. Egil had not been around the woman much before, but she seemed grayer than the last time he had glimpsed her. Holding the keep against the Jotun's men had taken its toll. He wondered how many years she had left in her bones.

Closer at hand was Mistress Aelthena and her man, Frey. The guardian was pale-faced, his broken arm cradled to his belly by a sling. Injured as he was, he would not be much use as a protector. Not that Aelthena looked to need it. She stood with her chin raised, her posture erect, and her emerald eyes aflame. The blows to her authority had not banked her fire. Egil now doubted anything would.

A few others were less known to Egil. Lord Siward Jonson, Jarl of Greenwuud, he knew as the Black Ram for his exploits during the Sack of Qal-Nu. He looked every bit the ancient warrior, precious metals jangling along his arms, though his years seemed to weigh on him. A young jarl,

Ingvar Alrikson, had taken his father's place after the battle at Petyrsholm. His mother, Nanna Of'Alrik, and another jarl's widow, Sigrid Of'Harald, stood nearby. Lady Sigrid was, by all appearances, the leader of Skjold now. Both women seemed on friendly terms with Aelthena. Perhaps they would be her allies if circumstances turned in her favor.

Egil eyed them all warily. Would any speak up for him when his reckoning came?

Thurdjur and Balturg elders lingered at the peripheries of the room. Vedgif stood among them, still clad in armor, though it had been cleaned since the battle. Closer at hand was a more surprising pair of faces. Edda Skarldaughter smirked at the surrounding highborn, her flame-haired shieldmaiden, Bodil the Blaze, towering behind her with a matching expression. As Egil's eyes alighted on Edda, the Vurg leader winked. He looked away before he could stop himself, face flushing.

Yet under the current grave circumstances, it soon faded. Officially, this was his father's trial, but Egil still bore his father's name. He might as easily suffer the consequences of his sins.

Lord Asborn, as the ruler of the lands on which they stood, would be in charge of the proceedings, since the prince, Alabastor Ragnarson, lay elsewhere in the keep, fighting for his life. The pale jarl watched as the keepers brought Egil's father to the edge of the pedestal. When he spoke, his voice was soft, yet edged with iron.

"Yaethun Brashurson. You stand accused of many crimes against Oakharrow and Baegard. Foremost among these is conspiring with our enemy, the Jotun. From this unfolds the other transgressions. Destruction of the Harrowhall. Murder of the former jarl's sons, his wife, his servants and sworn men. Ravaging the Teeth Gate. And the

Jotun's occupation of the city, which led to many more lives lost."

Egil glanced at his father. The night in prison seemed already to have hollowed his cheeks, and he had never had a full complexion. Yet there was no remorse in his expression, only indignant ire. He wondered if any humanity lingered behind those cold eyes.

"I only touch upon all that is set at your feet," Lord Asborn continued. "As the former lawspeaker, tell me: what does the Harrow Law dictate should be done?"

Yaethun curled his lips. Egil's stomach sank. Ever before, his father had been pliant, going whichever way the winds of fortune blew. Now that he was cornered, his reason seemed to have departed.

"That would depend on if the accused were guilty of their crimes or not," he spat. "It is clear you have decided which I am!"

"Because you are."

All in the chamber turned to look at Aelthena as she stepped forward. Egil watched her, equally astonished and wary. She spoke out of turn; if there was any doubt of that, the jarl's furious gaze settled it. But the daughter of Bor the Bear did not face Lord Asborn, but remained turned toward the accused.

"I do not know every letter of the law, but I know its spirit. The depth of his treachery demands one penalty: death."

Egil had thought he would feel something as his father's fate was spoken, but all inside him was ice. He had always tried to be frost-bent, yet only now did he feel truly frozen through, numb to his very core. Even Aelthena's glance his way did little to stir his feelings.

"Egil Yaethunson."

He looked up at Lady Kathsla's address. His voice stolen from him, Egil acknowledged her with a nod.

"You are Yaethun Brashurson's scion. I do not say he is guilty of the same crimes," she added as murmurs started up among the Thurdjur elders. "His actions have spoken otherwise, both in that foolish hunt into the mountains and afterward. No, I only wish to hear him speak. Have you anything to say in your father's defense?"

The attention of the room brought down on him broke the spell. Egil shifted under their gazes. He had never been one for speeches, always preferring action to words. But just now, he had no other weapons that mattered. Clearing his throat, he grasped after something, anything to say. As his frustration mounted, speech finally burst free.

"I cannot defend him. My father will take any master that brings him more power."

"No—Son!" Yaethun hissed, loud enough to set the chamber to muttering again.

His father's goad spurred Egil on. "He schemes and plots and plans for his own benefit. He is two-faced and honorless. He knows no god but ambition."

Lord Asborn, face still flushed from Aelthena's interjection, spoke in a clipped tone. "Then he deserves death."

"You're no son of mine!" The lawspeaker had not ceased his insults.

"He does. But," Egil said louder as whispers multiplied, "my father also knew the inner workings of the Jotun's reign over Oakharrow. He knew those with whom he was in contact, those who helped and hindered. If any remain loyal to the giant within the city, Yaethun Brashurson can expose them."

The elders' mutterings shifted, and the mood of the room with them. Lord Asborn's eyebrows shot up, and he tilted his head as if in contemplation. Mistress Aelthena stared at Egil. He wondered if his intervention had renewed him as an enemy in her eyes. He could not even say why he had bothered to defend him.

All the same, no word had been untrue.

Egil looked at his father to see him smiling. As with most of Yaethun's smiles, this one was far from pleasant.

"Ah, my fellow conspirators," the former lawspeaker said, voice soft and honeyed. "Those who helped undermine Oakharrow, you mean? Not unlike the very prince you serve, Alabastor Ragnarson."

There was no mistaking the shocked whispers now. Egil stared at the former lawspeaker, wondering if it could be possible. He was used to his father wielding secrets edged with truth, but this one seemed too far-fetched to believe.

His eyes caught on Mistress Aelthena, and her wide eyes gave him pause. A moment later, her expression smoothed, but something remained that made him wonder.

"Egil Yaethunson speaks wisely for one still young," Lady Kathsla said into the disquiet. "If my son agrees, I believe we should keep him in chains a little longer. But only so long as he is useful." She said this last with a dagger-filled glare in Yaethun's direction.

For once, his father said nothing.

"Yes, very well." The jarl seemed distracted, his gaze distant for a moment before falling on Yaethun. "I trust Yaethun Brashurson will prove compliant."

"Of course, Lord Jarl." The former lawspeaker bared his teeth in a grin.

Egil listened to the rattling chains as the keepers escorted the prisoner from the room. Only as they reached the doors did he look, catching one last glimpse of his father before he was whisked out of sight.

47. LESS

Death holds no fear for the brave
Death is but a specter
A ghost to haunt where he is not
Claws tempted by all he loves

- "Shard of a Runestone," transcribed by
Alfjin the Scribe

I will not leave him to the Jotun. It is our clan's duty to bring Bjorn home."

Frey watched Aelthena as she spoke. An ache grew in him that had nothing to do with his broken arm. Her courage and passion, born of love and pain, were as excruciating to behold as they were inspiring. Always, she pressed on, no matter the odds facing her. Always, she strove toward what she believed was good and right.

No wonder he loved her. No wonder he would follow her into Ovvash's hells and back.

He shifted his arm, wincing as it settled. They stood in Vedgif Addarson's house, Thurdjur elders crowded around.

Other than Aelthena, their host commanded the room, as he often did; the Rook was nothing if not a leader of men. Though most of the elders were loud in their opinions, they deferred to the scarred veteran when it came to matters of war.

Other highborn from their clan attended as well, including Egil. From the corner of his eye, Frey observed the young man. Now the head of a house that had once ruled Oakharrow, he had become far more than a sentry. Though, with a snake such as Yaethun as his father, his fortunes could still turn. He had only known Egil briefly, yet remembering how he had torn through their enemies, he found it difficult to believe him a traitor as well.

"Mistress Aelthena," one elder wheedled, "it is with the deepest regret I say this, but I must. Bjorn Borson is no longer part of the ruling family — nor, I fear, are you. To risk so much to reclaim him now is not following Baltur's wisdom."

Aelthena turned her glare on the weaselly man. "It is not wisdom we need, Elder Fiske, but courage and honor. Would you abandon any man to our enemies when we have the strength to take him back? I am a woman, yet I will not flinch from this path. Will you?"

The members of the council muttered, their feathers ruffled by her bald accusations. Frey hid a chuckle behind a cough and regretted both as his arm spasmed.

"Nor was my brother taken alone," she continued. "According to the word of every man I've spoken with, Brother Yonik was taken along with Bjorn by the Jotun. Would you leave a gothi to be torn apart by wolves? Then it will not be Baltur you must worry about, Elder, but Skoll. The Wolf God would be ill-pleased by you abandoning his priest to die."

The elder sat back in his chair, arms crossed and a surly

expression on his pinched face. Other elders, however, were less chastened.

"It is not a matter of courage, mistress, nor valor, but authority," another said, this one with a buckskin hat and a gruff manner of speech. "Lord Asborn rules as the jarl now. How can any Harrowman go without his blessing?"

Mutters of agreement sounded from across the room. They silenced as the Rook spoke.

"We will go. Not only to take back the men of our clan and land, but to strike at our enemy while they remain weak. Leave the Jotun to those mountains, and the beast will gather strength again. Reports place him at less than half a thousand men left. Bring Nuvvog's Rage and a large company and we can put an end to this threat before winter falls."

It was as rousing a speech as Vedgif seemed inclined to. Even the elders who had disagreed moments earlier started nodding. But the last one to have spoken proved the exception.

"And will our warriors be condemned upon their return?" the squat elder pressed. "We must have Lord Asborn's permission; on this point, I remain unswayed!"

"No. We must not." Aelthena's lips curled. Her disdain for her former betrothed was plain for Frey to see. He hoped it was less obvious to the others.

"As soon as Prince Alabastor rises," she continued, "he will again have the highest authority within the jarlheim. The jarl will not speak against him."

"If he rises," someone muttered, low enough to remain anonymous.

Aelthena frowned in their direction. "He will. I know the prince. He is as strong a man as I've ever met."

Frey wondered if he should take offense at that, then grinned. How could he compare with Bastor on that front?

The man practically had giant's blood running through his veins.

Though not so much as those jotunmen.

"I will do all I can to care for him," a voice spoke from near the door. "With the gods' favor, he will prevail."

All eyes turned toward the woman. Mother Ilva, Frey saw her to be. Her silver-striped hair tumbled out of a riverrat hat, framing her grim expression. It struck ice deep through him.

For the first time, he wondered if Bastor truly would survive.

A glance at Aelthena showed she shared his doubts. The next moment, she seemed to toss them aside. "Asborn — that is, Lord Asborn — cannot be relied upon to send warriors as he should. That duty falls to us. And when have Thurdjurs ever flinched from what must be done?"

That loyalist appeal was the last stroke. A hearty call arose from even the most elderly attendee. In contrast to their enthusiasm, Frey found his own mood souring.

These plans of attack would have to take place without him.

He glared down at his injured arm, still months away from being useful again. Rare was the moment that his body was incapable of doing what he set his mind to. He had grown up with a stick in hand, playing at being a warrior, before he proved himself in the common yards of the city. The Harrowhall's late blademaster, Raldof Koryson, had seen something in Frey and given him a chance to prove himself. He had not wasted it, training harder than any other boy, though he always hid ambition behind a smile. When the time came to choose guardians, Frey had been among the first.

He had thrown himself into harm's way a hundred times, but it would not be courage to do so now, only vanity.

Frey liked to play others for the fool, but he had long thought prudence the better course.

His thoughts took an abrupt turn as Aelthena spoke.

"Who will go with me, then? Who will fight the Jotun to save the gothi and my brother?"

Go with me. Frey stared at this woman he loved, this fierce she-wolf who never flinched from a challenge, no matter how towering or deadly. Little made him afraid, but hearing her speak those words had him near trembling.

The room erupted into excited chatter and shouts from volunteers. Frey used his good shoulder to push his way to Aelthena's side. She did not look his way, though he knew she noticed him. Only once he cleared his throat did she meet his gaze.

"If you go, then I must," he murmured.

"No, Frey." Her eyes flickered down to his slung arm. "You're injured. Stay here and heal."

"Please, Aelthena." He had not meant to beg; now, he could not stop. "Don't go where I cannot follow."

"I have to."

"Why? Why must you go? Look around! A thousand men will jump at the chance of renown and earning the favor of so many highborn, your family especially. What can you do that they cannot?"

She turned to face him fully. Her smile did not match her downturned eyes. "It is not strength I fear they'll lack, but wit and common sense. Do you think we will fight our way to Bjorn? They could kill him before we reach him." Aelthena closed her eyes. A shimmer started up at the edges as she opened them, but her gaze was as hard as granite. "Someone must know the right words to say."

"And that's you, is it?"

"You know I have the best chance of finding them."

He did, even as he objected. Yet Frey could not bear

this conclusion. Somehow, he had to be by her side. But could he carry a pack? Hike leagues uphill, possibly through snow? Even setting up shelters would be a task left to others, to say nothing of fighting. He would only be one more concern weighing on Aelthena's mind.

A gusty sigh escaped him. Aelthena set a hand to his good arm. In the public setting, it was a gesture too familiar. He was pathetically grateful for it all the same.

"Look after my father, and Bastor, and the city. That will help me rest easier, alright?"

Frey had no choice but to smile. "Of course. You need not worry about them." He paused, considering. "Take Bjorn's companions with you, Loridi and Seskef. They look as if they'll watch your back. And Egil as well. Don't tell him I said it, but he fights better even than I."

Aelthena's brow creased, but she nodded. No doubt she still had reservations where Egil was concerned, though the intervening days since their confrontation seemed to have warmed her to the former lawspeaker's son. Frey glanced at the solemn man. As Egil looked back, Frey gave him a nod, hoping he would understand.

It was as much as he could do to protect her. The rest was left to the gods.

48. UNTIL WORLD'S END

"Cunning can multiply one's strength, but it is spears and swords that kill men."

- Lion Ankhu, Paragon of Pawura's Sorrow in the 171st Flood of Gazabe

S*he knows.*

The thought stalked Sehdra, compelling her to pace the carpets of her pavilion, each step on her twisted leg sending needle-pain rippling up her body. No word of Teti's could soothe her, nor any tidings from Amon. The sight of what her hard-edged mercy had won her, the woman Gertrud sitting in the tent's corner staring sightlessly into the air, gave her no satisfaction.

Oyaoan and her servant knew all of it, all her plans, perhaps down to her every movement. All along, she had plotted resistance, and the Ibis had laughed it off. She turned the matter over and over in her mind, yet she could see no way around it. No way but the most foolish and rash.

What could dupe those with foresight but unpredictability?

She ran through her advantages, slight as they seemed. The Ibis had been surprised by Seth, as if he were an unanticipated piece in their game. Something about the burned boy put her enemies off-kilter. Could they see him in their visions now that they knew of him? She remembered the trance she had seen Oyaoan in before her brother died, reeking even more with the stench of sulfur than usual. Was that when she saw the path before her, through scarabs scuttling in sand?

It did not matter; none of it did. The situation was simple when it came down to it. The giantess and her translator knew she was disloyal. They would only keep her for as long as it was convenient. They had already murdered one karah; why hesitate at killing another? Pruning the last of Sehdra's line might prove problematic, but few would protest before the huamek's iron fist, with all of Hua's fury at her fingertips.

Step, wince, step, wince; it formed the rhythm of her plans. Implementing them would be more painful still. There was a narrow path forward, one that could lead to a modicum of control, but it might come at great cost.

But she had a chance. The slimmest of chances, but what other option did she have? She was all but tied to a pyre and waiting for the oil to catch flame.

I will not wait to burn.

"Sehdra. Please, sit for a moment. You must not overexert yourself."

"Overexert." She stopped and faced him. "What does it matter if I 'overexert' myself? We may all be dead come morning. Perhaps this very night."

He rose from his seat at her writing desk and grasped her hands. "This is why you must calm yourself. Think clearly. Remember what your mother always counseled: Plant your plans where they might blossom. When has rash action ever benefitted you?"

Shame edged in. No doubt he referred to that recent rashness whose reminder sat in the far corner. Sehdra pressed his hands back.

"I do not know anymore, Teti. My mind feels like the Nu in a flood, spilling over with all I must hold in it." Her eyes fell to his chest, vision grown blurry. "I am supposed to be a goddess, yet I have never felt like one. Tradition cannot replace the truth."

His hands traveled up to grip her shoulders. The force of his gaze drew her head back up.

"No, the truth cannot be denied. But though your body may be mortal, Sehdra, I do not believe that to be true of your spirit. There is a light in you that shines like no other. I have seen it in countless moments. In time, others will as well."

For him, she tried to smile, though it fell far short. "But that is just it, my friend. That time must be now."

"And so it will be — but in a moment. Just now, you must breathe."

Sehdra folded into his embrace, closing her eyes and letting her breath follow his own slow pattern. She did not care that Gertrud might see them and wonder, did not care if any other servant walked in and saw them in the intimate embrace. Teti was the one constant in her life. He was a brother, father, mother, friend. Where no other could comfort her, he had ever succeeded.

"You have always seen the way before," he murmured into her hair. "You will see it when it is time."

As if he spoke prophecy, Sehdra suddenly did. She drew away, gently prying his arms from about her, and looked up into Teti's face. Tears still moistened her cheeks, catching in the ridges of the cursed flesh, yet she did not wipe them away.

"Can I ask you to trust me?" she whispered. "This one last time?"

Teti smiled, his eyes sad. "Until the world's end, dearest one."

———

Hidden by the night's cowl, Sehdra stepped inside a tent.

Her leg, already aflame from her time spent pacing, now burned from the walk over. She had refused a palanquin, opting instead for as much stealth as she could muster. No doubt she would be seen, anyway; the Ibis was not so arrogant as to neglect spying on her tent. That did not stop her from posting Teti outside as a guard and weaving an excuse that might hold for one night longer.

Amon Baka stumbled to his feet and swayed. She smelled the wine even before she saw the open jug and half-filled cup. The disgraced general's eyes were bloodshot. A dark beard spread along his chin that had not been there when she last saw him. Even in this state, though, he was a handsome man.

If only pleasure were my purpose.

"Divine One. I wasn't expecting you." His words were slightly slurred, his tone informal. In public, it would have been considered an insult. Here and now, Sehdra was relieved to be addressed without pretense for once.

"Good. Perhaps our enemy does not, either."

At the mention, Amon seemed to rally. "Then it is business you're here for."

She arched the eyebrow not hidden behind the royal mask. To anyone else, the gesture would have been a damning censure. He only grinned at the sight of it.

Sehdra spoke quickly, hoping he would not see the blush spreading across her cheeks. "Do you still have men loyal to you?"

"Yes." His smile faded. "Only a small company, but all trusted and capable soldiers."

"Good. Gather them quietly. There is a place outside the city to the west near the foothills of the mountains called the Spine. You and your men must seize the pit there from Oyaoan's soldiers. An acolyte named Seth will show you the way. You will know him; his flesh has been burned in service to the Ascendant Crown."

Amon's dulled wit showed again, for it took several moments before his eyes lit with understanding. She hoped the wine had not gone too much to his head.

"Am I right in understanding," the general said softly, "that the Holy Karah rebels at last?"

"I am taking back what is mine."

The force of her words surprised them both. Sehdra had never been one to speak fiercely. She wondered where this lioness had come from, when she had been so long a cat slinking in shadows.

"It will be done, Divine One." Amon gave her a brief bow, then turned to his arms and armor mounted on the stands behind him.

"Good. May the Divine watch over you, Amon Baka."

Sehdra turned for the exit, heart fluttering. Like a chariot cut free and speeding downhill, her plans were in motion. For better or worse, there was no halting them now.

49. WITHIN THE FLAMES

There is an additional matter of which an effective shaper must be wary. Above all else, every servant craves one thing, however much they might confess otherwise: freedom. This desire must be stamped out early, made into a despicable dream, so the Tusk cannot imagine any other life but servitude, nor abide to live but under its yoke.

- Shaping Tusks, by Chanter Kapes of Bek

The space between Seth's shoulders itched.

It was not only because of the sleet dripping cold down his neck, nor the fear of a knife in his back, though he was far from trusting of the soldiers mounted behind him. No; it was the men's eyes that made him squirm. He felt like a fresh disciple facing the switch for the first time: nervous, afraid, uncertain. He was not used to leading, nor being anywhere in sight. The shadows were his cloak and his friend; all the light had ever done was burn.

Faith is pain.

Ever did he repeat the mantra. Seth chastised himself for his unworthiness, then sent up a silent prayer to Bek. Only through service could he purify himself. Only then could he be deserving of Gazabe's Delight.

Oh, how he yearned for that rest, that empyrean place. How he longed for a day, an hour, a moment without pain. But faith without pain was empty, a sentence without words.

I will be worthy of you, Divine One. He pictured the Holy Karah's face, halfway hidden by her celestial mask. The scarab loomed large in his mind; the tusk seemed to jab toward him, menacing, reminding him of the price of failure. *I am your Tusk.*

"How much farther is it?"

Seth startled. That was another thing he was unused to: others addressing him. He looked down at the tarnished general, the one who had spoken. Amon Baka rode in a chariot next to him. They had exchanged no word beyond what was necessary thus far. To Seth's eye, the man was all vanity and puffed up pride. Yet who was he to judge? It was for the gods to peer into a man's heart and know the strength of his faith.

Amon raised an eyebrow at him, so Seth forced out words, just loud enough to be heard over the racket of the wheels. "Not far."

The man snorted. "Helpful. Remind me to see you have a promotion upon our return."

He stared at the general for a long while before he understood. *A joke.* Such a vain man would make light of their grave duty. Seth frowned and looked away.

Amon was not his only irritant. Fifty soldiers came behind in yet more chariots, a company of men claimed to be worthy of trust. Yet when Seth looked at each, he doubted. Like their general, they had neglected their soldierly appearance. They had grown out their beards and hair. Their armor was scuffed and stained. Their eyes were bloodshot from smoke and drink.

Despite his doubts, Seth obeyed his goddess. As he always would.

Back to khnuum, *to Silver.* He wondered at their task and how he would accomplish it. There had been nearly fifty people when Seth had left the quarry, and though only half of those had been fighters, the Great One could have very well reinforced it by now. Soldiers and giants constantly flowed in and out of the city, both to the east and to the west. Seth had seen at least two huame that had failed to return before that evening and long ago lost track of the soldiers and slaves.

He cleared his mind as chanters had long ago taught him to, waving thoughts away like smoke from a windowless room. Worries would not aid his task, but hamper it. He would go, and see, and do what needed to be done.

The dark ride proceeded in relative quiet. The general had ordered his soldiers to talk as little as necessary, and the men had mostly complied. As the horizon began to brighten, however, the muttering grew louder.

They doubt. Seth almost smiled before he expunged his smugness. He was no better than they, but sinful to his bones. Only through service could he cleanse his soul.

And be more worthy than they?

Another filthy thought. His head was full of them this night. Baring his teeth, Seth battled the demons back into the shadows.

Dawn broke. Trees sprouted from the endless plains. Seth caught Amon's eye and said, "Soon."

The general's eyes widened, then he nodded and twisted around in the chariot. "Ready, men," he called back, a strained quality to his voice, as if he wished to whisper rather than shout. "We arrive soon."

The soldiers transformed, self-restraint emerging from unknown depths. Seth nodded to himself. This was his proof; he could not judge men for their outward crassness. The Divine could find tools in even the lowliest of places.

The forest thickened. The shadows grew long, then short. Seth slowed his horse to a walk, and the general and his men did the same. The creaking of the chariots was the loudest thing around. Seth's breath came quick. His skin itched and burned, irritated by the ride. Yet another thing to endure. The road narrowed. Soon, it would turn off...

There. The final path lay before them.

Seth dismounted and tied off his horse. Turning, he saw Amon had silently ordered the same of the men — or half of them, rather, for a score remained in their chariots. Seth waited for them to finish and the general's nod before stalking forward.

Seth trained his eyes on the spaces between the tree trunks. Moisture dribbled through the canopy to track across his face. The icy wetness made his clothes chafe against his skin. Though they must be suffering the same, none of the following men voiced complaints. Silence meant keeping their lives, and all of them wanted to live.

Noises echoed through the woods. Voices — men shouting harshly with hard words. Seth's shoulders tightened, his body remembering all the times he had been screamed at, and the pain that had often followed. The switch, the hand, the fist, the foot — each held their own brand of agony, and he had endured them all.

I am her Tusk. He smoothed his mind and pressed forward.

The sky opened. Sleet fell sideways in the wind, a gust that threatened to freeze the moisture on Seth's clothes anew. Even in the weather, the foul steam rose into the air, though dampened from how it had appeared before.

He lowered his eyes, then went still. Men were not the only ones to guard the clearing.

Huame.

Two giants stood at the perimeter of the pit, rising as high as the nearest trees. Their expressions were masked, but as one swiped at a human that stumbled too near to it, Seth judged the weather had put them in as foul a mood as the others. Fear and doubt assailed him as he stared at the indomitable creatures. These were direct descendants of Hua, the Bright Creator. To defy them might mean risking worse than death.

But he saw the thought for what it was and tossed it away. He served a goddess, a Sliver of Divine made flesh. His orders came from the highest authority, and the Holy Karah had made it clear what he must do.

Oyaoan must not have the pit, she had said when giving his last instructions. *However you can, Seth, no matter the cost, you must take it from her.*

There had been pain in his goddess's eyes, this not born of her body. She was afraid; afraid of her own words, it almost seemed. But that would mean the karah doubted, and Seth knew her to be above such feelings.

No; it was her benevolence showing through, a compassion he could never hope to achieve himself. She feared for him: him, an undeserving servant. The thought almost made Seth smile.

"Bek blight us all," Amon hissed. "We cannot fight huame!"

Seth took shelter behind a tree and looked at the general. Fear was etched into every line on his face. It was plain in how he cowered against the trunk. A glance behind showed Amon was not alone in his doubt. For all the discipline they had recently shown, the soldiers' courage was lacking now.

"We must," Seth said. "Our goddess commands it."

"The Divine One didn't know giants stood guard!"

Seth turned back to the pit. There was no arguing with a man ruled by terror. This mission was one he would have to do alone.

My last.

Seth had seen how the northern giant he had first served had kept fire well away from the *khnuum* pit in the mountains. He had seen what flames could do to even the raw silver sand. Feeling at his waist, he touched the flint secured on his belt along with a knife. A spark could do as well as a flame, so long as he had the chance to strike it.

Drawing in a steadying breath, he rose.

Movement flashed in the corner of his eye. Next he knew, Seth was shoved against the tree, shaven head scraping against the rough bark. A man held him. Seth bared his teeth and braced himself to fight, then went limp as something pressed against his belly.

He saw it by rolling his eyes around: the bared knife pushing against Seth's clothes. He was one wrong move from having his belly ripped open.

"I'm not letting you get me and my men killed, you imbecilic fanatic," Amon Baka hissed. The general's eyes were wide with more than fear now; hatred, it almost seemed. "Struggle, and my knife slips. Understand?"

Seth only stared back. He did not fear his knife. Fear of death had been burned away back when he destroyed the castle among the Winter Holds. But he could not fulfill his task if he were dead, and if he failed his goddess, he would not reach Gazabe's Delight.

Amon roughly shoved him back and away from the *khnuum* pit, guiding him with a hand on his shoulder. Seth tried not to gut himself on the knife bobbing around his middle as they stumbled along.

The soldiers were muttering aplenty now. They had been unified in their purpose before, cleaved to honor, but it had been too fragile. Only cowardice united them now, and Seth had seen how frail a binding that was.

The general did not yield his hold on Seth until they reached the horses and other men. Then he shoved him toward his beast, knife held at the ready.

"Mount," Amon Baka ordered. "You ride back to Ragnarsglade with us."

Seth did as he was instructed. He watched as the general handed his horse's reins to one of his men, then trotted over to his chariot. The soldier glanced at him. He was a burly fellow with a heavy beard on his chin, long past military regulation. Scowling, the soldier bunched the reins tighter in his hand as he stepped onto his own chariot.

"Do not try anything," he warned, then looked forward as the horses kicked into motion.

The moment he looked away, Seth acted. Leaning forward, he wrenched at the reins. His footing unsteady, the soldier fell back against the fencing, yet he clung to the straps still. Seth rammed his heels into his horse's side, then threw his arms around its great neck as it reared with a protesting neigh.

As the horse settled, Seth saw the gamble had paid off: the soldier had released him. Around him, chariots stuttered to a halt, but it would take them precious moments to turn around.

Seth grabbed his horse's reins and yanked them in the direction of the forest path.

"Stop him!" Amon shouted, but it was too late. Seth's horse, panicked by the commotion, already galloped down the lane, carrying him swiftly beyond the general's reach.

Soon, the shouts faded behind him. Seth did not try to slow his mount, but let it sprint unchecked. The pit was just moments down the road. Already, he could see the clearing approaching.

He bared his teeth. His moment had come. His service would soon be at an end.

But first, a final sacrifice.

Wind cut at his face. Sleet blinded him. His horse tossed its head, more frenzied with each stride. Only the path kept it to its course, the beast taking the way of least resistance. Seth clung on, though it felt as if he rode upon a storm. Despite it all, his mind was clear of all but his purpose.

The camp appeared around him. Seth and his horse tore through it. Soldiers shouted at him, then struck. Wounds scored across the horse's flanks. Some of the sharp steel struck Seth's legs as well. He barely felt them.

From across the pit, the huame roared.

Their voices and thundering footsteps finally proved too much for the horse. Screaming, Seth's mount reared.

Seth lost his grip and flew free.

As he landed, agony shrieked through his body. For a moment, he could not think or remember his purpose.

But he had come through fire once. This was just a conflagration of a different kind.

Seth pushed to his feet. He could barely stand, but he kept moving forward. His vision was blurred and his body broken, but he had been molded for this. The strength of Bek flowed through him. The purpose of the Divine One filled him.

I am enough.

Steam rose before him. He stumbled into its depths. Behind, the shouts grew distant. Even the bellows of the giants seemed muted. Seth wiped the blood from his eyes with a limp hand and stared. He had limped his way down the initial slope and into the pit. Rotten eggs filled his nose, his mouth, his head.

He grinned, though it hurt to move his face. He was close, so close to fulfilling his goddess's wishes now.

Something struck his side and sent him reeling.

Falling to his knees, Seth grasped at the thing sticking from between his ribs. It cut his hands as he felt it. *An arrowhead.* It felt strange and foreign, an unwanted invader.

Fire bloomed through his midriff.

The task! Frantically, he tried dragging himself deeper into the pit. Though obscured from sight, he was still vulnerable to bows. He could not risk being killed before striking a spark. His limbs felt clumsy, his mind scrambled, but he was the servant to a goddess. His duty was blessed by the Divine.

Another arrow pierced his leg.

Coughing, Seth spat up blood and wheezed as he dragged himself upright. He leaned against the quarry's wall. Every breath felt an impossible labor. He wondered when the last would come.

The spark. Strike the spark!

The voice spoke with command, as if the Holy Karah herself guided him. *Perhaps she does.* Sluggishly, he tried to obey. His hand fumbled at his waist, trying and failing to untie the pouch there. A glance down showed scarlet had spread all down his legs. The arrowhead glistened where it emerged from his side.

Despair dragged his eyelids closed before a clearer picture drew him in.

Tall grass surrounded him. To his right, a river, wide and deep, glistened in the sunlight. The scents of fresh-grown things filled his nose. The air was warm against his skin.

Home. He had never felt that feeling before, but he knew it down to his bones. The Land of Bounty was so very close. The reward he had awaited his entire life was near.

But he had not reached it yet.

A surge trembled through him. Seth's eyes flew up. His vision was no clearer than before, his body no stronger, yet his clumsy fingers at last pried open the strings on the pouch.

Fumbling out the flint, Seth coughed wetly and unsheathed his knife. Holding each in a hand, he wondered how he could do it. A spark, a single spark was all that he needed. He just needed to raise his arm, strike it on the stone, and all would be done.

Raising his arm felt like lifting a boulder. Darkness edged in. Each breath was wet and shallow. Seth could only hold the flint on the ground; anything more was beyond him. He ground his teeth so they felt they must crack and turn to dust. He tried to aim, then brought down his arm.

He missed the flint, yet the knife struck stone. Orange dots flew up from the ground. Like seeds sprouting, flames flickered up from them. Seth watched as moths became birds, then merged with each other, spreading faster and quicker with every moment.

Fire. He had feared it before, feared its touch against his flesh and the pain it would bring. Now, it was a messenger, its crackle a chorus of singers beckoning him to what waited beyond.

Home.

Seth reached up, and the inferno embraced him.

50. THE WISH

Death rarely comes to those who wish for it. It spares the undeserving and passes over the yearning.

Few choose their moment to die. Even among those miserable, some instinct remains, drawing us to the surface from dark depths, as if seeking a sun barely visible through the water's edge.

So must I keep swimming, though I wish to drown. So must I survive.

- The diary of Siva Of Torvald, Wife of King Torvald Geirson, Matron of the Harrowhall, the Last Queen of Baegard

Gertrud stared at the ripple in the fabric as a gust passed by the tent.

She had studied its every movement, knew the way it writhed and wriggled. Bound to its supports, it was confined to those small motions, little more than twitches. As captive to its fate as she.

Only one thought occurred to her, again and again.

I am alive. My son is dead.

Death could not be summoned through wishing. Were it possible, she would have perished as soon as she had awoken. A Sypten servant named Teti, a gaunt man with a kindly smile, had told her what had occurred. That the queen had spared Gertrud's life at the final moment. Gertrud had failed to muster a reply. Eventually, the servant had given up and left her.

They had not bound her, yet Gertrud had not tried to leave. She had remained in the chair in the corner, content to take whatever food and drink was given to her. She did not speak when others spoke to her, not even the foreign queen. Like her servant, Sehdra Karah seemed kind. Gertrud had cursed her name before, yet she had become her savior. Still, Gertrud could find no gratitude in her heart.

Why did you not spare him? she longed to ask. *Why did you break your word to him, but not me?*

The queen had done her no mercy by keeping her alive. This "Holy Karah" had stolen away her son, her purpose. What did she have left to live for?

Yet she breathed and ate, drank and slept. Even now, Gertrud could not help but live.

After watching the fabric for some time, sleep again stole over her. She did not rest easy, but was plagued by dreams, sometimes even during her waking hours. Just then, she saw a mouse in a dark, stone room, scurrying among the shadows. From somewhere to her right, a dog snarled, then leaped into view, attempting to pin the rodent. This was no ordinary dog. Its fur was black fading to ashen gray. Its eyes burned with orange fire, and its mouth leaked wisps of smoke. With every step, dust that sparkled silver rose from its feet.

The hound howled, then leaped at the mouse again. Its

paws found it, and the mouse squealed. Growling, slavering, the dog lowered its mouth to the creature, then—

Gertrud was shaken awake.

Or she thought she had been. Yet when she looked around, no one stood near. Sunlight made the tent stiflingly hot, even though winter would soon be upon them. The queen and her servant were inside with her. Sehdra Karah had paced much in the past two days, and did so now as well, her gait uneven as she traveled across the sprawled carpets. When the queen had been dressing before, Gertrud had seen her deformed leg, and a small stirring of pity and admiration had awoken in her. This was a woman familiar with pain and hardship.

Yet she did not save Ragnar.

Both the queen and the servant noticed Gertrud had awoken. Teti hurried over, eyes wide. "So you felt it as well."

"Felt it?" She was surprised that she spoke. From the others' expressions, they were astonished as well. Not wishing to think overlong on it, Gertrud tried to remember what had awoken her. "Was it a tremor?"

The kindly man grimaced and looked around at his queen. He still spoke in Djurian as he said, "Something has happened."

"We knew something would. But we must wait to know for certain."

"Divine One, my pardon for disagreeing, but I fear we must flee. If Amon could not capture the pit, you know what Seth was to do."

Sehdra Karah stopped and faced her servant. "No formalities, Teti, not now. Of course I know what I asked of Seth — how could I not? When it would lead to his..." She cut off, eyes closed, lips pressed tightly together. Her body trembled for a moment before her eyes snapped back open. "It was likely their only option. But if a few must die for the many, so be it. I will not surrender. I will not yield my kingdom to Oyaoan. My people have been tyrannized by her and her fanatics for too long."

Gertrud stared at the woman and the color flushing her face. She did not wear her mask just then, showing the right side of her face to be mottled and scaled. Yet it was not that sight that arrested her, but the passion with which this woman spoke of defending her subjects.

A ruler who cares. No matter how she loved her son, Gertrud had never had delusions of him being a compassionate ruler. Nor was he meant to be. A warrior was supposed to be strong, and warriors ruled the Seven Jarlheims. Yet this foreign queen had a gentler tact.

"Sehdra..." Teti bowed his head. "At least allow me to make precautionary preparations."

The queen's mouth twisted. "I doubt I could stop you."

The servant bowed again, then hurried from the tent. Sehdra Karah glanced at Gertrud, the right side of her face twitching. It seemed an involuntary movement. Gertrud wondered at the thoughts it betrayed.

"You seemed to dream," the queen said. "You muttered about a mouse, I believe."

Gertrud stared mutely at her, words run dry. She wondered if she should hate her, this woman who had a hand in her son's death and her home's destruction. Yet even that much emotion seemed impossible to muster.

Sehdra limped closer. "I know something about being a mouse. Of hiding in the shadows, afraid of being seen. I suspect you know something of this as well." She paused. When Gertrud made no reply, the queen continued. "My brother delighted in exposing me, parading me before his court so they might laugh at their cursed princess. Few insults were said to my face, of course, yet the whispers were just loud enough to overhear.

"I did not wish to leave the darkness. I did not want my brother's death, though the Divine know he deserved it. This crown" — she gestured to the elaborate mask displayed behind her — "was a burden I never expected to bear. It weighs heavier with each choice I make. Yet there comes a time when you must step into the light, or wither."

The queen sat in the chair next to Gertrud, eyes never wavering. Gertrud shifted, unwilling to meet her gaze.

"I am sorry I could not save your son. I know it is a pain that will never leave. But you cannot remain in his shadow now that he is gone. You must find something else to live for."

Gertrud had thought she was scrubbed clean of feeling. The anger flaring in her breast proved her wrong.

"No. I will not let go of my son." Gertrud spoke through clenched teeth. "He... it is all I have left."

"Not all. You have your life."

And what is that worth? Yet already, weariness returned, numbing the heat as swiftly as it had come. Exhaling, she slumped back in her chair.

Sehdra rose. "Rest for now. But be ready, Gertrud. We may soon have to fight for our lives."

She closed her eyes, doubting she cared.

———

Trampling feet woke her a moment before the tent flap tore open.

"Sehdra! Sehdra Karah!" A man stood there, disheveled and armored. Gertrud stared at him, bleary-eyed, her mind in a fog. She felt as if she had been in another dream, this one a storm of contrasting lights battling itself, but she could not recall it clearly now. She shook her head free of the fog and squinted. It was dusk, judging by the dim light in the tent, which was now illuminated by a fiery brazier.

The queen strode over to the man, her mask donned and her limp almost hidden by her haste. For several moments, they spoke in rapid Sypten. Gertrud rose to her feet, heart a storm in her chest.

Sehdra looked at Gertrud with eyes wide. "Quickly! We must go—"

Her words were lost as the sky was ripped away.

Gertrud fell to her knees and cradled her arms over her head. Harsh winds whipped up around her, reeking with the stench of the camp and rotten eggs. As they faded, she found the courage to raise her head. It was not the sky that had left, but the tent. Like a mighty gust had blown in, the fabric had been yanked away.

A silhouetted figure loomed high above.

Oyaoan glowered down at them. Dozens of feet tall and with hands like slabs of stone, her brutish face bore an unmistakable glower.

The hound and the mouse. Her gods-given dream no longer seemed a mystery.

"Sehdra!" A man called the queen's name from beside the giantess's feet. Tearing her gaze away for a moment, Gertrud saw him to be the same as had stood by Oyaoan when her son was condemned.

Anger blossomed through her. He had delighted in his burning. Yet her fury meant nothing to the enemy looming above.

There was only one way this night would end.

51. WRATH OF THE SUN

Those who taunt the Sun get burned.

- Common Sypten saying

Sehdra stared up at the giantess.

Her plans had been foiled. Her reign, the shortest in Ha-Sypt's history, had ended. Yet, even with death looming above, she refused to surrender to fear.

I was a mouse, once. No longer.

Sehdra drew up straight with her cursed, twisted body. If she was to die, she meant to be a goddess to her last breath.

"Oyaoan!" she called up. "How kind of you to visit at last!"

The giantess threw aside the pavilion's fabric and rose to her full, towering height, trunk flinging wildly from side to side. Brazier light caught upon her black, beady eyes, igniting them like coals catching flame, and set the jewelry upon her tusks to glittering.

"How did you do this?" the Ibis demanded, drawing

Sehdra's gaze back down. The translator smiled no longer. At last, she had struck a blow that he and his mistress had not expected.

"You knew of *ishilva!*" he screeched. "Knew even a spark could send it to the skies! How did you come by this knowledge? Tell me, puppet, or my men will lash the answer from your worthless hide!"

Sehdra held his thunderous gaze. Pain had been her most constant companion. The threat of it now failed to awaken even a tremble.

"You are not the only one with prescience, Ibis," she said, voice falling softer.

The translator's face twisted. At Oyaoan's feet were other Suncoasters, armed and ready to press forward. But for Amon and the few straggling men who had come with him, Sehdra had no defenses, none but her words. Further out in the torch-lit camp, soldiers gathered around, but none came closer. She did not blame them. They could not harm Oyaoan; only silver — or *ishilva*, as the Ibis had called it — could accomplish that. Perhaps she should have fled with Teti when he had asked.

And go where? a part of her objected. *No, Scarab. Even a beetle takes a stand when cornered. Even a mouse may wound a giant.*

Her friend was absent. Teti would survive. A smile claimed her lips. She could face death knowing he would be spared.

Oyaoan bellowed toward the sky, then stomped one massive foot. Sehdra almost lost her balance before the tremor, yet she just held her ground.

The Ibis stalked closer, soldiers flanking him. "Tell me now, Sehdra!" he shrieked. "Tell me, or I will tear off your fingers, one by one!"

The answer burst from her. "It was the disciple! You

could not see him in your visions, could you? That was why he caught you by surprise!"

Was it pride or courage that made her speak? Either way, Sehdra smiled as the translator's eyes widened, realization settling in.

"Yes," she continued, "you failed your giantess. You thought a burned servant beneath your notice. But he turned out to be your downfall. How long will your mistress keep you now?"

With each word, she felt the balance between them tilting. The Ibis was lost. His advantage had been taken and twisted into the knife that stabbed him through. She could only hope Oyaoan would have enough fury to punish him after finishing with her.

The sky moved. All of Sehdra's newfound confidence drained away as the giantess snatched her up.

Enormous fingers crushed into Sehdra. Her feet left the ground. Her vision spotted with black. Sehdra tried to remain conscious as her body screamed in protest. Oyaoan's clenched fist brought her up, up to the huamek's face far above.

For the first time, Sehdra stared her directly in the eye. Those black eyes were not so small as they always seemed, only dwarfed by the gargantuan head.

Oyaoan's bellow ripped through her. Fetid breath poured out, the same stench as Hua-fire. The world rippled.

Just as suddenly, a hush fell. Vibrations told Sehdra of continued sounds she could barely hear. Only a lingering sense of pride kept Sehdra conscious. She turned her lolling head so she could meet the giantess's stare.

She had been a mouse all her life. She meant to die a lioness.

A familiar voice pierced the haze. Sehdra twisted around, fear spawning in her a feeble vigor. She would have known that voice anywhere. He was the only person she wished to see, and the last she wished to see there.

Teti ran toward them. In his hands were two items: a torch and a pouch nestled into his palm.

She understood a moment before he fell against the Suncoasters.

No! she would have screamed, but her lungs were crushed. *Teti, no!*

Light flashed. Heat billowed up. Oyaoan's hand loosened its grip.

Sehdra fell.

For a moment, she was weightless, limbs loose by her side. Then she came crashing to a halt.

I am dead. I must be. Yet air whooshed into her lungs, telling a different tale.

Yet someone *had* died.

"Teti," she whispered through blood-flecked lips. Body screaming in protest, Sehdra struggled to look around and see what had become of her friend. All around her had devolved into chaos. Fire blossomed upward like the Jackal's Blight rose from the underworld, hellish and choking with smoke. Shadows writhed before the flames, men fighting one another, the sides impossible to distinguish. With her returning hearing, she heard the trumpeting of giants and felt their heavy footsteps tremble through the earth. If Oyaoan lived, she could not be certain, only that one huamek stomped dangerously near to her.

None of it seemed to matter much. Even if Teti had felled Oyaoan, Sehdra would not survive the wrath of her followers. She was broken and alone, the silver sand that birthed Hua-fire beyond her control. Teti had bought with his life the smallest of victories. All her struggles, all her people's sacrifices, had come to naught.

Sehdra closed her eyes and laid back her head. The

rotten stench of the fire drowned out all others. She breathed it in, not caring, waiting for the end to arrive.

Teti, Teti, why did you come back?

Her body shrieked, from her twisted foot to her ribs to her spine, but somehow, it had morphed. It seemed not just the agony of breaking, but mending. It was impossible. She knew it for what it was: an idle fancy, a dream brought by her coming death.

Hands roughly seized her and pulled her upright.

Sehdra's eyes flew open. For a moment, she stared, uncomprehending, at the man who held her, until her swimming vision finally let her recognize him.

"Amon?"

"Come!" Amon barked. Without waiting for her to respond, he began dragging her to her feet. "We have to go!"

She stumbled after the general, scarcely able to believe her legs still worked. He gave her little time to consider it, hauling her toward a chariot positioned just behind them.

Someone came up on her other side to clutch her arm. Sehdra turned and was astonished to see Gertrud there, her face pinched with equal parts fear and determination. No longer was she the empty shell from before, but a woman choosing to live.

With their combined efforts, Sehdra stepped up into the chariot bed and collapsed to the floor. She clung to the walls as Gertrud climbed in and Amon secured the door behind them.

"Drive, man, drive!" the general bellowed.

A man called an assent, and horses cried out. Then the chariot surged forward into the fire-brightened night.

52. HUNT

"For a brother, a lover, a mother — for them, is there any atrocity we would not commit?"

- Asger Fireside, a skald of Djurshand

Egil crested the rise before looking back. Oakharrow had disappeared behind the craggy peaks, gray and topped with white. The rest of the company trudged up the slope behind him: five hundred men and two women, Acolyte Tyra coming along with Mistress Aelthena. It was a far larger group than the last Egil had traveled with, especially when adding in the fifty-odd horses lent to them by the Thurdjur elders.

In the thin dusting of frost upon the ground, the tracks of those they pursued were still visible. Kuljash's were plainest of all, fitting the whole of a horse in each footprint. It was for the giant that they bore their most precious cargo: two barrels of dragonfire, lashed to either side of a mule that walked in the middle of the company. No matter how many men they had, they were unlikely to take down the Jotun through swords alone. Nuvvog's Rage was their true strength.

Egil relished the thought of using it, of burning Kuljash as the giant had burned Bjorn's kin. He would gain vengeance for the former heir and save him in the same stroke. The thought of it was almost enough to awaken a smile.

But that could wait until their reunion.

"Volkur smite me where I stand, did I just witness Egil Yaethunson looking wistful?"

Egil stifled the soft feelings as he turned to Loridi. The jokester grinned, his mouth seeming especially large on his narrow face.

Looking away without a response, Egil pretended to study the way ahead. He did not dislike Loridi, but his easy manner made him uncomfortable. He never knew how to carry himself around him.

"Don't tease him." Seskef came huffing up after his companion. "You know he doesn't like it."

"What else am I supposed to do? Stand next to him with a dourness to match his? If I fail to laugh, my friend, then my lifethread is running dangerously short."

Loridi stroked the muzzle of his horse — more of a mule, to Egil's eye. Since he had acquired it in Eildursprall, however, it could hardly be held to Harrow standards.

"What's he to you, anyway, our Lord Heir?"

Egil glanced sharply over at Loridi's question. Gone was the joking manner, replaced by a considerate look.

"Loridi," Seskef said softly, a chastising note in his voice.

"Don't know what you mean," Egil muttered.

The lump in his throat told otherwise.

The tall man stared a moment longer, then shrugged. "You just seem more loyal to Bjorn now than when we were the Hunters in the White. Wondered what changed."

Egil reached for a frost-bent calm, only just keeping a flush from his face.

"I'd better scout ahead." Mounting his gelding, Egil took off at a trot, chased all the while by the sense that he was fleeing.

The ominous surroundings soon drew his focus back in more productive directions. Though he ranged a league ahead, Egil encountered no enemies that evening. Their company made camp in the shelter of the sparse trees that night, the same place they had pitched their tents as the Hunters in the White. Egil watched Bjorn's sister across the camp as he chewed woodenly on a strip of smoked mutton. In most ways, she was entirely unlike her brother, but he noticed small resemblances. The curve of the lips. The prominence of the cheekbones. Certain mannerisms, like a shrug or a smile.

Aelthena glanced his way, and Egil looked aside, pretending not to have been staring. He did not dare peek another glimpse the rest of that night.

As the others found their bedrolls, Egil volunteered for the first watch. His back to the dying fire, he stared into the gloom. Though others struggled to see in the dark, he could still pick out the trees and the small creatures moving among them. His senses had always been sharp; it had been one reason he had been accepted into the city watch so swiftly.

His hearing was keen as well. The heavy, crunching footsteps signaled Seskef's approach before he lowered himself down next to Egil. They sat in silence for several minutes before the man spoke.

"We need not discuss it. Only, I think you should talk with someone. This sort of thing... it eats at a man from the inside out."

Egil did not need to ask what he spoke of. Anger flared

for a moment, but what good could come of it? It felt as if eyes watched and ears perked to listen, waiting for the defense against the allegations.

But for once, Egil did not want to be like the storied warriors of old. The night was bitter, and Seskef's solid presence was a draught of comfort.

Egil fished out a skin of mead from his saddlebags and offered it. Seskef nodded his thanks and took a swig before handing it back. Egil took a drink himself, a heartier one than he usually opted for on watch. The leather had slightly turned the mead, yet it still brought a pleasant warmth to his belly.

"Are you two happy?"

He had not meant to ask the question. Egil swallowed and looked around, compelled to be doubly sure no one eavesdropped. Yet their surroundings had not shifted; the night was hushed and still.

"Yes," Seskef murmured. "We are very happy."

Egil nodded. It was all that needed to be said. Seskef sat a while longer, then rose with a clap on Egil's shoulder. He did not meet the stout man's eyes, unwilling to face what he had just admitted aloud for the first time.

But if he had learned one thing from watching Bjorn Borson, it was that a man could only hide from himself for so long.

Halting the company, Vedgif gathered its leaders around. "Jünsden lies two leagues ahead."

Egil tightened his hand over his sword's hilt. The pass they traveled up was wide at the moment, but the steep slope and uneven ground made it difficult to congregate closely. Nevertheless, the Rook commanded their attention as surely as if they were atop a wall before a battle.

"You believe the Jotun has fortified there?" Aelthena stood near the center of the circle. Taking charge seemed a habit of hers, from all Egil had seen during their brief time together. It should have bothered him, yet somehow, he felt just the opposite. If she were a fool, it might have been otherwise, but her opinions were sound. Besides, a Bear in charge was a return to the way things ought to be, and Egil wanted nothing less than that.

"Likely so." Giving no sign if he accepted the former heir's intrusions, the elder turned to Egil. "Take five men and scout ahead."

Egil nodded and motioned back to the few men he had picked out before. Loridi and Seskef had come to mind, but he decided to leave them with Aelthena. Bjorn would not thank him if Egil allowed his sister to be killed.

"Come," he said once the five men had gathered around. "And keep quiet."

Young though he was, the men deferred to him. Not only was Egil highborn and they low, but he was the head of his household and descended from a line of jarls. He was used to being a mere sentry, but this new role was quickly becoming familiar.

He turned for his horse, hiding his scowl. The hunt for power had led his father astray. He refused to let it corrupt him as well.

Once mounted, they rode into the forest in silence, then kept within the trees. Though it made for slower riding, they were less likely to be observed from afar. Egil watched their surroundings for any sign of movement. The air was crisp and smelled of winter. Wind moaned between the trunks, rustling the pine needles. No tracks of boots or giants touched upon the sparse snow or mud. If the Jotun and his men lay ahead, Egil saw no sign of it here.

A league passed, then part of a second. His pulse quickened with each step that brought them closer to Jünsden. At any moment, they might stumble upon their enemy.

A part of him hoped they would.

Egil slowed their pace to a crawl, then gathered his men close. "We'll split up to cover more ground. You three, cover the southern approach. Latham and Destin, north with me."

It was a risk, but with their enemies no doubt keeping watch, he had to double their chances of warning the main host. Leaving the other three warriors, Egil led his two men across the open ground to the northern side of the pass, where a strip of trees hugged the cliff face. He watched the sky for smoke as much as the surrounding ground, it being a sure sign of habitation.

Soon, they reached the end of the copse. Egil edged his horse forward and squinted up the slope. There, over the next hill, he saw it: a tinge of deeper gray against the overcast sky. He wondered if Bjorn was there, just ahead. He wondered if they had hurt him.

His hands bunched into fists over the reins.

"We'll take a closer look," he said, pitching his voice low. "Be ready to flee."

Without looking back, Egil pressed in his heels, coaxing his mount to a walk. He spotted tracks on the ground a short time later. Yes — their enemy was close now. He hardly dared to breathe lest he miss a sign. His eyes throbbed from the strain of vigilance.

"M'lord," Latham murmured, "isn't this far enough? We saw the smoke. The Djur-damned giant and his men are there, no doubt."

"We cross," he said, and started forward. He saw no

need to explain that they needed to confirm it was their enemy and not the ordinary occupants of the town.

"And get ourselves killed?" Destin spoke now, fear palpable in every word.

Egil halted his horse and turned back. He looked at each, men older than him by a decade. Had it been time that turned their hearts craven? He did not expect to live long enough to find out.

"We protect the jarlheim," he said finally. "That is our duty."

"My wife would disagree," Latham muttered.

Destin smiled at that. Egil stared at him until the smile slipped away.

"Obey," he said softly, "or you will face the jarl's justice upon our return."

"Which jarl—?" Destin started to say, but quieted at a look from his companion.

"We'll go, m'lord." Latham's lips twisted at the title. "Mind you don't get us killed, though. I have daughters to think of, and Destin has his farm."

"Paltry though that's been," the thinner man muttered.

Egil turned away. He did not care to know of their lives, only to have their obedience. "We've delayed too long," he snapped, then started back up the hill.

This time, at least, his party remained intact.

Tracks appeared underfoot, many of them looking not a day old. Egil only glanced down at them, more concerned with who might linger among the cliffs. For the moment, they remained alone.

A boulder field sprouted ahead of them. The silence became stifling. He itched to draw his blade, but even the dull sun behind the clouds could reflect off steel and reveal their position. At each boulder, Egil peered around it. The men behind him had largely fallen silent, resigned to obedience. He could hear their fear in each soft mutter, but as long as they followed, they could say what they liked. The ground turned to pebbles, too large to detect tracks among them.

To his left, a shadow rose from a boulder.

Egil had his sword and shield in hand before his men cried out a warning. The figure atop the boulder, silhouetted by the bright sky, raised his arms. An arrowhead flashed at the end of his draw.

Egil raised his shield. A mere dozen feet away, the impact jarred up his arm as the arrow pierced a hand's width through the wood.

As he stared at the arrowhead, inches from his face, a sensation like a summer breeze billowed through Egil. He lowered his shield and saw the world was cast in pink hues, as if a tinted haze had settled over it. It affected not only his eyes, but seemed to suffuse his body as well, evoking strange sensations.

He remembered this feeling. Its strength. Its fury. Its need to paint the stones red. Distantly, he saw a door cracked open and yawning wider with each passing moment.

He threw it wide.

Surging to his feet, Egil stood atop his horse's back, heedless of his mount's protests. Leaping onto the boulder, he scrabbled up the rock face. The barbar tried to loose another arrow, but Egil's sword was quicker, darting in to stab his belly.

The man screamed, dropping the bow and clutching the wound, but Egil did not slow. Striking with his shield, the rim crushed the barbar's windpipe. The enemy fell to the stones below and lay there, motionless.

Something flashed in the corner of his eye. Egil threw up his shield to catch a second arrow, this one driving in shallower. It had barely made impact before Egil leaped from the boulder ten feet down, legs braced. The impact of landing resounded up his body, but he barely felt it. Parrying the barbar's strike, he countered, but this foe had been quicker to draw his weapon. A single-edged axe, he wielded it inexpertly, but well enough to block Egil's first strike. Egil feinted, then pivoted to cut open his opponent's arm, causing him to howl and drop his weapon. He silenced the man a moment later, knocking him to the ground with his shield, then skewering him in the back.

Looking around the looming boulders, Egil noticed two figures approaching. Blood dripped from their weapons.

Raising his shield, he stalked toward them.

"Lord Egil?" one said. "You take a blow to the head? We have to warn the company."

Red flashed in his vision. His muscles strained to lash out. Yet something in the man's tone made Egil draw to a stop.

A trick of Nuvvog's! Will you be duped so simply?

He took another step forward.

"Lord Egil..." The man's words trailed away. He looked at his companion.

They know you won't be fooled. Kill them!

Egil surged forward.

The men shouted in surprise, but their shields and weapons rose. Egil barreled into one, shoving him to the ground before swiping his sword at the other. His blade shaved wood and glanced away.

"Gods-damned bastard!" the enemy shouted. "Should have known you were a traitor like your father!"

Don't listen to their lies!

But the red fog was leeching from his mind, pierced by that word. Egil stumbled back until his back hit stone. He spoke in a whisper.

"I'm no traitor."

The strength bled away. His sword and shield fell to his sides. Only an edge of wariness remained as he watched the two men he now recognized as his own. Latham and Destin had not lowered their own arms. Both recovered, they kept their distance, confusion wild in their eyes.

"What in the hells was that?" Latham spat.

"He tried to kill us!" Destin sounded equally terrified and affronted. "He knocked me over! He fucking *swung* at you!"

"Cram it, Destin! Not swinging now, is he? Let him speak."

Egil could only stare at the pair. His mouth opened, but he couldn't find the energy to speak. His thoughts caught on the voice that had spoken in his head. Where had it come from? Why had he listened to its commands?

Latham slowly lowered his shield, eyes widening. "Sprites-touched. I see the signs now."

Destin still looked ready to fight. "What? So you're just going to let him kill you, then?"

"The madness comes and goes, from what I hear. Looks like it's over for now. Besides, what choice do we have? Don't you know what happens if you kill a highborn?"

"Better than dying, I'd wager."

"Not likely. You'd be lucky if you hung. Though I'd bet the wheel would be your fate."

Destin finally let his shield fall. "Then what? I'm not turning my back on him."

Egil rallied himself to speak. "I... I won't..." He shook his head, frustration returning a bit of his spirit. "I'm fine now."

"Fine." Destin loosed a high-pitched laugh. "Hear that, Latham? He's fine!"

"I'm warning you, Destin. Not another word." Latham looked Egil up and down. "What just happened, m'lord?"

He grimaced. It was the very question he needed answered. The very one for which he had no excuse. Yet, remembering some of Bjorn's explanations, he had a glimmer of one.

"Battle-madness." He let out his breath in a heavy exhale. "It had me, for a moment. But it's gone now. I'm in control."

In control. The words seemed to echo in his head. Was the thought his own? Or had the voice reemerged from some hidden depths?

Latham raised his arm, and Egil tensed. Though he was in the wrong and had caused all this mess, he had no intentions of dying for it. But the man only sheathed his sword.

"Fine, m'lord. Destin and I will forget this ever happened."

"We'll *what?*" Destin screeched.

Latham glared at the second man until he wilted. "But we have two conditions. First, we're never under your command again. And second, you make it so my family will live comfortably to the end of their days, and Destin doesn't have to worry about his poor soil. Do we have an understanding?"

Bribery. Not a week as the head of his house, and already, he traded in deceit as his father always had. But he had tried to kill these men; there was no backing away from the truth. One way or another, he had to pay for his mistake.

"Yes." Egil forced the word out through gritted teeth. "I'll do it."

Destin glanced between them, looking slightly dazed at this change in fortune. Latham's gaze remained hard, but he only nodded, then jerked his head back the way they had come.

"Lead the way, m'lord. Best bear back our news to the company."

With a weary effort, Egil levered himself upright again. Slowly, he sheathed his sword again, the two men watching him as he did. He had seen his horse flee in a different direction than Latham had indicated, but at the moment, he did not think himself in a position to protest.

What would Bjorn say if he saw you now?

Tottering forward, Egil set off on the long walk to return to the company, Latham and Destin's footsteps a reminder of all the burdens he carried back.

53. BOUND

"Though it defies reason, this I hold to be true: He who knows the future may change it."

- Torvald Geirson, the Last King of Baegard, days before his disappearance

I n, damn you, in!"

Bjorn ducked, narrowly missing the edge of the rough tunnel ceiling. He had kept heart during the long march before, but his courage flailed as he stared into the abyss yawning before him. Against all his wishes, he had wound up back in this hole of nightmares.

Jünsden Hall. Bjorn recalled to mind the massacre he had led his men into, which had once seemed his life's greatest folly. That scene that haunted his dreams over the past year. Seasons gone, he could still smell the battle, cooked meat and blood perfuming the air.

Yet could he truly regret what happened here? Without Jünsden Hall, would he have stumbled upon the Chasm and destroyed it, robbing the Jotun of his most potent weapon? Would he have gone to Eildursprall and learned of the Sight, met Mother Sign and the King of Ice?

He might never have traveled the path of the Four Shadows. Enea might have been doomed without even a chance for survival.

Bjorn sucked in a breath. This was his path to walk. But knowing one's destiny and following it were two very different things.

At his gaolers' insistence, he proceeded down the tunnel. The darkness was so thick even his heightened sight could not penetrate it. From the shadows cast by the flickering flames of the torches, horrors took shape. Axes and knives seemed to flash around him, and Bjorn flinched as each stroke fell.

You survived this before, he reminded himself. *You'll survive again.*

"Watch your step." Yonik's soft warning came from next to him. The priest seemed as steady as ever, his voice betraying none of Bjorn's fear. Bjorn wondered if he would have discovered Yonik's serenity had he been able to train under the Silvers for longer. But they were dead, and Eildursprall had burned. That was a future he would never know.

Their three escorts remained foul-tempered from the march before. Kuljash had driven them hard, prisoner and warrior alike. They had not rested for two days until finally, the barbar chieftains begged the giant to relent. Bjorn wondered about the haste. As tall and mighty as he was, did Kuljash so fear *khnuum*? Or did he seek to keep on his own path to victory, guided by Sight-gifted visions?

He had no opportunity to find out, not on the march or since arriving at the Yewling village. He had no pack, yet marching up a mountain with one's hands tied while being yanked along by a handler was no easy feat. Even had he not been exhausted, Bjorn and Yonik were kept away from any others and under a careful watch. Escape was not likely this time, not that Bjorn wished to flee.

I must speak with him, and soon. Aelthena would send men in pursuit; he did not need witchery to know that. Kuljash had to be brought to an understanding before she arrived or all would be lost. Baegard. Enea. The whole of the Runewar. All their fates rested on Bjorn's shoulders, bowed though they were.

He thought a prayer to Baltur, hoping his faith was not misplaced.

The tunnel ended, and the natural cave of Jünsden Hall opened up around them. In his mind's eye, Bjorn saw the battle play out again. Chieftain Kard, the first jotunman they had seen, cutting through the Hunters in the White. Egil leaping onto the table to swipe at the towering chieftain. Keld, Bjorn's young and lost friend, bravely holding his own, inspiring Bjorn to reach for the warrior slumbering within.

Since that skirmish, the hall had seen little repair. Chairs and tables lay broken on the cave floor, though scooted to the peripheries of the chamber. He and Yonik were dragged over to one edge where iron rings had been driven into the ground. Clearly, they were not the first prisoners who stayed here. Bjorn did not struggle as the barbars tied them up. With the knowledge he held in his heart, he could endure anything.

The barbars grunted a few last insults at them, then left, taking their torches with them. Bjorn watched the light recede, then disappear entirely. Despite his resolution, his throat constricted at being left in the vast emptiness. Even his improved eyesight failed to pierce the black. His hearing was scarcely more useful; silence pooled up to the top of the domed ceiling, but for the fading sounds of their captors.

More than anything else, Bjorn smelled his unwashed body, reeking with fear-sweat. It was not long before he could no longer endure it stoically.

"I cannot speak with Kuljash while we're stuck here," Bjorn murmured.

"No," Yonik replied. "Nor are we likely to escape. But you have told him your purpose. If Kuljash has foreseen the same thing, he will summon you."

Bjorn bowed his head to the gothi's words. Privately, he worried he had missed his chance. Perhaps there had been but a moment to convince the giant back in Oakharrow, and now the opportunity was forever lost.

Torvald saw it would come to pass. Trust him. Trust yourself.

There, bound and cold and shivering in the darkness, trusting himself was the hardest task of all.

Seeking a distraction, Bjorn thought over all he had overheard on the march up. Mostly, the barbars had complained of the punishing pace, but some tidbits had spilled free among the detritus, Djurian being the common language among them. From the sound of it, they knew as little of the King of Chieftains' plans as Bjorn and Yonik. The whole of the Baegardian valley had been promised to them in exchange for their service, yet out of hearing of the Jotun, many doubted they would receive their reward. It almost made Bjorn smile. Splintering loyalties among Kuljash's followers would work to his advantage.

If I can only gain an audience.

Hours slithered by. Leaning against the wall, the cold stone sapping the warmth from his bones, Bjorn dozed until he jerked awake at Yonik's touch.

"Look," the gothi murmured. "A light nears."

Blinking gummy eyes, he saw it to be true. Working his stiff muscles out as best he could, Bjorn rose to his feet and waited. Whether he meant to fight or follow, he did not yet know.

The glow brightened until four barbars, one jotunman among them, emerged into the cavern. The jotunman led the others, growling at them in a barbar tongue, and they hurried to obey. Bjorn flinched as the men seized him, but a moment later, his feet were freed, as was the leash bound to the stake. Then he was being shuffled forward, almost faster than his weary legs could handle.

Despite it all, elation filled him. His time had come. Kuljash had called them to him.

Destiny neared.

When they stepped free of the tunnel, light lanced into Bjorn's eyes, for though the day was overcast, he had sat too long in the gloom. The barbars were merciless, pushing him on and hauling him back up whenever he stumbled. Bruises proliferated across his body, and hands struck when he did not move fast enough. Bjorn gritted his teeth, unable to do anything but endure it.

His vision had cleared by the time the Jotun came into view. In the town of Jünsden, no building rose tall enough to obscure him for long. The village was little more than a single lane with hovels lining either side. In the center of the muddy street sat Kuljash, his tree-trunk legs crossed; an oddly human position to find him in, though he supposed even a giant could not always stand. In a semi-circle around him stood the eight barbar chieftains, speaking loudly in Djurian with such vehemence that Bjorn wondered why the King of Chieftains did not squash them all on the spot.

Then he noticed the giant's eyelids were closed. The stench curling into his nose a moment later told him the truth of the situation. *Khnuum.* Either Kuljash had indulged in it for sustenance, or he was Seeing even then.

Bjorn's captors threw him to his knees at the outer edge

of the conference, one of the decrepit homes at his back. Yonik was placed next to him. Bjorn did not have to look around to know they directed spears at their backs, prepared to gore them at the slightest provocation. He ignored them and the chieftains, instead tilting his face up to the giant. Even sitting, Kuljash loomed far above, and it strained his neck to look up.

Knowing how visions might go, he settled in for a long wait.

While he waited, Bjorn noticed something that had escaped his attention before. Leaning against a house on the giant's far side was the Witterland Runestone. It appeared Kuljash always kept it close. Was it for the way it could make men into weapons? Or was there some further reason for it?

His neck seemed on the verge of snapping when, at last, Kuljash cracked open his eyes. At once, his gaze settled on Bjorn.

"Rune-man," the giant rumbled, his Djurian so garbled it took Bjorn a moment to understand. As their leader spoke, the chieftains quieted, though not without throwing resentful looks Bjorn's way.

Having not had a drop of water all that day, Bjorn had to work up moisture for a moment before he could respond. "Yes. I am a rune-man."

He hesitated, wondering if he should dive into his proposal at once. Kuljash did not give him long to ponder it.

"*Speak!*"

Heart hammering, Bjorn pieced together his scrambled thoughts. Only Yonik kneeling next to him, his shadowed eyes steady upon him, imparted the courage to press on.

"I understand why you are here, King of Chieftains. Why you came to Enea." He swallowed, girding himself to say the words. *"Khnuum.* You need it as humans need food and water, don't you? All giants do."

Around the circle, the chieftains exchanged guarded looks. A weakness — no doubt that was how they perceived this new information. But would they see it as a weakness to buttress, or an opportunity to topple a once-infallible leader?

For the Jotun's part, he loosed a deep rumble in his chest. "You," Kuljash said, drawing out the word into an accusation. "You bring fire to *khnuum.*"

Had he ever felt so afraid to speak? Still, his path forward was forged from honesty, perilous as it might be.

"Yes. I had a part in it. I thought only to deprive you of a weapon."

The weapon that slayed my kin.

He kept the words locked behind his teeth. This beast was responsible for his brothers' and mother's death, true, but vengeance would be a brief balm. His society, his people, his own honor demanded he take it however he could, but none of them could afford that luxury.

He was the Stoneseer. Someone had to see beyond human frailty to the future. If not him, then who? If not now, then when?

Only as he surfaced from his inner turmoil did he realize the giant had, in a rare moment, expressed his own emotions. The chieftains flinched back, and even Yonik stiffened with fear. Kuljash had not risen, yet he seemed to loom larger. The slabs of muscles beneath his thick fur twitched; his great mouth drew back around his tusks. Bjorn became conscious that he kneeled within reach of the crea-ture. Kuljash could crush him before he had time for a second thought.

But, in surrender, there was strength. He would see this moment through to its end.

The Jotun exhaled a fetid rush of air, bitter with *khnuum*. "Why," he grunted, "come to me?"

Bjorn's voice shook, but now from a thrill as if he went to battle. "It is as I told you back in Oakharrow. Another seer — that is, rune-man — saw the end of this world. Yet he also saw a path to a new age. That path begins with an alliance, one between you, King of Chieftains, and my people."

This seemed a step too far for the barbars. The chieftains rose, all speaking over one another to the giant. Between the clamor and their heavy accents, Bjorn only caught some of their words.

"We will not ally with soft-bellied valley dwellers!" one fumed, his white-wolf headdress tilting eschew in his fury.

Another, barrel-waisted and ornate with feathers and beads, declared with more pomposity, "We have slain their cattle, butchered their bairns. They would never be our allies!"

Kuljash ignored them. His unblinking gaze remained on Bjorn. Did he debate what to do with him? Or was it an invitation to continue? Bjorn took it as the latter.

"We Baegardians have found another source of *khnuum*, King of Chieftains." He only knew this by inference, yet it seemed a sound one. Bastor's army had used dragonfire in the assault on Oakharrow, and it had also won the day at Petyrsholm, from what he had heard. It was possible it had been ported from the Chasm among the Teeth, but Bjorn doubted Kuljash would be so generous with a substance he had sailed across half the world to secure.

"With your supply gone," he continued, "you will need another to sustain yourself. Should we become allies, we can provide it."

The chieftains were quieting. Even outraged, they sensed their leader's interest.

"In exchange, we would require knowledge only you possess. Knowledge to help us preserve our home." Bjorn swallowed, bracing himself for his next statement. But there was no veering from the path now. "I would know more of the jotunar, and the surtunar, if possible. How to reason with them, or, if necessary, fight them."

A ringing silence greeted his words, broken only by the moaning wind. Bjorn wondered if he might hear an omen in that gust if he listened. He wondered what stories it would tell.

"I suspect," he pressed on, "it would be in your interest to protect *khnuum* from the other giants. You gain from their loss, do you not? You came not as the vanguard for your people, but as an exile, searching for that which you need to survive."

It was a guess, a conjecture based on the facts he held. But when the Jotun did not protest, Bjorn pretended it was correct.

"We would require more, however. In your last defense of Oakharrow, you used *khnuum* and the Witterland Rune-stone to make weapons of your warriors. You made them into berserkers. I wish to learn this secret along with all others known to you of *seidar*."

He might have pressed on, but Yonik edged close enough to settle one bound hand on his arm. Bjorn grimaced, but held his tongue. There were many more things to discuss, details which could make or break even the possibility of an alliance. But the gothi was right to council caution. Better first to paint in broad strokes and see if they shared a common picture. He had to hope their mutual interests were strong enough to hold.

One chieftain, the one with the wolf headdress, roused again. "Never! We Haddik will never bow—"

The man fell silent at once as Kuljash held up one enormous hand.

"They come," the giant rumbled.

Bjorn wondered at his meaning. Almost, there seemed a bemused twist to the words. It took only a moment for the cloud of mystery to disperse.

The sound of horns filled the air.

54. JUDGMENT

When the giants had been caught, they were brought before Baltur to stand judgment. Looking down upon them, Baltur frowned, his feather quill twitching in his hands.

'Only one price may be paid for your crimes,' said he. 'Our ways have always been the justice of the wilds: hand for hand, eye for eye, blood for blood.'

He ordered their manhoods taken for violation of the woman; their eyes gouged out for looking upon their victim; their hands cut off for touching her. Their pleas for mercy fell on deaf ears. Baltur's justice is as cold as iron.

- Tales of the Inscribed, by Alfjin the Scribe

Aelthena hunched over, miserable from the hard hiking and riding up into the mountains. The sound of galloping hooves, however, made her come back upright.

Egil pulled up his horse short of Vedgif, who traveled just ahead of Aelthena. Two of the five riders that had left with him came behind. All three were bloodied and wore hard expressions. Clearly, the thought of what they had faced had not yet lost its edge.

Misery forgotten, she urged Winterlily forward, eager to hear their report. Behind her, she heard Loridi, Seskef, and Tyra hurrying to catch up.

"Barbars," she caught Egil saying as she came abreast of the elder and scouts. "Ambushed us in a boulder field on the northern side a league and a half advanced."

For all the elder reacted, the sentry could have been speaking of his meal the night before. "Did any escape?" Vedgif grunted.

"None that I saw, but more may have been out of sight."

The veteran turned, barely glancing at Aelthena as he spoke to the arrayed warriors behind. "The Jotun and his armies lie ahead! Be ready for an attack. We move!"

The men gave a stirring cheer before obeying. Aelthena felt she could scarcely breathe as she turned her horse after the others. The most eager members of the company pushed ahead, while she drifted toward the middle of the pack. Courage, she had aplenty, but she knew better than to think she belonged on the front lines of a battle.

Still, the clarity of their purpose instilled fresh strength in her. She hardly minded the wind whipping her hair free of its braid and into her face, nor her dress flapping and tangling about her legs in the frigid wind. Soon, she would take back her brother.

So long as Bjorn still lives.

They had not gone far before horns, deep and echoing, filled the pass. Aelthena's chest felt as if Kuljash crushed it with one enormous hand as she scanned the surrounding cliffs, half-expecting barbars to stream down from them. As far as her untrained eyes could tell, they were empty but for frost, stones, and trees. Ahead was where their enemy lay, over the crest toward the gloomy sky.

The forests widened. A boulder field sprouted up, then died out. From the expanse ahead rose a stone hill, buildings crouched before it. Jünsden, she gathered it to be. The Yewling town was even shabbier than she had imagined.

Then she saw him.

The Jotun stood in the middle of the principal thoroughfare of the shabby town. She had thought seeing the giant would fill her with dread, as her first glimpse of him had, but wrath instead threatened to overwhelm all sense and reason.

This was the creature responsible for her kin's deaths, for her birthright and home being stolen. This was the beast who had made her people suffer. Her blood shrieked for recompense, all the old ways instilled in her chanting: *Hand for hand, eye for eye, blood for blood.*

But anger would not slay a giant, nor could it save her brother. Aelthena ground her teeth and sought clarity, though it felt far out of reach.

Vedgif drew their company to a stop just short of bow range. Barbars lined the way before the village; three hundred, she guessed at a glance. It was fewer than she had feared, but more than could easily be overwhelmed, particularly while they held the defensive advantage. The foremost had shields and weapons in hand, while those behind held bows nocked and ready to draw. Their lines were uneven and their formations haphazard. Aelthena hoped their own warriors would prove more coordinated if it came to battle.

If. With her enemy looming above, how could it not?

Aelthena urged her horse forward through the host. Behind, Loridi and Seskef cursed as they tried to catch up. Ignoring their calls, she made her way to Vedgif and Egil, who carried on a murmured conversation. The two looked up at her approach. Vedgif openly frowned.

"Now is not the time, mistress," he said, his tone brooking no argument. "Fall back behind the others."

"Now must be the time, Elder Vedgif." She turned her steely gaze from the older man to the younger. "Call for a negotiation."

Egil's expression, already thunderous, darkened further. "They took him," he said, voice almost a growl. "We must win him back."

His passion surprised her, but not enough to put her off. "If we fight, they could easily kill him. Treat with them, and perhaps we can compel them to give him up. Then we may crush them."

"They may attack us during negotiations," Vedgif said.

"That will not stop you from going. Nor will it me."

The elder's brow creased, but he did not deny her.

Egil crossed his arms. "We all go, then."

The matter decided, Vedgif ordered a torch to be lit. The warrior stepped ahead of the company, then waved the torch in slow arcs to either side. Though it was the Baegardian sign of truce, Aelthena wondered if it would translate for their enemies.

They waited several moments before the barbar lines split down the middle. Between them emerged a set of extravagantly decorated men. Yet it was the two men shuffling beside the barbars that made Aelthena's breath catch. She stared, unable to peel her eyes away from the one she had long yearned to see.

Bjorn.

He was difficult to make out in the distance, but he seemed to stand much taller than those around him. He had been only seventeen winters when they parted; it seemed the past year had yielded yet another growth spurt. She longed to hold him, touch his face, look into those somber eyes and know her brother was safe.

But he was not safe yet. Only she could make him so.

She stepped forward, ignoring Loridi and Seskef's warnings and disregarding Egil and Vedgif's stares. She walked a dozen paces into the empty gulf between the warriors, then shouted across the distance.

"Jotun! I would speak with you!"

Her shout echoed for a moment before the wind stole it away. The giant made no move. Had he heard? Large as he was, she could make out more of his face than any of the humans, and the snarl pronounced upon it.

When several seconds passed without an answer, she spoke again. "I give to you this warning, giant! Ignore our demands, and we will ruin you and those foolish enough to follow you. We have killed your kind before! You have seen our dragonfire; you know we can summon it again. Unless you wish to taste it, you will do this: release my brother and the priest."

"No!"

The shout was tinny and thin over the distance, but she knew Bjorn's voice even so. Still, she could not believe she had heard correctly.

No? How could he say that, now, of all times?

Her temper rose as she shouted back, "Let me handle this, Bjorn!"

"You must not kill Kuljash, sister!" he answered. "We need him as our ally, just as he needs us."

"Our ally!" A wild laugh threatened to burst free of her, though she felt not a shred of amusement. "He killed our mother, Bjorn! What of Annar, and Yof, and everyone else from the Harrowhall? He's behind it all! All the deaths in Oakharrow this past year, all the suffering is on him. And you want him to be our *ally?*"

"I have seen it, Aelthena." His voice cracked in that familiar, adolescent way. "I know the way to save us all!"

She was lost for words, trying to understand. *Save us all.* Her shock melted as comprehension set in.

"Your visions are not real, Bjorn! They never were! You almost killed a man because of what you imagined. It is madness, brother, madness! Do you not remember Father?"

There it was: the barbed arrow that had struck her from the first moment he had spoken, that she had scarcely noticed pierce into her soul. *He's mad. Sprite-touched. Like Father already.* Despair welled up in place of anger. Even if she preserved his life, she could not save her brother.

But she knew one thing to be certain. There remained one enemy she could fight.

She raised a hand toward the Jotun. "I do not understand what you say, but I know one thing to be true. This 'King of Chieftains' slew our people and attacked our jarlheim. His crimes cannot go unpunished!"

"Even if an alliance would save us?" Bjorn called back.

"He is a butcher, Bjorn! He will only kill more. His reign must end here!"

She had scarcely finished speaking before a deafening roar filled the pass. Aelthena flinched from the giant, her bluster broken before the sound. The Jotun cut off and glared down at her again. His upper lip curled, revealing the base of one yellowed tusk. But though it seemed the harbinger of an attack, no one on either side moved.

Before she could recover, someone stepped up next to her. Aelthena met Egil's gaze and flinched. Hatred burned like blue flames in his eyes, but it did not appear directed at her.

"I trust Bjorn," he said. "Do you?"

The accusation struck her with a cutting force. *Trust him? How can I?* She had seen the insanity take root in her brother before his departure. Their father showed its eventual result. How could she trust him when she did not know how far down that path he had ventured?

Yet one thing had not changed. There was one place where she, Bjorn, and his allies had interests aligned.

Aelthena faced the giant once more. "Jotun! First return my brother and the priest to us. Only then may we discover if we share common ground."

As she spoke, she studied Vedgif from the corner of her eye, wondering why the elder had not already intervened. He had become even more rigid than usual. Almost, he seemed afraid, impossible as that was to comprehend. Though she negotiated on Oakharrow's behalf with no real authority to her name, he said nothing. Whatever the reason, it suited her purposes.

The vale filled with wind. Aelthena clenched her jaw, watching and waiting. The squall died down, but no attacks came in its absence. The Jotun stirred and spoke.

"Free them."

She stared at the beast, knowing she must have misheard the garbled words. The barbars at his feet began babbling as if in protest.

Slowly, the truth sunk in.

Aelthena watched in a daze as the giant's men swarmed around Bjorn and Brother Yonik. Moments later, they parted, revealing the two men to be unharmed. Her brother seemed to hesitate, but the gothi touched his arm. Together, they strode unsteadily across the open ground.

She longed to run to them and envelop her brother in her arms, to hold him like he was little and she was the big sister keeping the world at bay. Self-preservation, however, kept her rooted to the spot.

But no arrow fell upon them, nor did any warrior strike them down. When they had come halfway across, Egil ran to them and escorted them the rest of the way. Bjorn grew closer and closer until he stood not two paces before her.

She did not dare look away as she took in all the changes wrought upon his flesh. Recent deprivation was obvious by his hollowed eyes, but he otherwise seemed hale and strong. Not only did he stand taller, but broader, and a full beard sprouted across his chin. He looked much like Bor the Bear as she remembered their father from her childhood. A warrior of song and tale.

But no matter how he had changed, he would always be her little brother.

"Bjorn."

He smiled at her, his eyes still turned down in that sorrowful way. "Hello, sister."

No sooner had he greeted her, however, than did Bjorn turn around. She stared at his back, then at the giant looming beyond him.

"I meant every word, King of Chieftains," her brother called. "I hope, by freeing us, it means you believe me."

The giant rumbled for a long moment before answering, the sound like an avalanche beginning to fall. "Bring *khnuum*, rune-man. We will speak."

Before he had finished, the Jotun was turning to stride away. With every step he took, the earth trembled under Aelthena's boots. She stared at the beast's broad back, scarcely able to believe it.

We won without shedding a drop of blood. And my brother still lives.

Vedgif stirred back to life. His face flushed as he leaned toward Aelthena. "The council will not bear this. We came to conquer our enemy while they were weak, not let them recover their strength."

Aelthena rounded on him. "I came to save my brother, elder, and I have done that. For now, it is enough."

The elder's jaw spasmed, but he only turned away. She might have pressed the issue, but Bjorn was striding toward her. To her surprise, he wrapped her in a hug.

"Thank you for coming for me, sister."

Aelthena smiled into his shoulder. "Of course. Haven't I always protected you?"

He chuckled into her hair, then pulled back. Looking into his eyes, she saw an eerie elation had replaced the sadness. Worry poisoned her relief.

"We still walk the path, Aelthena," he murmured. "All is not lost. Enea can still be saved."

She had to look away. Almost, she could see the sprites of ice circling his head. *One step at a time.* Her brother's mind was not entirely gone yet.

So she hoped.

"We had best depart," Aelthena forced out. "Before the giant's goodwill shifts." She wanted nothing more than to sink to the ground and close her eyes, to rest for the rest of the day through. But that was not an option, not until they had gone far from this place.

Once more, Vedgif did not argue before shouting the orders to march out. Aelthena glanced back at her brother and saw he had plenty of other people greeting him. If she was fortunate, he had not noticed her reaction.

With a gusty sigh, she turned after the others, setting off on the long journey home.

55. A DIFFERENT FIGHT

In all their years of war, men have never realized bravery can be found off the battlefield as well as on. There is no shame in staying to guard a family farm or stand watch at a ferry crossing. Perhaps, if we minded our own more often, the fields would not be sodden with blood and our young men whole and alive.

But my sons did not listen to me, nor my husband, nor the jarls pretending to serve at my leisure. This is a dying land. For all my platitudes, I cannot save my people.

- The diary of Siva Of Torvald, Wife of King Torvald Geirson, Matron of the Harrowhall, the Last Queen of Baegard

"G old... gold and shadow, falling down..."

Frey rubbed his eyes and sat up. His neck had a fresh crick from napping in the chair, but he was becoming used to pain. Carefully adjusting his broken arm, he stared at the man in the bed before him. The curtains were drawn, so the room lay in gloom, made more suffocating by the perfume of sickness and medicine.

Yet he could see Bastor shifting beneath his blankets, muttering nonsense in a feverish slumber. Barely a week had passed since he had taken ill, yet already, the prince wasted away before his eyes. Rising a head taller than Frey and with a big mouth to match, he had always been like a man from the sagas, full of deadly vitality. This dwindling felt even more dire for who Alabastor Ragnarson had once been.

Someone else drifted around the room: a servant attending to their prince. As the man moved to the bedside, Frey cleared his throat.

"Has his draught come yet?"

"No, guardian. Not yet."

Frey sighed. He wondered what could possibly be keeping the healer away from tending to his prince.

"I'd better fetch it, then."

Head pounding, Frey groaned and rose to his feet. He had spent too many days and nights in that damned chair, but Aelthena had asked him to watch over Bastor and her city. This was his only way of doing that. Not to mention, though he would never say it aloud, he had come to think of the roguish prince as more than his liege lord, though "friend" might be too far a stretch.

Picking his way through Vigil Keep's halls, still familiar from his previous stay, Frey found the tower where the healer was cloistered. The man moved about the frowzy room like a crow in its nest, his dark cap and clothes accentuating the effect. Frey dodged hanging herbs, often unpleasant in odor, to make his way to the healer's side.

"It seems you've forgotten something, healer. Again."

The man glanced up. His dark eyes darted over Frey

before settling back on the table he leaned over. "Cannot do anything more for your arm. Just have to wait for it to heal."

"I'm not talking about my arm. Have you so easily forgotten the prince?"

"Ah." The medicine man looked up again. "Prince Alabastor. Not forgotten — nothing more to be done."

Frey failed to stifle a grin. "Surely, you are jesting."

"I am not."

"This is your prince we're talking about. Your Djur-damned prince! Do you truly think it's a good idea to just let him die?"

Though Frey all but shouted in the man's face, the healer remained nonplussed. "The jarl asked that no more resources be spared. I am sorry."

He did not sound sorry at all, but it was a different thought that struck Frey, as if dagger-sharp ice pierced his chest.

The jarl.

"I see," he breathed. "We'll see about 'sparing resources,' shall we?"

Frey turned away from the healer's dubious expression and strode down the halls. Servants dodged out of his way; thralls cast him wary glances. Frey wondered how mad he must look, grinning to himself as he hurried along, his hair mussed and his clothes bedraggled.

Not half as mad as I'll soon be.

Four keepers guarded the chair-room, but they allowed him to pass at the mention of the prince. Within, Asborn paced before Hawk's Perch, absorbing something his mother was saying. They were not alone in the room. Besides the jarl's huskarls, several Balturg elders filled the eaves, two bobbing their gray heads to Lady Kathsla's words. Frey recognized one with a start: Hervor Silverfang, the duplicitous owner of the largest drascale mines. Though Aelthena had coerced him into admitting his collusion with Yaethun Brashurson, events had collapsed too quickly afterward to hold him accountable. Now, it seemed the man had clawed his way back to the heights of power.

Spotting Frey, Silverfang flashed him a smile. The glint of his silver tooth seemed a promise Frey was none too eager for him to keep.

Ignoring the traitor, he picked out the remaining attendees. Their Vurg allies were present, Edda Skarldaughter and her fiery shieldmaiden most notable among them. Bodil the Blaze leered at Frey, which he did his best to ignore.

This was not the friendliest of audiences, nor was Frey the ideal emissary for this mission. But Bastor could not wait for a better opportunity. Frey set his shoulders, adjusted his arm in its sling, and strode up the carpet to the jarl.

By the flicker of his eyes, Asborn noticed his approach, yet the jarl saw fit to ignore him until he stood before the stone chair. Frey stopped and smiled as he waited. Only as Asborn turned did he sketch a bow.

"Lord Jarl, if I could have but a moment of your time."

Rising, he noticed Lady Kathsla staring at him, her thin lips pursed. His back prickled as the attention of the chamber settled on him, but he had never been one to freeze before an audience.

"What is it, Guardian Frey?" The jarl's disdain was written across his features: his narrowed eyes, his haughty stance, his acid tone.

Frey pretended not to notice. "It is regarding Crown Prince Alabastor's care. I hear from the healer that you see him as unworthy of being, what was the phrase, 'spared the medicine'? Surely, the man misunderstood your orders. I cannot see any sound reason to withhold treatment for your prince."

Murmuring erupted across the room. Asborn's jaw spasmed. Before the jarl could respond, his mother intervened.

"Of course, the prince must be tended to. We will inform the healer at once."

The words sent his mind turning like a boat in the Whiterun's rapids. It seemed a fine response, but shite was often gilded among highborn. Only by breaking the crust could he release the stink.

"Perhaps, m'lord," he said in his most reasonable voice, "I might accompany this messenger now. The prince's condition calls for urgent action. I would not want the boy going astray."

Asborn descended the dais, each step slow and deliberate. Frey forced himself to stand his ground as the jarl stopped not a pace away. Asborn rose only a little taller than Frey, yet his fury and authority in that moment made him seem towering.

"Are you questioning my word, guardian? Implying I will not do as I say?"

Even then, Frey kept his smile. "Of course not, Lord Jarl. It is widely known you are an honorable man."

They stood there, matched in their stares. Frey knew Asborn could order his death at any moment. There would be hell to pay for it, but just then, Aelthena's former betrothed looked as if he did not care a lick.

"My son." Lady Kathsla spoke the words like a reprimand.

Asborn ignored her. "Go now. I have said I will send a runner, and so I will. You would do well not to question my word again."

Frey wondered if he could push his luck any further,

but decided there was little point in it. He could not force Asborn to listen, not with the present court at hand. Much as he wished Lady Kathsla would act more justly, he knew her to be too shrewd to rely upon her goodwill. They would make every appearance of caring for the prince, but in the end, they preferred him dead. Asborn was not Bastor's choice of jarl; as soon as he rose from his bed, Oakharrow might be taken away from him, even if it went against the king's wishes. In fact, it seemed all too likely that King Ragnar had once more ordered his son's death to prevent this very possibility.

"Thank you, m'lord." Frey backed up a step before bowing, then strode quickly from the room, ignoring the stares following him.

A little way down the hall outside the chair-room, Frey paused, his head spinning. *What now?* Bastor would not last more than a couple more nights by the look of him. He needed care right away.

But who could provide it?

Then he realized there was one person who could help, one who had remained conspicuously absent from the prince's bedside all that long week. Sucking in a breath, Frey braced himself for the task ahead.

He began to run.

The pain was excruciating, every step jostling his arm, yet Frey did not slow. He jogged past incredulous guards and gaping highborn, through the gates of Vigil Keep, then out into the streets of Oakharrow. The mood had shifted from the terror of the Jotun's occupation to a relieved ecstasy, but Frey had no time to soak it in. Up the streets and through the districts he ran, until at last, his destination rose before him.

The Tangled Temple had transformed from a rebel stronghold back to its former purpose. Its doors were open, and its windows trailed smoke from sacrifices made to the Inscribed Gods. Frey entered to see folks milling about the nave. At their feet lay those who had been wounded in the battle. The stink of their ailments combined with the smoke to make a particularly noxious bouquet.

Many of those present looked at him askance, no doubt wondering at his panting and sweaty face, but seeing him to be a warrior, most gave him a respectful berth.

At last, he saw the person he had been searching for standing just before the altar. "Mother Ilva!" he called across the chamber, squeezing through the crowd to approach her. "Mother Ilva, a moment, please!"

The gothi turned toward him, thick eyebrows raised toward her riverrat cap. As the head of the Inscribed Order within Oakharrow, she seemed occupied with reestablishing religion in the city even as she cared for the wounded.

"Yes?" she said, attempting and failing to hide her impatience. "What is it?"

"Prince Alabastor, Mother. He needs your help. The care he's been receiving, or lack thereof — it'll soon kill him."

At the words, her expression morphed. The priestess frowned at those closest to them. Drawing her meaning, they soon melted away.

"I was worried about this," she murmured once they could no longer be overheard. "The keepers turned me away at the jarl's insistence. Apparently, I would have only gotten in the way."

"Much to the contrary, Mother. The healer is depriving him of medicine. The fever... You must come and see it for yourself."

"I will try." Her face hardened as her eyes darted toward the back rooms. "What shall we need... Mugwort, nettle and fennel, watercress..."

"I leave that to you — only hurry. Even a day might be too late."

His thoughts were less polite. *Fight, you stubborn bastard,* he thought to the dying prince. *Fight like you always have.*

56. THE SIGHT

"Seeing is believing, until it comes to magic. That's best left to the stories."

- Asger Fireside, a skald of Djurshand

Bjorn kept his eyes on the pass below. The mountains opened up like the cover of a book, and he was eager to read its pages. This marked the end of a story, or at least a chapter of it. It had taken many long, bloody leagues, but at last, he might have a moment of respite.

Then he saw it. Oakharrow looked resplendent that sunny afternoon. Clouds and sleet had plagued them during the march, but the weather broke as they covered the last stretch. The view of Baegard from atop Ikvaldar had been glorious, but present circumstances made the scene before him surpass it.

His home was liberated. His friends abounded around him: Loridi and Seskef, Egil and Yonik. He was reunited with his sister after almost a year apart, and soon would be with his father as well. Clap, his loyal gelding, still carried on despite plunging through deep banks of snow and coming close to several battles.

And, seated behind him, her arms wrapped around his middle, was the woman he was coming to love.

He had been afraid Tyra would turn from him when he approached after the Jotun freed him. At first, she had only stared, her green eyes and red curls obscured by a low hood. Yet, when the others parted around him, the former acolyte surged forth and buried her face in his chest. It had only taken him a moment to return the embrace, chest feeling stuffed full of hot coals.

Yet this moment of return was not unblemished. Bjorn had done all he could to follow Torvald Geirson's visions, but he could not be sure he remained on the Four Shadows' path. Would Kuljash accept the alliance upon his return, or change his mind? Was it all a gambit to gain more *khnuum?* He could not know until he ascended the pass again, supposing he could secure an offering of such a precious substance.

Making matters more uncertain was that the giant had denied him the return of his runestones, including the Four Shadows. What Kuljash intended to do with the runestones, Bjorn could only speculate, but it did not bode well for a productive partnership. And Bjorn's attempt to divine the path forward without consulting the King of Ice's legacy would most likely flounder.

Even so, he did not feel that he strayed from his fate. The winds coming down from the Teeth whispered not of omens and iron, but summer and light. Bjorn smiled, frost crinkling in his beard, willing himself to believe.

"Makes for a beautiful sight, doesn't it?"

He looked over to find Aelthena watching him. A glance back at Tyra showed her to be smiling as well.

"Yes. It does." Bjorn looked back at his sister. "Thank you for letting me see it again."

Though her intervention might have ruined Torvald's prophecy, Bjorn knew he owed his sister gratitude. She had been brave to come after him, even facing down a giant to retrieve him. Even now that he stood taller than her, she still sought to protect her little brother.

"You wouldn't have to thank me if you hadn't needed saving."

Aelthena's tone was light, but there was an undercurrent to her words he could not ignore. They had divulged all their experiences over the past year during the five days' ride, and he had explained what he had seen as best he could. Yet even now, he saw the way she looked at him, like at an injured beast she did not know how to heal.

The same way she had always looked at their father.

He hid his thoughts behind a smile. "Then you wouldn't have something to hold over me."

Aelthena laughed, loud and unguarded. How he had missed that laughter.

"You've changed much, little squirrel. Grown much, too. And not just the beard — which you may want to trim at some point, by the way."

"I like it," Tyra whispered in his other ear.

That widened his grin until it ached. Bjorn rubbed at his jaw. It had been doing that more of late, both sides of his mouth throbbing from a constant pressure. He wondered if it was because he was smiling more than he had in all the year before.

"I'll clean it up," he said to his sister. "But we may have more important things to do first."

"Yes." Aelthena's expression darkened. "We may."

Thinking of all the obstacles lying before them, Bjorn's joy at seeing his home swiftly leeched away. Closing his eyes, he listened to the wind, clinging to its whispered assurances for a little while longer.

"He's dying?"

Aelthena's question sent chills down Bjorn's spine. He was already uneasy from standing within Vigil Keep. His admittance into it had been reluctant; even with wars abounding, his wounding of a keeper had not been forgotten, nor forgiven. Yet with greater threats ahead, Asborn had agreed to overlook it — for the moment, at least.

One of those threats, Bjorn guessed, was the ailing prince beyond the door.

"So Mother Ilva says." Frey Igorson looked haggard: blonde curls hanging limp, left arm in a sling. The guardian was far from the carefree fellow he had once been. Bjorn might have suspected it was from guarding his sister had he not noticed the way they looked at each other.

So I'm not the only one indulging in forbidden love.

Aelthena shook her head. "No. We cannot allow it. Without Bastor..." She looked up, guilt in her eyes. "Of course, I wish to save him for his own sake. But without him hampering his father's plans—"

"I know," Frey murmured. "There are many reasons he must stay alive."

"Then how are we to do it?"

Bjorn scanned their small company. Yonik and Tyra had entered Alabastor's chambers to see if they could assist Mother Ilva, leaving Bjorn, Aelthena, and Frey in the corridor. He had expected Egil to join them, but the sentry had split off as soon as they reached the city without even a farewell. Though it rankled him, Bjorn knew better than to hold it against the former sentry. Egil was the head of his house now; it only made sense he would have other duties to attend to.

When the priest and acolyte had entered the room, Bjorn had glimpsed the feverish prince and smelled the miasma of his sickness wafting on the air. From the first glance, he had known what must be done.

Yet he resisted his own conclusions. There was so much more he had to save his strength for, so much he wanted to do. Visit his father, whom he had not seen in a year. Spend some time alone with Tyra, a rarity since their reunion. Perhaps even steal a moment to read a book again, a long-denied luxury.

But there was no time for what he wanted. Duty sounded its horn, and a Bear always answered its call.

"I can attempt to heal him."

The pair stared at him. Bjorn sighed. He did not blame the guardian for his doubts, but he wished at least Aelthena would understand by now.

"You mean," Frey ventured, "you'll use... magic?"

"*Seidar*, the gothi call it, or the Sight. But yes, magic."

"Bjorn..." His sister pursed her lips. "I know you mean well, but... the Inscribed Beliefs forbid sorcery. More importantly, it is punishable by death."

"Will you condemn me?" He tried to make the question teasing, but it came out wrong.

Aelthena shook her head. "It's not worth the risk. We'll find another way."

"You heard Frey; there is no other way. I am trained, sister." An exaggeration, perhaps, but just now, Bjorn knew Aelthena needed to hear his confidence. "I have healed before; I can do so again. Please, just let me try."

Her scowl deepened, but it no longer seemed leveled at him. He pressed his advantage.

"I understand — you've never seen it done. You do not

know it truly exists. Then let me reason with you: if this is all in my mind, is there any harm in the attempt?"

"There could be. But... given the situation, I fear we've little choice."

Bjorn bowed his head, hiding the fear flitting through him. Though he had sought this course, it did not make it any easier to bear.

"I won't let you down," was all he said aloud.

"It will be enough if you do not burn for this." Her smile did little to lighten the heavy words.

With one last look at the guardian, Bjorn slipped inside the door.

As soon as he entered the room, Yonik caught his eye. Keen as his mind was, the priest seemed to understand at once what had been decided. Sighing, Yonik wiped his hands on a cloth and beckoned him over to the writing desk tucked into a corner. Bjorn was glad Tyra was preoccupied with a task set to her by Mother Ilva. He feared her slightest look would cause his courage to falter.

"I wondered how long you would wait before making the attempt." From the desk, the gothi drew forth a sheaf of parchment, an inkwell, and a quill. "If it helps, I can draw the rune as I remember it, then you can amend it as you see fit."

Bjorn nodded. He thought he remembered the symbol for *forsja*, but with all the nuances to it and the towering task ahead, caution was the best approach. "I'll see if I can find drascale ore."

"No need — I already secured some. It's just over there in my satchel."

Fetching the stone, Bjorn stoked the fire in the hearth a little hotter, then placed the stone among the flames. Ignoring the curious stares from the others in the bedchamber, he hung the water pot and waited for it to boil.

"Bjorn..." Tyra made his name a plea.

He slowly stood and faced her. The firelight exaggerated her long expression, though it already struck him to his core. He swallowed, trying not to let the strain show in his voice.

"It'll be fine, Tyra. Don't worry."

She only looked aside. Silence crowded the room as the water began to steam. When Yonik finished drawing the rune, Bjorn took a turn at it. Yet even before his embellishments, he could tell it would be effective. The Hall of Doors flashed before his eyes in fragments. Already, he could glimpse the door he would soon open.

Raising his head, Bjorn turned and found the others staring at him.

"It might be better if there are fewer here." Confident as he was in his Seeing, it was best to avoid any distractions they could.

"That it would be," Yonik said. "Please, everyone..."

After some convincing, all but the priest were persuaded to leave. Aelthena eyed Bjorn strangely from out in the hall, but parted without a word. Tyra hugged him close and whispered in his ear, "Be careful," before slipping out.

When the door had shut, Yonik turned back and gave him a small smile. "Shall we?"

Bjorn nodded, then used a fire poker to remove the ore from the flames. Yonik poured on the water. Steam billowed up from the hot stone to wash over Bjorn's face. He breathed in deeply, hardly flinching at the rotten smell coming off of it. Almost, he welcomed it, for it washed away his constant doubts.

The Hall of Doors appeared before his eyes, obscuring the shrouded room from sight.

"I'm ready," Bjorn murmured.

"Then come over here and look."

Reaching for his natural vision, Bjorn found his way to the chair next to the bed. Sitting, he gazed upon the prince's sweat-beaded face. Though he was sure he had never met him before, Alabastor Ragnarson had distinct features in which there was a strange marriage of Djurian and Sypten. Somehow, they seemed familiar, though he did not know where he would have seen him before.

But that was an idle thought, a distraction. Bjorn cleared his mind of all but the Hall of Doors and rested his hands on the prince's bared forearm. For a moment, he felt his feverish skin and the corded muscles beneath; then he purged himself of sensation and moved from his body into his mind.

"Look, Bjorn," Yonik murmured. "See the rune."

He opened his eyes. The rune was there on the page below him. No sooner had he looked upon it than he stood before its door in the shadowy corridor. The door trembled in its frame as the mark etched into the wood was set ablaze with flames. A light seeped out from the other side, like a sprite of fire seeking to escape.

Forsja. Forsja. *Mend.*

Bjorn set his hand to the door handle, then opened it wide.

57. GOLD & SHADOW

"There, the Dragon, tall as the skies! There, the Bear, wide as the seas! But a pest's bite may fell even the mightiest. A rat, if not crushed, can kill a giant."

- Torvald Geirson, the Last King of Baegard, a day before his disappearance

He ran swiftly, yet the Shadow still closed in.

Bastor nearly stumbled as he twisted around to sneak a look. It flew above him, that Shadow, coming ever nearer in its descent. Talons glinted beneath its body, extended and eager. Teeth glittered within its long maw.

He faced forward again and tried to run faster. But it would never be fast enough.

The Shadow grew large around him. Fire lanced through him, its claws piercing his back. Bastor cried out and lashed about him, flailing. He thought he had been weaponless, yet it seemed he clutched an arrow in one hand. Tearing the wounds in his back, he thrust the arrow up into the creature.

The world turned dark. A roar filled the void, then silence spilled back in.

For a moment, he was interred in darkness, as thick and complete as in a cave's belly. Panic rose, clawing up his throat. He thought he might scream, but in that ringing silence, he doubted he could make a sound.

Then, like mist before a gust, the darkness parted. Bastor blinked. He stood on top of a creature, an arrow planted between its shoulders. Surely, it was the Shadow, for the arrow looked to be the one he had wielded. Only now, the beast was not wreathed in umbra, but golden and gleaming and as long as a drakkar.

A dragon.

Panting for breath, Bastor scrambled off the creature. An expanse surrounded him, empty and forlorn. Yet as soon as his feet touched the ground, a host rose from the dirt. Spectral soldiers composed of swirling dust lurched toward him, weapons and shields raised. Their edges were sharp with swift winds, and he knew they could kill as easily as steel.

As the first blow fell, Bastor threw up an arm. A white shield appeared that had not been there before, and the bright steel deflected the attack. Snarling, Bastor lashed out with his other hand, which now clutched a sword as black as night in the heart of winter. The blade pierced the dust-man's chest, and the soldier loosed a howl as it drifted apart.

Battle-thrill rose in him then. Bastor cried out in delight as he cut through the next of the sediment soldiers, hacking them into clouds. Their weapons nicked him, but he barely felt the wounds, only continuing to press forward.

The rumbling ground roused him from his frenzy. Raising his head, Bastor saw a beast bearing down on him, just as massive as the golden dragon he had left behind. Ten times the size of any greatbear, its fur flared around it in muddy curtains, and its teeth curled out from its maw in yellowed tusks.

Bastor faltered before its charge. Throwing aside his weapons, he ran sprinting through the battlefield, though he did not know where to escape his fate. The Beast was too swift. Its panting grew louder behind him, and the earth threatened to tremble apart beneath its paws.

Then something flew before his vision: a beetle, black as ink but for its wings, which were shimmering and translucent. At once, Bastor followed its flight, knowing this tiny creature was his only hope for salvation.

The edge of a cliff appeared ahead. As the beetle flew toward it, Bastor put on a burst of speed. If he could only leap over the edge, the Beast could not catch him. Its hot breath was on the back of his neck. Twisting around, he looked to see how close it neared.

Then the greatbear embraced him, claws rending him apart.

All he could do was wrap his arms around the Beast and fall off the cliff's edge. Clutched close, the Beast could only roar, its fury vibrating through Bastor's body. He felt his blood seep into the fur as the wind whipped cold at his torn back.

He had expected darkness to lie below, but instead, light grew around them. Looking down, he saw flames rising toward them, red and all-encompassing. The Beast stiffened and stilled. Bastor looked down toward the oncoming fire and smiled. Loosing his bloodied arms from the creature, he raised them toward their coming destruction.

Fire burned through his body, but it held only pain.

With a strangled cry, Bastor sat up. Flames did not surround him, nor bears and dragons and soldiers of dust, but only a gloomy bedchamber. He himself was abed, blankets pooled about him as if just thrown off. Ordinary surroundings, and firmer and more distinct than those that had come before.

Dreams, only dreams.

Running his hands up his arms, he found that, while there were the seams of wounds, most had already scabbed over. Bastor shuddered, a chill running through him. The dream-pain had subsided, but a dull ache remained behind. He felt as if he had slept both too long and not long enough. The room stank as if someone had left eggs in a forgotten corner for the entire length of a season.

Groaning, wondering what mischief he had gotten up to this time, he moved to lever himself out of bed, but his legs knocked into something. No, *someone*. A man, with hair long and tangled in his beard, his clothes and skin unwashed as if after a long journey, lay slumped over the covers. Only then did Bastor realize a second man was speaking; it had seemed a meaningless murmur before.

"Bjorn," the stranger said, shaking the prone man's shoulder. His face was even more enveloped in dark brown hair than the first. "Bjorn, answer me."

Bjorn. Bastor frowned. A familiar name, though he could not quite place it.

"Bjorn, I'm going to bring you back." The second man moved his hand to his waist and produced a knife.

Before he knew what he was doing, Bastor lunged and seized the stranger's wrist, holding it tight. It was gratifying to feel his strength returned. "No killing anyone until I know what in Ovvash's red hells is happening."

The man looked him full in the face, and only then did he recognize him.

"Brother Yonik." Bastor loosened his grip. "Volkur's tits, what are you doing here? And where am I, for that matter?"

"I'll explain all in a moment. Right now, Highness, I need to save your healer."

Bastor released the gothi and scooted back, looking at the unconscious man with fresh eyes. As Brother Yonik shifted him around, the hair fell away to reveal another familiar face.

Bjorn Borson, the self-exiled heir. And my healer?

Questions burned on his tongue, but he stifled them as the priest set the knife to the young man's forearm, then cut across it. Bjorn's eyes flew open for a moment, then fluttered closed again.

"Bjorn." Brother Yonik lowered the knife and leaned in close. "Bjorn, close the door. You must close it."

Bastor held his breath. Blood trickled down the young man's arm, dripping onto the blankets and floor. Did his chest even move? Was he still breathing, or lost to whatever stupor claimed him?

Then Bjorn jerked. Sucking in a ragged breath, the young man let it out in a cough.

Bastor released his own and grinned. "Good. I would've had a hell of a time explaining a man dying in my bed. Or whoever owns this bed."

Brother Yonik only spared him a glance. "Are you with us, Bjorn? Have you left the Hall of Doors?"

"Yes." The word came out in a whisper. Bjorn's eyes were slitted, but they were open.

"Not to interrupt," Bastor started again, "but if you would explain the situation now, I'd be most grateful."

The gothi pursed his lips. Though his eyes were cast in darkness, they seemed to have some inner light of their own.

"You were gravely injured, Prince Alabastor. Dying of soured wounds. You were brought here to Vigil Keep where you were wasting away. Bjorn is the only reason you still breathe." The priest paused, seeming to size up Bastor for a moment. "He did it by *seidar*, Highness, the rune sorcery of our ancestors. These powers healed you, but at significant cost to himself."

Though steam still filled the room, the clouds were clearing from Bastor's mind. "A prince's savior requires princely care himself. Ho, there!" he bellowed at the closed door. "Come in, if anyone's lingering out there!"

He had suspected his retinue had not entirely abandoned him, but it still came as a surprise when the door flew open. His serving man, Mido, led a few other servants in with him, an apologetic look on his face. The reason for it became apparent as a host of other people flooded in behind.

"Bjorn!" squealed a girl Bastor could not identify at the moment. She darted to the young man's side. "Gods be good, they spared you!"

"He did it." Aelthena stood at the foot of the bed, bright hair in disarray and her clothes rudimentary and dirty. She looked as if she had traveled for a week straight and not yet washed. "I should have believed him." Her eyes lingered on her brother, then rose to meet Bastor's. "Prince Alabastor. I cannot say how glad I am to see you alive."

"An unexpected greeting." Bastor flashed her a full-toothed grin. "But not an unpleasant one."

He took in the others around him. His servants hung about the peripheries in uncertainty. Mido stood with them, looking peeved at being prevented from nearing the bed. The girl, he now remembered, was one of the trio who had come to the war camp; Tyra, he thought her name was. A middle-aged woman with a fur hat and robes came to the fore: Mother Ilva, if memory served. Frey Igorson was also there, shadowing his beloved lady as usual. His arm in a sling and dark circles ringing his eyes, he looked to have seen better days.

Though I doubt I look any better.

Bastor shrugged his stiff shoulders and cleared his throat. "I'm sure Bjorn would be more comfortable in his own bed. Mido, go find him a room, if he hasn't one already. Make sure he has his every need attended to. The rest of you, go with him. It stinks in here, and not only from whatever the priest has cooked up. And fetch me a meal," he added as his stomach rumbled. "Damn me if I'm not starving!"

The room's occupants leaped at his commands. The servants shot out the door. Bjorn was carefully lifted to his feet by Brother Yonik and the girl, then the three shuffled out of the room along with Mido. Mother Ilva lingered a moment, but at Bastor's wave, she bowed and also departed. Soon, only Aelthena and Frey remained.

Bastor looked between them before speaking. "Let me guess: something happened while I slept."

Aelthena grimaced. "Many things. Not the least of which is a jarl condemning you to a slow death."

As swiftly as that, all his amusement filtered away. He sighed and leaned back against the headboard.

"Go on, then. Tell me everything."

58. MADNESS

War or madness. That is the choice the jarls have laid before me. Like wolves, they smell the blood from the kingdom's wounds and prepare to tear into its carcass. Never mind that we shall be weaker for fragmenting; each has eyes only for his own gain. The reins of monarchy chafe their pride, and no number of corpses will dissuade them.

Torvald, perhaps you would have known how to unite them. Perhaps they never would have challenged you had you remained the man with whom I took vows.

But I have learned not to live in the past. It is the future I forge, and I will do what none of these men can.

I will save our people — for a little while.

- The diary of Siva Of Torvald, Wife of King Torvald Geirson, Matron of the Harrowhall, the Last Queen of Baegard

Aelthena tilted her head back against the stone wall and closed her eyes. For once, she did not think of appearances, but allowed the cauldron of emotions to storm inside unimpeded.

"Don't tell me you're going to need your brother's healing, too."

She opened her eyes to Frey's tilted smile. She wished she could find their situation as amusing. Her brother lay in the next chamber over, Tyra and Yonik watching over him as he slept. The priest had seemed confident he would make a full recovery, but with witchery involved, Aelthena felt less certain.

"It almost killed him, Frey."

His smile slipped away. "But it didn't."

"This time. What if it does the next?"

He pressed her arm gently. Here in the privacy of the room, with only those she believed to be allies to see, the show of intimacy did not seem so dangerous. And she needed to feel his touch.

"We will come through this. Bjorn's alive, and so is Bastor. In a few short hours, our dear prince will confront Asborn and set things right."

"Without spilling blood?"

His grimace told her all she needed to know.

Aelthena sighed, then leaned into his side, mindful not to knock his arm in its sling. "I'm just glad you survived. And your family, too."

"As am I. Mother was furious when she saw the condition I was in. But even that was a relief, in its own way. Things might return to the way they were."

She thought of all the battles she had seen, the death that had come with them. Her home and family gone up in flames.

Life would never be the same as it had been. But that did not mean she could not forge a better world from the ashes.

Pulling away, Aelthena drew herself back upright and smoothed her dress. She was still only passingly presentable, but it would have to do.

"We had better check on our prince. Wouldn't want him to act rashly."

Frey let out a soft chuckle. "As if there's any preventing that."

Aelthena kept her chin high as she walked next to Bastor down the corridor to the chair-room. Fears worried at her, and only a lifelong study kept her composure knitted together. She had to remain poised; if not for herself, then for Frey and Bastor, for her father and her brother. A reckoning was coming, and she had to ensure it did not swallow up the men in her life.

Soldiers surrounded her. Even before the prince had eaten, washed, and risen from his bed, Bastor had summoned them to his side. Now, two dozen loyal huskarls formed their company. Along with Aelthena and Frey came Elder Vedgif and a handful of Thurdjur warriors, including Loridi and Seskef. Brother Yonik and Tyra remained at Bjorn's side. She was glad her brother had such friends to watch over him, and her father as well; Uljana had taken the old jarl to Bjorn's chambers out of an abundance of caution.

But she could not worry about them now. Her eyes slid over to the man leading their party. Pride alone carried Bastor now. Though he still had much of his bulk, illness had diminished the prince. His stride was shorter, his shoulders rounded, his head bowed as if weighed down by an anvil. Yet he wore his dark armor, and his axe hung from his hip. A feverish light filled his cerulean eyes. Whatever it cost him, she knew he would see this task through. Even if it came to blood.

A hand touched her arm. "All will be well," Frey spoke in her ear. "Asborn will see reason."

"I'm not sure he knows reason anymore."

"He does. He'll remember it if he faces the wrong end of a blade."

Aelthena could not hide her grimace. Frey's eyes remained steady upon her.

"Our prince is not a monster," he murmured. "He'll show mercy."

A low laugh sounded from her left. Aelthena looked over to see Bastor looking sidelong at them.

"Am I not?" The prince flashed a weary grin. "I wouldn't be so sure."

Like the infection that had ravaged Bastor's body, fear took hold of her. She could do nothing more than swallow it back down to sit heavy and cold in her belly.

"Either way," Frey muttered, "I wish I had the use of my arm. Don't suppose your brother can do anything for it when he wakes up?"

"No." The response leaped from her lips. "We should not use more witchery than we must."

"Witchery?" Bastor looked fully at Aelthena. "That 'witchery' purged poison from my veins. I'd be a corpse by now if not for what your brother did. Be it a gift from Nuvvog, Ovvash, or some unknown, dark god, I don't much care. I won't leave such a useful tool to rust."

She looked away and tried to put the thought from her mind. The last thing she needed just then was another worry.

437

Conversation died as they reached the chair-room's doors. The keepers before them stepped forward, though hesitantly. The oldest one, a veteran by his shaved head, spoke up.

"Prince Alabastor. I was told you were bringing armed men before Hawk's Perch."

Bastor's men muttered like a hive of hornets. A glance showed none were so foolish as to draw weapons.

Yet.

"Were you?" Bastor sneered. "Well, keeper, I don't give one shite what you were warned of. Step aside, unless you wish to stand in the way of your prince."

The veteran wavered for a moment. Then, with a bow of his head, he waved at the other keepers so that all four stepped back. Bastor snorted a laugh, then nodded at the man to his left — his new drang, by Aelthena's understanding. The scarred man stepped forward and threw open the double doors, and the prince led his retinue inside.

Aelthena swallowed at the sight within. No audience of highborn awaited; instead, keepers lined the walls, a score at a quick count. Asborn stood before the keep's chair, clad in Balturg red up and down his person. The Winter Mantle hung from his shoulders, the white bear fur glowing in the sunlight cast down by the tall windows. His mother, Lady Kathsla, was by his side. Beyond them, only two others occupied the room: the Vurg leader and scion of Skarl Thundson, Edda Skarldaughter, and the Balturg warrioress who always shadowed her. These two seemed the only ones at ease, both smirking as if expecting an amusing performance. Though Aelthena admired women seizing power, those smiles rankled her to the bone. Just then, however, the pair was her last concern.

Bastor stopped half a dozen paces before the dais. His

posture drew up, and though he could not tower as he had before, his voice boomed throughout the chamber.

"Asborn Eirikson! I almost didn't live to see you again."

Aelthena tore her gaze from Bastor's back to stare at her former betrothed. Asborn had changed much since their time together, yet she still knew him intimately. Behind the creased brow and narrowed eyes lay a twitching, nervous apprehension. But that did not mean he would yield; to the contrary, it could make him even more stubborn.

"Prince," the false jarl replied. "I am glad to see you well."

"Are you?" Bastor took another step forward, the movement like a greatbear's lumber. "I've heard of the care you gave me while I lay dying. Didn't sound like well-wishing."

"As soon as I heard of my healer's error, I ordered it set right." Asborn's eyes flitted to Aelthena, then settled on the man standing next to her. "Did I not, Frey Igorson?"

Frey loosed a wry chuckle and glanced at her. Nodding, Aelthena stepped up next to Bastor, keenly aware of how close the keepers' spears loomed.

"Yet my guardian says the healer did not come, nor his draughts. He had to fetch Mother Ilva in his stead."

Surprise lit up Asborn's eyes for a moment before his expression hardened. Had he expected some measure of loyalty from her, even now? She could not deny feeling a glimmer of guilt, yet she knew better than to trust it. Asborn had betrayed her. The worst she had done to him was to be honest in following her heart.

Bastor took another step forward. Keepers stood only two paces ahead, as did the dais upon which Asborn stood.

"Tell me plain, Asborn. Swear on your father's stone. Did you mean to let me die?"

A corner of Asborn's jaw spasmed. "No."

Bastor lunged, the prince moving so swiftly Aelthena

could scarcely follow. Asborn yelped, while the keepers closed in. Bastor had already pushed his way through and gripped the false jarl by the clasps of the Winter Mantle. He nearly held Asborn off his feet, though he had not looked to still have the strength.

Gods, no...

Lady Kathsla backed off the dais. Her face turned red as she shouted something, but the words were lost in the sudden tumult. Keepers moved toward their liege, spears lowering, but most had to turn back as Bastor's warriors drew their weapons and moved toward their liege.

Bastor ignored them all. *"You lie!"* the prince roared in Asborn's face, spit flecking from his lips. "Tell me, *Lord Jarl,* one fucking reason I shouldn't smash your head on that gods-damned chair."

Asborn had gone as pale as a winter mountain. "Your father named me the Jarl of Oakharrow."

Bastor laughed. "Piss on my father and his commands! Or wasn't it my father who ordered you to leave me for dead?"

None of the prince's warriors even flinched at the mutinous words. Little wonder; it was not Bastor's position that had won them over, but his courage in battle. They would follow him to death and glory, fighting all the way up to the heavens.

"There will be hells to pay." Asborn's voice had grown faint. Aelthena almost couldn't hear him over the blood pounding in her ears.

Bastor bared his teeth. "I'm well-acquainted with the hells."

At last, Aelthena's mind thawed. *Do something!* If this came to blows — and Aelthena could not see how they would avoid it now — she would be defenseless. There was only one thing she could do.

Aelthena stepped forward. "Stop this at once! Put down your weapons — you're not boys brawling in the yard!"

She stood ahead of all the warriors, between the bristling steel on either side. One wrong move, and her life would end. But she was done cowering. If she was the only one with sense remaining, she had to wield it for as long as she could.

Bastor looked over his shoulder at her. "Best leave this to me, m'lady," he said, a laugh in his voice. "You need not stain your dress with a traitor's blood."

"No one will bleed this day, Prince Alabastor. My people have bled enough."

Something in her voice made the large man turn. Asborn, still in his grip, lowered a fraction, but he did not make any move to free himself.

"He was your betrothed, Aelthena, and yet betrayed you," Bastor said slowly. "He stole your father's mantle — *your* mantle. Were you in his power, and you stood in his way, would he spare you?"

Aelthena kept her doubts tightly hidden. "It does not matter. We do not spare him for what he would or would not do, but because it would be wrong to kill him. Not in the gods' eyes," she added as Bastor's eyebrows rose, "but because it would split apart my jarlheim. We must stand together, strong and whole. See reason, Alabastor, and release him."

The prince stood motionless, gazing at her with that baleful look of his. Then he twisted around and threw Asborn down the stairs.

Her former betrothed sprawled at her feet. Aelthena stared down as he raised his head. Gone was any expectant hope, replaced by hurt and rage. The keepers' spears lowered a fraction more, but none had yet struck.

Bastor descended the stairs, one at a time, to stand over

the false jarl. "Asborn Eirikson, I have spared your life for the sake of the woman you betrayed. But everything else, I strip from you, down to the very cloak on your back. Remove the Winter Mantle and cast it to the stone, as you have trampled on the position you hold."

Asborn did not speak nor rise from his knees. Slowly, with his head bowed, he raised his hands to the clasp on the mantle and undid it. The heavy fur cloak fell from his shoulder to pool about his legs.

"Good." The prince's voice dripped with disdain. "Now go. Leave Oakharrow in exile and shame. Never return here for as long as your jarl deems it to be so."

Your jarl. Aelthena raised her head to meet Bastor's eyes. Before she could speak, however, Asborn found his voice.

"You think yourself above me. But I know what you are, prince." Asborn put one foot on the ground, but did not yet rise. "I know what you've done. Your transgressions are far more grievous than mine. Because of you, giants entered Baegard. Because of you, men, women, and children died by the thousands. Their blood stains your hands, Alabastor Ragnarson!"

Aelthena froze where she stood, the damning accusations falling like stones upon her. She had known them, known them all, yet she had not been ready to hear them spoken aloud, here and now. She looked at Bastor, suspecting Asborn's words would incite him to violence, but the prince only sagged as if his illness had at last caught up to him.

"Blood stains deep," the prince murmured, then raised his gaze. "Leave, Asborn. While you still have your head."

Wrath flashed in Asborn's eyes. Aelthena thought he would draw his sword. Instead, he rose to his feet and stalked through Bastor's warriors, who parted before him.

The keepers surrounding the room glanced at each other, then one gave a signal. The men raised their spears and followed their leader from the chamber, all silent but for the stamping of boots and the rattling of armor.

When the last man exited, Bastor said to his drang, "Follow them. Make sure they do not cause trouble."

The warrior nodded, then waved to the prince's men. Most went as they tailed Asborn's procession.

"Well," Edda Skarldaughter declared as she emerged from a corner of the room, "this'll make quite the tale."

Aelthena glanced at the Vurg, but made no response, her mind focusing on a more pressing matter. Slowly, she turned to Bastor.

"What did you mean when you said, 'your jarl'?"

Bastor smiled, then bent over. When he rose, the Winter Mantle was in his hands. "Your brother saved my life. And you saved me in your own way. But this isn't about paying debts. You're a leader, Aelthena, born and bred. You'll do a damn sight better at this than I have being a prince."

She scarcely dared to hope, though Frey leaned forward expectantly by her side. "The words, Bastor," she whispered. "You must say the words."

The prince grinned. "Oh, not yet. You'll have to wait for the ceremony for that."

59. TO BIND

The Desolation is a recurrent subject among the revela-
tions, for sound reason. The return of Hua's Children will
bring the end to all we know, the world scoured clean by
the sun's eternal fire.

Yet not every prophecy predicts this cleansing will be
our end. Ineni of the Eye, widely known to be accurate in
her auguries, saw in the sands a time after the Desolation.
The peoples of Enea, even our enemies to the north, stood
with the People of Dust. Violence had settled in their
hearts at last, and peace reigned over all the lands.

I cannot say in what manner Ineni's divination may
come true. But when the fear of what awaits us steals over
my heart, I think of her words and I pray they may be so.

- Revelations, by Kheti, High Chanter to Qa'a

his is a dream.
She wanted to believe it, tried to believe it.
During the long journey, jostled in and out of

consciousness by bumps in their path, Sehdra felt it must be a dream. What had happened could not possibly be real.

If what she remembered was real, Teti was dead.

No! No. This is all a dream.

But when the chariot rolled to a stop, reality set back in. Sehdra blinked open her eyes. The canopy was sparse with winter's coming, naked branches scratching at a gray sky. Only the pine trees remained green, though in muted hues of those readying to endure long hardship. She had experienced little of winter before, it being the flood season along the Nu instead, but in that moment, she understood it. Life dimmed and faded in this time. She herself felt numbed to the world.

Get up, she commanded herself. *Rise. Or will you lie here forever?* Had Teti been there, he would have gently coaxed her up, then helped her to her feet. She could picture his smile, hear his laugh, smell his earthen scent. She felt his absence as a phantom touch on her arm: ever-present, yet never truly there.

He's gone, truly gone. Will you let him die for nothing?

At last, she arrived at an intolerable thought. She could not let his sacrifice be in vain, nor the others who had given their lives. Seth, that boy she had so callously sent to his death. Amon's soldiers. All the people who had fallen victim to Oyaoan's whims.

Maybe Teti had died for her actions. Maybe it was a judgment passed by the gods to punish her for all she had done. But she would not accept their verdict lying down. Not if she was supposed to be their equal.

Gritting her teeth, Sehdra rallied her scant strength and sat up.

"So you are alive."

She looked over to find Amon Baka staring at her from

where he leaned against a tree near to the chariot. His appearance had been disheveled before; now, it verged on frightening. Sweat and ash stained his face and tangled the hair of his unshaven cheeks. Worse still was his bloodshot eyes and the tremble in his hands. Going without wine would be good for him, but it would not make for a pleasant transition.

"Somehow." Recalling the fall she had taken from Oyaoan's hand, she wondered how she was not dead, or at least badly injured. But that thought strayed too close to memories that might rob her of the little sanity she had left. "Where are we?"

"North." At her look, he sighed. "It was the only option. South would have taken us through the camp. East was barred by the river. West would lead toward any remaining soldiers from that cursed pit, or to the mountains beyond that, and chariots are not suited for rocky terrain." The disgraced general spread his arms and smiled. "So here we are."

North. It left few options for how to proceed. *If it leaves any.*

Sehdra skirted the despair that threatened to draw her back into its embrace and looked around them. A forest like most other forests in the Winter Holds surrounded them. Through gaps in the trunks, she could see a gray stream not far away. From it drank two lathered horses, while a man she did not recognize crouched next to them filling water-skins. She guessed him to be one of Amon's soldiers by his shabby uniform. Nearer at hand, Gertrud bent over again and again, gathering kindling for a fire. The Baegardian woman glanced up, then darted her eyes away before Sehdra's gaze.

These were all that remained of her subjects, she who

had once been a goddess. She thought of what Teti would have said.

You are still a goddess, Divine One. Does a leopard cease to be a leopard out of a tree? You will always be the Holy Karah, for as long as you draw breath.

She smiled. Even now, she remained the karah. Feeling sorry for herself would not drive the huame from Ha-Sypt. And drive them out, she must. Even if Oyaoan had died — though she doubted they were that fortunate — other giants would take her place. Enea would not be safe until they were rid of them all.

Lacking a throne and army did not change who she was. Who she would always be.

Like the calm period of the Nu after the floods, her mind settled into clarity. And like the Nu-watered fields, the seeds of ideas began to sprout.

She looked at the general. "Why did you come back for me, Amon Baka?"

He stared back at her, unblinking. "You question my loyalty, Divine One? After all I have given up for you?"

His attempt at guilt fell like droplets on a broad pool. They were nothing to the pain she already endured.

"Please, do not toy with me," Sehdra said softly. "We have been honest with one another thus far, and I like to think we each know the other's character. I understand your earlier assistance was to reclaim your career and accepted it as the bargain. But risking your life and giving up the lives of your men for me... It seems a step too far even for a gambler."

The disgraced general stared at her for several moments longer. Then he looked away with a ragged laugh, crossing his arms and tucking his shaking hands out of view.

"Yes, you know me, Sehdra Karah. This is more of the

same. You were and are my ladder out of the pit of disgrace. Without you, my life is worthless."

Despite his agreement, Sehdra found herself frowning. There was a false note to Amon's words that told her all was not as he made it to be, nor as she had presumed.

"And Gertrud?" she pressed. "Why save her?"

The rings around his eyes seemed to grow more pronounced. "What would you have expected me to do, shove her from the chariot? She came with you. Besides, I thought you might require a servant."

Again, she felt he was leaving things unsaid. She wondered if there was more loyalty and goodness in the man than he cared to show, or she had bothered to look for.

"Very well." Sehdra looked aside, seeking a way free of the awkward silence that had fallen. "What, then, is your appraisal of our situation, Amon Baka?"

This seemed territory he was more comfortable with, for he straightened slightly before answering. "My honest opinion, Divine One? We are fucked, well and truly."

That provoked a small smile from her. "At least I still have my subjects' respect," she said lightly.

Amon smiled, but it faded swiftly. "I doubt the huame will let us off easily, especially after what your man did to Great Oyaoan. She will hunt us to the ends of Enea. I suppose she will rule directly now that you are gone. So it does not leave many options." He sighed gustily. "We might seek sanctuary in Xen'tia if we can cross the mountains, though with the seasons in this Gazabe-cursed valley, ice and snow would likely kill us first. We cannot move south for obvious reasons. East is impossible unless we contrive a way to ford that damned river, though doing so would only take us deeper into the Winter Holds. Further north would be just the same."

"Deeper into the Winter Holds..." Sehdra frowned off

toward the trees, staring at where the water moved in the growing darkness in a low, rushing hum. Her thoughts had caught on a half-formed idea, but she could not comprehend what it was until her gaze settled on Gertrud again.

"Gertrud, if you would come here a moment," she spoke in Djurian.

The woman paused and stared at her. In silence, she set down the small bunch of branches she had been holding and approached. Amon looked back and forth between her and Sehdra with a furrowed brow. For the moment, Sehdra ignored him.

"You know something of these lands," she spoke to Gertrud. "Do you know where Alabastor Ragnarson would be presently?"

Gertrud's eyes widened. "Yes," she said, voice hushed. "The crown prince took half of Baegard's forces east to reclaim Oakharrow."

Sehdra nodded and adjusted her mask. It had been ruined during the battle, stained with blood and ash and its tusk bent, but it would have to suffice.

"Why ask after this man?" Amon asked in their own tongue, though he evidently knew Djurian. "Is he not the son of their king?"

"He is." Sehdra forced a smile. "But blood does not always bind."

"Even so, enemies make for poor allies. If you mean to beg sanctuary from him, you will be completely in his debt — a hostage. We have nothing to offer this savage prince."

"To the contrary, general. We have the power of a nation behind us, if he will aid us in taking it back."

Amon dropped his gaze and shook his head. The soldier had returned and stared at her, water sloshing out of the unstoppered skins. Gertrud chewed on her bottom lip, her hands intertwining with a nervous flutter.

They were worried, all of them, each in their own way. But it was for them to follow, and for her to lead. She only prayed she did not lead them astray.

"We will cross the river," Sehdra said. "Then we make for Oakharrow."

60. A LITTLE LONGER

"Ever do those who love warriors ask them to stay a little while longer. And so they make us liars, for we must always say 'yes'."

- Highlord Carr Gunnarson, Fifth Arkjarl of Baegard

Once more, Bjorn opened his eyes to an unfamiliar ceiling.

Blinking away the last tendrils of sleep, Bjorn rose slowly onto an elbow. It felt as if iron had been embedded under his skin, his movements heavy and clumsy, but it was a fair sign that he was moving at all.

After what he had done, he was lucky to be alive.

He gazed blearily around the room. It looked to be a simple but well-kept chamber, with all the necessary fixtures for one to live in comfortably. His bed was more agreeable than any he had slept in since departing from Oakharrow, filled with feathers rather than straw and boasting a robust frame. His clothes, which had been changed while he lay unconscious, were similarly fine and soft against his skin.

His observations were cut short as his gaze caught on the woman dozing in the chair by his bedside. For a long minute, he was content to watch Tyra rest. Her head was lolled back against the chair, her mouth hanging slightly open, and her breathing was slow and even. Every once in a while, she twitched, as if a fly had just landed on the tip of her nose.

He smiled as he whispered, "Tyra."

She inhaled sharply, then her eyelids fluttered open. For a moment, she stared at him without comprehension before a smile split across her face.

"Bjorn!"

He rose a little higher as she leaned toward him. As she winced and touched a hand to her neck, he smiled sympathetically.

"You didn't have to sit there all night."

"Yes, I did." She gave him a look that forestalled further objections.

"Not that I'm ungrateful," he added hastily.

Tyra let out a short chuckle and shook her head, hand falling back to her lap. "It's not that. Only... I thought you might not come back this time."

Bjorn winced. "Yonik was there. He wouldn't let anything happen to me."

"You cannot promise that." Her eyes shone with enough reproach to silence him. "I know you have seen visions that you feel compelled to follow. No, that's not fair — that you *must* follow. I know you do it for the good of all. But I'm not sure I can..." She looked aside.

Fear, blessedly absent until then, returned as an icy gale, and all within him seemed to freeze at its touch. But he knew what he had to say, for her sake. After all she had given up for him, it was the least she deserved.

"I understand. I would never want to hurt you. You don't have to stand by me while I risk my life—"

"What? No!"

Bjorn stared at her, baffled, as she laughed and touched a hand to his arm.

"Quiet, you silly man, before you say something you regret. I'm not abandoning you — much the opposite. I want to come with you, wherever you go."

He was not sure if he wanted to laugh or weep. "Tyra, wait. I've told you—"

"*You* wait, Bjorn Borson, and listen to me. Mother Ilva offered me a place at the Tangled Temple. I could be an acolyte a little longer there, then soon a gothi like her and Brother Yonik. I could help people, help them heal. But... There are too many hurt, too many dying, and more will only follow. I don't want to try to put the pieces back together as everything falls apart. I want to stop the world from breaking in the first place."

A lump grew in Bjorn's throat. He hardly dared to breathe, much less swallow, as he stared into the acolyte's shining eyes.

"What do you mean?" he forced out.

Tyra let out a shaky breath. "I'm not sure yet. I don't know what the future holds for me. But I don't think it's the path I've been on for as long as I've been out of a child's frock. That frightens me more than anything."

It shouldn't frighten you more than our enemies, or even our allies. But even with his mind still coming awake, Bjorn knew better than to say that aloud.

She grasped his hand in both of hers, her gaze capturing and holding him. He rested his other hand on top, calluses rough against her softer skin.

"I know one thing, though," she continued, soft now. "I don't want to lose you. Your path will put you in the way of danger, but when you leave, from now on, I go with you."

"Tyra — no, I must say this," he rushed to say as she tried to shush him again. "Despite all the visions I've glimpsed, I don't know what my future holds, either. But I know just as you do that it won't be easy or safe. How could I put you through that?"

"I care for you, Bjorn, and I love you." A blush spread across her cheeks, but she shook her head and continued. "That would be enough for me to go, too. But you're also our future. If I protect you, I protect all of Enea."

How can you protect me from giants and war?

But again, he kept the words caged behind his teeth. Instead, he released her hands to cup her face and bring her close to him. Tyra folded against his shoulder, heavier than his wearied body could easily bear, but he voiced no complaint.

It was unfair to her to hold her close. Unfair to let her love him when he might die any day. But he wondered if he had the strength to push her away and still do what must be done. Wondered if he could stop loving her back.

"Promise me," she whispered into his hair. "When you go, I go with you."

"I promise."

Only as he spoke the words did he realize they were a lie. No matter her best intentions, no matter how he wished for her to stay close, he would never willingly put her in harm's way. He meant to stand by a jotun and delve into ancient magic from which there might be no return.

He had lost so much already. He couldn't bear to lose her.

After several long moments, Tyra sniffled, wiped at her

eyes and nose, then drew up his gaze again. "There's something else I should tell you. Probably best I tell you now."

Her tone made him think through all that might have gone wrong while he slept. "The prince didn't survive?"

"No, he did. It's what he said that you should know."

Bjorn frowned, wondering what that could be. But before either of them could say anything more, the door to his room rattled, then opened.

Aelthena appeared in the doorway, though she paused as her eyes flitted over both of them. "Sorry to interrupt. I was coming to check in."

"No, you're not interrupting." Tyra cuffed her eyes again and smiled up at her, then seemed to realize something and shot to her feet to curtsy. "I mean, m'lady."

Aelthena laughed and slipped inside to set a hand familiarly to the acolyte's arm. "Please, no need. Not between us." She gave Bjorn a significant look, though what it signified was beyond him.

"Very well." Tyra looked back and forth between them, caught in indecision.

"If I might have a moment to speak with my brother..."

"Of course, m'lady. That is, Aelthena. I'll fetch us some food, Bjorn. You must be starving."

With a lingering look Bjorn's way, paired with a fleeting smile, Tyra swept from the chamber.

Aelthena looked bemused for a moment before stepping forth to take Tyra's seat. As she did, comprehension slowly dawned on Bjorn.

"It's finally happening, then."

He had expected her to smile. Instead, Aelthena only tilted her head. "That depends."

"On what?"

"You, mostly."

He would have laughed but for her serious expression.

"What do I have to do with you wearing the Winter Mantle?"

His sister waved a hand. "We can speak on all that in a moment. Are you truly well?"

"I think so." He held up his hands and turned them over, as if to demonstrate their normalcy.

She leaned forward, elbows propped on her knees. "Then I should say I'm sorry."

"Sorry?" Bjorn tried to remember the last time his sister apologized, to him or anyone else, but even his keen mind flailed at the task. "What do you have to be sorry for?"

"For not trusting you. Not believing in you."

Growing uncomfortable, Bjorn slid up to lean his back against the headboard. "Can't say I blame you."

"But I blame myself. You're my brother. I shouldn't have doubted you."

He chuckled and shook his head. "Aelthena, when we last saw each other, I'd attacked a man, then fled into the mountains. Those aren't exactly the actions of a sane man."

"But you are well now?"

"As much as anyone can be in these times, I suppose." Bjorn put on his best reassuring smile. "Though a bit peaked. Sleeping takes it out of you."

She smiled, but it swiftly slipped away. "Then I suppose I cannot dance around it any longer."

"Dance around what?"

For a moment, she only stared toward the curtained window. "Bastor asked me to be the jarl."

They had danced around the matter since the moment she entered. And he had been prepared to be delighted for her.

What he had not prepared for were conflicted feelings that arose.

He had never wanted to be the jarl. Such a position of

power neither suited his disposition nor filled him with anything but anxiety and apprehension. Yet he had always known it might be his duty to become the jarl, and he liked to think he would have risen to the occasion had it been his burden to bear.

Now, he would never have that chance. He had been passed over. Everyone else had seen he was as wanting as he always believed of himself.

Aelthena reached a hand forth to press tightly over his own. "I know this cannot be easy. And if you don't want me to—"

"No! Please, Ael, it's not what you think." Bjorn drew in a breath, then tried letting out his insecurities with the air. "I want you to be the jarl. Oakharrow needs you to be. You've always been better suited to it."

Her eyes flickered between his, searching them. "Are you certain? Absolutely certain?"

"Yes." He spoke with every bit of conviction within him. It was made easier that he did not have to lie. "Bear fur always suited you."

She smiled and leaned back. The depths of her elation, restrained before, was now on full display. "Thank you, brother. Though you should know, you'll still be my heir."

Bjorn groaned and put a hand to his forehead as his sister laughed.

"If I must," he answered at length.

Her mirth quickly faded. "I'm glad you'll be there to stand by me, little squirrel. Glad you've survived."

"Same for you." He did not want to speak the rest of what was on his mind, but the words lifted from his tongue all the same. "Though you know it's only just begun, right? We still have much more to live through."

Her jaw tightened. "I know. And as much as I wish to, I won't command that you stay out of harm's way. But I will ask this: do all you can to stay alive. For my sake, if not Tyra's."

"I can agree to that."

"Good." With a pat on his leg, Aelthena rose to her feet. "Now, don't be late to the afternoon's ceremony. And if you wouldn't mind washing and trimming your beard before then..."

61. WHO WEARS THE MANTLE

He who wears the Winter Mantle shall be known as the Jarl of Oakharrow, to rule and safeguard the jarlheim and its people.

- The Harrow Law; On Hierarchy

A elthena stood at the foot of Hawk's Perch, her gaze upon the doors, waiting as all in the chamber stared toward her.

All that attention should have made her nervous. Instead, she found that she reveled in it. Those in attendance were many things to her: friends and family, allies and enemies, soldiers and servants and more. Soon, nearly all would be united in one respect: as her subjects.

If only the priestess would hurry.

She had been careful in selecting her outfit for the occasion, stitched in a hurry at Bastor's expense. Thurdjur aqua formed the bulk of the color, while white fox fur trimmed the sleeves, hem, and neckline. Around her neck hung a delicate silver chain, an aquamarine stone set in the pendant, and with earrings to match. She wore no cloak in preparation for the one that would soon weigh heavy on her shoulders, but she did not shiver, the day's chill kept at bay by the warmth of anticipation.

To her right stood Bastor, clad in a princely purple regalia and with a lynx's pelt lining his cloak. He had already recovered much of his strength, though his eyes were more heavily shadowed than before. Almost, he looked haunted by some internal struggle when he thought no one was looking. As her gaze lingered, however, he cast her as wide a smile as he usually wore, eyes lit by some untold amusement.

To her immediate left stood Bjorn, with their father and Uljana just beyond and Frey a step past them. Her brother wore the simple garb she had selected for him paired with his laundered wolf's cloak. Neither were fine enough for the position he held, but with time short, it had been the best she could arrange. Her father's clothes had been less worn, and Uljana had seen to him becoming handsomely attired in their clan's colors and his beard and hair finely trimmed. But for his vacant stare, she almost could have believed him to be the man she had once looked up to.

If only you could see what I've become, she thought, eyes tracing his wasted features. *I swear to safeguard your legacy, Father.*

Frey wore his armor, washed and oiled since the battle, even as his arm remained in a sling. At her look, he cast her a small smile. Of all in this room, he perhaps knew best of all what this meant to her.

Aelthena looked back up, worried her stinging eyes might soon spill forth all she strived to hold back.

The crowd beyond provided plenty of distractions from sentimentality. Among them were the majority of Oakharrow's notables. Thurdjurs, of course, had flocked to her with unanimous support. Even those elders who had once balked at a woman's rule now cheered the loudest. All yearned for a Bear to wear the Winter Mantle once more, and for Oakharrow to become as it had once been.

Her brother's companions had also come at her invitation, despite Loridi, Seskef, and Tyra not being highborn. Loridi, at least, seemed thrilled to be among such august company, and as comfortable as if he were born with the nobility he pretended to possess. When Aelthena looked in the direction of the acolyte, Tyra gave her a warm smile, which she returned without reservation.

Egil Yaethunson had also come in support. Aelthena had watched with curiosity as her brother went up to the houselord upon his entrance. From both Bjorn and Frey, she had heard the two had grown close, and Frey had expressed even deeper feelings might be flourishing on the part of the lawspeaker's son. Now, warmth seemed wholly absent from their interactions. Egil acted distant, his responses short and his gaze constantly darting away. Guilty, she wondered if her actions toward his father had driven a wedge between them. Though she could have done nothing different, she knew how few friends Bjorn had had over his life. To be even partly responsible for losing him one was not a burden she wished to bear.

Still, she was relieved that the jarlheim's traitors were not in view for once. Yaethun Brashurson remained in the Keep's dungeons, awaiting her visit to pry as much information as she could from him regarding the giant Kuljash. Though she had sent men searching for Hervor Silverfang, the merchant had gone conspicuously silent. The best rumors she could gather placed him at his country estate near his mines. Sooner or later, she would have to hunt him down and confiscate his possessions, if only to replenish her empty coffers — a duty she would delight in, to be certain.

Balturgs in general were absent from the keep, none having taken kindly to the deposing and exiling of their jarl. The clan elders voiced loud protests, and those keepers who had not traveled with Asborn were said to be fomenting more violent resistance. One way or another, Aelthena would have to quash the dissidents before she had another Skarl Thundson on her hands.

Vurg leaders, however, more than filled their absence. Edda Skarldaughter wore her usual smirk and armor as she stood before those held in the highest regard in her clan. Her red-haired protector stood at her shoulder, seemingly unimpressed by what she saw. Though she could not help an instinctive distrust of Skarl's scion, Aelthena remembered Edda's aid in taking the city. Thus far, she had proven to be nothing but loyal to Oakharrow. If time should continue to prove her trustworthiness, she suspected the hard-edged shieldmaiden might have a place of high honor, indeed. At last, women might rule themselves, as they had not since the brief reign of Queen Siva Of Torvald, widow to the King of Ice.

A wrong long in need of righting.

Oakharrow's own were not the only ones in attendance. Nanna and Ingvar had come, as had Sigrid. Even Lord Siward stood there with his family gathered around him, though he looked far from pleased about it. His wife, Iona, beamed at Aelthena with her usual cheer as she bounced her young son in her arms, inured to her husband's skepticism. Perhaps Greenwuud was not yet her accomplice in their burgeoning rebellion, but that he lent support to her ascension was a fine sign for future negotiations.

Many of the other highborn who had ridden with the army, on the other hand, had left for Petyrsholm in protest, Lord Petyr's daughter foremost among them. As they went, she decried the refutation of the king's will, promising, "There will be blood to pay!"

Despite the ominous portent, Bastor seemed even more relieved by their departure than she, for he was finally freed of his many admirers. Aelthena could only smile at that. It was only a matter of time before Oakharrow's nobly-birthed women came out of the woodworks to court him afresh.

Aelthena drew her eyes away from the audience and set them back on the double doors. All of these relationships to be nurtured or soothed could wait. For once, she meant to try to enjoy this moment so she could remember it for all the cold nights ahead. Winter would descend upon them all too soon.

And with its thaw, the wars still to come.

At long last, the doors opened, and Aelthena's straying attention focused on the figures who stepped through them. Mother Ilva led the small procession, her riverrat hat removed in place of a fur-lined hood. She kept her gaze slightly up and past Aelthena as she walked slowly down the aqua carpet bisecting the room, fetched from some dusty corner for the occasion. Behind her walked Yonik, who looked his usual grizzled self. He also had his hood pulled forward, the half a greatbear's head shadowing his face and making his eyes glitter in the gloom.

But it was the object draped across his arms that drew her stare.

The Winter Mantle.

She studied it as Mother Ilva stopped before Aelthena, then turned to address the crowd. The white fur had been washed so it almost seemed to glow in the afternoon light streaming in through the windows. The bear insignia on the silver clasp shone as well.

This was the highest symbol of the jarl's authority and power. *He who wears the Winter Mantle shall be known as the Jarl of Oakharrow,* the Harrow Law dictated. It was one of the few passages she knew by memory, used to fuel daydreams of one day wearing it herself.

Now, at long last, that day had come.

While she had indulged in her thoughts, Mother Ilva had been speaking to those gathered. "...to shelter and protect this great jarlheim," she was saying, "and you, the people within its boundaries. To her dying breath, this duty and privilege shall remain here. Does Aelthena Of'Bor have your fealty?"

"Aye!"

The response was resounding, and it seemed to reverberate in her chest, amplified by all the times she had never dared believe she would hear it.

Mother Ilva turned to Yonik and gestured at him. The priest turned back to Aelthena, a ghost of a smile on his lips. But before he could approach, another stepped up before her.

"Wait!" Bastor bellowed as he spread out his arms.

Aelthena stared at the prince, wondering what devilry he was up to now. After all they had been through, she had just begun to fully trust him. She hoped his next words would not change that.

He let his arms fall to his side as the room fell silent. "You all know I'm your prince. While I remain in Oakharrow, I expect I'll be sitting in that chair as well." He pointed back at Hawk's Perch, then slowly lowered his arm so he indicated Aelthena. "But this is the woman you should remember to look up to."

All her fears flushed away before his words.

"'Time and again," he continued, "she has inspired me to be a better man. And the gods know I have room to improve!" He paused as if expecting laughter, but his audience remained transfixed. "Yes, she's a woman, and that's not a common thing in a jarl. But in the days ahead, I expect you'll see her the same way I do, and be glad for it."

Murmurs started up now. To her relief, they sounded like assents. Bastor spoke over them.

"The war is far from over. Much as I hate to say it, it's likely only beginning. But if I could have anyone by my side through the Eternal Night, it's Aelthena Of'Bor!"

As the audience hall once more erupted with applause, Bastor flashed her a grin. Aelthena returned it, though her heart still thumped hard in her chest. She could not help but look to her left, and seeing Bjorn and Frey's smiles, she quickly recovered her courage.

The prince stepped aside, and Mother Ilva, a look of bemusement claiming her features, motioned once more to Yonik. This time, the priest approached her without interruption.

"If you would ascend the dais, m'lady," the priest murmured in her ear, just audible over the continued noise.

Aelthena complied. Each step felt a weighty undertaking, as if her burdens redoubled with each pace advanced. But as she reached the chair and turned back, she stood tall and unbent.

Yonik moved behind her. White flashed in the corner of her eye before the heavy cloak settled over her shoulders. Aelthena remained staunchly staring across the room and over the heads of the assembled, even as their din grew ever louder.

The priest moved around to her front to fasten the clasp at her collarbone. Withdrawing his hands, he stepped aside and swept an arm toward her.

"Hail, the Jarl of Oakharrow!"

She did not smile before the din that followed. A smile would have been too thin to show all that brimmed within her. Eyes shining, she let her gaze fall from the opposing wall to each of her closest confidantes. Frey. Bastor. Her father. The jarls' wives and her other companions.

At last, she looked at Bjorn. As their eyes met, her brother grinned as she had not seen him do since he was a boy. Only then did Aelthena allow herself to believe it.

She was Oakharrow's jarl.

Now, she thought with a twist to her lips, *I just have to keep us all alive.*

EPILOGUE

P arick's eyes drifted close. Only as he tipped over did he jerk back awake.

Sniffing, Parick cuffed his drooping eyelids until they seemed like they would stay open — for the moment, at least. He had only indulged in a swig or two of whisky since coming to his shift that night, yet it seemed enough to tip him toward the other side of drowsy. Now, he was falling asleep on his feet, and no amount of salt-bitten wind from the Treacherous Sea blowing in his face could keep him conscious.

All the pleasures's of our great country, he thought miserably.

Benwold had its charms, but on the whole, Parick reckoned most in Enea thought little of it. Few ships ventured so far north, nor did many invaders come over the land. Ha-Sypt was too busy brawling with Baegard to cross the Breath and the Fell Hummocks to reach them. Talgarten, that island of riches that groveled at the karah's feet like an overfed hound, might have caused them trouble by the sea, but they were content to sit on their piles of coins.

Patriots were keen to declare their love for capital and country, but Parick knew Skaug and Benwold held little of interest for anyone. Little, that was, that could not be found inside a bottle.

"Pie-Eyed! What's that, you think?"

Blinking the fog from his eyes, Parick glared at the pimply boy, who squinted at the wide, dark waters. Though Gorry could not have seen more than fifteen monsoons, the watch captain had seen it fit to saddle Parick with the lad.

Or maybe because of it.

Parick had never gotten along with authority and often paid for it. This was only his latest penance.

"Told you not to call me that," he grumbled. "And it's nothin'. Birds, driftwood, a fleck in your eye — nothin' worth botherin' me over."

Turning away, Parick snuck another swig from his flask, hiding it more out of habit than any other reason. Gorry knew he drank, the captain knew he drank, the whole gods-damned Seawatch knew he drank, but they needed eyes on the water. Whatever else he lacked, Parick still had eyes.

Gorry leaned through the crenel. "Really, Pie — I mean, Parick. I think somethin's there."

He contemplated tipping the lad over the wall, then shook his head and stole another drink. "Keep goin' on about it, boy, and I'll make sure you got somethin' to see."

"What?" The boy turned to squint at him. "What d'ya mean by that?"

"You know, that I'll — shite, never mind." Parick knew he had been clear on his intentions to sock the lad. It wasn't worth trying to hammer the concept into his dull skull.

Gorry had lost interest in the conversation and returned to looking over the wall. "Has the shape of a ship," the lad said, his voice losing its sense of urgency. "Though I suppose it would be too big for one. But there would be the masts; there, the sails; can even make out the riggin', I think."

Parick realized he had let his eyes drift closed again. Lifting his head, he shook it and stared morosely at where the boy imagined a ship. Then, frowning, he squinted and looked closer.

Cowled in darkness was the very boat Gorry prattled on about.

It was as the boy said — a ship far too large to truly be there, yet complete with details all the same. The hull, the masts, the sails — all were exactly as a seafaring vessel should be.

"A ghost ship?" Parick muttered under his breath. There were tales among the sailors of such things and worse on the open seas. He had always thought them to be inventions of bored and fearful minds, or perhaps just to lead on gullible boys. But with the evidence before his eyes and no other explanation at the ready, he was starting to think the sea tales might not be far wrong.

A howl cut through the air.

Parick froze, unable to do anything but listen. As the first howl died off, a second and third rose, then a dozen more after it. They were deeper-voiced than any dog Parick had heard. The part of his mind not shocked to stillness wondered if it might be a wolf's call.

"P-Parick?" Gorry stuttered. "Is that c-comin' from the ship?"

The observation finally thawed him. "Sound the alarm!" Parick hollered. "Rains damn you, boy, *go!*"

The lad took off running, though it was hardly necessary. Shouts had risen up and down the wall as other sentries heard the howls and noticed the odd direction from which they came. His job done, Parick's gaze drifted back to the ship.

Maybe they're punishin' me, the gods. Punishin' me for my damn vice.

Something caught the light in the air above the ship. Parick screwed up his eyes at it, but an uncommon sight caught his attention.

Further down the coast, the wall erupted into flames.

Screams soon joined the crackle of fire, and the guttural howls rounded out the terrible song. Behind the wall, the city was rousing, the panic of the besieged swiftly falling.

No, Parick thought as he stared at the blue-tinged flames. *This ain't your fault, Pie-Eyed. This is just the end times. The Eternal Night fallin' and all that.*

The thought was oddly reassuring.

FROM THE AUTHOR

An author's career isn't built by the writer alone. It takes every reader who has bet hours of their time on a cover, a blurb, and the hope that this will be the story that grips them and sweeps them away. A story that gives them something new.

Thank you, dear reader, for taking that risk on my book.

I hope *The Stone of Iron & Omen* has been everything you were looking for and more. If you did enjoy it, please consider leaving a rating or review, particularly on Amazon and Audible.

Most readers don't know the difference a review can make for a book. I know I never gave it a thought until I became an author myself. But here's the truth: it makes or breaks a book's success. By reviewing, you can help other readers determine if they'll like the book, and hopefully a virtuous cycle blooms.

I'd like to be doing this till I have one foot in the grave. I wrote my first (terrible) book at twelve, and I don't intend on stopping now.

So if you're feeling generous and want to help an author out, look up *The Stone of Iron & Omen* on Amazon or Audible to leave a review. You'll have my infinite gratitude!

APPENDIX I

THE WORLD

COUNTRIES AND CONTINENTS

The Witterland - An ever-frozen continent to the north from which Djurians, the ancestors of Baegard and Benwold, are said to have long ago migrated.

The Sumerland - An eternally hot continent to the south from which Zakai, the ancestors of Zakowa and North and South Vinaxi, are said to have migrated. Known as "the Suncoast" to Syptens.

Enea, or The Middle Land - A continent positioned between the Witterland and the Sumerland where the events of the story take place.

Baegard, or The Seven Jarlheims - A nation founded among the mountains and the wide valley cradled among them. The jarlheims are city-states within Baegard that share similar cultures and unite for the purposes of common defense. Known as "the Winter Holds" to Syptens.

Ha-Sypt - A nation that has long been the antagonist of Baegard. It is a land of deserts and oases, founded primarily along the rivers Nu and Qal. It is ruled by a monarch held to be a god, the Karah. Syptens are descended from Eneans, the native people of Enea.

Benwold - A nation that shares a common descent from Djurian culture with Baegard and often allies with them.

Zakowa - A nation of Sumerland descent that often allies with Ha-Sypt.

North and South Vinaxi - Two nations of Sumerland descent that are in constant conflict with their sister nations.

Xen'tia - A powerful republic of Oessa, the continent to the west of Enea; sometimes participates in the wars between Baegard and Ha-Sypt.

Jin'to - A widespread empire of Oessa, the continent to the west of Enea; sometimes participates in the wars between Baegard and Ha-Sypt.

CITIES OF BAEGARD

Oakharrow - Formerly ruled by its jarl, Bor Kjellson.
Petyrsholm - Ruled by its jarl, Petyr Petyrson.
Ragnarsglade - Ruled by its jarl, Ragnar Torbenson.
Djurshand - Ruled by its jarl, Hother Alverson.
Greenwuud - Ruled by its jarl, Siward Jonson.
Skjold - Ruled by its jarl, Harald Sigurdson.
Aelford - Ruled by its jarl, Alrik Adilson.

OAKHARROW

The Squalls - The poorest district; primarily populated by Vurgs.
The Dusty Wares - The street-side markets along the main thoroughfare, the Iron Road.
Oakheart - The richest district; primarily populated by Thurdjurs and Balturg highborn.

Greenstead - The primary gathering place in the city for large-scale events.

Dawnshadow - The cliff that looms over Oakharrow.

Harrowhall - The former bastion of the last king of Baegard and the home to the present jarl; the center of Thurdjur power.

Vigil Keep - The citadel of the thane and center of Balturg power.

Honeybrook - The river that runs through the city.

EILDURSPRALL

Heim Numen - The compound of the gothi located within the Yewling town of Eildursprall. The center of the Inscribed religion in Baegard.

The Silvers - The three leaders of the gothi who rule from Heim Numen.

The Etching Wall - Every gothi contributes to carvings of the Inscribed.

CITIES OF HA-SYPT

Qal-Nu - The border city that was sacked by Baegardians just over twenty years before the start of the story.

Annax-Nu - The capital of Ha-Sypt, where the karah reigns.

CLANS

Thurdjurs - The ruling clan of Oakharrow; their clan color is aqua.

Balturgs - The secondary ruling clan of Oakharrow; their clan color is red.

Vurgs - The poorest and most oppressed clan of Oakharrow; their clan color is yellow.

TRIBES OF THE TEETH

Yewlings - The settled people of towns such as Jünsden and Eildursprall, who are on generally peaceful terms with Baegardians.

Skyardi - A nomadic tribe with a tenuous relationship with Baegardians.

Woldagi - A seasonally nomadic tribe with a hostile relationship with Baegardians.

Ovaldi - One of the tribes who has joined the Jotun's army.

Haddik - One of the tribes who has joined the Jotun's army.

Telduri - One of the tribes who has joined the Jotun's army.

Roks - One of the tribes who has joined the Jotun's army.

MAGIC

Volur - The Old Djurian word for one who can use magic.

Seidar **/ The Sight** - Magic as Baegardians know it; involves the ritualized use of runestones. When employed, it is called "Seeing."

Khnuum - A mysterious substance contained within drascale ore that causes hallucinations in those susceptible to its influence, such as *Volur*.

The Hall of Doors - the place seers visit to access the power of runes; appears as a shadowy corridor lined with doors that are inscribed with runes. Open the doors and their powers are conferred. *Hael Ek'dyrr* is the Hall of Doors in Old Djurian.

BAEGARDIAN CULTURE

Jarl - The highest social position in present Baegard; the ruler of a jarlheim and leader of the ruling clan.

Thane - The second highest social position in present Baegard; the next-in-command of a jarlheim after the jarl and the jarl's heir, and the leader of their clan.

Lawspeaker - The primary judge and arbiter of justice in Oakharrow.

Warden of the Watch - The primary leader of the city watch.

City Sentinel - One of the captains of the watch, focused on the protection of the city.

War Drang - The leader of Oakharrow's patrols and, in times of war, its warriors.

Drang - A leader of a company of warriors.

Huskarl - A man-at-arms, such as a guardian of the Harrowhall, or a keeper of Vigil Keep.

Gothi - Once a group of people dedicated to keeping old Djurian traditions alive, they have become in the modern era a codified priesthood. They have a centralized compound located in Eildursprall, where the three Silvers oversee the religion.

Yeoman - A man who holds and manages a small estate of land.

Thrall - A slave, often of Sypten descent and captured in raids.

SYPTEN CULTURE

The Ascendant Empire - Syptens' name for their country. Also refer to it as "the Plentiful Land" and themselves as "the People of Dust."

The Holy Karah - The god-king of Ha-Sypt; often referred to as "Divine One."

Ohkweht - The sister to the karah; translates to "Royal Sister."

High chanter - The highest priest dedicated to a specific Sypten god; referred to with the honorific "nautjer."

Vizier - The foremost advisor to the karah.

Chief general - The head general of the Sypten armies; honorific for generals is "baka."

Paragon - A notable champion addressed as "lion."

Afterlife - Syptens believe they either descend to the Jackal's Blight or receive an everlasting life in the Jackal's Delight, both ruled over by the god Gazabe.

Apostates - Those who defy the will of the Divine, including the karah.

Duaat - A Sypten game modeled after the real-life game "Senet," in which the aim to move one's pieces across a long board and into the afterlife.

Nomes - Districts of Ha-Sypt, ruled over by governors called "nomarchs."

Khopesh - The preferred Sypten sword; is curved halfway up its length like a sickle and single-edged.

DJURIAN PANTHEON: THE INSCRIBED GODS

Djur - The Wild God, the Greatbear, the God of the Stars and Wrath; father to many of the pantheon.

Nuvvog - The Trickster, the Dragon God, the God of the Sun and Deceit; father to the other half of the pantheon.

Skirsala - Goddess of the Harvest; one of the three Wild Wives of Djur.

Yusala - Goddess of the Forest; one of the three Wild Wives of Djur.

Lerye - Goddess of the River; one of the three Wild Wives of Djur.

Ovvash - Goddess of the Underworld; the daughter of Nuvvog and the surtun Finyurrle.

Lavaethun - God of the Sea Moon; thought to take the shape of a giant sea serpent.

Skoll - God of the Blood Moon; thought to take the shape of a giant wolf.

Baltur - God of Poetry and Justice; the son of Djur and Skirsala.

Volkur - Goddess of War and Glory; the daughter of Djur and Lerye.

Mostur - God of Stone and the Forge; the son of Djur and Yusala.

The Spinners - Three immortal beings who are said to spin the thread of each person's life when they are born and determine the timing of their deaths.

SYPTEN PANTHEON: THE DIVINE

Pawura - The Dreaming Antelope; Goddess of Art and Love.

Yeshept - The Prowling Lioness; Goddess of the Hunt and Wealth.

Qa'a - The Wise Scarab; God of Justice and Foresight.

Bek - The Red Behemoth; Goddess of Might and War.

Aya - The White Cobra; God of Cunning and Deceit.

Gazabe - The Black Jackal; God of Death and Decay.

Hua - The Bright Maker; Father of the People of Dust; Mother of the mighty Huame; Creator of All. Also known as the sun and claimed to be the mother of the huame, the southern giants.

OTHER

Jotunar - Giants of Frost; the mythic behemoths of the Witterland

Surtunar - Giants of Fire; the mythic behemoths of the Sumerland. Known as "huame" to Syptens, or "Children of the Sun."

Jotunmen - Barbars who have have been changed into bestial men that resemble the Jotun

Nuvvog's Rage - The mysterious inferno that appears to manifest from Chasm-dust

Woolith - A livestock animal that resembles a mixture between an aurochs and a wooly mammoth.

APPENDIX II

CHARACTERS

OAKHARROW

Thurdjurs

Aelthena Of'Bor - Daughter to the jarl of Oakharrow.

Bjorn Borson - Youngest son to the jarl of Oakharrow.

Bor Kjellson - Jarl of Oakharrow.

Bestla Of'Bor - Wife to the jarl of Oakharrow.

Annar Borson - Eldest son of the jarl of Oakharrow; the jarl's heir.

Yofam (Yof) Borson - Middle son of the jarl of Oakharrow; the war drang.

Frey Igorson - A guardian of the Harrowhall.

Yaethun Brashurson - The lawspeaker of Oakharrow; son of the deposed jarl.

Brashur Felson - Former jarl of Oakharrow; deposed and executed by Bor Kjellson.

Egil Yaethunson - Son of the lawspeaker; a sentry of the watch; a member of the Hunters in the White.

Vedgif Addarson - An elder of the Thurdjur clan; first drang to the Hunters in the White; known as "the Rook" for commanding role in the Sack of Qal-Nu.

Keld Erlendson - Youngest member of the Hunters in the White.

Morif Morifson - The warden of the watch.

Brant Elofson - An elder of the Thurdjur clan.

Fiske Yarison - An elder of the Thurdjur clan.

Raldof Koryson - Blademaster of the Harrowhall

Menif Laethson - A sentry of the watch.

Skarif Graynson - A guardian of the Harrowhall.

Menith Karlson, or "Pine" - A guardian of the Harrowhall.

Pestur Yroelson, or "Ratclaw" - A guardian of the Harrowhall.

Colden - A guard at Eagle Estate.

Hemming - A guard at Eagle Estate.

Latham - A loyal man coming to the call of war of the clan.

Destin - A loyal man coming to the call of war of the clan.

Balturgs

Asborn Eirikson - Son of the thane of Oakharrow.

Kathsla Of Eirik - Wife to the thane of Oakharrow.

Eirik Havardson - Thane of Oakharrow; leader of the Balturg clan; known as "Bloodaxe" for his ferocity during the deposing of Brashur Felson and the Sack of Qal-Nu.

Loridi Kelnorson - The self-proclaimed "Lord Sword"; a jester of the Hunters in the White; Balturg.

Seskef Gulbrandson - Named "Skiff" by Loridi; companion to Loridi and member of the Hunters in the White; Balturg.

Tait Knudson - A young keeper whom Bjorn attacks and injures.

Snornir Baelson - A city sentinel of the watch

Hervor Halvorson - Known as "Silverfang" for his silver false tooth; an elder of the Balturg clan; also a wealthy merchant and owner of drascale mines.

Sven Arvidson - A loyal keeper serving Asborn Eirikson.

Vurgs

Edda Skarldaughter - Fierce warrioress, daughter of Skarl Thundson, and the new leader of the Vurg clan.

Bodil the Blaze - Ruthless shieldmaiden to Edda Skarldaughter.

Skarl Thundson - Known as "the Savage" and "Dragonskin"; deceased leader of a rebellion.

Troel Magurson - A sentry of the watch.

Thralls

Uljana - The loyal servant to Lord Bor.

Darby - Servant to Edda Skarldaughter.

Horses

Clap - Bjorn Borson's loyal gelding.

Winterlily - Aelthena's white mare.

Other

Yonik Of Skoll - A gothi (priest) of Oakharrow; famous for his greatbear cloak won from a hunt.

Ilva Of'Skirsala - The head gothi (priestess) of Oakharrow.

Kuljash - A jotun ruling among the barbar tribes of the mountain range the Teeth. Also known as the "King of Chieftains" and the "King-Chief."

PETYRSHOLM

Ipu - A thrall young woman who works in the Elkhorn kitchens.

Pyhia - The thrall head cook of the Elkhorn kitchens.

Bennu - A young thrall girl.

Neith and Soben - Two young thrall boys.

Ragnar Ragnarson, or Ragnar the Younger - Bastor's younger brother and the youngest son of Ragnar Torbenson, Jarl of Ragnarsglade.

Thorpe and Kustaa - Two guards of the Elkhorn.

Destin - A huskarl to the jarl Siward.

Helka - Lord Siward's eldest daughter.

Olle - Lord Siward's infant son.

Yerrik - A wall captain.

Endre Kettilson - A huskarl to Lord Ragnar.

Tove Of'Petyr - Daughter of the jarl Lord Petyr Petyrson.

Mido - Thrall to Alabastor Ragnarson; gifted by Lord Petyr Petyrson.

EILDURSPRALL

Tyra - An acolyte at Heim Numen who works in the library.

Flint - The captain of Eildursprall's sentries.

Wuldof and Dagar - Two sentries of Eildursprall.

Embla - A priestess stationed at Heim Numen.

Torvald Geirson - The Last King of Baegard. Legends tell of him wandering into the Teeth and never returning.

RAGNARSGLADE

Bastor, or Alabastor Ragnarson - A rogue first encountered in the Wolf's Den, revealed to be the Heir of Ragnarsglade. Now the Crown Prince of Baegard.
Kare Lone-ear - First drang to Alabastor Ragnarson.
Vern Leaf - The second first drang Alabastor Ragnarson.
Stein - Huskarl to Alabastor Ragnarson.
Gertrud - Mother of Ragnar Ragnarson and a washer-woman at Lynx Manor.
Eydis - A servant at Lynx Manor.
Takhat - A thrall at Lynx Manor.
Brenna - A servant at Lynx Manor.

The Silvers

Mother Sign - An enigmatic older woman skilled in the Sight.
Mother Iron - A bold older woman who positions herself as the de facto leader of the Silvers.
Father Temperance - A cautious older man who counsels a conservative approach.

JARLS OF BAEGARD

Bor Kjellson - Jarl of Oakharrow.
Ragnar Torbenson - Jarl of Ragnarsglade.
Petyr Petyrson - Jarl of Petyrsholm.
Alrik Adilson - Jarl of Aelford; deceased.
Harald Sigurdson - Jarl of Skjold; deceased.

Siward Jonson - Jarl of Greenwuud.
Hother Alverson - Jarl of Djurshand.
Ingvar Alrikson - The new Jarl of Aelford; son of Alrik Adilson.

Wives and Widows of the Jarls

Sigrid Of'Harald - Widow to Lord Harald, the Jarl of Skjold; now ruling as the de facto jarl.
Iona Of'Siward - Wife to Lord Siward, the Jarl of Greenwuud.
Olga Of'Petyr - Wife to Lord Petyr, the Jarl of Petyrsholm.
Inkeri Of'Hother - Wife to Lord Hother, the Jarl of Djurshand.
Nanna Of'Alrik - Widow to Lord Alrik, the Jarl of Aelford.

HA-SYPT

Sehdra - The "ohkweht," or "Royal Sister," of the karah, the ruler of Ha-Sypt.
Hephystus III, or Physt - The karah, or god-king, of Ha-Sypt.
Oyaoan - A surtun (or huamek) acting as the shadow ruler of Ha-Sypt. Also known as "Great One."
The Ibis, or Ganiah Phaza - The Suncoaster translator to Oyaoan.
Teti - A servant and friend to Sehdra.
Zosar - The vizier to the Karah.
Renab - The high chanter of Qa'a.
Nekau - The restored chief general.
Amon - A now-disgraced general; formerly chief general.

Amasis - A chanter of Bek.
Ebana - The shaper, or priest tutor, to Seth.
Iset - A chanter of Hua.

BENWOLD

Patrick "Pie-Eyed" - A sentry of the Seawatch of Skaug.
Gorry - A young sentry of the Seawatch of Skaug.

ACKNOWLEDGMENTS

The team is the same, but the gratitude shifts with each book they help to create. A jotun-sized thank you to:

Kaitlyn, my wife and the biggest cheerleader for The Runewar Saga. Thank you for never letting it be far from mind.

Shawn Sharrah, my dogged proofreader, who not only caught all the missed errors, but put up with an insane deadline to boot. I cannot thank him enough.

René Aigner, my cover illustrator, who outdoes himself each time. Truly, this might be his best work yet, for which I'm entirely in his debt.

And lastly, to my advance reader team, *the Chapter*, whose reviews and encouragement ease the travails of book publishing.

BOOKS BY J.D.L. ROSELL

Sign up for future releases at jdlrosell.com.

THE RUNEWAR SAGA

1. The Throne of Ice & Ash
2. The Crown of Fire & Fury
3. The Stone of Iron & Omen

LEGEND OF TAL

1. A King's Bargain
2. A Queen's Command
3. An Emperor's Gamble
4. A God's Plea

RANGER OF THE TITAN WILDS

1. The Last Ranger
2. The First Ancestor

THE FAMINE CYCLE

1. Whispers of Ruin
2. Echoes of Chaos

3. Requiem of Silence

Secret Seller (*Prequel*)

The Phantom Heist (*Novella*)

GODSLAYER RISING

1. Catalyst

2. Champion

3. Heretic

ABOUT THE AUTHOR

J.D.L. Rosell is the author of The Runewar Saga, Legend of Tal, Ranger of the Titan Wilds, The Famine Cycle, and Godslayer Rising. He has earned an MA in creative writing and has previously written as a ghostwriter.

Always drawn to the outdoors, he ventures out into nature whenever he can to indulge in his hobbies of hiking and photography. Most of the time, he can be found curled up with a good book at home with his wife and two cats, Zelda and Abenthy.

Follow along with his occasional author updates and serializations at jdlrosell.com or contact him at authorjdl rosell@gmail.com.

CPSIA information can be obtained
at www.ICGtesting.com
Printed in the USA
BVHW041457240223
659176BV00003B/586

9 781952 868313